"Fresh, sexy, and laugh-out-loud funny. A refreshingly hilarious paranormal romp."

—Angie Fox, *New York Times* bestselling author
of *The Last of the Demon Slayers*

"Unique and fun with a magical kind of romance the genre needs more of... Rowe's gift for ironic humor will make any reader's day."

—*RT Book Reviews* Top Pick, 4.5 Stars

"An action-packed tale of star-crossed high-risk lovers... hits the spot."

—*Publishers Weekly*

"Hilarious... a very entertaining tale with witty characters... The tantalizing attraction between Blaine and Trinity was emotionally complex."

—*Night Owl Romance*

"An over-the-top satire that hilariously lampoons the subgenre... Fast-paced readers who appreciate humorous urban fantasy will know already Ms. Rowe is one of the best, as affirmed by her latest tale of love and misdeed."

—*Genre Go Round*

Also By Stephanie Rowe

Kiss at Your Own Risk
Touch If You Dare

HOLD ME IF YOU CAN

STEPHANIE ROWE

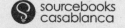
sourcebooks
casablanca

Published by Sourcebooks Casablanca, an imprint of Sourcebooks, Inc.
P.O. Box 4410, Naperville, Illinois 60567-4410
(630) 961-3900
FAX: (630) 961-2168
www.sourcebooks.com

Printed and bound in the United States of America
QW 10 9 8 7 6 5 4 3 2 1

*For MIG, for everything. I love you
with all my soul and all my heart.*

Chapter 1

NATALIE FLEMING HAD DONE THE IMPOSSIBLE, AND SHE couldn't quite believe it. But as she stood there with her hands on her hips surveying the gleaming storefront of Scrumptious, she knew it was true. With less than three days to spare, she'd restored her boutique chocolate shop from the decimation and looting that had occurred after she'd been briefly murdered by a deedub.

The demonic leprechauns of hostile origin had declared her precious store a free-for-all after they'd mistakenly thought they'd finally brought her down, and it had taken a highly bribed restraining order and two weeks of twenty-four/seven work to clean up the utter devastation they had wrought to her dreams.

But she was only halfway there. Three days was all she had until the Michelin-O Gold Star Rating Team (the Otherworld branch of the esteemed ratings company) arrived to bless her establishment or shut it down forever.

How she was going to do it without her sous chef, she had no clue, but Gina Ruffalo had cheerfully volunteered to die instead of Natalie, and she was dancing in Afterlife with her true love and was entirely unavailable for emergency dessert creation.

Which meant it was up to Natalie to do the impossible. Of course, surviving a deedub attack had also been impossible, and she'd done that, so how hard could it be to create a mountain of mouthwatering, and highly magicked, desserts practically overnight?

Natalie grabbed her list of pre-looting inventory and hurried over to her walk-in freezer. She studied the list as she pulled the door open. She should start with the virility balls, because that was her most powerful creation—

"Hello, my dear."

Natalie jerked her gaze up. A young man was camped out in her barrel of high-testosterone Belgian cocoa, chocolate smeared all over his face. A black Yankees cap sat askew on his head. A platinum skull and cross-bones dangled from his left ear. A row of diamonds along the crest of his right ear. All youth with attitude. Invading her precious space!

Indignation rolled over her. Seriously? "I just got this place clean! You don't have the right to eat my food! I have a restraining order from the Triumvirate. Punishment for violation is death, for heaven's sake!" Yes, she'd felt a little uncomfortable with the death part, but she also knew that their fear of death was the only thing that would keep her safe. She hadn't thought any of them would actually try to cross the line, not with that punishment. "Are you crazy…"

The words died in her throat as an old, well-repressed memory flared in her mind. "Oh, dear God." Her hand went protectively to her throat. "You're the one who murdered me."

He bowed. "And your whole family, of course."

Her mother and sisters bleeding on the kitchen floor, each of them infected by the deedub poison, cursed to die. The funerals, one after the other. Year by year, her family dying off, one by one. Her own gravestone, awaiting the moment when she finally succumbed—

"Didn't you turn out to be quite the unexpected surprise?" He cocked a jaunty eyebrow and flashed his vampire-wannabes at her. "Surviving a deedub bite? How on earth did you deem yourself worthy of such an affront to the laws of the universe?"

His cocky voice was like a shock of lightning to her cotton candy brain. "You don't get to have me!" She leapt back, threw the freezer door shut, and slammed the lock down.

The door to the freezer thudded as he slammed himself against it, and she jumped. The door bulged and strained against the hinges.

"Oh, crap!" She raced across the store and grabbed her purse, rifling through for her keys. She didn't want to abandon her store, but if she stayed, he would kill her and then the Michelin-O appointment really wouldn't matter, would it?

The deedub howled, and steel claws raked a triple stripe down the middle of the door. Steam rose off the steel, and it began to vibrate. "Oh, God." She found her keys and raced across the store. Her car was right outside. If she could make it there—

There was an explosion behind her, and then the freezer door catapulted past Natalie's head and crashed through the front window. Bins of chocolate flew through the air, clattering to the floor. One hit Natalie and knocked her down.

The deedub appeared in front of her in a burst of purple smoke, leaning casually against the doorjamb.

He grinned. "What? No hello? After all we've been through."

Natalie scrambled to her feet. "I have a temporary restraining order. You're not supposed to be here—"

He shoved off the doorway and charged her. Natalie lunged over the counter and grabbed one of her cooking knives off the counter. She spun around and—

He yanked the knife out of her hand and hurled it into the wall. "Don't you Sweets ever get that we can't be stopped? The fact you dodged death simply makes you more of a challenge. You know what men are like. The tougher a woman is to get, the more we want her." He leaned forward and sniffed, no doubt trying to get a high off the scent of her blood, which was way too chocolaty for her own good, courtesy of her Sweet heritage.

She palmed his jaw, slamming his head back, summoned her magic, and directed her most powerful suggestion at him. Not that her power of suggestion had ever worked on a magical being, but theoretically it was *supposed* to. "Get away from me!"

But instead of succumbing to her command, he grabbed her hair and pressed his nose to her throat. "Just like Godiva. Richer than when you were a baby. You smell like a luscious, decadent woman now." His fangs elongated, and he began to salivate.

She grabbed one of the diamond-crusted coffee cups reserved for her special customers and smashed him in the side of his head. He backhanded the mug and it flew across the room and clattered to the floor.

Was this really how it was going to end? At the dungeon-breath claws of the same monster whose poison had been killing her for the last twenty-five years? For three weeks she'd been free of him and his taint, and boom-ba-da-boom, it was over again?

He yanked her against him and aimed his teeth toward her throat, and she knew she'd just lost her chance at her second life, and she hadn't even gotten started. Dammit! This wasn't right! She—

"I'm afraid I can't condone that kind of behavior," a male voice interjected. "It's not polite."

"Nigel!" Natalie's insides furled with hope and warmth as her attacker lifted his head to see who had interrupted them. She couldn't see past the deedub's shoulder, but she didn't have to. She knew exactly who that voice belonged to.

The deedub growled. "Back off—" But before he could finish, a dozen tulip-shaped throwing stars flashed past Natalie and slammed into the deedub's forehead, marking out the shape of a heart. He bellowed and clutched his cranium as it caught fire. He stumbled backward, and then the air was filled with sparks of light as more metal objects in assorted floral shapes whipped past her, hitting him in every part of his body.

The deedub screamed, the unearthly bellow of a demon thwarted. He stumbled back, flashing like bad disco, and then he blinked out of sight. "I'll be back," he shouted.

But she barely even noticed his howled promise of retribution.

Because now that the deedub was gone, she could see her rescuer. Standing before her, a small frown quirking his brows, was Nigel Aquarian, the best friend of her sister's true love.

Never had the sight of the contemplative warrior been more beautiful. His dark hair was tousled, his leather pants creased, and his shoulders broad beneath his black T-shirt. On his cheek pulsed a pink rose tattoo that infused peace and serenity into the face of a man who should, by rights, be a cauldron of seething fury and anger, you know, given the fact he'd been tortured and betrayed for a hundred and fifty years by Death's psychotic grandma.

But not Nigel.

Never Nigel.

He sauntered across the floor and crouched beside her, and her heart began to race. She'd seen him around the house dozens of times, but they'd barely spoken, even when they were in a room alone together. She knew him. He knew her. But they'd never connected. Not until now.

"Thanks." Her body relaxed instantly, as it always did when he was near. "Your timing was fantastic."

He winked. "I'm known for my timing. It's one of my assets."

She blinked at the sound of his rich voice. She'd heard him talk to others. But having him direct that deep tone at her was different. It felt like he'd reached inside her and plucked chords she didn't even know existed. Suddenly all the tension she'd been holding the last three weeks vanished, and she knew she was safe, for the moment. "What are you doing here?"

"Your sister asked me to keep an eye on you while she was gone." He crouched beside her, his thigh muscles flexing as he supported himself. "I was picking up some pizza from across the street and thought I'd stop in." He cocked his head. "A man likes to feel needed, but I must admit to being a little surprised to find you being attacked by a deedub. Your sister implied you had that handled."

"Yeah, well, the restraining order didn't work." She

struggled to a sitting position, and Nigel's hand moved as if he were going to help her. She caught her breath, exhilaration rushing through in anticipation. He'd never touched her before, and she'd thought about it often.

Then he dropped his hand, his gaze intensely watching her as she stood, as if ready to catch her if she needed it. "A restraining order," he echoed, a small frown etched between his dark eyebrows as he stood along with her. He was so tall, looming over her. "You came back to work based on the assumption that a restraining order would keep you safe from homicidal demons with a chocolate addiction?" Fire simmered in the depths of his eyes, but it was a quiet flame. One that was utterly in control, soothed by the serenity of his spirit.

She'd always basked in the tranquility of his aura and inner peace, feeding upon his spiritual tranquility when her own soul was roiling with turmoil, and she cherished that. Thoughts of him had been her salvation so many times when she'd been succumbing to the deedub poison, terrified and spiraling toward death. She smiled, breathing in the peace she always found in his presence. It was as if he simply blocked all the negative energy, allowing her soul to rest. "But the TRO carries the threat of death—"

"It's almost impossible to kill a deedub." A few remaining steel tulips vanished into his blackened palms, absorbed back into the flesh that had created the weapons. "You must know that."

"Well, that's why I got the restraining order, because I can't kill them myself, and I needed to open my store." She sighed when she saw her front window was shattered. Brand new, with freshly painted gold lettering. It was now glittering on her floor and the sidewalk, like hundreds of rainbow crystals. But they weren't rainbow crystals. They were carnage.

Scattered across her floor were barrels of her specially imported chocolate, the decadently expensive and powerful contents oozing out onto the floor. She couldn't stop the wave of defeat that settled on her shoulders. "Look at this mess. How am I going to fix this in time?"

Nigel followed her glance, and he swore under his breath. "You're lucky it was only your freezer and your chocolate—"

"No! I'm not lucky! It shouldn't be any of it!" She grabbed a broom from the closet and strode across the room, biting back tears as she began to sweep up the glass. It was mixed with the chocolate, so she couldn't even save the ingredients. "Do you think people would be upset if there were glass fragments in their desserts?"

Nigel raised his brows for a second before he apparently realized she wasn't serious. "Opening your store isn't wise right now. You're still too hot—"

"I have to do it." He thought she was hot? Sadly, she suspected that he wasn't referring to her hourglass figure or flawless skin, but more likely the fact that her name had been on the front pages of all the papers after she'd dodged her deedub fate.

"You don't *have* to do anything." His boots crunched on glass as he walked across the floor and picked up one of the two-hundred-pound chocolate barrels as if it were a glass of milk. "Take a year off. Let things settle. The deedubs know where to find you here. Go on a tropical vacation until they forget about you." He carried the steel tub to the freezer, striding across her store as if he'd been there a thousand times and had already staked his claim on it, even though this was the first time he'd ever set foot in it.

"A year? Are you kidding?"

"I'll book you a ticket," he said, his deep voice unyielding. "I'll take you to the airport tonight."

"What?" No! Panic rippled through her, and she knew these were her sister's machinations. She and Jarvis had no doubt convinced Nigel to cart her off for her own good, because they all knew she couldn't stop him. "Nigel!" She grabbed his arm as he passed by.

He stopped immediately, a huge warrior responding instantly to her light touch. It made her feel powerful, but not nearly as powerful as the burning gleam in his eyes as he stared at her, waiting for her to speak. His T-shirt was so soft to touch, and she could feel the hardness of his muscles beneath it. Something fluttered inside her, something at the core of what made her a woman. For a split second, she was tempted to move her hand two inches and touch his skin—

Dear God! What was she thinking?

She jerked her hand away, her cheeks flaming. God help her if she went down that path again. She didn't want to awaken that side of her ever, ever, *ever* again. She took a breath and tried to focus. "My soul needs to work with chocolate. I need to craft my desserts and use my magic to help customers." She willed him to understand, to let her be. "It's like your art," she explained urgently. "I need this store like you need art."

Nigel ground his jaw, and he didn't look pleased by the revelation. "I sure hope you don't need it the way I need my art," he muttered.

"What?" She was confused. This was the man who

carried a sketchbook everywhere he went, who took time to bask in the beauty of his art right in the middle of battle, because it gave him such peace and focus. "What's wrong with your art? It's your salvation."

"That it is, my sweet girl, that it is." But his voice was quiet, as if there was a heavy weight behind his words.

My sweet girl? Her? Something shifted inside her, a softness that felt good. She didn't feel sweet. She was desperate, she was still carrying way too much fear, terror, and generally debilitating phobia from her trek down "murder victim lane." For him to even use that word... God. Maybe there was a chance that there really was a normal girl underneath somewhere. If she could resurrect her business, reconnect with her chocolate mojo, and find a way to ward off the deedubs, maybe a normal life was possible.

But it wouldn't be possible if she ran away. She had to own what made her feel alive, and that was this store. It was tapping into her magic. It was helping those who needed her. She folded her arms across her chest. "I won't leave."

Nigel set the heavy barrel down so carefully there wasn't even a sound. He propped his shoulder up against the stripped freezer door and folded his arms. "If you stay here, you'll get killed. He'll be back, and others will too. Deedubs can't stay away from chocolate." His eyes darkened, flashing with a protective violence that rippled through her. "And they can't stay away from Sweets. You're a Sweet. They will find you and attack you, just like before."

Natalie swallowed and realized her hands were shaking. Of course they were. She'd spent a lifetime fighting the deedub poison, waiting to die. And now it was only a matter of time until they came after her again. "I'll find a way." She lifted her chin. "I've been afraid my whole life, and I won't live like that anymore. I have a chance to live again, and this time I'm taking it. If I walk away now, I won't ever be able to come back. They won't forget me. Not ever."

Nigel swore, and she knew that he recognized her truth. They would wait at her store, and they would search for her. "Then you don't come back."

"What? No!"

Nigel strode across the room with sudden purpose. He grabbed her upper arms and pulled her close. Heat was vibrating off his shoulders, and his face was fierce. But she felt no fear. Just a tremble of excitement at this other side of him, a side she'd never seen. His hands were burning through her sweatshirt, his grip so powerful and strong, but also gentle. She could feel his strength, but also his protectiveness. "Your soul is too beautiful to die," he declared. "I won't let you die."

She stared at him, shocked by the intensity of his words. By the power rolling off him. He was a man of intensity, a warrior who had risen to protector status. Because of her? A thrill echoed through her, a heat that buried itself right in the depths of her soul. "Thank you," she said. "That was beautiful." And it was. No one had ever looked at her like that, as if they saw a beauty that no one else could see.

Nigel blinked and then released her suddenly, as if he'd realized what he'd said. "I'll be back to pick you up tonight. Be packed and ready to go."

"What? Nigel! No!" Dammit! She could tell that he

wasn't going to be dissuaded. Her sister had probably convinced him it was for her own good. Actually, her sister had probably bribed him to do her dirty work while she was out of town. "I don't need to leave. I can influence them to leave me alone!" Theoretically, completely true. In reality, not a chance. But dammit, if he took her away, he would steal her chance to live.

Nigel raised a skeptical brow. "Then why didn't you do it just now?"

Excellent question. "I wasn't ready. I'll be ready next time." She folded her arms. "I won't run, Nigel. I need to stay here."

Nigel studied her, and he finally shook his head. "You speak from the soul."

"Of course I do!"

Nigel slid his hands softly across her skin, rubbing softly. "You carry your own curse," he finally said. "Just like me."

She blinked. "My chocolate? It's not a curse. It's a gift. It's the only thing that has kept me alive all these years. I cherish it." She frowned. "You think your art is a curse?" She didn't understand. "But you love it."

His eyes darkened with denial, but he didn't voice it.

"Listen," she said. "It'll take that deedub at least a day to recover from what you did to him, so I'm safe from him for now. I expect the others will defer to him, since he found me first."

He rubbed his jaw, and she could see him evaluating her point. Finally, he nodded. "I agree."

Yay! "So, we don't need to do anything yet. Give me time to figure out a solution." No need for anyone to be carted off to the airport!

Amusement flickered in his eyes, as if he knew exactly what she was trying to do. "I'll be back to check on you."

She breathed a sigh of relief. "Why doesn't that surprise me?" Yes, she didn't want him teaming up with her sister in overprotective mode, but it was nice to know that he'd be by to toss metal tulips into the forehead of any assailants.

He laughed softly as he traced his finger across her brow, not quite touching her. She caught her breath, willing him to make contact, to feel his skin against hers.

His gaze met hers and his eyes darkened. He moved his hand, his thumb hovering over her lips. She waited, afraid to breathe, afraid he wouldn't touch her. But also terrified of the intensity of her desire for contact with him.

Then he shook his head once, an almost imperceptible movement, and dropped his hand. Disappointment surged through her. She should feel intense relief, really, but she didn't. All she wanted to do was to take his hand and lay it against her cheek. Feel his touch. Why did she crave him so badly? It was so dangerous. She'd learned her lesson. She couldn't be that kind of woman. She couldn't tap into that side of her. She'd tried it once, and it had killed her, so yeah, not the best results so far. And what she'd felt that time was nothing compared to the intensity of her reaction to Nigel.

"You have to stay alive, Natalie," Nigel said, drawing her attention back to him. "There's no other option." There was a fierceness to his words that made her think that maybe he wasn't actually acting on her sister's behalf, but that his stubbornness about deporting her was his own idea.

But why? They'd barely spoken before today. Why would he have made her safety such a priority? "Nigel—" But before she could ask, he spun around and stalked out of the store, leaving her staring after him.

He would be back. She knew he would. He wanted to keep her safe, which, of course, was a deliciously admirable trait in a man. But he would also steal her dreams, her soul, and her life, and that was just not acceptable. And if he ever decided to touch her, to tap into the intensity of her attraction to him... God help her.

The answer was clear. He couldn't come back. He had to leave her alone on all fronts.

But she knew he would never concur. How could she possibly stop a warrior like Nigel?

Chapter 2

AFTER ALMOST TWO HUNDRED YEARS UNDER THE KIND and nurturing (ahem) tutelage of Death's deviously psychotic grandma, Nigel was thoroughly aware of the overbearing nature of his decision to relocate Natalie to a safe location.

There was no doubt that his arrogance in making such a high-handed and singularly inflexible decision would have gotten him severely punished if he were still locked down in the Den of Womanly Pursuits, the bastion of estrogen, torture, doilies, and black magic hell run by Angelica and her team of equally untenable female apprentices. Nigel and his team had been their unwilling guests for a century and a half before orchestrating a successful break for freedom.

His stint in the Den enabled him to recognize and freely admit he was being a stereotypical male in the very worst of ways with his need to protect a female. But Angelica was no longer in control, and Nigel had damn well suffered quite enough loss in the last one hundred and fifty years. Natalie was not going to be added to that list, and that was the end of the story. She was simply too damn important. If he had to be Not a Quality Male to make sure she stayed safe, then that was the way it was.

Nigel would give Natalie the day of respite she'd requested, and then he was going to make sure that she went someplace where the deedubs would never find her. He simply would not allow them to destroy that beautiful light inside her, that amazing glow that had been his salvation since the first moment he'd met her.

And as Nigel hoisted the pizza boxes over his head and walked down the hallway of his penthouse, he couldn't quite suppress the pleased smile at the thought that there was one thing in this world, one beautiful treasure, that would always be safe, not only from the deedubs, but also, and possibly more importantly, from him.

"What's the smile for? You look like you just inherited an entire warehouse of art supplies." Pascal Magnussun, a young warrior Nigel and his team had recently rescued from the Den, looked up from his football game as Nigel walked into his favorite room in the place. Arched ceilings, huge windows, crown moldings. Pure artistic perfection.

"Just loving the beauty of the things in our world, P-Man," he replied. "Just feeling the love."

"Amen to that, brother. The world outside the Den is a thing of beauty."

"That it is." Nigel glanced at the stack of pens and sketchpads on the poker table, wishing he had a couple minutes to sketch. Being around Natalie always made him want to bring her spirit to life on the page.

But he was a man, and food had to come first. Nigel strode into his guest-suite-turned-infirmary, a sizable room that had been hosting the younger warrior since Nigel and his team had pried him free of the Den. "Pizza delivery."

The other five rescued warriors were spread out

across his penthouse suite, and Nigel had already dropped off pizza to those who were conscious. As the team's resident healer, Nigel had opted to host them at his place, instead of allowing the other three members of his team to offer their homes.

Nigel might be an artist. He might like his peace. But first and foremost, he was his team's safety net when the shit became more than they could handle. He was the healing magic that none of them could live without, and he'd saved the life of everyone they'd rescued so far.

Most were still somewhat out of it, but Pascal had finally started to get some of his spark back.

Nigel glanced at the tag on one of the remaining pizzas. "Triple XL white pizza with spinach, basil, and whole wheat crust?"

"Yeah, that's mine." Pascal waved a battle-ax decorated with golden lamé braids he'd woven with great care and impressive skill. "Does it have parsley? I ordered fresh parsley sprigs."

"Of course it does." Nigel frisbeed the top box at the blond-haired warrior propped up on a black leather futon watching the super-sized flat-screen TV Pascal had surreptitiously ordered off the Home Shopping Network. Using Nigel's credit card, the slippery bastard.

Not that Nigel had bothered to cut him off. They all deserved some serious man-things in their lives after almost two centuries of flower arranging, poetry writing, and other attempts to turn them into Angelica's perception of worthy mates with a truly sensitive side.

Screw that. They were men, real men, and it was insane, illogical, and unremitting torture to try to turn them into anything else.

Pascal flipped the lid, then closed his eyes and inhaled deeply, an expression of utter peace and delight on his face. "Francesca's Organic Pizza Garden always gets it right."

"That's why I go there." Nigel had tried ordering from Butch's Pizza & Ribs and from The Real Man Pub, but the shit was too greasy and fatty. When he'd seen Natalie eating a pizza from Francesca's, he'd immediately been inspired to try it.

As with everything relating to Natalie, the pizza had been sheer exquisiteness.

The others had tried to man up and suck down Butch's pizza, but in the end, Francesca's had won. Yeah, sure, it might have homegrown organic garlic and tofu specialties, but pizza was a man's food, so they figured it was still good. Their testosterone was running just fine now that they weren't having to eat arugula and beet salads or escargot delicacy in the Den of Womanly Pursuits.

"I've been waiting all afternoon for Francesca's brilliance."

Pascal leaned his ax against the wall beside the assortment of weapons that he could call out of thin air in the middle of a battle. Currently reposing were three spears, six swords, at least fifteen daggers, and some other implements. All of them were decorated with intricate coils of gold floss that Pascal had woven. The warrior could create butterflies out of thread in less than a minute, and he always kept his pink heart pillow nearby when he was napping. But he could also decapitate a scorpion with a thumbtack from ten miles away, so it was all good. "Check it out." Pascal jerked his chin toward the window.

Nigel tossed Pascal a beer as he glanced over at the French doors that led to his patio with the panoramic view of Boston. Gazing out at the muddy Charles River, his foot up on a hacked-up wooden bust of their former captor, was his teammate, Christian Slayer.

Christian had his back toward Nigel, but his skin was glittering as it always did before battle. His hands were flexed, and his neck was rigid.

"He's been like that all morning," Pascal said as he popped open the organic apple-plum beer brewed by opera-singing monks in Belgium.

"Hey, Christian." Nigel set his own sushi pizza on the poker table beside his sketchpads, then sauntered across the room and tapped the corner of the last box into Christian's back. "Got your—"

Christian whirled around and slammed his fist at Nigel's face.

"Hey!" Nigel dodged the unexpected assault with a tuck and roll he'd perfected in Gymnastics for Warriors 101 in the Den and landed on his feet after two flips and a handspring, pizza still upright and steaming. "You forget your coffee this morning or something?"

"Shit, man! Sorry. Didn't realize it was you." Christian's skin had taken on a purplish metallic shimmer that suggested there was more than a little adrenaline stirring beneath the flesh. "Don't sneak up on me next time. I don't want to kill you."

"Sneak up on you? I've been here for five minutes." Nigel scanned Christian's gaunt frame, the shadows beneath his eyes, his sunken cheeks, the unhinged fire in his blue eyes. "You okay?"

"Yeah, sure. Yeah." Christian ran his hand through

his short, perfectly coiffed hair, trying to mess it up. Angelica had mutated Christian so that he was in a perpetual state of gelled perfection whenever he tapped into his metallic side, and the warrior did his best to rebel whenever possible. "Just hungry."

Nigel handed the pizza to his friend. "Talk to me, Slayer. I can help."

"Not this time." Christian strode across the room and took up residence at the poker table.

Exchanging raised brows with Pascal, Nigel sat across from Christian and shoved his Sharpies across the table at him. "Give it a shot."

Christian snorted as he uplifted half the pizza and took an enormous bite. "If I need peace, I've got a greenhouse of flowers in my place to arrange."

"Yeah, well, it's not helping." Nigel flipped open his pad to find a blank sheet for Christian, then paused when he saw the drawing on the first page.

It was a sketch of Natalie sitting in the window seat of her living room, knees pulled up to her chest, looking out the window. Her pale pink tank top slipping off the curve of her shoulder, her delicate fingers entwined around her knees. Sensual and vulnerable at the same time. It was the pose she'd been in when he'd walked into the house the morning after she'd almost died, and he'd never forget the vulnerability in her eyes... until she'd looked at him, and she'd gotten that fiery expression in her eyes that she always got when she noticed him watching her. That spark of life that had enchanted him from the first time he'd seen her.

He brushed his thumb over her cheek, wondering what it would be like to feel that soft skin beneath his hand for real. But that was a line he didn't dare cross. It was one thing to bask in the magic of Natalie's aura from afar. He'd been careful not to speak much to her, to keep a distance between them, never to indulge his desire to cross the chasm and succumb to the allure of her soul.

If he did that, he'd never get himself back out. And she would pay for it. He knew she would. Never would he trust himself to get close to her. Because she deserved to live, and if he got close to her...

He swore. No. He wouldn't endanger her like that. He'd give her space and derive his peace from drawing her. Art would be enough. It had to be.

"Damn." Christian leaned forward to peer at the page. "You got a crush on Natalie or what? You made her look like an angel."

"Shut up." Nigel flipped the page, hiding Natalie and giving Christian a blank sheet of paper. "Maybe flower arranging isn't your shtick," he said as he held out the pad to his friend. "Try drawing."

"No chance." Christian shoved it away from him. "Art may be your salvation, but it's not mine—"

A loud purring interrupted them. *The Persians*. A perennial favorite of their former captor, and not in a good way.

At least not for them.

———

Well, that certainly wasn't going to win her the Michelin-O Gold Star of Love, was it?

Natalie folded her arms, leaned against the marble counter, and studied the broken freezer door she'd jerry-rigged shut.

On the plus side, she was suitably impressed with her ability to use the fourteen-carat gold ribbon ties from her gift boxes to hog tie the steel door back to the hinges, but when the inspectors for Michelin-O waltzed into her store, that wasn't going to cut it, was it?

Yes, granted, as a Sweet, she was gifted with that special touch with chocolate, but all that did was qualify her for consideration by Michelin-O. She still had to prove herself and her store.

Cursed deedubs. The sexual hopes of men everywhere depended on the success of her store, and if it got destroyed because a bunch of chocoholic demons—

She sensed movement behind her, and her heart jumped with both excitement and dread. Nigel was back already to have his way with her?

"So, this is the place where it all happens, huh?"

Natalie yelped at the female voice in her ear. She grabbed a serving spoon, spun around, and found herself paddle-to-jaw with a woman who made her think that maybe she was on the wrong side of the freezer door.

Yeah, sure, being stared down by a skinny, five-foot-four, twenty-something female with wire-rimmed glasses, a fitted white blouse, and a high-waisted black skirt would not normally be cause for distress.

It was the fact that she was clutching a bloody twelve-inch serrated knife in her left hand, her white blouse was covered in blood, and her high cheekbones were smeared with it as well was what was giving Natalie pause.

"Back off!" Natalie backed up slightly, wielding the instrument-o-love like she knew how to use it. Which she did, if it involved careful preparation of magically enhanced chocolate desserts. Not so much of an expert at using it for self-defense, as evidenced by her need to get a TRO instead of defending her own turf. So not feeling the love for having sent Nigel away right now. Big manly warriors were supposed to be present for protective purposes at all times!

The woman blinked. "Didn't we have a meeting set up for today?"

Natalie lowered the ladle a bit, realizing that if this woman wasn't a deedub, then, well, it would be slightly embarrassing to be caught trying to impale her on a kitchen utensil. Okay, so yeah, maybe she was a little bit jittery. Despite her bravado, Nigel's concerns had been niggling at the back of her mind all afternoon, and she was decidedly edgy now. "I'm sorry, I don't recall a meeting—"

"We set it up three months ago." The woman extended her nonbloody hand. "I'm Ella Smitweiser, PhD candidate, here to interview you about your business." She waved the bloody knife. "Sorry about the blade. I just came from interviewing a Jack-the-Ripper fan club. They really weren't what I'm looking for, so I'm hoping our interview goes better."

Of course. A Jack-the-Ripper fan club. Why hadn't Natalie thought of that? "An interview with me?" Natalie moved away from the freezer, putting a crate of empty crème bottles between her and the hidey-hole where she'd found the deedub such a short time ago. "That doesn't sound familiar, and I'm kind of busy right now—"

"Don't you dare try to put me off." Ella set her hands on her hips and gave Natalie a peremptory stare.

"You're my last study for my thesis, and I need to have my research done by next week if I'm going to graduate this summer and start teaching in the fall. There's only one open spot for Professor of Hedonism, and it's mine, but I need you."

"Professor of Hedonism?" Natalie noticed her hands were shaking. Hello? Living in terror was no longer acceptable. There would be no more trembling in fear for Natalie Fleming, remember? She'd survived a deedub bite, grabbed onto her second chance with both hands, and she simply was not going to live in fear like she'd done for the last twenty-five years. "What does that mean?"

"Hedonism is about making your own happiness your number one priority in life."

"Oh." Natalie set her assault weapon on the counter beside the paints and paper Nigel had left by her room one morning. She'd never used them, but she'd been comforted by their presence when she'd been here trying to get the place back in shape. It almost made her feel like he was there with her, keeping her safe.

But Ella seemed innocuous enough. Natalie doubted too many people had been murdered by geeky women who were devoted to self-pleasuring.

"My thesis is on practitioners who work in the field of bringing extreme and utter joy and exhilaration, and complete, selfish, pleasure to everyone around them," Ella said. "The Ripper fan club is completely deluded about what constitutes pleasure, I'll tell you that right now." Ella dropped the knife into a nearby trash can and headed toward the sink to wash her hands. "But since your business is to enable clients to enhance their sexual pleasure to limitless extremes, you're the perfect subject for my thesis."

"I don't advocate selfish pleasure," Natalie protested. "I give people the chance to follow their dreams, and the more sensual side of human nature is what I tend to be most successful at…" Her protest faded as Nigel's image appeared in her mind. The way he watched her, the sensual way he held his markers, as if he were caressing them. She picked up one of the paintbrushes Nigel had left her. It was fiery red with sparkles, so smooth to the touch. Passion and fire, just like Nigel. She imagined his fingers running down the wood, a featherlight caress of—

"Oh, come on. Hedonism is good. It's where we should all be headed." Ella interrupted Natalie's thought, jerking her back to the present. "Or do you believe in suffering, misery, and denying joy to your own heart?"

"God, no." A cold shudder went through Natalie at the thought of how she'd spent her whole life, haunted by the deadly curse of the deedub who'd bitten her when she was a child. Even since she'd shed the curse and had a second chance at life, she'd still been on edge and unsettled. Not quite able to focus. The only time she'd felt calm was when Nigel had been nearby. It didn't matter if he was in the other room talking to Jarvis. The deep resonance of his voice always eased her tension, made her feel safe.

But, of course, now that Jarvis and her sister were out of town, there had been no reason for Nigel to stop by, and she'd felt that absence. Until today, when he'd appeared so unexpectedly, almost as if he'd been drawn to her in her moment of need. It was sort of cool that he'd arrived in that moment. A coincidence? Or was he always watching, making sure she was safe?

She glanced out at the street, but of course he wasn't leaning against a lamppost playing guardian. She sighed and set the paintbrush back on the counter, carefully placing it beside the paper. "But it's not that easy to let go of the fear—"

"Of course it's not easy. That's why they need good professors, and I'm the best." Ella pulled out an iPad and began typing. "So, tell me how it feels when you use your chocolate-enhanced power of suggestion and tell a flaccid-impaired man that he can get a boner, and then you see his pants swell?"

"You want to know about erections in men?" A creak sounded from the freezer, and Natalie glanced sharply at it. Was that ice settling, or was there something in there? In the thirty seconds she'd been at the front of the store flipping the sign to open, a deedub could have snuck in. What if there was a lawbreaker in there right now?

Ella made a noise of exasperation. "I explained all this in the email."

"Hello? Is anyone in here?" The door opened and in strode a construction worker in a white hard hat with a bunch of tools hanging from his belt. "I've been by here every day for three weeks and you're finally open!"

Her first client in weeks! Natalie hurried over to him as Ella rushed back to her computer and began typing again. "Hi, I'm Natalie—"

"I'm getting married tonight, by God, and I haven't had an erection in six years." The man grabbed her shoulders, his grip desperate. "The Good Catholic Boy shtick won't help me after tonight. You *have* to help me!"

Excitement raced through her. This was what she was here for! This is what Scrumptious was all about! "Hang on." She raced to the newly cleansed freezer and yanked out the drawer for the Chocolate Virility Balls she'd launched just before she went insane and nearly died. Only ten left.

She grabbed two of them and hurried back. She set them in his hand. "What's your name?"

"Richard Small. You can call me Dick, though."

She blinked, resisting the urge to tell him that maybe his first step should be to start going by Rich instead. "Okay, well, Dick, eat the balls."

He tossed them in his mouth, and she leaned forward, staring intently at him. "The moment you think of your fiancée, you will get an erection that will last until she has orgasmed, at which point you will experience your own magnificent pleasure that rocks both your worlds." The words, the magic words, that had always sounded so beautiful, almost stuck in her throat. Her stomach clenched as she recalled with vivid clarity how she'd almost died at the hands of the Godfather, a man who killed women by sex.

Caught in the deedub thrall, she'd been irresistibly drawn to him, even though she'd known that to succumb to his allure meant certain death. Oh, she knew, but she'd been completely unable to resist the call of the orgasm. A nightmare, a horrific terrifying experience that had brought her own demise.

Never had she felt that kind of sexual longing before, and she would never allow herself to get out of control like that again. Not ever. Even saying the suggestion to Dick made her stomach turn. It was too close to the memories of being compelled to places she didn't want to go.

Which was why her reaction to Nigel earlier had been so unsettling. Her awareness of him as a man... it felt so good to feel the heat of his gaze on her. Too good. She couldn't trust herself. Not anymore. Not ever again.

Dick stared at her. "That's it?"

"I'm good. That's all that's needed." Sexual baggage or not, it did feel fantastic to be back in her place. Helping men who needed her. Bringing order to the world of sex. This wasn't sexual chaos and uncontrolled, deadly passion. This was precision and order, a systematic alignment of sexual balance in the universe. This was what her soul lived for. "What's your fiancée's name?" she asked, a question designed to force him to think of his fiancée and trigger his erection, just so he could know it was all going to be okay.

He frowned. "Lucille DeLuca."

Natalie waited expectantly for the blood to go south and the dough to begin to rise.

He stared at her blankly.

Ella watched.

And then an awkward silence grew. Finally, Natalie cleared her throat. "Aren't you getting an erection?"

He narrowed his eyes. "No."

Um... hello? He should be hard as a steel shaft right now. On his way to redemption and happiness. "But you're thinking of your fiancée?"

"Yeah."

Uh oh. Why wasn't he getting a boner? No man had ever failed to respond to her suggestions, at least not when they'd had their sexual resistance lowered with some of her specialty chocolate. She always helped every man who came to her, except, of course, those who had some Otherworld powers, because she could only influence those with no magical ability whatsoever, as evidenced by her utter failure with the deedub. "Are you Magick?"

He blinked. "Magic? Are you shitting me?" His face turned a brilliant shade of embarrassment. "This is all a hoax, isn't it? You got a hidden camera in here or something? The boys put me up to this, didn't they?"

"No, no!" Shoot! He *was* human, but she hadn't been able to help him. What had gone wrong? How could she have failed to help him? "I'm not sure what happened. Let me try again—"

"No chance, bitch! I won't be humiliated by yet another woman!" He yanked himself free and stormed out the door, disappearing in a furious rant down the street.

"I don't understand. I always help men like him." Natalie gripped the counter as she stared after him in disbelief. "I can help anyone." He'd been so receptive to her assistance that she should have been able to influence him even without the chocolate, yet she'd failed utterly.

"My word, girlfriend. You can't even influence an ordinary human?" Ella whistled. "That's bad news, girl. Really, really bad."

"I know." She didn't need an aspiring hedonism expert to tell her that something was wrong. Helping men with their sexual inadequacies was the core of who she was. It was her calling in life. It was her soul's mission.

Yeah, she was still alive and had a second chance at life, but something really, really important was still dying inside her. But what?

Chapter 3

A BLADE ERUPTED FROM NIGEL'S PALM, AND CHRISTIAN leapt to his feet. Christian's arm shimmered with metal, and he pulled a sword out of the scabbard that was his arm. The two warriors whirled around, armed and ready—

Pascal was laughing hysterically. "You should've seen your faces! I've never seen old guys move so fast."

Nigel sighed and lowered his sword. "Causing trouble again, newbie?"

But Christian didn't seem to realize that Pascal had worked them over. "Where are they?" The skin on Christian's shoulders shifted into metal scales, and the air began to hum. His blue eyes were flashing, and the skin on his jaw shifted briefly into chain-link metal before taking on flesh form again.

"Behind you," Pascal said. "Watch out. Big scary kitty."

Christian spun around, and Nigel slowly turned. Perched on top of the flat-screen TV was a fluffy white Persian kitty. Not a whole herd of the beasts, too numerous to handle. Just one, solitary kitty. It was crouched in assault mode, its tail flicking as it readied to pounce. "Angelica's found us. She's back." Christian raised his sword, and purple sweat streamed down his brow. His reaction was far too intense given that the enemy numbered only one. "She's coming to get us—"

"Is she now?" Nigel pointed his blade at Pascal. "What did you do?"

Still laughing, Pascal held up a tube of glittery pink lip gloss. "Fairy Tale Rose."

Nigel's veins burned at the sight of the polycarbonate container inside which Angelica stored her most demonic spells. How many times had Nigel been chained to a wall as Angelica had pulled out a tube of pink, bracing himself for whatever hell emerged? Might be demons, acid-laced candy canes, killer bees, or some combination thereof. You never knew what hell on earth was going to emerge when that sucker was opened.

"Thought it might help Christian if I gave him something to play with," Pascal said. "We all miss the battles we used to have in the Den, dig?"

Nigel glanced over at Christian, who looked like he was about to go into full assault mode over one kitty. The warrior had been off like milk left in the Sahara Desert at high noon, and Nigel wasn't sure his buddy was up to a little disco dancing with pink spells.

Nigel strode over to Pascal and swiped the tube out of his hand. "How many did you let out?"

"Just one." Pascal grinned. "Shit, man, I'm not crazy. We'd get our asses kicked if I let out a bunch. This is just for fun. Better than beating each other up—"

Before Nigel could answer, the purr deepened ominously, a loud boom filled the room, cat hair showered down over them, and then the real beast burst through the white cloud of fur.

It wasn't the cat. Not anymore.

It was a bronze-skinned demon of metal, with spiked skin and teeth the size of Blaine's number two knitting needles. Its claws were longer than the ones Angelica's enhanced wolverines had used to rip out Nigel's spleen during the summer of the Beasts from Beyond Hell, as he and his boys affectionately referred to dog days when Angelica had tapped into a new level of brutality that she hadn't previously accessed.

Except for the pink bows, peach lipstick, and the pompoms around its ankles, this creature was all wire, with no flesh, no body parts, just spiked coils sharp enough to cut through metal.

Nigel envisioned thousands of microscopic blades forming in his palms beneath his skin, and he instantly felt the sharp pricks in his palm as the blades began to rise to the surface.

"Wait." Pascal held up his hand to stay him and nodded at Christian. "Let him. He needs the therapy."

Christian's skin was shimmering as he slipped out of his human form into his attack mode. Skin cells shifted into microscopic chain links worthy of a deep-sea fight with a great white shark. The transformation continued, until Christian was nothing but one oversexed shark suit. When in that form, Christian was toxic to anything that touched him, unless it was protected by nylon.

Nigel hadn't seen Christian in full armor since they'd escaped. Maybe Pascal's plan had merit after all. They all needed some good battles from time to time to keep the juices flowing.

Christian was actually smiling. "Hallelujah!" He let out a whoop of delight, charged the demon, and cleaved it in half with one stroke. "Hot damn! I forgot how much fun that is!" Christian beckoned at Nigel. "Give me another one!"

"You got it." As Nigel dipped the applicator into the tube, he could practically see Angelica's eyes gleaming in anticipation. Her boys were playing with her toys, and she hadn't even forced them. Success, even from the prison she was locked away inside.

But not really, because they were in control now. He grinned, thrilled as hell to see Christian looking so cheerful.

"That lip gloss is a nice shade for your swarthy skin." Pascal cocked an eyebrow. "You might consider trying it on those lips of yours. Almost matches that pretty rose tattoo on your cheek."

"Nah, I'm holding out for a peach tone. I think it goes more with my lips." Wearing makeup was something that even Angelica hadn't dared force upon them. Thank the gods for small victories.

The applicator began to smoke, rosy pink billows puffing off it, and Nigel flicked it so two drops landed near Christian.

The warrior's metal skin shimmered as two more kitties appeared. "Bring it on, baby."

"This is better than football." Nigel leaned against the wall, relaxing as his buddy battled the two demons. "That's a sight I thought I'd never see again. Christian kicking ass—"

Pascal coughed, and his skin turned soot-colored as he suddenly fought for breath.

"Shit!" Nigel ditched the lip gloss and set his hands on Pascal's chest. Dark poison was circulating inside. Where had that come from? He immediately began to shove healing light into the warrior.

Christian swore. "What happened to him?"

"I don't know. He seemed fine." The dark energy inside Pascal was resisting Nigel's healing. "Something new has come to the party."

Draw.

Nigel jerked his head up. "Did you just tell me to draw, Slayer?"

"Hell, no." Christian was heavily engaged mano a mano with a set of twin demon-kitties, unable to assist Nigel until he dispatched them. "But if you think it'll help, go for it."

Draw the warrior.

It wasn't a command. It was his own instincts telling him how to focus his healing energy. Of course drawing made sense. Art was how he pulled himself together.

Nigel whipped out the pad he always kept with him, sat cross-legged on Pascal's bed, and began to sketch the young warrior. The moment he began to work, rightness filled his soul. This was what he was supposed to be doing.

"Do it fast," Christian said. "Pascal doesn't look good."

"I know." Nigel sensed Pascal's energy fading, his body rigid as it fought to hang on. Nigel's pencil flew across the page, driven by the adrenaline, by the torment on Pascal's face, the moan of agony deep in his throat.

Nigel transcribed the tension on Pascal's face, the way his skin was stretched by his battle with death, the desperation of his soul's fight to hang on. Pascal's fierce passion filled Nigel, bringing his energy into alignment. By the time Nigel had finished drawing the warrior's face, powerful healing energy was pulsing through Nigel. He set down the drawing and rubbed his hands together. "Okay, Pascal, I'm going to clean this up—"

Finish the drawing.

Nigel ignored the command. He didn't need to draw anymore. He'd gotten what he needed. He placed his hands on Pascal's chest and a rosy glow filled Pascal. The kid coughed, and then his chest heaved as air rushed back into his lungs.

"And we have liftoff," Nigel announced.

"Nigel," Christian shouted. "The lip gloss is leaking."

Nigel saw the tube lying on the floor, pink liquid oozing out of the end. "Shit!" He grabbed it and shoved the lid on, but there were already a dozen kitties perched on cabinets. "This is why men should never play with makeup."

"No shit. You're on your own now," Christian said as the room filled with the screams of demons coming to life. "Take care of our boy, and I'll handle these guys."

"I'm on it." Leaving Christian to play, Nigel forced more energy into Pascal, and he found an insidious black taint inside the warrior's body. "There's some kind of poison inside him."

"Clear it," Christian ordered as he took down three demons with one swipe.

"I'm on it." But he'd never seen it before. He needed to figure out how to clear it—

Finish the drawing.

Nigel lunged for the sketchpad. He *had* to finish the drawing. The answer lay within the picture. He sketched until Pascal's form was complete, and peace and rightness surged through him. Nigel tossed the pad aside and palmed Pascal's chest. Power poured from his hands into the warrior. Nigel's energy plunged into the poison, shredded it easily, and well-being rushed back into Pascal's body.

Pascal's green eyes snapped open.

Nigel grinned. "Welcome back, buddy—"

"Oh, man!" Pascal paled, looking past Nigel. "Tell me I'm hallucinating."

"Holy mother of hell," Christian muttered. "This isn't good."

Nigel turned. A glittering, diamond-shaped hole was forming in the wall. A portal to the Den. In his house! Nigel leapt to his feet as the woman who'd been Angelica's all-star apprentice for the last hundred years appeared in the doorway.

Mari's brown hair was still streaked with blond highlights, but gone were tight jeans and stack-'em-high T-shirts. Instead, she was wearing a navy blue suit and all-business heels, and there was a confident set to her shoulders that hadn't been there before she'd taken over after Angelica's incarceration.

This was not the needy, weak apprentice who had manipulated Christian and betrayed them all. This was a woman who would fight from the front lines, and she had taken control in Angelica's absence.

Excellent. Because the chicks had been altogether too boring before.

"Mari. What do you want?" Nigel allowed daggers to ease from his fingertips as Mari waved cheerfully at him, holding a piece of paper in her hand. On it was his drawing of Pascal.

Nigel grabbed his sketchpad off the ground and saw that the picture of Pascal was still there. But Mari was holding the exact same image in her hand.

"Get her!" Christian charged the hologram, sword blazing, but when he tried to tackle her, he went right through Mari's image without doing anything more than causing her image to flicker.

"It's a hologram," Nigel called out. "She's not real!" Which was good. Murdering the woman in cold blood wouldn't be the best therapy Christian could find. You know, given that they were all pretty much hardwired not to harm women in any way, even those decidedly lacking a reciprocal set of morals.

Christian whirled around. "What do you mean?"

"It's not her. It's just her image."

Christian swore and slammed his sword through the image in frustration. Yeah, old girlfriends were a real drain on a man's ability to get up and go. But Nigel sensed that something else was bothering Christian, something that ran a whole lot deeper. Because Christian was, quite simply, not the type to harm a woman. Even Mari. Even a hologram of her. Not once. Not ever. No matter what.

"Hey, dudes. A little help, maybe?" Pascal called out.

Nigel glanced over at him and was surprised to see he was apparently being dragged by some unseen force straight toward Mari, who was gripping the drawing tightly in her hand. "Whoa. She's trying to take you through the portal?" Damn. That just wasn't acceptable. Invading his digs and stealing his peeps? He shot a hard look at her. "No chance, Mari. You don't get to have us anymore."

She didn't respond. She just kept watching Pascal, who'd grabbed onto the footboard of his bed, hanging on with impressive strength for someone who'd been almost dead a few minutes ago. But they were warriors. They did shit like that.

Nigel stiffened, not liking the intensity of Mari's stare. How had she opened the portal in his place anyway?

"She shouldn't be here."

"Unfortunately, she's not." Christian leaned on his sword, still looking overly disgruntled that he couldn't grab Mari by the hair and drag her out of the portal. "That's the first time I've ever seen anyone get sucked into a portal through a drawing."

"Impressive," Pascal agreed, still hanging on tightly. "Maybe we should sell tickets?" His voice grew more strained. "I gotta say, though, going back to party with Mari isn't my first choice. I mean, she's hot and all that, but she is my buddy's ex-girlfriend and all. Violates man code to do her."

Christian barked with strained laughter. "She's all yours, newbie."

"Don't really want her, actually." Pascal gasped as one hand slipped off the footboard.

"Fight it, man. I'm coming." Nigel loped across the room and grabbed Pascal's wrist. "I've got you—"

Pascal was ripped out of his grasp. "Hey!" Nigel lunged after his comrade as Pascal tumbled across the room toward Mari and the hell that they'd all suffered for so long. Crap! What was going on?

Christian swore, and both warriors lunged for Pascal's outstretched hands. "Hang on," Nigel ordered. His fingers brushed against Pascal's. "Got him!"

Pascal met his eyes, a stricken look on his face. "First time ever that I didn't get pleasure over you being wrong." Then he was torn away from Nigel and sucked through the portal.

"Pascal!" Christian dove into the portal, but it shut too quickly, and Christian crashed to the floor, empty-handed. Except, of course, for his sword. He swore and whirled toward Nigel. "You trapped him." His skin was even tighter across his face, his eyes sunken. "You sent him back!"

"I know." A hundred and fifty years of sensitivity training had made Nigel able to admit when he'd screwed up. He had no clue how that could have happened, but it had. He swore and slammed his fist into the wall. "She had to have tainted the paper. Or the markers. Or maybe it was my healing." Christian had nearly been broken when he'd been yanked back. Not another one. Not Pascal. "I'm going in after him."

"You can't go in there by yourself." Christian gripped Pascal's footboard, his skin undulating with metal as Christian fought to keep control. "I'm going with you." There was agony, fury, fire, and a deep, deep terror on Christian's face. What could bring that level of fear to a man so immortal and so fierce that even the demons ran from him?

"No. You can't go back in." Nigel knew Christian was in bad shape. No way could he ask his teammate to return to the Den. It was too much, too soon. "It's my responsibility." Hell, yeah, it was his responsibility. He'd committed one of their own back to hell. *Shit!* His job was to take care of everyone, not bring them down!

Christian shook his head. "Blaine and Jarvis won't be back from their cruise for two weeks. You need backup, and I'm going in with you. We're getting him back."

"I can handle it." Nigel grabbed a Sharpie and a paper off the table and began to sketch Christian's torment. He was so pissed and frustrated he couldn't focus. Two minutes with the pen and he'd be able to create a strategy.

"What are you doing?" Christian demanded.

"I'm drawing. Need to clear my head." He added the lines of strain around his teammate's mouth—

"Stop!" Christian ripped the sketchpad out of his hand. "I won't let you send me back to the Den, too. Draw something else." The tip of Christian's sword touched his jaw. "Not me."

Nigel stared at Christian. "You think I drew him back into the Den."

"Yeah, I do."

Shit. Was that possible? Of course it was. Better not to take the chance. They all knew what Mari would do to have another chance at Christian. "Yeah, okay. I'll draw something else." Natalie's face flashed in his mind and he smiled. Oh, yes, he knew who to draw. The delicate visage of a woman with haunted green eyes, living with a fear so deep she didn't sleep. The passion in her eyes, the sensual way her body moved when she was doing something as simple as getting milk out of the fridge.

A sense of peace settled over him as he began to sketch. That delicate upturned nose, those full lips—

"Look at what you're drawing," Christian said quietly.

Nigel saw that he'd drawn Christian's face again. Not Natalie. "What the hell?" He flipped the page again, his soul getting restless. He needed to draw to pull himself together. He envisioned Natalie's lovely energy, the sparkle in her eye when she'd been in the moment of joy, the anguish in her face when she realized she was dying. The flush of her cheeks, the way she would watch him across the room, so aware of his every move—

Christian ripped the paper out of his hand. "Look."

He'd drawn Christian again. "Son of a bitch."

"Mari wants me, and somehow she's compelling you to draw me, just like she did with Pascal."

Draw Christian.

It was the same voice in his head as before.

Holy shit. Christian was right. Mari was manipulating his drawing. He had to stop. But even as he thought it, a burning need seared through him at the thought of not drawing. It was his salvation. It was how he cleared his mind enough to go into battle. It was how he summoned his healing arts. He needed a clear mind to rescue Pascal, and he wouldn't get there without his art. It was exactly as Natalie had said, that his art was a part of his soul.

But she had no idea how truly important it was. He absolutely could not afford to be without the respite that his art gave him. But as he looked at Christian's eyes staring at him from the paper on the floor, he knew he couldn't risk it. He couldn't draw. Sweat beaded on his brow at the thought of being without it. "No, I can handle this. She can't control me—"

"Hell, man!" Christian ripped the pen out of his hand, and Nigel saw he'd started to draw Christian on his own palm.

Christian raised his sword to Nigel's throat. "I love you, man, but I can't go back. Not on her terms." Tension rippled his body. "It'll haunt me for centuries to do it, but if you try to draw me again, I'll cut off your hands and pray you figure out how to regrow them."

Nigel swore and bunched his fist. Was he that weak that he couldn't stop himself from drawing Christian? And who would be his victim after that? Blaine? Jarvis? He was a danger to them all. But without his art, he was an even greater danger. To them, to Natalie, to anyone he cared about. "I can do it. I need to draw—"

"I don't trust Mari." Christian's face was hard, but there was sympathy in his eyes. "You've got no chance if she's decided to use you."

Nigel swore. A hundred and fifty years had taught them very clearly the limitations of their power against Mari and Angelica. Christian was right.

Christian nodded. "We have to preempt her now." He tapped his sword against Nigel's wrists. "Give me permission."

"No." He shoved Christian's blade aside. "She wins if you take away my weapons."

Christian hesitated, then slowly lowered his sword. "Get help, then. Someone who can be louder in your head than Mari."

They didn't have time for this. They needed to get Pascal back fast. Every minute he spent there was hell. "I can outtalk Mari—"

"You really want to take that chance?"

Nigel swore. Pascal was already gone. Christian was next. Did he dare risk it? His soul needed to draw anyway, and with Mari pushing at him… "Shit."

Christian nodded. "That about sums it up."

Who the hell could shut down Mari's voice in his head? Alleviate his need to draw? He needed to focus his mind so he could strategize and think of a solution. To give him the peace that art gave him without actually picking up the pen. Natalie's face flashed in his mind, and Nigel itched with the need to draw her. If he could have five minutes with her image, he could clear his head enough to find an answer. Natalie could help him, she could… Holy shit. *Natalie could really help him*. And not just by being an image he drew to calm himself.

Natalie Fleming had a gift, a special gift that was exactly what he needed. But hell, he couldn't ask her for help. She was the last person he dared to think about even when he had his art to keep him calm. Without it? Shit. She would be in such danger.

He couldn't risk her.

But without her, he couldn't save his team. He swore and lunged for the door. "I'll meet you in an hour."

Christian frowned. "Where are you going?"

"I gotta go see about a girl." A girl who should be on her way to a safe haven in the tropics. A woman he'd sworn not to endanger by getting close to her. A beautiful soul that he would put in jeopardy with every second in her presence.

He couldn't afford to turn to her for help. Not for her sake. Not for his.

But he couldn't afford not to. *God keep you safe from me, Natalie*.

But he knew that God couldn't keep anyone safe. Not from him.

Especially not Natalie Fleming.

Chapter 4

STILL REELING FROM HER FAILURE WITH DICK SMALL and his flaccid rod-o-love, Natalie shuffled numbly across the store and flipped the sign on the door to Closed just as a police officer reached for the door handle. She met his gaze, and she saw the hopelessness in his eyes, the broken visage of a man who couldn't figure out how to be a man on his own.

"Please don't close," he said quietly. "Please."

She hated feeling useless. But she wasn't going to humiliate anyone else until she could figure out what was wrong with her. "I'm so sorry."

"But I need your help—"

"I can't." She forced the door shut on him and leaned her back against the glass, steeling herself against his pleading requests. Her soul was screaming at her to help him. She was supposed to be his angel of virility. And she had to let him down.

Ella cocked her head, her gaze sympathetic. "Girl, you're in bad shape, aren't you?"

Natalie eyed the iPad sitting on Ella's lap and thought of her life being splayed out for public consumption in Ella's dissertation. "This really isn't the time for an interview. I have to figure some things out. I—"

"I've been there."

Natalie frowned. "Been where? Unable to give a man erection assistance?"

Ella smiled. "Oh, no, I can't say I've ever been for-tunate enough to affect men's sexual performance on a regular basis. But I've been in a pretty bad place."

Yeah, sure. This PhD candidate looked like she was far above such mundane things as failure to deliver the big boner or being stalked by demons with eating dis-orders. "You mean you were about to die ahead of your time? Failed to live up to your destiny? Unable to do what your soul is screaming at you to do?"

Ella nodded. "Yeah, pretty much. Only I was praying to die and couldn't make it happen."

Well, that wasn't an answer she heard every day. "Really?" Natalie looked more carefully at Ella. The prim and proper schoolmarm outfit, the straight brown hair in a pristine bun, the elegant and subdued makeup weren't what Natalie would expect a hedonism professor to wear. Maybe a flamboyant grass skirt. Or a scarlet red body suit. Platinum blond hair. Not this tightly wrapped example of how to suppress every piece of passion in your soul.

"Really." Ella set the computer aside. "Listen, Nat... Can I call you Nat?"

"Yeah, sure." Natalie moved closer, lured by the friendly lean to Ella's shoulders. By the welcoming warmth in her eyes. With her only remaining sister now spending most of her time with her new man, Natalie missed the companionship of another woman. "What happened?"

Ella shook her head. "Oh, no, you don't want to hear my story." She gave a smile that didn't reach her eyes. "But I just wanted to tell you that sometimes life seems to be more than we can handle, but it's really not.

There's always a way, even when it seems like there isn't." She picked up a chocolate bar and sniffed it. "The key thing is not to give up. Take action, even if it's little steps. It helps, it really does."

Natalie perched on the chair next to Ella. "I don't even know who I am right now. I feel like I'm floundering." Yes, she was alive, but after twenty-five years of being haunted by her curse, waiting to die, now that she had a chance to start over, she almost felt like she didn't know where to begin. She was envious of Nigel, who always seemed to be so at peace as long as he had a pen in his hand.

"You?" Ella raised her brows. "You're one of the most powerful Mystics I've ever run across. You're this amazing talent with this great business. Don't forget that."

"But I'm not powerful!" But it did feel good to have someone telling her she wasn't a total loser. "I couldn't even influence a human just now."

Ella squeezed Natalie's hand, genuine, urgent concern in her voice. "Play with your chocolate. Try to influence an ant. Anything it takes to keep moving forward. Action begets action." She balanced the chocolate bar on the tip of her index finger and began to spin it. "Watch."

It whirled around in a dizzy circle. "Never abandon forward motion," Ella said. "If you do, that's when you crash. So much harder to get going, to find hope again. Even if you feel like you're spinning in circles at least you're moving." Ella flicked the end of the spinning bar and it flew off her finger, spiraling through the air as it soared across the store, landing on the floor and sliding another ten feet before it came to a rest beside a vintage candy machine. "See? Even running in circles can launch you forward. Always keep moving. Always."

"I'm not giving up." Natalie fisted her hand. "I'm just a little out of ideas for how to move forward." How could she influence a deedub not to kill her if she couldn't even give Dick Small an erection? Nigel would come back for her, and she would have no defenses when he pointed out her inability to defend herself.

But if she couldn't heal men sexually, then what did she have anyway? Without it, her soul would die.

Ella smiled. "Doesn't matter. Just do something. Anything." She grinned and gestured at the store. "You have enough chocolate in here to combat the PMS of all the women in Boston. Start with a chocolate binge, then go from there. Doesn't chocolate always help?"

Natalie couldn't help but laugh. "Of course. Why didn't I think of that? Chocolate bingeing is the answer to all of a woman's problems."

"Always and always." Ella grinned back. Then her smile faded, replaced by a more serious expression. "Just know that I've been where you are, and if there's anything I can do to help, just let me know." She winked. "Off the record, of course."

Natalie smiled, feeling like she had an ally. Ella had come in waving a bloody knife. Who knew? Maybe the woman had talents beyond wielding an iPad and writing dissertations. "Well, as long as it's off the record—"

"Natalie Fleming? It's really you?" A young woman in cut-off jeans and a torn T-shirt shoved open the front door, her eyes wide with disbelief.

Natalie groaned. "Listen, I'm not open right now. I—"

"My name is Maggie Valtese." The visitor shoved

her tangled brown hair out of her face. Her face was peaked and drawn, her eyes worried. "I'm here about your job posting for an assistant chef. I have my resume with me." She began to rifle through her purse. "I'm a Sweet, so I'm really good with chocolate. You don't even have to pay me. I just need a place to sleep and maybe some food. Please. I really need this job."

Natalie felt a tinge of empathy for Maggie. She knew what it felt like to be desperate. "Listen, I'm not sure when I'm going to reopen. I've got some things I need to address first." Like how to get her mojo back in time for the inspection. A gleaming store wasn't the only thing she'd need to show them to get her rating.

Natalie began to pull out some ingredients to make another batch of virility balls. Maybe she'd failed with Dick because the chocolate had gone bad. Maybe fresh ones would do it.

But even as she set a mixing bowl on the counter, a dark dread pulsed inside her. One that said maybe it hadn't been the chocolate. It had been her.

Ella patted her shoulder and started to clear off the counter to make more room for cooking. "Good girl, Nat. Taking action is the first step."

"My ex-boyfriend is hunting me." Maggie inched closer to the counter, like a furtive puppy dog hoping to snatch a steak off the counter. "I didn't know he was a deedub until he lost it one night and tried to have me for dessert."

"What?" A bowl slipped out of Natalie's hand, and Ella barely caught it before it crashed to the floor. "Has he bitten you?"

"No." Maggie picked up a piece of chocolate and

turned it over in her hand, her fingers caressing it with a reverence Natalie had seen only in her family, only in other Sweets.

"Good." Natalie let her breath out and took the bowl back from Ella. *She's okay, she's okay, she's okay.* Maggie was not destined to the same fate as Natalie and her family. As long as she could get Maggie out of there, the girl would be safe. "You need to hide from him. We can't defeat deedubs."

"I've been on the run for almost two years, but he keeps finding me." Maggie shoved up her sleeve and held out her arm. Dark red claw marks raked across her arm, making Natalie's stomach lurch. "So, then I heard about you, and how you dodged death, and so I hoped you could help."

"Me?" Natalie looked more carefully at Maggie. She couldn't be more than twenty-two. She looked worn out and scared, scattered. Exactly how Natalie had felt her whole life, waiting for the deedub poison to kick in and take her out, watching each member of her family die off, one by one as the deedub poison took them. "I'm not a warrior. I can't protect you against *that*—"

"But you have to!" Maggie picked up the chocolate again and began shaving fine pieces off it, almost frantically, as if she needed the comfort of manipulating chocolate. Which, as a Sweet, she probably did. "If you put me out, I'll be dead."

Crap! She knew Maggie wasn't exaggerating. Now that she'd been scented, she would be hunted until they found her. But how could Natalie possibly keep her safe? "I want to, but—"

"And here is our newest attraction on our tour." The

door opened and in strode a woman in a black suit jacket and a cute little skirt, wearing a large white name tag that said Marjorie Stevens, All World Tours, Inc.

Maggie froze, Ella graced them with a curious inspection, and Natalie stared in confusion. A tour? Of her store? Holy cow. She'd become so famous that she'd made it onto a walking tour of Boston. "This is fantastic!"

"This is great data," Ella said, typing furiously on her iPad. "That's so interesting to know that the city of Boston places such a high value on great sex that your store has made it onto a tour."

A man in plaid pants and suspenders eyed the broken front window. "What happened to that?"

Oh, right. Granted, it was great to have made it onto the tour, but she and the store weren't exactly in show condition. Natalie hopped up, tucking her disheveled hair behind her ear and hoping she didn't have too much dust on her face. "Welcome to Scrumptious."

Marjorie beamed at her. "Why thank you, my dear. It's lovely to be here. Would you like to do a presentation? Maybe tell us a little bit about how you achieved such success?"

Such success? Warmth spilled through Natalie and she smiled. "I'm so delighted that my store is on your tour." She beamed at the half dozen potential customers with ball caps and sweater vests spreading out in her lobby, posing next to her display cabinet and snapping pictures. "I'll be thrilled to welcome you back next week when we're officially open. Right now we're doing construction and prep work for a very exciting, very elite opportunity to be considered for a Michelin-O Gold Star of Love." She picked up some of her gold-embossed napkins. "You are all welcome to take one of these with you as a souvenir as you leave—"

"Oh, don't worry about us," Marjorie said, waving her hands in dismissal. "You don't need to entertain us. We don't mind invading your privacy." She pointed at Natalie. "And this is Natalie Fleming, the only Sweet in history to survive a deedub bite."

The only deedub survivor? Cameras began to click again, and Natalie became aware of the scent of chocolate thickening in the air. Of a sense of restlessness building among her guests. The skin on the back of her neck began to crawl. Holy crap. This wasn't a regular tour. This was something else. She knew with sudden certainty that she needed to get them out of her building. Immediately. "Leave my store. Now." She moved in front of Maggie. "Get out of here, Maggie," she whispered. "The back door."

Maggie dropped the chocolate and began to edge toward the rear of the store.

"Everyone take your pictures," Marjorie chimed. "She won't be here for long, so this is a very exciting time—"

Maggie tripped on a barrel and a bronze candlestick clattered to the ground, its echo loud in the store. The entire tourist group jumped, and a man in red-and-white plaid shorts, a white polo shirt, and knee-high white socks snarled.

"Oh, yes," Ella said. "Men who snarl are generally not the boyfriend type. Maggie, let's go." She slipped behind the counter to help Maggie untangle herself from the upturned barrel and candlestick.

While the queen of hedonism helped the Sweet to

her feet, incisors began to stretch past checkered short man's lips. He had fangs? And they were coming out in a chocolate shop? Natalie's grip tightened desperately on the knife. "Tell me he's not a deedub." *Please, God, tell me he's not a deedub*.

Marjorie smiled. "Of course he is." She gave a cheerful, all-inclusive swing of her arm. "We all are."

"You all are?" Natalie realized everyone in the group was getting a little pointy-toothed. Oh, dear Lord almighty—

"I must have her!" Checkered shorts guy ripped his camera aside and leapt at her, teeth bared.

"No, no, no! Not permitted!" Tour guide Marjorie unleashed a deafening catcall and tackled the tourist. She sideswiped him into one of the bar stools, but one of the other tourists leapt over her and charged Natalie.

Ella started shouting, and then Maggie screamed. Knee sock guy hit Natalie hard in the chest, his claws sank into her shoulders, and a little old granny grabbed her ankle.

Natalie blocked his first bite with the knife, and then someone jerked her down from behind, and two tourists landed on top of her. She caught sight of Maggie disappearing under a load of plaid and Ella slamming her iPad into one of their heads, uselessly—

"Enough!" Marjorie bellowed in outrage. She sprayed purple dust across the store, and all the deedubs vanished.

Natalie stared in shock as the room went silent. Behind her, Ella and Maggie struggled to sit up, covered in purple dust. "You guys okay? Did you get bitten?"

Maggie shook her head. "No, no. Did you?"

"No, I'm fine." Dear God, that had been so close. A whole room full of deedubs? And Maggie, poor Maggie! The girl would be traumatized for life.

Marjorie curtsied. "My deepest apologizes, Ms. Fleming. I will do my best to avert such behavior next time."

"Next time?" Natalie shook her head. "No, no, no next time. My store is off limits—"

"Not to us," Marjorie said with a smile. "We're all in this together, my dear."

"What? No—"

But in another burst of purple smoke, the tour guide was gone, taking with her Natalie's only chance to stop her from coming again. Would she back in a day? A week? Five minutes?

"And you still expect me to believe you've got it all under control?" Standing in the doorway, staring down at her was the most beautiful, broad-shouldered, deadly artist she knew.

"Nigel!" She blurted out his name, unable to keep the relief out her voice. Let the tour come back now!

"Oh, wow," Maggie whispered. "Who is he?"

Ella shushed the girl and bundled her back behind the counter, but Natalie didn't bother to look at them.

She was too entranced by Nigel.

The warrior had changed.

Not his clothing.

Him.

He looked completely badass and mean, far more cranky than she'd ever seen him. Even the pink rose tattoo on his cheek looked darker and angrier than a flower had a right to be. He didn't look anything like the serene warrior she was used to seeing. He was on edge, he was violent, he was restless, and he was vibrating with energy in a way that sent pulses of excitement through her. *Yes*. The word whispered through her soul, unbidden.

His brows raised, as if he'd heard her whisper. His eyes darkened, and he held out his hand.

Oh, God. She shouldn't do it. She shouldn't touch him. Simply being around him stirred longings inside her that she wanted to stay dead. If she touched him... too much. But she wanted to. She wanted to feel his skin against hers. She *needed* to. Caught by the depth of his gaze, Natalie slowly raised her hand. For a moment, she hesitated, willing him to pull away. To take the choice away from her.

He didn't retract his hand. He simply waited. And slowly, her heart thudding in her chest, she set her hand in his. The shock was instant and electric as he closed his hand around hers. His skin was warm, his grip strong, his expression so intense she could feel it reverberating in her soul.

"Up we go." He tightened his grip and pulled her to her feet.

She wound up right in front of him, chest to chest, barely any space between them. He carried the faint scent of vanilla, and her body warmed. Energy seemed to crackle between them, and she realized he was still holding her hand.

His gaze flicked to her palms, as if reading her mind, but instead of letting go, his grip tightened. She realized suddenly that he wasn't going to let her go, and she liked it.

The fact that she was so thoroughly delighted that

Nigel wasn't going to let her go was quite possibly even scarier than the tour of deedubs.

Physical attraction was not something she could afford.

Not now.

Not ever.

And certainly, most definitely, not with Nigel.

Chapter 5

TOUCHING NATALIE WAS NOTHING LIKE NIGEL HAD anticipated.

And he'd thought about it a lot.

Because he was a guy, and guys did shit like that.

He'd been around Natalie a fair amount in the last few weeks. Not *with* her. Around her. In her presence. Enough to notice. Not crossing her path. Despite the fact that he was ruthlessly compelled by Natalie's luxurious brown hair and the turbulent depths of her radiant green eyes, and even though he hadn't liked the compression of her aura after she'd nearly died a few weeks ago, he had exercised his warrior discipline and hadn't reached out to her.

But he'd watched her carefully. He was well aware of the intense conflicts raging within her. You know, because he was an artist, and artists were sensitive to the intricate complexities of emotionally rich souls, and Natalie was all that, and then some. He'd sketched her repeatedly on the sly (she had no clue), but he'd never been able to capture her tormented spirit in his art to his satisfaction.

When his pen had drifted across the page bringing her to life on his paper, he'd envisioned what her skin would feel like. It wouldn't be cool and rough, like the apprentices in the Den. Natalie's skin would be warm and soft. It would be gentle and silky. She would feel the way a woman was supposed to feel.

But now, when he was finally touching her, when all the fantasies in his head became the fiery reality, as he folded his fingers around hers, he realized he'd been wrong about what it would be like to touch her.

He'd failed utterly to anticipate the raw electric shock that ripped through him, igniting every cell of his body, juicing the testosterone until he could think of nothing but going to the mattresses, with her beneath him.

For a man who was pretty damn sold on the benefits of celibacy, his reaction was a little surprising. Maybe it was her fingers. They were smaller than he'd expected. Dainty. Delicate. If he wasn't careful, he could snap them in half by accident. His fingers enfolded protectively around her hand.

He rubbed his thumb over her palm, stroking the silken skin as she stared at him, her face riveted with shock that suggested she was as startled by his touch as he was by hers. Her skin wasn't cold, yeah, he'd got that right. But warm didn't describe it. It was hot, pulsing with energy, with fire, with adrenaline, with passion. She was alive with so much energy he half-expected it to burst out of her skin... except he could tell it wouldn't. She had it ratchetted down with enough force to blindside a tsunami in a hurricane.

She had her spirit in a merciless grip, but there was no peace in Natalie Fleming. He knew exactly what that was like.

He tugged, and she moved, allowing him to pull her closer. Her T-shirt brushed against his arm like the whisper of an angel's wings, and he was hit with a sudden, soul-deep passion to draw her. Not to keep himself under control, but for the sheer, beautiful experience of bringing her to life on his pages. He would take her out to his balcony at sunset, when the sky was vibrant and alive. She'd be wearing a red silk dress that clung to the curves of her body. He'd slide the strap over her shoulder, revealing skin so soft, so womanly, so precious.

A tourist on the street caught his attention, and he immediately went into vigilance mode. As he surveyed the store for threats to her, he noticed that she didn't try to move away. Because she wanted him to keep her safe? Or because she was feeling the same fire billowing through her?

Much as he wanted it to be the latter, they would both be so much better off if it was the former. So, for the moment, he'd just pretend that's what it was. He was her protector. She was his client. He would do his job.

He checked the surrounding area carefully, but all he saw was a lanky gal in wire-rimmed glasses watching them and typing furiously on an iPad, and a slightly ajar cabinet door that hid a third woman who'd crawled in there during the battle. "You okay?" he asked Natalie.

"Yes, yes." Her brilliant green eyes were wide with vulnerability, but she finally pulled her hand free to brush the purple dust off her arms. "Everything's fine."

He narrowed his eyes, not buying her bravado. She'd been trembling when he'd taken her hand, and she'd been scared. Plus, he'd been there long enough to know she'd been in major trouble, and he didn't like the idea of what would have happened if that one woman hadn't gotten control of the situation. "Who were they?"

"Apparently, I've been put on a deedub tour. I'm all the rage since I managed to avoid dying." She set her hand on her hip, indignation chipping away at her fear.

"Do you realize that I have a TRO against any deedubs coming into my store? Did you see any respect for the law? Did you? Because I certainly didn't."

He grinned as she began to work herself up. He knew she was trying to chase away the fear, and he appreciated that. Anger was empowering. Fear wasn't. "Yeah, weird," he agreed. "Seems like deedubs would normally respect Otherworld laws designed to control them."

"Arrogant, lawbreaking pinheads. They should all be sent to a treatment center for chocolate addicts." She surveyed the store that was in somewhat disarray. "Just because they bit me once doesn't mean they get free rein over my chocolate, you know?"

"Of course they don't." Nigel leaned against the counter. Her voice was beautiful and sexy, and he loved the indignation. Because it wasn't self-righteous, it wasn't moral. It was passionate and vulnerable, but there was truth to it. She *was* mad that her space was being violated, and that was far better than the woman who had been hiding in fear before her death and immediately afterward.

He wasn't blind. He could see she was unsettled, but she was searching for ways to manage that fear. Of course, she should be scared. No good could come of deedubs stalking her. "It has to end."

She smiled then, the first spark of real life in her eyes. "You think? I don't know. It seems like rather a good way to spend the day. You know, being attacked by the same creatures that haunted me my whole life."

He grinned back, captivated by the way her cheeks curved when she smiled. He hadn't seen many smiles from her, and he liked it. Liked that he'd caused it.

"Well, it was just a thought. I could potentially be convinced to change my mind." Huh. He hadn't meant to inject his statement with an undertone of innuendo and sensuality, but from the sudden flush in her cheeks, he was guessing he had.

Must have been because he'd been visualizing her trying to persuade him with a seductive dance involving silk scarves, black lace, and talented lips.

"So, yeah. Okay." Suddenly flustered, Natalie turned away and tucked her hair behind her ear.

He smiled, appreciating the little gesture that said she was affected by the heat he knew had been blazing in his eyes. "I don't like the idea of a herd of deedubs crashing your store." No, he definitely didn't like it. They'd invaded her sanctum, and that was just not on his list of acceptable activities by demon leprechauns.

"I don't either." She tugged at her hair, and that's when he noticed a flash of gray on the tip of her fingers.

"What's that?" The skin on the back of his neck tightened in warning, and he lifted her hand to inspect the discoloration more closely. The nails were the color of the ash that sloughed off his hands in battle, a stark contrast to the healthy flush of her skin.

"What is what?" She peered at her finger, and then frowned. "You mean the gray?" At his nod, she shrugged. "I don't know. I never noticed it before. Maybe it's residual from when I almost died."

"I don't think so. It's a living energy." He ran his thumb over it, and it came away tingling. He knew that tingling. He'd been on the receiving end of it before. "Shit."

"Shit?" Worry furrowed her brow. "Tell me that you just remembered you left the oven on or something, because I really don't have time for any more challenges in my life right now."

"Sorry. I don't cook." He tapped her fingers. "The gray is black magic residue." He resisted the instinct to whip out a blade and ready it for self-defense. He didn't respond well to women who dabbled in black magic, but this was Natalie. He'd watched her until he knew the depths of her soul.

"Black magic?" She jerked her hand free and wiped it over her thigh, her shoulders relaxing. "That's it?"

Black magic made her chill out? Hell, black magic was enough to wake him screaming from a sound sleep. Rhetorically speaking, of course, just to be clear. He was not a screamer. "Do you practice black magic?" He kept his voice impressively casual, completely masking his instincts to plunge into battle right then and there.

"Of course not." She set her hands on her hips, clearly not nearly as concerned about black magic as he was. "I must have brushed against it on my way here. I was afraid it was something bad." She met his gaze and must have seen the darkness on his face. "I don't practice black magic," she repeated again, her voice gentle. "I'm not one of those women from the Den." Her face softened and she touched his hand. "I promise you, Nigel, I'm not one of them."

Her touch was gentle and reassuring, and it broke through the tension that had started to build the moment he'd felt that black magic. He concentrated on the warmth of her hand. There was no magic in her skin. It had just been her fingernails. "Okay." He shrugged his shoulders, trying to shake out his tension. "I believe you."

Yeah, he bought that she wasn't mixing up demon

spells in her freezer, but that didn't change the fact that it was still black magic, and it was on her. Somehow, it had gotten in and that meant it was around. He flexed his hands, shifting the blades into place.

"Well, good." She grabbed a tasseled towel and rubbed her fingers, but the taint stayed put. It shouldn't have. Not unless it was emanating from inside her. She cocked her head. "You know, would you have any interest in working for me?"

His eyebrows shot up. Well, hell, there were a whole lot of things he could imagine doing for her. All of which would not be a good idea. The only good idea was staying away from her, but he had a bad feeling that that was just not going to happen. But that was okay. He had discipline. He could be in her presence and keep under control. He had to do it, because he needed her. "Doing what?"

"Enforcing the temporary restraining order." She glanced at the knife on the floor. "Just for a little bit. I have a big inspection in three days, and I don't have time to be cleaning up after the deedubs." She met his gaze. "Or being carted off to the tropics."

"Or being eaten by deedubs."

Her cheeks paled ever so slightly. Not much, but he knew her well enough to notice. Despite all her bravado, her reaction told him that she understood her vulnerability. "Yes," she said quietly. "Just for a little while. It's a better choice than trying to make me leave."

"And then I should let them eat you?"

She almost laughed. "God, no, just until I figure out how to protect myself."

"Figure out how to protect yourself?" He cocked his head, trying to picture the delicate Natalie wielding a pickax to take out a deedub in hand-to-hand combat. Nope. Couldn't see it. Which was good. The women in the Den were very easy to imagine in hard-core violent situations. He liked that he couldn't picture Natalie with a bloody blade and a gladiator helmet. "I thought you're going to influence them."

"Um…" She squared her shoulders, a defiant stance that was belied by the vulnerability in her green eyes. "Yes, I am."

He studied her carefully, trying to ascertain what she wasn't telling him. "You really can do that?"

"Of course."

"Good. Then you don't need me." And what an exceedingly easy segue into what he needed from her. He knew she was hiding something, but he didn't have time to figure it out. "I need you to influence me first."

The iPad woman stopped typing and narrowed her eyes, watching him unabashedly. He frowned, realizing that he'd seen that look before. From her, or in general? This woman was trouble, and it wasn't just because her shirt was covered with blood.

The woman's cheeks flushed at his stare, and she ducked her head, shielding herself from his inspection. The reaction of the guilty.

He would watch her.

"You need *my* help? Why would you need my kind of assistance?" Natalie's gaze flicked to his crotch. "I mean, you seem really quite virile and—"

"Shit, no! Not that kind of help." The pitying way Natalie had looked at his crotch made a guy want to get a boner just for bragging rights. To prove he could. "I'm fine there. Trust me, I'm all set with that." Well, he was the last time he'd tried. He really hadn't bothered for a long time. "It's my art."

Now Natalie looked surprised. "Your art? What do you mean?"

He ground his jaw. "I need you to cut the addiction. Like smoking or chocolate or sex or whatever." Shit. He shouldn't say "sex" when he was around Natalie. Got him thinking about things he shouldn't be thinking about. "I need to stop drawing."

Her brows knitted in concern. "But it makes you whole."

"No. I make myself whole." Or at least, that was the way it needed to be, and fast. He saw a red marker on the counter and had to shove his hand in his pocket to keep himself from pilfering it. His hands were suddenly burning with the need to draw, but it wasn't natural. It made him feel out of control and that was not where a warrior needed to be. "My art has become dangerous. I need to stop drawing and rescue Pascal."

She frowned. "Pascal? But you already rescued him."

Nigel shook his head. "He's back in the Den."

"Oh." Natalie's face contracted with worry and she touched his arm. "I'm so sorry—"

"Yeah, me too." He felt her genuine concern. She understood how bad it was, and he appreciated it. Her touch on his arm seemed to ground him, to help him focus. "It's fine. I'll get him. I just need my drawing under control."

"Um, sorry. I can't help you." She grabbed a broom and began sweeping up the purple dust.

Nigel swore under his breath. "Why? Because it's not about sex?"

She finally looked at him, and her green eyes were stricken. "No, I can't. I can't influence Magicks."

Well, that was a load of crap. "Of course you can. All Mystics can influence Magicks. It's automatic. Besides, you just said you were going to influence the deedubs not to attack you."

She cleared her throat. "Well, yes, I did say that, but I can't do it yet, exactly—"

"Really, Nat?" iPad woman had stopped typing to listen, her face soft with concern that Nigel didn't trust. "Even under normal circumstances? You know, when you've got your mojo?"

Natalie's cheeks turned pink. "No, but it's not a big deal—"

"Of course it is. All Mystics can influence anyone," the woman said. "You've never been able to? Ever?" She set the computer aside. "Sweetheart, I had no idea you had that problem. Why didn't you tell me?"

"Hey." Nigel frowned at the gal. "Who the hell are you? I'm kinda busy here."

"My name," the woman said, sitting up and pulling her shoulders back haughtily, "is Ella Smitweiser, PhD candidate in Hedonism and—"

"Shit! I knew I'd seen you before." Nigel stiffened. "You've consulted for Angelica."

"Angelica?" Natalie whirled around. "You worked for Angelica? In the Den? You didn't tell me that!"

"No, no, I didn't work for Angelica." Ella suddenly looked ill, but oddly enough, Nigel didn't feel overwhelmed with pity. "My parents did. There's a difference."

"No, it was you." Nigel scowled, realizing why her face had looked familiar. She'd been in the room on more than one occasion, muttering things under her breath... yeah... "I remember, very clearly, being locked down with one of the young warriors, and he was supposed to fight me to the death, and neither of us would fight. And then you walked in, whispered something, and then he attacked. He came after me until he died."

Ella's face was ashen. "No, no, no! It wasn't like that—"

"I trusted you." Natalie had her hand over her heart, and she looked stricken. "And you're one of *them*? You hurt Nigel? And the others?"

"You're a Mystic." The females who worked for Angelica weren't women. They were monsters, and too many young warriors had died at their hands before Nigel had finally accepted that the only way to save himself and others was to no longer see them as women, but as despicable creatures who had invited their own destiny upon themselves.

"Get out of my store," Natalie snapped, her voice laced with hurt and betrayal, but there was also fury, anger, protectiveness. She moved in front of Nigel, as if guarding him from Ella. "I thought you were my friend, and it was all a ruse just so you could get to Nigel and the others."

Oh, now, wasn't that sweet? Natalie's defense of him made him grin. Not that he needed defending, of course, but it was still interesting. Women never turned on women to protect a man. That female/female bond was pretty much inviolable. Men came second. Always. But Natalie wasn't playing by those rules. Damn, but didn't that just make a man feel like he owned the entire world.

"I have no designs on any of the men!" Ella rose to her feet and set her hands on her hips. "And I don't owe anyone explanations for my past. It's over and done," she said. "I *am* your friend. I—"

"I don't believe you." Natalie's hands were fisted.

"How could you sit there and tell me that you understood what it was like to suffer, when you're the one who hurt other people? How can you live with yourself?"

Ella pursed her lips as she swept the iPad from the counter and shoved it into her backpack. "I can help you both." It was a last-ditch attempt, and Nigel didn't buy it. *Nice try, but no cigar.*

"We don't want your help—" Natalie said.

"I can teach you how to influence anyone," Ella interrupted as she swung the bag over her shoulder. "Even Nigel."

Nigel stiffened. Of course Ella would know how to influence him. Would he even realize she was messing with him before it was too late?

"What?" Hope flared in Natalie's eyes. "You can teach me? I could take down a deedub?"

"Technically, yes," Ella said, but Nigel heard the hesitation in her voice.

"But what?" he demanded, allowing her to hear the anger and aggression in his voice. He wanted her to feel his willingness to do whatever it took to protect himself and Natalie from her, and he wanted her to know that he was now free to do whatever he wanted. He spun the blade between his fingers, letting it catch the light, as he took Natalie's arm and pulled her closer to him, inside the circle of his protection.

"How do I do it?" Natalie asked Ella.

"It's not easy." Ella glanced at Nigel's blade, swallowed, then focused on Natalie. "You have to release your resistance and tap into your power." Her voice grew more confident, stronger, and Nigel realized she was moving into her comfort zone. The world where she was the expert. "It's scary, and that's why you haven't done it. Because you haven't let go."

Natalie's cheeks turned pink. "I let go."

Ella laughed. "Sweetie, you don't even come close."

He knew Ella was right. He'd felt Natalie's strict control on her emotions. But there was no way he was letting Ella get her claws into Natalie. "Natalie doesn't need your help," he growled.

Ella's expression grew shuttered, then she turned and faced him. She looked him right in the eye, and she allowed him to see her self-hate. "I am truly, truly sorry for whatever I did to you," she said.

"Whatever you did?" he repeated. "You don't even remember, do you?" Men had died because of Ella Smitweiser, and she hadn't even bothered to remember a name or a face. But she thought that an apology would do it?

No chance.

"Three hundred and forty-six warriors died while I was there," he said. "And I can tell you the life story of every single one of them." And he had pictures to prove it. Portraits he'd made of every single fallen warrior, all of them framed and hanging on his walls. Memories of those who he hadn't been able to heal, whose souls had been too broken for him to resurrect. Even the greatest healer, which he was, couldn't save a soul that wanted to die.

But this time it was different. The men stashed in his condo wanted to heal, including Pascal. And it was time to get the kid back. No more time wasted on Ella and her baggage. He turned to Natalie. "Tell me I don't need to draw," he demanded. "Influence me now."

"I can't!" she protested. "It won't work—"

"It can." Ella was leaning forward again. "Let me help. I *need* to help you." She glanced at Nigel. "I need to help you both."

"No way." Nigel took Natalie's arm and pulled her away from the poisonous creature. "Touch Natalie, and you die. Touch me, and you die. Natalie might not be able to kill you, but I can—"

The cabinet door behind Ella opened, and a scared face peeked out. A young woman looked right at Natalie. "We're both going to die, aren't we?" Terror was etched into the lines of her young face, and she was staring at Natalie, asking to be told she was wrong. Desperate to be told she had a chance to live.

Natalie bit her lip. "Maggie—" Then she paused.

"You can't save me, can you? Or yourself?" Tears filled Maggie's eyes. "Oh, God," she whispered. "You really can't help me. I'm going to die."

Shit. She was an innocent. Another innocent about to die. He didn't have time for this. He really didn't.

Natalie got a stricken look on her face. "No, Maggie! You won't die! I promise!"

"How can you promise?" Maggie shoved her way out of the cabinet and lurched to her feet. "You've got nothing, do you?"

"No, I—" Then she stopped, apparently unable to deny the accusation. She looked at Ella, and looked back at Maggie. Then, like the big bad monster coming at him in slow motion, she turned toward Nigel. He saw by the look on her face that she was going to say something he really, really didn't want to hear.

Chapter 6

"WE NEED TO LET ELLA HELP US." NATALIE KNEW HER idea wasn't going to be popular with Nigel, but it was the right choice. For both of them.

"No." Nigel's face darkened, and he grabbed Natalie, his words a fierce growl. "She murdered my friends. There can never be trust. Ever."

"I know, I know." She searched his face and understood where he was coming from. "But I'm not ready to die." The words burned in Natalie's throat, words acknowledging the true dimness of her future. It wasn't irrational fear. It was logical and smart, because those deedubs would kill her, they would get her store shut down, they would get her deported to the tropics, and she couldn't even use her own magic anymore. She didn't have defenses, but she was putting precautions into place to make sure it ended up the right way this time. "I want to live, and I can't do it by myself."

He swore under his breath, hesitating, and then seemed to make a decision. One that fired him up and made him tense at the same time. "I'll help you." He pulled a black felt-tip marker out of his pocket. "You don't need her."

On the one hand, it felt sort of delicious to think of him helping her, but that feeling of excitement made her nervous. She didn't want to get that close to Nigel. Well, she did, which is why she didn't. Besides… "You can't always be by my side. Someday you won't be there and they will, and then what?"

Nigel cursed.

Oh, yes, he knew. She did, too. Teeth in her throat. Poison coursing her veins. And then embarking on round two of watching herself become stronger and more powerful and happier until she became deluded with her own power and attempted something that killed her. She'd watched her family die, one by one on their deedub suicide missions. And then she'd done the same. Tried to get herself killed by orgasm at the hands of the Godfather, for heaven's sake! Death was bad enough, but to get yourself killed because you can't live without the high of an orgasm?

That was the fate of a deedub bite. Instead of dying right away, it made the victim stronger and stronger and more powerful until she was so consumed with her power that she felt the need to push the limits, and then got herself killed. The path each death took depended on the natural inclinations of that victim.

Natalie's power was sensual in nature, so pursuing a man who killed with orgasm had been the curse's choice for her. She'd gotten her wish, the Godfather had killed her with an orgasm (which really wasn't as fun as one might think), and then she'd been saved at the last second when her sister had switched her soul into the body of her sous chef, Gina Ruffalo. Gina gratefully went to the Afterlife and Natalie got another chance.

Too close. Too scary. And too horrific to know she was chasing her own death for a sexual high, and yet entirely unable to stop herself. "Never again. I won't do that again." She gestured at Maggie, who was still peeking out of the cabinet. "And they're going after Maggie, and I can't keep her safe. It's all going to happen again, unless I do something to stop it, and I can't do it alone."

"Ella is not the answer—"

"No?" She poked at his chest. "How are you going to get Pascal, then? How are you going to control your drawing?"

He swore again and ran his hand through his hair. "You can do it. You don't need her."

"I can't even influence a Dullet right now!"

Nigel frowned. "What are you talking about?"

"I've lost it." She shoved her hands in her pockets, hating to admit her ineffectiveness. "There's nothing inside me but this great emptiness. There's no power. Nothing. Just emptiness." As she said the words, she realized that was indeed what had happened. There was no more sensual power within her. It was as if it had died with her old body.

"You can't lose your power. It's yours, and it's still inside you." Nigel grabbed her shoulders and turned her to face him. "You exude so much passion and fire, I can hardly stop myself from drawing you at every given moment." He laid his hand over her heart, his palm warm and strong. "But you've got it ratchetted down. Stop fighting your passion. It'll come out."

"Stop fighting?" She started to laugh. "Did you not see me when I was under the deedub thrall? When my inner passion was driving me toward my own death?" She folded her arms, hugging herself against the memory.

Nigel met her gaze. "But did it feel good? To unleash your inner being and hold back nothing?" His question was urgent, demanding, as if his soul needed to hear that answer.

She hesitated.

"Tell me."

Finally, she nodded. "Unbelievable," she whispered. "Like I was alive for the first time." Granted, she'd been on a quest that was going to end in self-destruction, but the *feeling* of indomitability had been magnificent. After a lifetime of fearing every moment of health, strength, and good moods, it had been so liberating to embrace her strength.

"I bet it was," he said quietly, with an undertone that almost sounded like yearning.

She shuddered, remembering her inner self screaming at her to stop, and her complete inability to tear herself away from the man who had already killed so many women before her. "I don't want to be afraid anymore, but as God as my witness, I never want to be out of control like that again, and I never want to be a victim like that. I can't go backwards, Nigel."

"Going backwards." Nigel closed his eyes for a moment, his grip tightening on his marker. "That's a crappy place to be."

The depth of his voice struck her, and she realized he understood how she felt in her desire to be able to live freely, all the way to the depths of her soul. She had no clue how a man as powerful as Nigel could understand what it was like to hide from life or the power within, but she sensed that he did. She took his hand, needing his touch, the feel of another person who understood what she was saying. "If Ella can help, I want to let her."

Nigel swore. "She can't be trusted." He took the cap off the marker, a move so quick it seemed almost desperate.

Ella's face tightened, but she said nothing. She was waiting.

"I know she supported Angelica—"

"I don't anymore," Ella interjected, then shut her mouth when Nigel glared at her.

"But if we stand together, we can protect ourselves if she tries anything." Tears began to burn in her eyes as Natalie contemplated fading back into the woman she used to be. "I have to take any chance I can get, because I can't go back to who I used to be. Could you go back to the Den? Could you?"

"I'm going to as soon as I leave here." His voice hardened as he began to draw on his hand. "I have to rescue Pascal—" He stopped, staring at the marker in surprise, as if he had no idea how it had gotten into his grip. "Did you give this to me?"

"The marker?" She blinked, confused by the change of topic. "You took it out of your pocket."

Fear flickered over his face, chased by raw longing. Nigel was afraid? Dear God, what could be so bad that *he* was scared?

He thumbed the tip of the marker. "Give me your hand."

"What?"

He looked at her, and she saw the need in his eyes. "Your hand."

She knew what that kind of desperation felt like. She'd lived it. So she set her hand in his, hoping she could give him respite or peace. No one should feel like she'd felt, and like he apparently did.

His touch was firm, just like before, but this time, his grip was cold, as if he was treading the edge of an emotion he didn't like. He wasn't burning with energy and adrenaline, like he had been when he arrived in her shop. He was tense and on edge. His jaw set in a grim line, he studied her, and then he began to draw on her palm.

Her body tingled at his intense scrutiny, at the way his gaze bore into her, as if ferreting out all her secrets. This was the Nigel she knew. The one who intrigued her. The one who made her feel like there was more to her than the woman who huddled in fear and ran from shadows. A woman worthy of his attention.

His pen was flying across her palm, the touch feather-light, as if she were the greatest treasure and he was afraid to harm her. He wasn't looking at what he was sketching. His gaze was riveted on her face, and she knew he was drawing her. He was drawing her the way he saw her, not the way she looked. "What do you see?" she asked.

He was almost in a trance, his place of utter peace, of absolute serenity, of ultimate power. "A woman who beats with fire, who's flushed with passion. A bird who wants to fly, but has chained herself to the earth with ce-ment." His eyes darkened and he caught her chin, even as he kept drawing with his other hand. "You have so much fire inside you, Natalie. And so much restraint. Cold, hard restraint. Fear." His thumb moved over her throat, his touch so soft and tender that it made her belly jump. "Fear sucks, little one. It will break you."

"I know." Dear God, did she know. "That's my point. I don't want to be afraid anymore. I want to own my life."

He nodded. "Good. That's the first step—" He swore suddenly, and his fingers tightened on her throat, press-ing more firmly. Not hurting at all. But reminding her of the intense, deadly strength in this man. How easy it would be for him to kill her with no more than a breath. "Take your hand away from mine," he said. "Get it out of my reach. Right now." His command was ruthless, unflinching. Demanding.

She tugged, but his grip tightened as he fought to keep drawing. "You're holding me too tightly—"

"Now!"

Galvanized by his command, she yanked her wrist out of his grasp. He whirled around and grabbed the counter. He gripped the marble and bowed his head, his muscles rigid in his arm, the tendons bulging in his neck.

She rubbed her wrist where he'd held her so mercilessly, her skin still throbbing with the strength of his grip. She wasn't afraid. He wouldn't hurt her. She knew that. But something was not right with him. "What's wrong with you?"

He didn't lift his head, his shoulders still flexed. "I was drawing you. I was focused on you, and I was drawing you."

Heat washed through her body, like a hot spring had exploded in her belly and poured over her. "I know you were. I could feel you inside my soul, probing me."

He raised his head to look at her. His eyes were dark, smoldering with heat. "I'm always inside you."

She swallowed. "I know."

He didn't take his gaze off her. "Look at your hand. Tell me what I drew." His voice was raw, desperate. "Tell me it's you."

Natalie flipped her hand over. At first, she couldn't quite tell, and then she saw muscles that weren't hers, shoulders too broad for a woman, a jaw that was too defined, cheeks too gaunt. Then she looked into the eyes, and she knew. "It's Christian."

Nigel's grip on the counter tightened, and anguish flashed across his handsome face. "Is it finished?" He gritted out the question, as if each word was poison, ripping at his throat as he spoke it. "Did I finish it?"

She looked at it. "I think so—"

"No!" Ella was leaning over her shoulder, peering at the drawing. "His left foot is missing." She pointed to the base of Natalie's palm. "See?"

Instead of Christian's foot, there was a red imprint from where Nigel's thumb had been gripping her so desperately. "Oh, yes, I see—"

"Sweet Mary." Nigel let out a breath and leaned his head back, as if he'd just been granted the gift of a lifetime. "You're certain it's not finished?"

"Yes." She started toward him. "I'll show you—"

"No!" He threw up his hand to block her, quickly backpedaling, as if terrified of her. "Keep it away from me."

She stopped instinctively and folded her hand over. Her heart ached for the anguish she saw on his face. Her serene, poised, powerful warrior was struggling. Waging an internal battle. "Nigel? What's going on?"

"Wash your hand. Wash it 'til it's gone. Now. Before I can finish it."

His tension was evident, and she went cold at the fear on his face, the self-hate. God, she'd been there. She knew what he was suffering, and her heart softened for him. "Okay, okay. I'll get it off." Natalie hurried over to the sink and began to scrub. The marker wasn't permanent, and it flowed off easily. By the time she finished, Nigel was gripping the counter again. Sweat was dripping down his temple, and his muscles were shaking with the effort of controlling himself. From coming after her? He looked like someone was flaying his back with a whip, and only sheer force of will was keeping him on his feet.

"It's gone," she said quietly. "It's okay, Nigel."

"Take the pen." It was between his fingers. "Take it now."

"Okay." She moved quietly across the room and set her hand on the back of his. His skin was ice cold, the flesh taut across the bones in his hand. The moment she touched him, he sucked in his breath, and his body tightened. But he didn't lift his head or open his eyes. Carefully, she slid the pen free and handed it to Maggie. "Go throw that away."

Maggie scrambled to her feet and hurried into the back room.

Natalie put her hand on Nigel's shoulder. It was rigid, his muscles bulging as if he were fighting a battle. "Okay, so the pen and the drawing are gone."

Nigel's shoulders shuddered and he lifted his head. He met her gaze, and his face was haunted. "I really thought I was drawing you."

She nodded. "So did I."

"I couldn't stop it."

She frowned. "Yes, I noticed." And then she understood. It was exactly like it had been when she'd been dying from the deedub poison. Her mind had been conscious, aware, but she hadn't been able to stop herself from doing things that were so dangerous, so deadly, and so not in her best interest. But they had felt so good, and that had been the addiction.

Like his drawing. Oh, no. Not him, too. Being out of control like that was a horrible feeling, and for him? A warrior who'd been fighting his captor for control his whole life and finally gotten it? She knew exactly what it felt like to go backwards, to a place of being out of control.

She rubbed his shoulder, wanting to give him comfort. "Why is drawing bad?"

Nigel smiled grimly. "Long story, sweet girl." He took a breath and unpeeled his hands from the counter. There were cracks in the marble spiderwebbing out from the pressure. He met her gaze. "I need you."

Something tightened in her belly at the raw need on his face, at his admission, at the idea that this warrior, this vision of passion and heat and strength, needed her. The thought that she could help him made her feel strong and powerful, and she clung to it, needing that illusion. She could not let Nigel suffer, not when she knew what it was like. "Okay."

Nigel nodded and turned to Ella. "You will teach Natalie how to influence me."

Ella's cheeks flushed and her eyes filled with sudden tears that she blinked away almost instantly. "Yes, yes. I will."

Nigel put his hand on the back of Natalie's neck and pulled her close. "You hurt Natalie, and you die. For her, and for all the others."

Natalie didn't pull away. She liked his protective stance. He was going to keep her safe, and that felt good. She hadn't felt safe for a very, very long time, and his firm grip on her was a gift.

Ella's cheeks grew redder. "I won't hurt her. I promise." She met his gaze. "Or you."

"I don't need assurances for myself. I can defend myself from you, and now I'm free to do it." He turned Natalie toward him. "How long do your suggestions last?"

Oh... wait a second. What was she promising? She couldn't even influence a Dullet anymore. What made her think she could suddenly do what she hadn't ever been able to do before? "I think Ella should influence you."

"Ella?" His grip tightened on her. "No chance," he growled. "I will never permit her near me. *Ever*. It has to be you. I won't trust anyone else."

Okay, so it was incredibly sweet and touching that a man who had no reason to trust anyone in this world trusted her, and it made her want to help him so much. But she wouldn't promise something she couldn't deliver. Regretfully, wishing she could be the woman who would help him, she shook her head. "I already told you I can't do it anymore. Even if I figure out how to do it, there's no way to know how successful I'll be. You can't count on me for something that important—"

"I don't have time for a can't. I only have time for cans. You can. I can. Pascal lives. You live. That's the end of it." He looked past her at Ella. "How long will it take to teach her?"

"Five minutes or never. Depends on her."

"Make it three minutes." He ignored Natalie's protest. "How long will her suggestions last?"

"Thirty seconds to a few days. It's different for everyone." Ella cocked her head. "You'll be a challenge. It won't last for days with you. You'll push it away."

He nodded and turned to Natalie. "Then you're coming with me. In case you need to do a second round."

She blinked. "To the Den?"

"Don't be afraid." He grabbed her hand. "No one else under my care dies. Starting with you."

No one else? People had died while under his protection? Like her sisters and her mom. Dying while she tried to make them live. God, he understood, didn't he? "Oh, Nigel." She laid her hand on his cheek.

"I swear on the soul of every warrior who died in my care that you'll survive." His fingers dug in.

All she needed was a chance. An opening. And she could do the rest. "Okay."

He nodded once, relief evident in his eyes. "Okay."

And with that short exchange, she was bound.

———

Well, hellfire and damnation, when had he turned back into a man?

Charles Morgan, former dream genie of subpar reputation, peered carefully around the corner of the couch. He examined his reflection in the stainless steel toilet he'd been drinking out of for the last three weeks, since he'd been so rudely lured into imprisonment by an attractive young woman wielding a ham bone.

It didn't seem possible, but as he double and triple-checked his reflection, it was undeniable. He was no longer a smut-infested dog. He was a man. And not a demon-infused-smut-monster loaded with taint.

It was his own visage, one he hadn't seen in far too many decades.

Stunned, he touched his face. Whiskers, and not the canine kind. The manly kind that women swooned for. Cheekbones. Lips.

"Hot damn," he whispered. After three hundred years of being contaminated from the smut of a certain witch's black magic spells, he was finally clean again! "I'm really back!"

"How do you like it?" Standing in the doorway was the sensual beauty who'd waved that tasty bone and promptly locked him up. In the three weeks since she'd deprived him of his freedom, she'd been scratching his butt and delivering white standard poodle girlies to him. Poodles with pink bows who had been very friendly to a big, black, shaggy dog that stank of smut, black magic, and death.

Yes, yes, he appreciated the thought and all, but inside that canine body had been a man's awareness, and he'd been thoroughly horrified by his furry side's amorous designs on the poodles.

His captor's auburn hair and blue eyes looked much better in color than in dog-vision black and white, and the man was more appreciative of her curves than the dog had been, but that hardly snagged her absolution for what she'd done to him with the poodles. "You should be tortured—"

Stunned, he stopped and pressed his hand to his throat. Holy crap. That was his real voice. Not some smutted up raspy voice that had been haunting him for the last three hundred years. That was his own beautiful tenor, the one that had wooed women, calmed frenzied patrons, and whispered words of advice into the sleeping ears of his hopelessly misguided clients. "My name is Charles Morgan," he said, just to test it.

His voice. His name. His body. He was back. Truly, truly back.

Without another thought, he dropped to his knees and bowed his head. "Thank you, Lord of All Genies, for bringing me back. I will remain true to our creed and will never deviate from our mission again. I honor you—"

"It was me that cleared the smut from you, not a genie lord. But I'm glad to know it makes you happy." The Bone Queen stepped inside the door, carefully closing it behind her as she had done every day for the last three weeks.

He lifted his head. "You freed me from that smut-ridden existence?" Well, hell, that was a lot better than bringing the dogs. He might even forgive her for that.

"Of course I did." In her right hand was the fuchsia curling iron that she used to shoot poisoned bobby pins into his family jewels and nipples. The razor-sharp bastards burned like hell and left behind deformed red lumps that itched like crazy. It had taken only one escape attempt to realize it wasn't worth it. "You're a much better looking man than I thought you'd be," she said, cocking her head at him. "You have a nice smile."

"A nice smile?" Well, granted, it was a far cry from being adored, sought after, and idolized, but he'd take it as a first step. And he always had had a particularly devastating smile. So, at least she was insightful.

"Oh, yes." She gave him a warm grin, and he noticed that her eyes were an interesting shade of violet. Not pure blue.

He pulled himself straighter, trying to remember how to appear appropriately arrogant, even though, quite frankly, all he wanted to do was sit down and stare at himself in the toilet, and maybe kiss her toes in sobbing appreciation for a day or so.

But after a three-hundred-year sabbatical, the dream genie had a reputation to rebuild, and it started now. What had his reputation been? Oh, yes. Devastatingly handsome, a great lover, and one of the most powerful mythical beings in all creation.

He let out his breath. God, that felt like an effort to rebuild, but he could start with his amorous reputation, he supposed. His captor was a significant improvement over the poodles. Maybe she would cleanse the residual taint. "You want me, don't you? Fortunately, I'm already naked, so we can just—"

"Get naked with you?" She shook her head quickly and held up her hand as if to ward him off. "No, I'm in love with someone else."

"You are?" Her angled face was haunted and miserable. None of that glow of love. Charles sighed. Oh, yes, he'd seen that look before on so many of his clients' faces.

"He doesn't love you, does he?"

Raw agony flashed across her face, the kind of soul-deep pain that could be caused only by the evisceration of one's heart. Then the vulnerability was gone, replaced by the cold mask of survival. "My love life is none of your business."

Oh, yes. He remembered now why he'd gone AWOL from respectable genie behavior. Because it was just too frustrating to try to help people like her. That's why he'd gone on his mission—

Hellfire and damnation! How had he forgotten his mission?

He leapt to his feet. It was time for his vision to come back to life, for the sake of women like this sweet young thing. "My darling, listen to me, and listen carefully."

It had been over three centuries since he'd had to face down some besotted lovelorn who didn't know how to manage her dreams. Turns out, it still got to him as much as it used to. "You're destroying yourself by dreaming of something you can't have. Unless you can clear your aura, it will eat away at your soul like acid on beautiful, fragile silk."

She blinked, her face softening until it was almost pretty. "You think I'm like beautiful silk?"

"Of course I do." He touched her cheek and was surprised by how soft her skin was. Who said poodles were soft? Not even in the same ballpark as this.

"But that's not my point." He could not afford to be wooed by a pretty girl. His mission was too important to be derailed by the need to help a single young woman in distress. He had bigger plans than that! "You obviously can't manage dreaming successfully, so you have to let it go or you'll torture yourself into a miserable and early death, like my sweet Prunella." Ah, Prunella. How many moons since he'd been sane enough to remember her. He laid his hand over his heart and looked to the heavens. *I will never forget you, my love.*

The woman blinked. "Prunella? Who's Prunella?"

"My daughter." He sighed, remembering her bright blue eyes looking at her papa with adoration for so many years. "Some bastard put dreams in her head and she fell in love, and he did not love her back—" Anger surged through Charles, anger he hadn't felt in so long. "She couldn't let go of her dreams, and I couldn't make them come true for her. And she died, torn apart by a soul broken by unfulfilled dreams." Oh, hell, how awful that had been! It had to stop! How many people had died from broken souls in the three centuries since he'd gone canine? Charles grabbed his captor's shoulders and shook them. "Ditch the dreams, woman! Ditch the—"

She shot him in his golf balls of love.

"Hell!" He grabbed for his nuts and dove behind the couch, out of range of the weapon from hell. It had hurt like shit when he'd had shaggy dog hair covering his balls, but now that he was naked with fragile human skin? Words were inadequate to describe the living hell he was currently experiencing.

"I'm so sorry!" She ran over and leaned over the couch, her face crumpled in dismay. "I didn't mean to do it, but you were getting violent and I sort of panicked." She touched his shoulder. "Are you okay?"

"No, I'm not okay! You just shot my nuts!"

"I'm sorry!"

He glared at her. "Then hand me that damn curling iron."

"Oh." She glanced at her hand, and then glanced back at him. "I don't think I can do that."

"Sure you can. Just hand it over."

"No, no, no." She scrambled back to her feet. "See, I looked you up in Angelica's files, and I think you'd try to keep me from doing what I need to do. I mean, I really don't want to hurt you, but I *have* to get this fixed. Too many people were hurt when Angelica was running this place, and I helped. I have to make it right. And I need you to do it."

"Angelica?" The name knifed through him like a hot fork through a melted marshmallow.

Angelica was the witch he'd tried to assist when she'd been suffering from tortuous dreams of unrequited love. Had she appreciated it? Hell no. She'd turned him into her black magic garbage disposal, rending him an insane, homicidal maniac, right when he'd been on the verge of saving the world, starting with her. "Where is that bitch?"

"She's gone. I'm in charge of the Den now. And I'm changing the rules." The new Queen of Hell leaned over the couch to peer at him, her eyes gleaming with anticipation. And hope. She wanted something from him.

No chance. He clenched his teeth and shoved a couch pillow between his legs, fighting not to cry like a baby. "I don't play by rules."

"Don't rules suck?" Mari grinned and holstered her curling iron, but he already knew how fast she could get to it. "I like you already, dream genie."

Charles tensed at the salutation. "Dream genie?" She knew what he was? Oh, hellfire and damnation, no wonder she was threatening him. Everyone wanted something from dream genies.

Seriously. Was it hard to figure out why dream genies protected their anonymity so ruthlessly? Because if their identity was known, desperadoes like the woman before him would harass, torture, and abuse the genies in a misguided attempt to force the dream gods to grant the nearest and dearest yearnings of their hearts. And then blame them when the dream genie couldn't perform.

The one time he'd revealed his true self was to Angelica, and she'd promptly smutted him. And now her sex-providing replacement was in on the game? Time for the Caution Dance. "I used to be a dream genie," he said conversationally while he assessed the odds of being able to disarm her before she shot his nuts into a state of utterly debilitating pain.

"Oh, good. That is so fantastic." She smiled and held out her right hand, and he noticed that she had her nails painted in the softest pink. A color of vulnerability and femininity. Not what he'd expect from a protégé of Angelica of the silver-and-scarlet manicure.

"Hello, Charlie," she said. "My name is Mari Hansen, and I'm here to offer you a deal."

Chapter 7

SOMEHOW, SITTING IN CLOSE PROXIMITY TO A PILE OF garbage that had gone ripe during her three-week siesta didn't seem an appropriate venue for tapping into an inner strength and talent that had eluded Natalie for a lifetime.

Seriously. Years from now, she would look back on this defining moment, when her life changed forever, and instead of sunshine and glory, she would smell rotted bananas, mouse poop, and the sound of a garbage truck doing its morning collection, all of which were drifting in through the open window. The front side of Newbury Street was ooo-la-la galore, but the alley behind? Not so much. Granted, she'd moved the trash outside this morning, but the stench still owned the joint. "I really feel like we should go somewhere else—"

"No time." Nigel was crouched in front of her. His neck muscles were rigid, his face in turmoil she'd never seen before. "Ella needs privacy, and I need air. We don't have much time, so the back of your store wins. Deal with it."

Natalie raised her brows at his uncharacteristically abrupt dismissal of her concerns. "Deal with it? You've never been that crass in your whole life, have you?" Nigel was the most mellow dude ever, a warrior who never got worked up about anything enough to order someone to "deal with it." She frowned. "You're not okay, are you?"

Awareness flashed over his face, as if he had just noticed he'd snapped at her. "Sorry." Then his jaw tightened. "Don't worry about me. Just focus."

"Okay, so I've got the front shut down." Ella hurried into the back room of Natalie's store. Her skin was pale, and she looked worried. "Nigel, you need to go out there and fend off anyone who tries to come in." She pulled up a step stool, dusted the flour off it, and sat down in front of Natalie.

Nigel didn't move.

"Nigel, please." Ella looked at him imploringly. Her hands were trembling. "If someone saw me do this and realized who I was, it would have very bad repercussions for me. You need to make sure no one comes in."

"There's no chance I'm leaving you alone with Natalie. And I can't say I'm overly concerned about repercussions for you." A tendril of smoke began to drift up from Nigel's palm, and the tip of a metal blade poked out at the end of his fingers. "Teach her, now."

He sounded desperate, and Natalie touched his arm. "You're going to be okay," she said quietly.

He squeezed her hand, his grip warm and reassuring, but his face was grim, as if some dark future was chasing him, and she was the only one who could stop it. Oy. What if she couldn't? How bad was the hell chasing him?

"I can't be discovered." The hedonism student looked like she was about to keel over. "No one can know that Ella Smitweiser knows about mysticism. It's imperative."

Natalie saw the fear in Ella's eyes, and her heart tightened for her. She knew what it was like to have a past you didn't want. She also understood that it was possible that the choices of Ella's past maybe hadn't really been Ella's choice. "Who is after you, Ella?"

But the woman shook her head. "No."

Nigel looked back and forth between them, and she saw him quickly analyze the situation, sift through the facts, and assess what he was going to have to do to make things happen the way he wanted. "I'm monitoring," he finally said, his tone making it clear that he wasn't feeling the love for the fact he had to give Ella comfort. "I've got it covered. No one's going to come in that store without me knowing about it." There was such finality in his voice, such raw assurance, that Natalie immediately relaxed.

Some of Ella's tension eased also. She clearly realized that one of Angelica's warriors in battle mode was a force worthy of reckoning. "Okay," she said. "I'll do my best." She shook out her arms to loosen her muscles, then took Natalie's hands.

Her fingers were ice cold. Too cold for a living being. "Are you okay?"

Ella laughed quietly. "Sweetie, I haven't been okay for a long time, but I'm working on it." Her gaze flicked to Nigel. "Assisting you guys will help."

Natalie sensed a huge weight on the woman's soul, and she squeezed Ella's hands. "It'll be okay, Ella."

"Maybe." Ella leaned forward. "But this is your time." She smiled lightly. "Stop worrying about me. I'm fine. Really. Just haven't done the mysticism thing for a while." She tapped the back of Natalie's hand. "I need you to concentrate on you, not me. Can you do that?"

Natalie noticed that there were little gray circles

on the back of her hand where Ella had tapped them. They faded quickly, but why had they been there at all? She would have to ask Nigel later. "Okay," she said. "I'm ready."

Ella nodded. "Suggest something to Nigel. Something easy."

Natalie looked over at Nigel, and something twitched in her belly. He was entirely focused on her, and she could almost feel his energy pulsing at her. "You will blink twice."

He didn't blink.

"Oh, I forgot. You need chocolate." Natalie pointed at the tray near him. She'd brought in the last of the virility balls. "Have a virility ball."

Nigel eyed the chocolate spheres like they were noxious beasts of hell about to attack him. "Got anything that doesn't have to do with sex? I don't want anything messing with my manhood."

"You don't need to worry about your manliness." Natalie exchanged knowing looks with Ella. Men were so sensitive about their masculinity. It was sort of endearing. That's why she loved her job so much, because she had insight into the one thing that made men vulnerable. "It increases your sexual performance, so you can only benefit."

"I got that covered, sweet cheeks." Nigel's gaze swept over her with piercing intensity, as if daring her to find out exactly how much he did have it covered. Such a guy!

But his look worked. Heat pulsed in her belly, and she tried to hide her reaction by gesturing at a box on one of the shelves. "That's some raw chocolate. You could go with that." Yeah, playing with fire wasn't a good idea when Nigel was concerned. She needed to be over the sex thing, thank you so much. If a man she didn't even like could get her worked up so much that she couldn't stay away from certain death by orgasm, then what would a man like Nigel do to her self-control?

She didn't want to know.

She just wanted to be safe, in control, and a force to be reckoned with, thank you so much.

"I'll get it." He shoved himself to his feet, hauled a box down, ripped it open with a knife that appeared out of nowhere, and then resumed his position. He bit off a large chunk and swallowed it. Nothing sexy in his approach. He was all business right now. And the fact he was in warrior mode was just as mouthwatering as the sensual perusals. Dear God. What was wrong with her? Could she get her mind out of the gutter for one minute? She wasn't that kind of girl, remember?

It was too dangerous.

"Try again," Ella said.

"Okay." Natalie leaned toward Nigel, cleared her mind, and concentrated all her energy on him. "Blink your eyes twice."

No blinkage.

"See?" She sat back and threw up her hands in frustration. "I can't do it! I can't even influence a Dullet. Why would I be able to influence him?"

"No." Nigel grabbed her arms and hauled her over to him. "Ella said every Mystic can influence Magicks. You can do it."

"I can't—"

He put his hand over her mouth. "You're blocking your powers. You gotta let it go."

"He's right." Ella leaned around him. She was focused now, her face calm and confident as she allowed herself to be consumed by this world she knew so well. "Every Mystic has a power source, an inner passion, that drives their ability to influence others. It's what fuels you." She nodded at the virility balls. "Yours is sex, and you've got to tap into that."

"Sex?" Oh, Natalie was so not liking the sound of that. "What do you mean?"

"It means you need to unveil the sensuality within your soul and let it soar," Ella said. "Feel the eroticism deep in your belly, allow it caress your soul and seduce your own body."

Natalie became aware of Nigel's intense scrutiny. She peeked at him, and her breath caught at the expression of raw lust on his face. He met her gaze, then his attention dropped to her mouth. She swallowed and licked her lips before she could stop herself.

Nigel let out a faint growl, and her entire body tightened. "Oh. God." She turned away from him and focused desperately on Ella. "I can't go there right now."

"You have to." Ella made a noise of exasperation. "It's your path. It's how you do it."

"Well, yeah, I know, but I'm not doing it. There has to be another way."

Ella scowled at her. "You're not frigid, but you're sure acting like it."

"Frigid? I'm not frigid!" Oh, well, this was certainly fantastic. Nothing like being completely embarrassed in front of Nigel. "I just want to maintain complete and utter control of all hints of passion or sexual need within me. That is completely different from being frigid!"

Nigel coughed, a pathetically inadequate attempt to hide his amusement at her protest. Perfect. Just perfect.

"You're blocking your sensuality." Ella nodded at Nigel. "Use him to tap into your inner vixen."

Nigel raised his brows. "Yeah, feel free to use me however you want."

Something began to pulse deep in her abdomen at his dark and hooded look. "I—"

"He's sexy, he's masculine, he's got so much testosterone that he'd turn a nunnery into a lusty den of iniquity, for God's sake," Ella said. "With all his sexuality and yours, you should be able to get him to give you a naked lap dance by only thinking about it."

Oh, God. She was thinking about it. She was really thinking about it. Nigel, his torso bare, his decadently soft leather pants low across his hips. His abs flexing as he moved his hips in a suggestive invitation, his hand reaching for her breast—

"All she needs to do is ask," Nigel said, his deep voice rippling through her. "No influencing necessary for that."

"Yes, yes. Can you feel that sensuous current building between the two of you?" Ella's voice was quiet, almost husky. "Feed upon it, Nat. Let it wrap around your belly. Allow it to crawl up your thighs, caress your belly. Feel the delicious pulse of desire and awareness. Close your eyes and imagine Nigel's hands on your body. Starting with your hips, moving over your butt."

"Oh, lordy." The throbbing inside Natalie's belly was deep and penetrating. Her skin was hot and prickly. And then she felt it. A stab of uncontrollable *need* for Nigel's touch. For intimacy. For connection.

She'd been here before. Felt this same deep, dark sexual attraction when she'd been under the deedub thrall and drawn so lethally to the Godfather. But this was worse, more powerful, because she *knew* Nigel and she liked him. She took a step toward him, and his hands lifted, reaching for her—

"No!" She leapt back, tripping over the crate. "God, no, no, no. I can't do that!"

Nigel caught her arm just before she fell. His grip was solid, warm, and reassuring. Secure. Not threatening or scary. "Hey, babe," he said quietly. "It's okay. I won't let anything happen to you. I swear it."

"No." Her heart was pounding, her mouth was dry. It was too close, too vivid. She was panicked, scared, and back in that hell when she'd been staring into the eyes of the Godfather, knowing that to go with him would mean she would die, and yet she'd been unable to stop. He'd been a stranger, she'd hadn't even liked him, but she'd been willing to trade her life for his kiss.

Yes, yes, she knew that it had been because of the deedub curse, but the curse only tapped into that which was already there. It had been *her* that had been so drawn to the high of letting herself go, of indulging in her dreams and fantasies, of allowing herself to fly without fear of repercussions—it had been too much to resist, especially after a lifetime of living in fear.

God, how many times in her life had she fought down euphoria, forced herself to remember to be serious, to fight, to stay in control? Afraid that any sign of ebullience or physical well-being was an indicator that the deedub poison was going active?

Her rigid self-control had allowed her to stave off the

onset of the deedub symptoms for years longer than her sister, and then it had been sex that had pulled her out of her safe zone. Sex! There was nothing like orgasming yourself to death to make you realize that you have an addiction to the high that will fast-track you toward your own demise. "I can't open that door." She pulled her arm free, and Nigel allowed her to go. "There has to be another way."

"Ella." Nigel didn't take his gaze off Natalie. "Is there another way for Natalie to tap into her powers?"

"No." Ella stood up. "We all have our power base, and Natalie's is sensuality." She gave Natalie an encouraging smile. "Nat, sexual passion and desire are the strongest power sources in existence. The fact you can tap into them means you have practically limitless influence."

"Well, that's great news." Natalie bit her lip and hugged herself. Limitless power? It was her dream. But through sex? It put it out of her reach.

Ella looked at Nigel. "She would be powerful enough to help you, and not many would be able to get through your will. She's enough for you, Nigel. I can feel it in her."

Brief hope flickered through her, and then Natalie's stomach turned. She was all too aware of the ruthless allure of sensuality. She knew how powerful it was. How destructive it was. "There *has* to be something else for me to tap into."

"No, there isn't, so you need to access your tools." Nigel grasped her shoulders, his thumbs caressing small circles. "Don't disempower yourself, Natalie. You're a warrior."

"I am not a warrior!" She pulled herself free. "I just

want to find a way to stay alive and run my store. That's it! I don't want to go jumping naked all over furniture just to tap into some inner power." Oh, God. Had she jumped naked over the furniture when she'd been under the deedub thrall? She couldn't even remember—

Sudden pain congealed in her belly and she grabbed for her stomach. "Oh, no. Not again."

Ella and Nigel were suddenly in front of her, concern etched on their faces. "What's wrong?" Ella asked.

"Tell me what hurts." Nigel caught her, his powerful arms supporting her as the pain shot through her again. "Has this happened before?"

"A couple times," she gasped. "But not like this." She'd dismissed it before as stress and assorted emotional baggage, but not this time. This time was different. The pain was insidious and stabbing, twisting through her body. Agony bounced around inside her like a pinball gone haywire. To every corner of her body, her fingers, her toes, her belly, her chest. "Oh, God." She went down on her knees, but Nigel pulled her to his chest, easing her down gently.

Then he swore, and his protective embrace loosened. "Mother of hell." Raw shock stunned his voice. "You smell like Mari."

She didn't have time to respond before the blackness hit her mind and the world disappeared.

Having a woman swoon in his arms had never been on Nigel's top ten list of things he wanted to accomplish in a lifetime. Yeah, true, an unconscious female was somewhat limited in her ability to hurt him, but the fact she was limp and vulnerable put the responsibility on him to go into nurturing mode. With a woman.

That was against everything he'd ever learned.

You respected women.

You acknowledged that one or two might be a decent human being.

You always remembered their ability with a knife, black magic, and poison darts.

And you never, ever saw them as a fragile bundle of femininity that needed support, because the minute a man dropped his shields to give her some TLC, the chick would turn that vulnerability on him in a heartbeat.

He'd go from cradling her in his arms to having his balls in a vise faster than it took to lose a boner at the sight of Angelica or her girls. He knew, because it had happened to him. The other warriors had learned faster not to nurture a woman, but it hadn't been until number sixty-one that Nigel had finally gotten smart enough to realize a man never, *ever* saw a woman as vulnerable and treated her that way.

But as Natalie sagged in his arms, all he wanted to do was cradle her to his chest. To bring her peace. To keep her safe. To protect her as he'd never protected anyone in his life. In that moment when Ella had been bringing them together, connected their energy, he'd felt something come to life inside him, a warmth that had eased the hardness inside him.

It had been dangerous to allow himself to burn for Natalie like that, but he'd realized that it was necessary. Natalie needed to feel a safety net around her, and she needed his help to tap into the power within her. It had been a calculated risk to reach out to her like that, and it had made him apprehensive... until he'd felt her spirit reach for his.

And then he'd simply known it was right. That moment, that choice, it had been beauty unlike anything he'd ever drawn in his life. The he caught a whiff of a scent he knew all too well.

Mari. The woman who had tumbled so fragilely into his arms smelled like Mari. He lifted her hand and inspected her fingers. Black magic residue pulsing even more strongly than before. He swore as blades instinctively came to life beneath his skin. The shit racing around inside Natalie was everything he'd spent the last hundred and fifty years fighting against so he would live one more day.

Natalie Fleming was black magic, and she was Mari's black magic. His skin was tingling everywhere they touched, and his palms were smoking. A knife sprang up in his hand before he'd had time to think.

"What are you doing?" Ella grabbed at his arm, trying to wrest the knife out of his grip. "Something's wrong with Natalie! Can't you see? She's not attacking you, for God's sake! Look at her!"

Nigel instinctively glanced down, and her eyes fluttered open. The emerald green depths weren't Mari's. They were Natalie's. How many times had he drawn those eyes, the turmoil within? From across the room he'd watched her, compelled by those eyes—

"No." He knew what women were like, and this woman was bleeding Mari from every pore of her body. His instincts ordered him not to be taken in again. *He would not.*

But as he held Natalie in his arms, as he felt her body

convulsing in agony, heard the moan of dismay deep in her throat, as his warrior side ordered him to drop her, stand back, and pull out his weapons, he couldn't stop thinking of her eyes. Of the woman who had such ghosts in her soul.

He knew what ghosts were like.

"For God's sake, drop the knife," Ella ordered. "Give her to me. I can help her—"

"Don't touch her." He suddenly realized his blade was inching too close to the tender skin of Natalie's throat. Son of a bitch! He was better than that!

Swearing, he hurled the knife against the wall. It hit with a loud thump and sank deeply into the wall. He hooked his left arm around Natalie to anchor her against his chest, then rubbed his palms together as she convulsed again. The moment a faint glow began to emanate from his palms, he set his hand on her chest, over her heart, to heal her from whatever was eating away at her.

He closed his eyes and opened his soul to hers, to the pain within her. The taint within her hit him hard, and he swore as the darkness swirled over him. The blackness. It was raw black magic, and it was Mari's, and... mother of hell. *Angelica*.

Now both women's auras were swirling inside Natalie, thick and black. He could taste the bitterness, like black licorice mixed with sulfur, burning his mouth, his nose, his cells. It was acrid and harsh, bleeding through him. It wasn't just magic, it was the darkest part of black magic. Images flashed in his mind. Of the bronze metal beasts that had attacked him such a short time ago.

Demons.

There was demon magic inside Natalie.

Chapter 8

CHARLES MORGAN HAD NO TIME FOR DEALS. NOW THAT he was back, he was going to be a little busy saving every living creature from themselves. No one would ever suffer the fate of his darling Prunella. Not ever.

Mari eyed him. "Don't you want to hear what the deal is?"

He gave a lofty snort that felt delicious. It was wonderful to be sane enough to remember how arrogant he was supposed to be. "I am far too powerful to resort to deals."

"Are you so powerful?" Mari sighed and waggled her weapon with a decided lack of enthusiasm. "Because it seems to me that if you were that magnificent, you wouldn't have been stuck as Angelica's smut monster for the last three hundred years."

"She caught me off guard." And that would never happen again. It was time to go on the offensive and tap into his best weapon: dream manifestation. Charles began to search Mari's mind for a dream he could use against her long enough to shift the balance of power between them.

Every creature was a constant swirl of dreams. Some desires were little, like wanting to reach the itch in the middle of her back. Some were big, like pining for some bastard who would never love her. Most were fleeting, not focused, not pure of heart, and he couldn't do a damn thing about them.

But sometimes, there was a dream that the wisher was in complete alignment with, even for a split second, and if Charles caught that moment, he could make it come true.

In Mari's dream field, he saw the name Christian again and again and felt the desperate love surrounding it. Her unrequited love for Christian was destroying her.

By all saints, she was just like Prunella! Pining for a man she didn't believe she was worthy of. And just like Prunella, there was nothing he could do to grant dreams that were so bogged down with denials of self-worth, with doubt, with that agony of undeservedness. The poor child. She was blocking so many dreams—

One flared into focus—bright, bright focus.

I am so hungry. And then she thought of a pizza with pure, unfettered, beautiful longing.

Bingo! He snapped his fingers and a spinach salad appeared out of nowhere. It hovered in front of her for a moment, and she yelped in surprise. Shit. Where was the pizza? It *had* been a pizza, right?

Then he noticed the shocked look on her face. Yes, yes, he was impressive, wasn't he? Pizza or greenies, it was still quite a move, eh?

The salad leapt off the plate and flung itself toward her mouth. Because, you know, she was hungry, right? And she wanted to eat it, right? Dreams come true, baby.

"Hey!" She ducked and batted away flying spinach leaves as he lunged for her pink baton of hell.

He yanked it out of her hand just as the food went flying. "Victory to the king!" He held it above his head and grinned as she wiped blue cheese splatterings off her face. "You will bow to me. I am a god."

And hot damn. He was. Three hundred years without granting a dream and he'd gotten it almost right on his first try. He'd tried for food and actually gotten food! He was magnificent. It really was time to save the world.

Mari peeled a piece of spinach off her right eyebrow. Surprisingly, she looked disappointed. "I was thinking of pizza, not salad. I thought you were better than that."

"I'm rusty." Then he realized the implications of what she'd said. "You wished for a pizza on purpose?"

"Of course. I wanted to test you." She cocked her head, studying him thoughtfully. "So, that's really all it takes for you to do your work? One thought of pizza and you turned into Chef Gourmet?"

"Oh, yes. I need only a split second of pure longing, and I can tap into it." He spun the baton. "Now open the door, salad girl, and release me."

Mari sat down on the couch and patted the seat beside her. "Come talk, Charlie."

He brandished the weapon he'd stolen from her. "I'll shoot you."

She froze. "Oh, no, don't shoot that gun. It'll turn on you."

"Hah! Why would I believe that?" He sensed that Mari wasn't half-bad, but he could not fulfill his mission while he was locked in her dungeon. "I appreciate you relieving me of my smut, but I have important things to accomplish. Let me out."

"I can't." She folded her arms, and her chin jutted out. "I need your help to fix everything that I've done to the men here. You aren't leaving until we're finished."

"The world needs me!" He picked up the gun. "Open the door or I will force it."

Mari sighed and leaned back. "Fine, be that way."

"Fine." He aimed the gun at her heart and pulled the trigger.

The pink stars of pain shot out, whipped around, and hit him right in the nuts.

"Mother of pearl!" Charles dropped to the ground, grabbing for his manly regions again. "That wasn't supposed to happen!"

"My spells go to the nearest XY chromosome in the room," Mari said as she picked up the baton. "None of my weapons can be used on me. Now, are you ready to talk?"

His nuts had already swollen to the size of grapefruits, and they were red and inflamed. Elephantiasis on the way. "A man's jewels of ecstasy are personal zones of safety, woman! Attacking violates every rule of combat in the universe!"

"You did it to yourself! I tried to stop you!" Mari shoved the baton into her pocket. "For heaven's sake, this kind of thing isn't supposed to happen in the Den anymore! Men are supposed to be safe here! Don't you understand what I'm trying to do? Don't make me do this kind of thing!"

Dear Lord. His nuts were like watermelons with poison ivy. "You are a crazy bitch."

Mari's face crumpled with dismay. "I am not crazy, and I am definitely not a bitch. I'm trying to fix things."

"You develop weapons to turn a man's pride and joy into leprosy. Crazy and bitch, all in one."

"But it's for good reasons. It's not to hurt you." Mari sighed. "As much as I think Angelica had her values all screwed up, sometimes I understand her frustration. I am not doing this because I like to hurt you. We all must sacrifice for the greater good."

"Ah… the greater good." Yes, yes, that was what he lived for. He liked the greater good. Charles unbent himself enough to get his elbows on the couch. "Shangri-La, you mean?"

"No." She frowned. "Loving, lasting partnerships."

Oh, *that*. He rolled his eyes in disgust. "Not love again." He struggled to his feet, keeping his thighs well spread so his overly inflated regions of pleasure had room to throb. "Listen, hotlips, let me tell you something. Dreams destroy." He eased down to the couch next to her with a groan he couldn't stifle. "People get so obsessed with what they aren't getting that they lose the ability to appreciate what they do have. The unrequited yearnings eventually ruin them. And unrequited love is the worst culprit of all." Darkness settled in his chest as he thought of his dear, sweet daughter. Destroyed by a love so deep.

"Love can be painful, I admit." Mari glanced down at his manly bits, and she bit her lip. She walked over to his fridge, pulled out an ice pack, and handed it to him. "Here."

He set the cooling panacea on his groin. "Ah, yes, that's much better."

"I try to mitigate the effects of my spells," she said. "I keep first aid in all my men's rooms."

Charles closed his eyes. "You're still a bitch."

"I am not!" Mari's voice grew tense, and then she took a breath to calm herself. "Look, Charles, I agree that dreams can be harmful."

He looked up, startled. "You do? No one ever agrees

with me. The dream genies put me on administrative leave when I started talking like that." He moved closer and winced as his swollen balls got squished under his thigh. "Do you want to hear my plan? It's brilliant." He glanced around the room for any eavesdroppers. "I can grant dreams, right?" He lowered his voice. "But I can also destroy them."

Mari's eyebrows shot up. "What?"

"Oh, yes. I can suck them right out of someone." He rubbed the ice gently over his testicles. "I still remember the first time I did it. A young man named Ricky was deeply in love with a woman who had scorned him." Ricky, who had been Charles's best friend since childhood. "He was depressed, he'd lost his job, he'd stopped taking showers, and he'd adopted six feral cats. He was dying, and all because of his dream."

Ricky's dreams had been so powerful that when Charles had been riding his horse past the cabin, he'd literally been forced to rein in and rush into the decrepit abode. How he'd raced up the stairs, his heart thumping when he'd rounded the corner and seen his friend. "It was just like Prunella," he said. "Seeing Ricky dying, because he dreamed of a woman who didn't love him back." He could still feel the pain as he'd fallen to his knees and grabbed his friend's hand. "He begged for me to grant his dream, but I couldn't give it to him."

"Why not?" Mari looked so disappointed. "I thought you were good."

"Hey! I tried!" he snapped. God, had he tried. Impotence was the worst hell indeed. "But he didn't believe in his dream, and unless you believe, I can't do it." Something inside him had simply snapped, and he'd done the unthinkable. He hadn't tried to do it. He'd just freaked out and it had happened. "I took his dreams and tossed them aside."

"Really?" Mari leaned forward, her face riveted. "How'd you do it?"

Charles shrugged modestly. "Just my natural talent, I guess. It's technically impossible for a dream genie to steal dreams, but I have always been an overachiever, so it really was no surprise that I could do the impossible." It turned out that it was a lot easier to steal dreams than to grant them, because it didn't depend on the wisher having his thoughts in perfect alignment.

Mari waved her hand impatiently. "So, what happened to Ricky?"

Charles thought back to that moment, and peace settled over his body. "Ricky looked at me and said, in this voice of pure awe, 'It's gone. The pain is gone.'" Charles grinned. "And then he went on to invent a new method for coloring women's hair, made millions, and died a happy man with many women servicing him repeatedly."

Mari smiled. "That's beautiful."

"It is." He sighed. "It was too late for Prunella, but if I can save others from her fate, then her death was not in vain."

She nodded. "I understand that. The awful things that happen sometimes are made less terrible if we use them to do good things." She hugged herself. "That's what I keep telling myself when I get upset about the things I did under Angelica's orders."

He studied Mari. "If you take away people's dreams, then you take away the frustration and agony of wanting something they can't have. And then they can find the inner peace and serenity that will allow them to be who they truly are."

Mari smiled. "So, you plan to turn the world into Shangri-La by stripping all living beings of their dreams?"

"Yes, yes." Now that he was free from smutville, he could actually do it. He stood up. "Let's do it, woman. Let's—"

She didn't move. "But you're not that good at the dream thing."

Charles narrowed his eyes. "I am a god."

"Who creates spinach salad instead of pizza."

"It still worked."

"Sort of." Mari rose to her feet and stretched. "What if you try to steal dreams, and you screw it up? Don't you need to get it right the first time? Because once you start monkeying around, then the dream police will get into your head and come to arrest you. One-shot deal, right?"

Ah, it was always unfortunate when someone else had a valid point. "This is possible. They do not have my vision. They lost track of me when I went into demon dog assault mode, but I suspect they will be able to find me now that I'm playing in their sandbox again."

"They can't get you in here." Mari gestured at the walls that were glistening with black magic. "You can practice stealing dreams in here."

Charles looked around at his prison. At the light blue walls, at the dog bed in the corner, at the bowl of kibble on the floor. "I don't want to be in here. It stifles my creativity."

"Well, I have news for you, Charlie." Mari folded her arms over her chest. "You're in here until I let you out."

He narrowed his eyes. "What do you want?"

"I want you to cleanse the dreams of the men I bring to you," she said, her voice growing in excitement. "Every dream they have except romantic love. They all deserve to be loved, but we damaged them so badly that they can't love. Love will bring them peace."

"Absolutely not." Charles folded his arms over his chest. "Romantic love is most dangerous. I cannot stand by and watch more people suffer when they could be saved."

"These warriors are already broken inside." Mari leaned forward, her voice urgent. "To heal, they need to be able to release their dreams of revenge, of destruction, of harm, and they need to open their hearts to love. Surely you can admit that fulfilled love is beautiful?"

Charles sighed, remembering that moment when he'd saved Ricky. The feeling of his heart swelling, when he'd realized he could save the world. That was when he'd first fallen in love with himself. "Yes, yes, love can be wonderful—" He stopped when he saw the flash of triumph on Mari's face. "Would one of these needy warriors be Christian, by any chance?"

Pain flickered across her face. "Eventually. I owe it to him. He suffered greatly because of me." Mari's voice was quiet. "He deserves love. It doesn't have to be me. I just want him to have peace." She held up a black pole he hadn't noticed before. Where had she been hiding it? "This is my smut rod. I've used it on you three times to pull smut off you. I'll trade cleansing for your help. Each load I take off you, you'll get more of your talents and powers back. No more salads instead of pizza."

Charles narrowed his eyes. He'd already been

snookered by Angelica once. "Why would you make me more powerful?"

"Because you will need to be at your strongest to help Christian. His dreams are extremely bitter and entrenched." She hunched her shoulders, looking fragile and vulnerable. "I really betrayed him," she said. "He's pretty consumed by hate and revenge now."

Charles rubbed his whiskers, contemplating. Mari had dreams, big dreams, and he admired that. She reminded him of Prunella, with her courage and her strength, and the way she was suffering from unrequited love. He could help this woman the way he hadn't been able to help his own daughter.

And practicing his skills under the radar of the genie lords would be fantastic. Because, as amazing as the spinach salad was, Mari was right. He was rusty.

They could help each other. She would give him opportunities to practice until he was ready to wipe the world clean in one swoop. And then he would give her dreamless peace the way he hadn't been able to save Prunella.

At last, perhaps, he would be given the chance to atone for the fact he had not been able to save his own daughter. Save Mari. Save the world. All in the name of his beautiful daughter.

He smiled and felt the world shift to his power for the first time in centuries. The dream genie was reawakening, and soon the world would receive the greatest gift of all.

It was time.

He held out his hand. "I agree to the deal, my dear."

Mari shook his hand, and he smiled as he scanned

her mind. Oh, yes, she would be easy to cleanse when it was time.

The world would soon be resting in dreamless serenity.

Chapter 9

Dreams of hot, sexy warriors were good.

Nightmares of being sucked into bottomless pits of fire, poisonous smoke, and monsters with really big teeth? Not so much.

Or at least, she *really* hoped it was an illusion.

Scalding hot air rushed past Natalie's face as she catapulted down a bottomless pit of blackness. Glowing red eyes flashed in the darkness, claws ripped at her skin. Piercing shrieks of agony and howls of the damned ripped through the darkness. She screamed, scrambled to stop the fall, but there was nothing to hold on to. Her fingernails tore as she grabbed for the rocky walls, her grip failing as she plummeted toward the fire, toward the darkness, toward *hell*. The scent of sulfur burned her nose, tears stung her cheeks, and her skin bubbled with heat.

"Natalie. Come back to me." Nigel's voice penetrated the fire and brimstone assault, and she clung to it, gasping as she fought for air, for consciousness.

She caught the scent of chocolate, and it overrode the acrid pungency of the demon-infested sinkhole. The pit of hell sucked at her, trying to drag her back into it. She inhaled more deeply, latching desperately onto the smell of decadent chocolate, using the familiar scent to draw her back into consciousness, into safety.

It's only a dream, Natalie. It has to let you go. The

heat began to fade. The screams retreated. She became aware of a cold, hard cement floor against her back. It hadn't been real. There would be no scratches on her arms. No burns on her skin.

Not real. Not real. Not real.

"Come on, Natalie. Back to me now."

Nigel's urgent demand jolted her the rest of the way into full consciousness, and she jerked her eyes open. She was lying on her back on the floor of her back room, fluorescent light glaring. She threw up her arm to protect her face, half-expecting a demon to leap out at her, teeth bared—

"Natalie! Look at me." Nigel moved, and suddenly a shadow broke up the blinding glare as Nigel leaned forward, his broad shoulders blocking the light.

She saw he was sitting on a crate, looming over her. It was Nigel. Not a demon. Not a monster. He smiled and laid his hand on her cheek. "You're okay. It was only a dream."

"Oh, God." She put her hand to her forehead, felt the sweat beading. Relief shuddered through her body. *Nigel was with her*. His boot-clad feet were on either side of her head, and he was leaning over her, his forearms propped on his thighs. His presence was huge and powerful, chasing away the final remnants of the hell she'd just visited.

"Nigel," she whispered. "You're here." Her voice was raw, as if she'd been screaming, and it hurt to talk, as if she really had been falling down the hole of hell before Nigel had commanded her return. "I had another episode, didn't I?"

"You had something," he agreed. "But you're

okay now." He brushed his fingers over her cheek, and his touch eased her. "Are you working with Mari and Angelica?"

His touch might be gentle, but the pink rose on Nigel's cheek was so bright it was almost glowing, and muscles were ticking in his cheek. His palms were dark with embers, and his eyes were hooded and dark. The man was on edge, and he was fighting to stay in control.

"I'm not working with them. I'd never do that." She started to sit up, but Nigel's hands went to her shoulders, holding her down on the bed of newspaper.

"Your face is still gray. Stay." His touch softened, urging her not to move instead of ruthlessly forcing her to bend to his well. But she knew it was still an order. He was in her space, and it didn't feel all that nurturing and protective. The darkness in his eyes was edged with a dark unrest.

"I need space." She twisted out of his grip and sat up.

He caught her before she pulled away, and he tugged her toward him until she was wedged between his knees. He was pure, lethal force, danger, and anger. Not directed at her specifically, but swirling like a rising tide of aggression. His gentle concern seemed to have vanished, replaced by a dangerous undercurrent of power.

"Turn it off," she said. She was way too on edge to deal with this kind of attitude from him. She tugged, trying to free herself to give herself distance from the energy swirling around him. "Nigel," she said gently, "let me go."

Sudden awareness flashed in his eyes, and his gaze went to his hands, where he was gripping her so tightly. He jerked his hands back and loosened his knees, as if he were shocked to discover he'd been holding her so aggressively. "Shit. Sorry."

"It's okay." She scooted back instinctively, even though a part of her wanted to reach out to him and help him chase away the shadows. "What's wrong with you, Nigel?" This aggressive side just wasn't like him. She knew him, she'd been watching him, and he simply didn't do that kind of thing.

"More than you want to know." He didn't stand. Didn't move. Just kept his forearms resting on his thighs, his knees apart, as if she was still sandwiched between them. She could still feel the pressure of his legs on her hips when he'd held her between them. Heat poured through her at the reminder of how much more powerful he was than she. She supposed it should be terrifying, but it wasn't. Because it was Nigel, and that made the knowledge compelling. Exciting. Stirring.

"Tell me," she said. "What's wrong?" But even as she asked, she realized what it was. Relief rushed through her. "You need to draw, don't you?" Without his art, he had no outlet for the darkness inside him. "Do you want a pen?"

"No! I can't afford to draw." For a long moment, he simply breathed, as if he were trying to pull himself together. Fighting off an inner demon. His ribs expanded, his shoulders broadened, his muscles flexed.

She took a step toward him, wanting to touch him, to help him... but she didn't dare reach for him. Her urge to do it was too compelling and too scary, reminding her too much of how she'd felt with the Godfather. So, instead, she began to edge toward the door. Away from her desires, and away from the adrenaline surging inside him.

Finally, he raised his head, and his eyes were softer. Not nearly as lethal as they had been. He was back under control. "Do you practice black magic?" he asked quietly.

"Of course not. I already told you that." When he didn't come after her, she stopped slinking toward the door and forced herself to stand still. To face him. To face herself and the desires racing through her to touch him, to tap into the storm brewing inside him. She wanted to help him. Wanted to restore his peace. "I don't know anything about magic. It's not my shtick."

He nodded once and ran his fingers through his thick hair. "I knew that."

She frowned at his acquiescent tone, and she knew he really did believe her. "Then why did you ask?" But even as she posed the question, something inside her relaxed at his acceptance of her answer. He trusted her. He wasn't a man who put any stock in the claims of women, and yet he had faith in her, even when she was apparently leaking Angelica smut all over everything. As he always did, he saw her as the woman within, not the person on the surface.

Instead of answering her query, he held out his palm. It was still blackened, and embers were sloughing out. The ashes were no longer red hot. Just white, as if the fire had gone out, leaving behind remnants and soot. "Give me your hand."

She started to reach for him, and a chunk of charred ash dropped off his hand onto the floor. It sizzled on the concrete and then flickered out. She stopped and closed her fingers. "I'm not fireproof."

He inclined his head once in silent acknowledgment,

and then raised his hand higher, inviting her to trust him. But who was he asking her to trust? The creative genius who used to sit pensively and draw, or the one who had yanked her close with unrest in his soul? Who was the real man?

The artist. Yes.

But so was the turbulent warrior.

"Give me your hand," he repeated.

She saw the dark, threatening depth to his eyes, the muscles flexed so rigidly in his shoulders. He crooked his index finger. One movement. One flick. So subtle. A plea for her help, a need so desperate he wouldn't ever admit to it. But she felt the tension in his body, his fear that she would say no. Beneath the violence and the anger was the man who had watched over her so carefully from a distance for the last three weeks, the warrior who had come to her aid today when she'd needed him.

This man, this warrior, this living creature of fire... he needed her.

It was who she was to help. Any man. But especially, *especially* Nigel. The need to help him was so much stronger than she'd ever felt with anyone else. "Okay." She unfurled her fist and set her hand in his.

For a moment, he simply held her, his grip light and tender, almost as if he was mesmerized by the feel of their connection. Her belly tingled with anticipation, and she realized exactly how much her soul yearned for his touch. For him to pull her into his strength and kiss her—

"Oh, God." A cold fear swept through her, and she started to pull away, but he tightened his grip.

"How long have you had this?" he asked.

She tensed at his demanding tone. The artist was gone. All that was left was the fierce warrior who'd pinned her between his thighs. Which, she had to admit, was a little bit exciting. Terrifying, but also deliciously compelling. "Had what?"

"Your fingers." He pointed at her fingers.

Spots now dotted along her cuticles. What had been a grayish tint before was now speckled and dark. "What is that?"

Nigel thumbed the discoloration and swore. "It's smut."

"Smut?" She wiped her free hand on her jeans, but the stain didn't come off. "Like the fallout from using black magic spells? The backlash?"

Nigel nodded. "Mari and Angelica use black magic for most of their experiments. Every spell they do gives off residue. If they don't put it somewhere else, it'll taint their auras."

"So?"

He smoothed Natalie's hair back from her face, an absent gesture that made her whole body tingle. His muscles were vibrating with tension, violence and aggression were still bubbling beneath his taut skin, and yet his touch was so gentle. A caress. "Both women," he said softly, "have auras that are completely clean. They send the smut elsewhere."

She stiffened, and a cold feeling of violation came over her. "To where?" A faint thudding beat through her, the ominous approach of something unpleasant.

"Angelica was off-loading to a guy we called the Chameleon because he was constantly shifting form to murder. He was killing dozens of people." Nigel rubbed her fingers, as if he were also trying to get it off. "But Angelica pulled him out of the field, and it looks like he's been replaced. I can feel the energy of Angelica and Mari in your fingers." He met her gaze. "You're being smutted, sweetheart. By Angelica and Mari."

"I am?" It sounded bad, but she tried to remain calm. How bad could smut be? It couldn't be worse than being haunted by deedubs and being so insane that you almost orgasmed yourself to death, right? "So, what exactly does that mean?"

"It means you're being contaminated with demon blunt." Nigel released her hand and stood up. She'd forgotten how tall he was, how imposing. If there was a man to have around when she was discovering she was being contaminated by demon blunt, he would be it.

Seemed like if anyone could take down demon blunt, it would be him. "What will it do to me?" She didn't really want to turn gray, but if that was the extent of the damage, she'd live with it for now.

"Everyone reacts differently. Depends on your pre-disposition, but it'll eventually take you over and you'll be in bad shape—"

"Bad shape?" She set her hands on her hips, struggling not to panic. "What does that mean? Don't be vague, Nigel. I need to know what I'm dealing with."

But he shook his head, his face frustrated. "I wish I could tell you, but it's different for everyone. We just have to wait and see—"

"Natalie?" Maggie poked her head around the corner. "I was looking at your recipe file so I could make more virility balls, and I had a couple ideas. Do you mind if I play around with the recipe? I think I can make them taste less magicky, so people who don't want suggestions will buy them just for the flavor."

Natalie caught the scent of the purest cocoa, so rich and so divine it transcended any scent she had ever experienced. It was the same olfactory delight she'd been smelling when she'd woken up, only much more potent. Her body ached with need, and she inhaled again, only this time she noticed the underlay of warmth, of humanity, of life. "Maggie? Is that you?" Her head felt light, almost giddy, and her stomach rumbled.

"Is what me?" Maggie frowned. "And why are you looking at me like that?"

"Like what?" Natalie inched closer. She sniffed again, and this time she was sure of it. Her newest staff member had a fragrance that was compelling beyond words. "God, you smell good."

Maggie backed up a step. "You're weirding me out a little bit."

"Why? Because I love your delicious bouquet?" Natalie reached for her sous chef, but Nigel grabbed her arm and pulled her back toward him. "Hey!"

"Quiet." His arms folded her against his chest, pinning her to him. "Maggie," he said calmly. "Go experiment with the recipe. Natalie would love any help you can give her to enhance her business. See what you can do."

"Yeah, okay." Maggie shot them a wary look, then turned and hurried out the door.

"Wait!" Natalie struggled to get free of Nigel, desperate to follow her employee to the front of the store. "I need to go after her—"

Nigel spun her around, pressed her back against the wall, and pinned her there with his body. "Natalie."

She tried to wiggle out of his grasp. "Let me go."

"No." He wedged his knee against her inner thigh, trapping her leg against the wall. "You're stalking her."

Natalie inhaled, trying to catch another whiff of that fading scent. It was vanishing, twisting out of her reach in tormenting fashion. "Of course I'm not stalking her. That's ridiculous—"

"Hey." He grabbed her chin and forced her to look at him. "You were compelled by her scent. Admit it."

"No, I wasn't." Was she? Her head began to clear, and she noticed the tension in her body, how hard she had been struggling against Nigel to get away. To follow Maggie and her delicious smell? "Um…"

Nigel's grip relaxed slightly. "Nat?"

She leaned her head back against the wall, becoming aware of how many body parts Nigel had pressed into her to immobilize her. His finger was caressing her throat, and his thumb was resting lightly on the swell of her breast. How had she not noticed all the physical contact, especially his knee wedged against her inner thigh? She hadn't noticed because she'd been caught up in Maggie's scent. "I guess I was obsessing over her a little bit."

"Yeah, you were." Nigel's voice was thoughtful even as he continued to caress her throat. It was as if he hadn't really noticed he was touching her, but was simply deriving comfort from their connection while he processed the events.

"What happened?" She should push his hand away, she knew she should. But she couldn't make herself do it. It was too tantalizing, his unconscious caress. It made little fires leap through her body, just small ones, not enough to scare her, but enough to feel good. "Did the smut make me aggressive or something?" Oh, man, she hoped not. She'd had one traumatizing experience with being compelled to places she didn't want to go. She was so not up for another one. "Didn't you say her last smut monster was a murderer? I don't want to be a murderer!"

To her dismay, Nigel didn't offer her reassurance, and his expression was grim. There was no repudiation coming from him dismissing such a ridiculous notion.

A dark dread pulsed through her soul, as if her deepest consciousness knew a terrifying truth that her mind hadn't grasped yet. "Nigel?"

He laid his hand on her cheek, as if trying to lessen his words with a gesture of comfort. "The smut from black magic is demon smut."

"I've heard that before." Macabre foreboding began to percuss, like rain thundering in the distance, getting closer and closer with each moment.

"Exactly how the demon smut affects a person will depend on their predilections."

"So? What does that mean?"

Nigel's voice became quiet and soothing, as if he was trying to talk down the horror he was about to deliver. His face flashed with sympathy as he stroked her hair. "Every smut receptacle succumbs to the demonic influence in their most vulnerable spot. You carried deedub poison for twenty-five years, and it's probably still in your soul." He met her gaze. "You were stalking Maggie. A Sweet."

"Stop!" She tried to pull away. She didn't want to hear what he was about to say. "I'm not becoming a deedub! That's insane—"

He gripped her shoulders. "It's actually very possible—"

"No!" Natalie began to shake uncontrollably, and she was suddenly back in that moment when she was seven, eating dinner, laughing with her sisters, teasing her mom, when there was that knock at the door. Her mom had walked over to it, laughing over a joke, and the doorknob turned, so slowly. The door opening, the claw, the growl, the way he'd leapt at her mother, his teeth bared, ripping through her skin, throwing her aside. The way he'd come after her sisters, one by one. How she'd raced so desperately for the trap door. That crushing weight as he'd tackled her to the floor. His crazed, hungry howl of raw pleasure, of sheer delight, of utter mercilessness as he saw her face, and then plunged his teeth into her throat—

"Natalie!" Nigel gently shook her, calling her back to the present.

She stared at him in horror. "There's no way—"

"Listen to me." He cupped her face in both hands and leaned close. "We need to know. I can handle it, but I have to know what I'm dealing with."

She shook her head, panicking. "No, God no. I can't become that monster. I can't—"

"Natalie." He stroked her cheeks. "Look at me, sweetheart."

Her insides were churning, her skin was clammy, and she wanted to run, but there was nowhere to go. Nowhere to hide.

"I can keep you safe," he said. "I've battled demon magic my whole life, and it's never taken me down." He winked. "Hasn't even left a scar on my magnificent body, right?"

She stared blankly at him. Unable to process. "I don't know. I've never seen your body."

"Well, I'll show you later." He grinned, his easy smile penetrating her panic. If he was so relaxed, it couldn't be that bad, right? "We're going to find out now." He didn't wait for her agreement. "Maggie," he called out. "Come in here."

Natalie leaned her head back against the wall. "No, don't."

"I make things okay. It's what I do." He thumbed her jaw. "It'll be okay. I promise." He leaned down and brushed his lips over her forehead.

Sparks rippled through her as he pulled back. His eyes had darkened, and his gaze went to her mouth. Her heart began to thud, and his hands tightened on her face. He moved closer. Lowered his head —

Maggie poked her head around. "Yes?"

Nigel pulled back, and a sense of loss rippled through Natalie. Loss that was quickly followed by relief. She couldn't afford to get involved with Nigel, not when she found him so compelling.

"Give me your hand," Nigel said to Maggie, not taking his gaze off Natalie.

Unlike Natalie, Maggie didn't hesitate to trust him. She beamed at Nigel and stuck out her hand without question.

Nigel took her gently by the wrist and pressed her arm up against Natalie's nose. "Smell her."

She turned her head. "No, I can't —"

He positioned his forearm across her chest, pinning her against the wall. He leaned his weight into her, allowing her to feel the power in his body. "I'm stronger than you are," he said. "I won't let you do anything to Maggie. We need to know."

"I already know," Natalie protested, even as fear hammered in her belly. "I'm not turning into a deedub—"

"What?" Maggie jerked her arm back. "You're a deedub?"

"No, I'm not—"

"Calm down." Nigel took Maggie's arm again. "Show me, Nat. Prove to yourself that you're not."

"Fine. You'll see that it's ridiculous." Natalie swallowed, then she closed her eyes and inhaled deeply. The scent of the most magnificent chocolate tingled through her, and her toes curled with delight at the amazing smell.

But that's all it was. Just appreciation for the scent of blue-blooded chocolate. Because she was a Sweet, and Sweets could appreciate chocolate in a way that no one else could. The fact she was a little smutted didn't mean she was turning into a psychotic creature who would attack darling innocents like Maggie. Seriously. Maybe she *used* to have demonic leprechaun poison sifting through her body, but that didn't mean—

"Natalie." Nigel's voice was a soft command, forcing its way into her thoughts. "Let her go, little one."

Let her go? She suddenly became aware of Nigel resting his forehead against hers, of his breath against the side of her face… and of the fact that she was sucking on Maggie's arm.

Chapter 10

THE MINUTE NIGEL SAW NATALIE'S SHOCK AND HORROR that she was French kissing her sous chef's arm, rage exploded inside him. It was that ancient, deep-souled fury, the dangerous emotion he'd managed to suppress for almost two hundred years, by manipulating his emotional state with his art.

But it was no longer dormant. It erupted inside him with the same force it had that fateful day so long ago. Outrage that he'd failed to protect her. *Her*. This wasn't some halfway suicidal newbie warrior in the Den.

This was *Natalie*. The woman he'd been ready to sacrifice to the tropics so she would live. He'd been willing to forego the calling of his very soul for her in order to protect her from himself and from the deedubs. And he'd failed her? He'd failed to foresee a threat that had snuck right past him?

He was a warrior. And he'd *failed*.

Son of a bitch. His muscles burned, and liquid metal scorched his cells with a fierceness that made his soul shudder.

"Nigel?" Natalie's green eyes were wide, burning with concern and worry for him.

For him? For the monster? God, the purity of her soul to be worried for him! The fury deepened, the self-hate that he could have failed this woman—

"No," he growled to himself. He would not let himself lose control again. Not with Natalie so close by, so vulnerable. The anger would not win. His sanity would prevail, no matter what the cost.

Art. The only answer was art. He jammed his hand into his front pocket... and it was empty. No pen. Oh, *shit*.

He shoved himself away from Natalie, stumbling as the madness intensified within him, as he fought to own his sanity. Jesus. It hadn't been like this in a hundred and fifty years. Because he hadn't let anyone matter to him that much since then. "I need a pen," he muttered. "Get me a pen!"

Natalie ran toward the front of the room. "I think there's one up here."

Please don't let me snap. He threw boxes off the shelves, desperate for something he could draw with. It was building inside him, that shit that he'd kept contained for so long with his art. He'd felt it stirring over the last few hours, and yet he'd been so arrogant he'd thought sheer willpower could keep it curbed without his art. He'd been an asinine fool. He needed to draw. *Now*. He'd have to control the drawing. Keep the image innocuous. He could do that. He had to do it. He couldn't beat this without his art.

He saw shiny dots on his arm and knew they were metal blades fighting to emerge from his skin. "Jesus," he whispered. Not again. *Not again*.

"Natalie! Stop it!" Maggie shouted.

Nigel jerked his head up and saw Maggie scrambling backwards, away from Natalie, who was clutching the metal shelving to keep herself from attacking Maggie. Her skin was white, her face sickened with self-revulsion and horror. Her beautiful face, that soul so filled with love and outrage, decimated.

And that's when the tenuous cord of control he'd been fortifying so carefully his whole life… well, the damn thing just snapped.

His vision went black, and he could see nothing. But he could feel it. This wrath, this violence, this uncontainable detonation blasting through his defenses, ripping at his body, at his self-control—

"Nigel!"

Natalie's scream of sheer terror cleaved though the raging onslaught eviscerating his mind, and he opened his eyes to see thousands of microscopic blades careening through the air. They were spewing from him. Not just out of his hands, but out of every pore of his body. Maggie was running for the door, and Natalie was hunched over, shielding her face with her hands. Metal blades clanged against walls all around her, barely missing her.

Mother of God. How long could he control them enough to keep from hitting her? Then, as he watched, he saw one hurtle through the air, right at her. "No!" He swore and willed it to the right, to force it to shift trajectory. *Don't touch her*, he ordered it. At the last second, he managed to divert to the left, but it was so close to her shoulder that it tore a hole in the sleeve of her shirt. Shit. He was losing it!

He had to get out. "Stay here," he ordered her as he charged for the door to the alley. Blades were erupting in all directions, hot metal incinerating his skin, embers sloughing off his shoulders, his face, his legs, his feet. His clothes were on fire. Knives everywhere—

He leapt into the air and slammed his shoulder into the steel door. Agony cleaved his body as the stainless steel burned him. Then the door exploded off its hinges and flew into a parked truck in the alley. He dove after the door and yanked it down over him as the blades continued to pour forth into the makeshift shield. The deafening ping of metal ricocheting into the door, into the asphalt. The thud of it hitting bricks. The tinkle of windows breaking. He had no control. Couldn't stop it.

"Mother of hell!" He was going to kill everyone. His body was creating weapons faster than it ever had before, as if it were trying to make up for a lifetime of being crushed and hog-tied. And he had no control over it. It was as if he were a five-year-old boy again, not a grown man. What the hell was going on?

And how was Natalie? He had to get back in there and check. If a blade had hit her, he could heal her, but first he had to arrest the cacophony of metal.

Then he saw his chance. A white cup with pink and orange letters. Dunkin' Donuts coffee. Upended on the alley. A wooden coffee stirrer floating in the spilled coffee. A chance for art.

He lunged for the stick, dipped the end into the coffee, then traced a line across the asphalt. Two inches before the coffee ran out.

Dipped it again.

Another line.

Dip.

Line.

Dip.

Line.

An eye took shape. He knew that eye. His teammate Blaine. Not Christian.

Relief rushed through him. He could control his art!

His hand flew across his urban canvas, the portrait taking shape faster than he'd ever drawn before. The destructive energy, the fury, the passion, all of it fueling the outpouring of blades. He seized that negative energy and channeled it all into his drawing, until the coffee image was nearly vibrating with life on the dirty alley floor.

Nigel dabbed the last stroke, his body shuddered with relief, and the blades finally stopped as all the darkness fled from his body into his art. Silence throbbed in the alley. Stillness crushed down on him. The aftermath of hell. Nigel bowed his head as exhaustion surged over him, his body depleted of all that it had to offer—

Glass crashed to the ground, and he looked up in time to see another pane of glass fall from its third story window and crash to the alley. Around him, carnage. Bricks severed, cars destroyed like they'd lost a battle with an army of nail guns, glass everywhere.

"Hell." It was just like last time. When people had died. People he had loved with all of his heart. His mother. His father—

"Natalie!" Ella's shout ripped through him.

Natalie. He leapt to his feet and sprinted back toward the store. He'd been too late to save his parents. Was he too late again?

Killing his own mama had been bad.

But losing his shit again, as a full warrior? Inconceivable.

Nigel leapt across the threshold of the store and his heart froze when he saw Natalie crumpled to the floor. Ella and Maggie were crouched beside her, using lace doilies from a nearby box to try to stem the flow of blood from her chest. Revulsion poured through him. He'd done that? He'd hurt her? *Natalie?* How was that possible?

"I can't stop the bleeding," Maggie said. "It won't stop—"

Her anguish galvanized him into action. "That's because it's my blades. Most people can't heal them on their own." People like his mother. Like his father. Like the only people in the entire fucking world that mattered to him.

Maggie gaped at him. "*You* did this to her?"

"I can fix it." He didn't waste time with her censure, on target though it was. Instead, he shoved in beside them and rubbed his hands together. His own body was bleeding badly and it hurt like hell, but he was glad for the pain. He deserved it.

His palms emitted a faint glow, and he set them on Natalie's chest.

He felt her fading spirit almost immediately. The utter devastation to her body. Several blades were inside her, working their way into her body as if they were alive. He hadn't released living blades in almost two hundred years. And into Natalie? "Jesus." What was happening to him?

"What did you do?" Ella was furious. "How could you not control yourself?"

"Good question." Nigel closed his eyes and fought to find the healing energy within him, but there was almost nothing there. Without his art, he was losing his healing as well. He didn't have enough to save her. Shit! He needed an influx of energy.

He jerked his phone out of his pocket and threw it at Ella. "Call Jarvis Swain. Tell him I need energy. Now."

Ella quickly dialed the phone while Nigel focused on Natalie. He found her heart and assessed the damage, while the blades kept ruthlessly digging deeper and deeper. "Come on, baby, fight it off." He summoned all the energy he still had. His hands flared a bright orange light, and he shoved it all into her heart. The organ flared, he heard the shrieks of the lethal metal as it pulled back and released its grip. He frantically knit her heart together, fighting to bring her back while he still had juice.

Ella held the phone up. "Jarvis is on the line. He says he's never done an energy transfer over the phone, but he'll try."

"Put it on speaker and hold it against my ear," Nigel commanded. He rubbed Natalie's chest. "Come on, Natalie. You can do this. Hang on, baby."

"Nigel." Jarvis's voice crackled in his ear.

"Need all you got, buddy. I got nothing."

"I'm on it."

The phone went silent, and then Nigel heard the hum of Jarvis's sword whipping through the air. He closed his eyes and pictured Jarvis's sword spinning around in circles, harvesting all the energy from his environment, pulling it out of people, nature, the earth. Every creature, every object, everything.

Nigel let the power ripple through him as Jarvis converted energy to sound waves. His body began to hum and his palms began to glow again. Nigel bent over Natalie and fed the energy into her body and quickly began working his way through her damaged cells. A blade worked its way to the surface and clattered onto the floor. One down. One more to go. He fought harder, worked faster, but he could feel Natalie slipping away. "I need more," he barked.

"Hang on," Jarvis said. "I'll feed it in one burst."

"I can help." Maggie eased up beside him, her face almost as pale as Natalie's. "I can generate a lot of energy."

Nigel didn't give a shit how the girl could do it, or if she was making it up. He was willing to try anything. "Do it. Touch me."

The humming from the phone intensified, and he knew Jarvis was gearing up. "I don't know if it'll go through the phone as well as if I stabbed you, but I'll try," Jarvis shouted.

"Give me a count," Nigel shouted.

"Help me get this box," Maggie ordered Ella, no longer the meek, scared girl she'd been. Suddenly she looked like a young woman who knew her own strength. A female in her power zone. "I need it near Nigel."

Ella jumped up and helped carry a three-foot box across the floor. It dropped beside Nigel with a thump. The women ripped it open.

The humming from Jarvis's sword got louder.

Natalie's pulse became fainter.

Nigel's healing energy faded even more, despite Jarvis's influx. "Come on," he shouted. "Bring it on!"

Maggie plunged her hands into the box, and he saw it was cocoa powder. Thick, dark, luxurious, it drifted up in the air like dust. Maggie shoved her hands around and stirred it up, until the air filled with a chocolate fog. Calling upon chocolate as her energy source.

"Three!" Jarvis shouted, starting his countdown.

Natalie's heart beat once, sluggishly.

Ella grabbed handfuls of chocolate powder and poured it on Maggie's head.

"Two!" Jarvis's humming got louder. Almost ready.

A blade pierced the lining of Natalie's heart, and

Nigel slammed energy in front of the invader, creating a wall to protect her. He shuddered as he felt it touch his energy. It was poisoned. Barbed. Dripping with death. If that blade touched her heart, it would be instant cardiac arrest. Mother of hell, what had he created? And when had he developed the ability to make *that*? And how in God's name had it made it into the body of the one woman he wanted to protect?

Because he wanted to protect her. Because he cared. That's why the blades had targeted her. It was exactly like the last time—

The blade burst through Nigel's virtual wall and plunged for Natalie's heart.

"One!" Jarvis shouted, and the force of explosion knocked Nigel on his ass. He bounded back to his feet and grabbed Natalie. Energy was racing through him and he plunged it into Natalie. He had almost enough. "Maggie! Give it to me now!"

Maggie's eyes were completely black, empty pits in her face, and her face was sheer white. Then she placed her hands on Nigel's face, and sheer electrical force blasted through his skin where she was holding him.

Yes! Power pulsed within him, and he began to work on Natalie, feeding the healing energy into her as quickly as he dared. He had enough now, but could he heal her before the blades killed her? It was a race with a deadly outcome.

He went faster, shoving the energy into her as fast as he dared, gauging her reaction. Her body lurched and he backed off, easing off the influx. Too much could kill her as fast as the blades could. He had to balance it just right.

Then her heart stopped.

"She's gone," Ella gasped. "She's gone!"

"No, she's not," he snapped. Screw the gradual approach. "You can do it, sweetheart."

He summoned all force swirling through his body, converted it to his healing frequency, and shoved it all into his hands until they were radiating so much energy that they looked like a bad nuclear waste movie.

Ella grabbed his arm. "She'll never survive all that."

"She won't survive without it." Nigel fully opened his connection with Natalie, and then he released the entire force into her, attacking the last blade and every bit of damage in the same instant, a whiteout blast of energy powerful enough to blow her to pieces if he didn't manage it right.

But Nigel was aware of every cell in her body, of every fragment of metal circulating inside her, of every breath of life, of every taint of death. He attuned himself to the very beat of her soul, until his own heart was beating in rhythm, until his spirit was vibrating at the same level of hers.

The connection was alive and intimate, a merging of the souls that stripped him raw and laid him out for her. But he didn't feel exposed. It was where he'd needed to be, where he'd always needed to be. His entire world was Natalie's body, her soul, her existence, the danger trying to take her. He could feel her soul calling to him, opening for his touch, and he allowed the warmth of her energy to fill him, empowering him.

There was no resistance from Natalie. She was opening herself to him, trusting him to help her. He could feel her calling to him, drawing his energy even deeper into hers, mixing their auras until they were indistinguishable. Her love, her warmth, her fears, her sensuality wrapped around, drawing from him responses so deep and so powerful he couldn't have stopped them if he'd wanted to.

But he didn't. No chance. He'd never felt this alive, this connected, this beautiful in his whole existence, and he never wanted to step away. And he wouldn't. Not as long as she needed him. *I won't let you down, Natalie. I swear it.* Wrapping his warmth around her spirit, he cradled her soul protectively as his healing raced through the battlefield, wiping away the insidious damage he'd caused, and he felt each moment her body inhaled with relief as he freed another part, and tightened the bond between them.

Again and again and again.

And then her heart stuttered, and it began to beat its rhythm, that beautiful, amazing rhythm that spoke of life, of future, of healing. His heart matched hers, and he bowed his head, allowing the power of her life force to roll through him. Her soul reached for him, and he met her, their energy holding onto each other as they both began to breathe again.

They'd done it.

Together, they'd defeated his darkest side.

For now.

Nigel liked to be right.

As a man, it was his calling. To be right. Always right. Especially about anything that might have to do with such manly pursuits as battle, weapons, or torture.

But as Nigel vaulted up the stairs from the basement

hideaway of Natalie's store, where he'd reluctantly left a recovering Natalie in the devoted care of Ella and Maggie, he knew it wasn't a matter of liking to be right.

He *had* to be right this time, and he had to know *now* whether he was. Once he'd gotten Natalie settled comfortably and knew she would soon be waking up, he had to go check. It had been all he could do to tear himself away from her when all he wanted was to sit with her on his lap, but he'd forced himself to leave.

It was just for a minute, but that minute was everything. It would give him answers about what they were facing, about whether he would have to call upon Natalie to trespass into areas she didn't want to go, whether life was a whole lot darker than he wanted it to be.

There was only one way to know what their future was holding, and that was to find out who he had really drawn on the floor of the ally. Christian or Blaine? Or someone else?

As Nigel sprinted out the back door of the store, he did a very careful and thorough scan to make sure there were no threats lurking nearby that could endanger Natalie while she was out of his presence.

The area was secure. No deedubs, no threats. Just the taint of black magic that was trailing after Natalie. Shit. They had to deal with that, and soon. No way could he let her turn into her worst nightmare. Just couldn't happen.

He sprinted into the alley and headed straight for the Dunkin' Donuts coffee and the wooden stirrer that had saved his sanity. He crouched beside the abandoned coffee and searched the debris for the picture he'd drawn. *Come on, let me be right.*

And then he saw it, and glory be, he was right. The face scowling up at him was Blaine's, not Christian's. "Hot damn." He sat back on his heels and closed his eyes.

After he'd tried to draw Natalie and had wound up drawing Christian instead, he'd been worried that he'd remembered wrong this time, that he hadn't noticed what he'd really been drawing.

But he was right. It hadn't been Christian. Christian was still safe. *Yes*.

He flexed his shoulders, feeling power rush through him. So, yeah, he was back in control. He was the master of his domain again. It would make sense that he was. He was a man, after all, and he was in utter control of who he was, right? Nigel grinned and rubbed out Blaine's feet with the toe of his boot. "Not to take any chances, though, buddy—"

The feet didn't disappear. He scuffed his boot over Blaine's face... but the dried coffee remained intact. Nigel frowned and kicked at the dirt, but the image didn't budge. It was permanently struck on the ally floor, forever. Coffee on dirt? Permanent? The sharp pulse of dread knifed through his back.

He pulled out his phone and dialed his team leader.

Blaine's phone went straight to voicemail.

"Call me now," Nigel barked into the phone.

Then he dialed again. Straight to voicemail.

Blaine never turned his phone off. He lived by the creed that you never turned your back on your team, and going offline could mean he wasn't there for someone when he was needed, so he never turned it off. Ever.

Nigel dialed Jarvis, who answered on the first ring. "Yo, painter boy. Did it work?"

"Yeah. Is Blaine around?" Jarvis and Blaine had joined forces to take their new women on a romantic interlude somewhere in the South Pacific.

"No, I haven't seen him today. Heard some screaming from their cabin earlier, but you know how those two get—"

Nigel's palms began to burn and smoke rose from them. "Check their cabin."

"What? No way. I'll get set on fire if they're in the middle of—"

"Check their cabin. Now."

Jarvis was silent for a moment. "What's going on, Nigel?"

Nigel told him.

"Hell, man, don't paint me." There was the sound of boots thudding on the wooden deck of the cruise ship as Jarvis loped toward the cabin.

Waiting, unable to do anything constructive, Nigel stared helplessly at the metal blades jammed in the buildings around him, evidence of his descent into insanity. He saw a well-dressed couple walking toward him, and he watched their faces morph into shock and fear when they noticed the millions of knives lodged in everything.

"It must have been a gang fight," the man said.

"What if they come back?" The woman clutched her purse to her side.

Oh, they're back. You're looking right at him. Nigel watched them turn and scurry back down the alley. Away from the monster who had left behind such carnage.

"Blaine! Trinity!" Jarvis hammered on the door cabin door. "You guys in there?"

Nigel let a small dagger ease out of his palm, and he crouched beside the drawing of Blaine and tried to chisel it off the asphalt.

The blade broke. The coffee drawing stayed intact. Indestructible. Yeah, and that was a good sign. "No answer," Jarvis said. "I'll break in." There was a loud crash and then the sound of wood splintering.

Sweat trickled down Nigel's back, and his skin began to burn. Not just his palms. His shoulders. His back. His face. Blades taking shape all over his whole body. Again. Come on! Where was his control? This was crap!

"There's no one here," Jarvis said. "The hair dryer is still on, and Blaine's electric razor is running. They got yanked."

Nigel swore and threw the dagger into the asphalt. It hit the coffee and bounced off, as if the drawing was magically protected.

Which it probably was.

Son of a bitch. Mari had corrupted his painting and used it to steal another warrior.

"I'll be home as fast I as I can," Jarvis said.

Nigel realized he was reaching for that same coffee stirrer again, and he jammed his hand in his pocket, taking away his chance to draw before he could burn someone else. "It'll be over before then."

One way or another, this was one battle that was going to die fast.

And Natalie was his only chance to survive it.

Would she even be willing to come near him after he'd almost killed her?

She'd trusted him to save her, yeah, but now that she

was okay, would she be foolish enough to risk herself with him?

If she had any sense of self-preservation, she would boot his ass out of her life forever. For good.

Chapter 11

"MAGGIE, I'VE CHANGED MY MIND," ELLA SAID.

Natalie rolled over as Ella's voice penetrated her subconscious.

"About what?" Maggie asked.

"I'm not going to help Natalie," Ella said.

"What?" Natalie forced her eyes open and looked groggily around. She was startled to find they were in the Creative Brainstorming Utopia below her store, her private retreat that she never allowed anyone in, or had even told anyone about. How had the women found it?

The Utopia had deep red tapestries, a handwoven tasseled rug, textured bronzed walls, and dim lighting. The room was only a few feet wide, a former boiler room or something, but she'd co-opted it as a place to clear her mind and create new recipes. There was no room for furniture, but she'd covered the floor with a decadent number of thick, luxurious pillows in an assortment of fabrics more expensive than most of the cars on Newbury Street. It was a place of sensual assault in all directions, with the lighting and the colors and the fabrics and the music.

The moment she entered this room, Natalie's soul always came alive. The deepest sources of her power would course through her. It was where she spent a half hour every morning before heading upstairs to start wooing customers. It was the place where she released a lifetime of fear of her oncoming death and doomed future. It was where she tapped into herself and her sensuality.

She hadn't come here in weeks. And she'd intended never to visit it again, ever since her experience with the Godfather had cleared her of any desire to tap into her sensuality ever again. But she had no immunity to this room that she'd designed specifically to tap into her sensual side, and she felt warmth stirring deep in her as thoughts of Nigel drifted into her mind. His broad shoulders, his intense gaze, the way he—dammit! "What are we doing down here?" She couldn't quite keep the panic out of her voice.

Ella's face lit up. "You're awake!" She flung her arms around Natalie and hugged her. "I'm so glad!"

"Me, too!" Maggie tackled them both, and Natalie caught a whiff of the girl's chocolate scent.

Oh, yeah, she'd forgotten about the "need to eat the young woman who had come to her for protection" thing. Natalie pulled back from Maggie and breathed through her mouth so she couldn't smell the delicious fragrance that was making her stomach clench. "No, seriously. Why are we down here?"

Ella's forehead was furrowed. "Okay, so I know we barely know each other, but I feel like sharing a near-death experience has created one of those instant lifetime bonds."

Maggie perched beside Ella. "I'm going to second that."

"Near-death?" Natalie started crawling over the pillows for the door. Her skin was itching, crawling with the need to tap into her sensuality. She had to get out before she succumbed. Where was Nigel? Was he nearby? What would it be like if he walked in here? Oh, God.

That was just too frightening and, of course, decadently thrilling. "Whose death are you talking about?"

"Yours."

Natalie stopped crawling for the door to stare at them. "Mine? Did a deedub bite me or something?" Oh, wow. She'd meant it as a joke, but the mere words caused adrenaline to rush through her. She wanted to leap up with swords brandished, ready to fight for her life. Except, of course, she had no swords or swashbuckling skills, so yeah, that wasn't going to work.

"No, not a deedub."

"Well, that's good." But the denial didn't reassure Natalie when she saw the wary glance the two women exchanged. Natalie started heading for the door again. She needed space. She needed fresh air, and she needed to be away from all the sensuous thoughts of Nigel that were crowding common sense and survival mode out of her mind.

Then Ella looked at her. "Nigel almost killed you, of course."

"Nigel? He would never—" Natalie stopped, her hand on the doorknob, at the sudden memory of all those blades erupting from Nigel's body. The look of fury on his face, his lethal anger, his roar of rage before all those blades had started pouring out of him. The sensation of that one slamming into her chest. He'd become a monster. The mellow Nigel she knew, the man of art and serenity... he'd been swallowed up by the beast, an assassin who had almost killed her—

The door opened, and Nigel stepped into the room.

Natalie jumped and then tumbled back as Ella yanked her away from him.

"Get out of here," Ella commanded. "You're dangerous."

His shirt was caked with blood, and it was ripped to shreds. New pink scars peppered his body, and his eyes were dark with a raw determination she'd never seen before. There was no sign of the artist. He was pure warrior and pure action.

And he was focused on her. "Everyone but Natalie, out."

Natalie's belly tightened. With what, she wasn't certain. Sheer unbridled terror? Raw, sexual attraction? Heart-wrenching empathy for this man whose inner monster had taken him somewhere he loathed to go? None of it good, whatever it was.

Ella stood up, her hands fisted by her side. Her skin rippled with blue-green luminescence, and power crackled in the air. "You will—"

He clamped over her mouth. "*Never* try to suggest anything to me," he said with lethal calmness. "Or you die."

Ella's eyes widened, and she pulled away. "I don't do that anymore," she snapped.

He met her gaze knowingly. "Not even to save Natalie from me?"

"No—" Then Ella's face paled with realization. "I was doing it, wasn't I?"

"I could feel the power of your words," he said. "Never, ever try that again."

Ella ran her hand through her hair, and Natalie saw her hands were shaking. "Ella!" She scrambled over to the pillows toward her friend. "What's wrong?"

"Nothing." Ella pulled her shoulders back and met Natalie's. She'd shelved the fear, but Natalie could feel it pulsing within her. She knew, because she had lived with that kind of terror her whole life, and she knew how it could eat away at a soul. It was fear of what monsters lay within. "Ella—"

"No." Ella squared her shoulders and faced Nigel. "Leave us," she said, but her voice was flat and calm. No force of suggestion. "You're too dangerous."

Recognition flashed in Nigel's eyes, and he inclined his head. "I am," he agreed. He met Natalie's gaze again, and this time there was acknowledgment in his eyes. "This is your opportunity to walk away, Natalie. One chance, and if you don't take it, I'm keeping you until this is over."

His tone was brutal and unyielding, and it sent a shudder through her, a quiver of longing. He wouldn't leave her. No matter what. He could keep her alive, and he would.

Of course he might snap and kill her, too.

What was a girl to do? Bad boys were one thing, but *bad* boys were something else entirely. She'd had enough men luring her to her death, thank you. She shook her head. "I can't—"

His face hardened before she even finished her denial, and guilt coursed through her. He needed her. He'd snapped, and in the most horrible way. She knew him well enough to know that he would never, ever turn on her intentionally, so she knew it had been out of his control. She could see the haunting horror in his eyes, the anguish of knowing that he'd lost a battle of the worst kind. Her fingers folded with the urge to reach out and touch him, to reassure him that he wasn't a monster, that whatever had happened wasn't him, and she knew it. For him to snap like that, dear God, what kind of beast was he fighting within?

Nigel was burning with passion, with strength, with power. He was life, and he wasn't going to lose, and he wasn't going to die. Maybe he could teach her how to be the victor. Maybe he could show her how to defend her own life and believe in herself. Maybe—

Ella took her arm. "Girl, I know he's hot, but some men just aren't worth it." She shuddered. "Don't go down that road. Not with him. You know what men like him are like. There are other ways—"

"No!" Maggie scrambled to her feet, stumbling over the cushions. "I touched him while he was saving. He has a good soul." She grabbed Natalie's other arm, her young face raw with a grown-up understanding that Natalie didn't expect. It was the face of someone who had been through hell and was still living in its shadow. She tugged on Natalie. "He saved your life, Natalie."

"He did?" Natalie suddenly recalled hearing his voice while she'd been catapulting down the crevasse. With the demons stalking her, the hell chasing her, she'd heard his voice calling to her. She could still feel his warmth plunging into her body, yanking her back from the free fall, ripping through the pain crushing her chest. He'd been there, and he'd brought her back. "Of course he did," she said softly. "Of course he has a good soul."

Nigel still hadn't spoken, but his brow furrowed ever so slightly at her words, as if he couldn't quite believe what she'd said. He made no effort to convince her to stay and help him. He was simply waiting for her answer. Allowing her to find her own path. His face was impassive and hard, as if he already knew she was going to abandon him. Abandon his friend he needed to save.

Abandon the man who'd had no one to count on for one hundred and fifty years of hell.

God, she wanted to help him, but being around him brought out the very traits in herself she was trying so hard to suppress. What would happen if she spent more time around him? If she liked him more? He already tapped into her womanly side in a way that—

Natalie caught a whiff of chocolate, of Maggie's scent, and a violent craving crashed through her. She whipped toward Maggie, grabbed the girl's wrist, and yanked her close. Her teeth began to throb, and she fixated on Maggie's throat. Heard the rush of the blood coursing through her veins. Knew it would taste like chocolate decadence. Her body tingled in anticipation of the high she could get.

"Natalie?"

Natalie jerked her gaze off Maggie's throat and saw the raw fear on the girl's face. Holy shit. Natalie looked at Nigel, and she saw the empathy in his eyes. The understanding. He knew what she was becoming, and he wasn't judging her.

She couldn't battle the demons on her own. Nigel was dangerous, but so was she. Apart, they were both turning into monsters of hell. Together? Maybe they'd be the demise of each other, but maybe, just maybe, they had a chance.

She took a deep breath, not taking her eyes off the warrior who had (apparently) killed her once and had (definitely) saved her twice. He was her best chance to live, and also to die. But everything else gave her the chance only to die. "It's okay, girls. You can go."

Nigel let out his breath and nodded, his eyes lighting

up. She smiled back at him, and suddenly teaming up with him didn't seem so dangerous. It just felt right, deliciously, powerfully right.

Maggie grinned. "I'm so glad," she said. "We need help, sister."

Sister? Natalie looked sharply at Maggie, and she warmed at her expression of trust. Maggie had no one left in this world, and she'd put her faith in Natalie. *Sister.* "All of my sisters except Reina are dead," she said.

Maggie nodded. "Mine, too." She held out her hand. "So, let's start our lives over. Sister?"

Natalie's throat thickened, and she thought of her sisters, dying one by one. She'd held out her hands to them to try to keep them safe, to bring them back, and each one had left her behind. No one had held on. No one had reached back for her help.

Until now.

Until this sweet young thing that Natalie was going to attack if she didn't find a way to stop herself.

But as Natalie looked into Maggie's hopeful and desperate face, she knew she wanted to help her. To save her the way she hadn't been able to save herself or her sisters. And she certainly couldn't bear to become the monster that had taken them all.

But until she stopped Mari and Angelica from off-loading smut onto her, Maggie wasn't safe, and Natalie was going to become the monster who'd destroyed her life. She knew what she wanted. She wanted to live, she wanted Maggie to live, and she wanted to be able to open her heart to people again. She wanted all of it more than she wanted to run away from who she was. And she couldn't do it without Nigel.

"Nat?" Maggie prompted.

"I'm with you." She squeezed Maggie's hand. "Sister." The word stuck in her throat, making her ache with longing for the sisters she'd lost, for the hope that maybe life was turning around.

"Great!" Maggie grinned. "I'll go work on some recipes upstairs." She gestured to Ella. "Come on! You can take notes on the proper ingredients to stir a man into total and complete ecstasy." She squeezed past Nigel, after giving him a look of adoration.

Ella was slower to leave, but she finally left, too.

Nigel stepped aside to let Ella pass, then he walked in and pulled the door shut behind him.

And suddenly, the room full of everything that tipped her off sensually seemed very, very small.

———

Nigel stepped inside Natalie's private hideaway and shut the door. He leaned back against wood, and she heard the click as he locked them in. His shoulders were as wide as the door, and his black leather pants and black T-shirt were taut across his muscled body. The rose tattoo on his cheek was shadowed, and his eyes were hooded. He looked dangerous and delicious.

And he was blocking the only exit.

Heat began to unfurl inside her belly as they stood there in silence, letting the weight of their presence hang heavy in the air. She shifted her position on the pillows. The velvet was soft and seductive against her bare feet, caressing the tender skin and making chills run down her spine.

Or were the chills from the way Nigel was looking

at her? Um, yeah, locked inside this sensual room with the man she'd already had a little trouble resisting? Wasn't this exactly the kind of deadly and explosive combination that people warned about? "So, um, are you okay now?"

"Apparently not." He didn't move from the door, but his gaze swept over her body. Possessive. Owning.

"I'm so sorry." She searched his arms but didn't see any blades on the verge of emerging. "Can I help?"

He didn't answer. Instead, he seemed to need to clarify her choice, as if he couldn't quite believe it. "You stayed."

She nodded, her heart softening for him. For this great warrior who was steeled for her to walk away. "Of course I stayed."

He was watching her intently, as if trying to see inside her soul. "I told you, if you stayed, you were mine until it's over."

She rolled her eyes. "I know that. I'll help. We'll do it together." She grinned at him. "I'm not afraid of you, Nigel, so you can stop worrying about it. I'm in. I'm staying. I'm not running away."

He closed his eyes for a moment, as if drinking in the beauty of her words. Her heart began to thud, and it felt so good to see his reaction. He needed her. She could help him. He could help her. Neither of them had to take on their burdens alone. Not anymore.

"Thank you." He opened his eyes and smiled. It was a warm expression, tender, but it was laced with a fierce fire, with male power, with the determination to dominate all obstacles.

Inside her, the womanly, sensual part that she'd tried

so hard to suppress purred and stretched and beckoned to him. *Down, girl! Get down!*

"I called Christian," Nigel said. "We're meeting him in thirty minutes at the last known portal to the Den. We're going in."

"Into the Den? I'm going too?" At his nod, her heart began to pound, and this time she knew it wasn't from the sexual awareness percolating through every cell in her body. Her heart was thudding because the thought of heading into the Den was a little daunting.

Yes, a part of her was sort of curious to see this hellhole that had damaged so many men, but she'd also heard an awful lot about the horrors there. Yes, true, she wasn't a man, so that might buy her some wiggle room with the women in there, but she would be *with* a man, a target, and she would be aligned with him, going on the full offensive against Mari. And even if her double X chromosomes gave her some indemnity, the Den and its occupants were a rather formidable opponent, and if they didn't succeed in disarming Mari, her entire future was going to be pretty grim.

A lot of pressure and a lot of unknowns! And the last time she looked, she wasn't exactly an All-Star when it came to battle situations. So, taking on the Den… Yeah, no problem. She could do this. Right?

Nigel smiled. "You'll be fine. I'll do the killing, maiming, and disarming, and all you need to do is hang around if I need you. Cool?"

She raised her brows. "Somehow, I doubt it's going to work out quite like that."

He grinned and inclined his head in acknowledgment. "Yeah, okay, more likely, you're going to have to tie me down and seduce me until you can influence me so I'm under control."

Her cheeks heated up and she swallowed hard at the visual Nigel had just put into her mind. "Um…"

"We need to leave here in a couple minutes." He pushed off the door and walked toward her. His body was tense, his face a mixture of turbulent heat and the cold, lethal focus of a warrior. The closer he got, the larger he seemed. Not just his bulk, but the sheer intensity of his presence. He was focused on a quest, and he would sweep her up into his mission ruthlessly.

"We're going to stop Mari from smutting me?" She stiffened as he neared, as desire began to ripple through her. "And Angelica?"

"Mari first. I think she's the issue. I think she's just redirecting Angelica's old smut. Angie's pretty out of commission right now." He caught her wrist and tugged her toward him.

Natalie stumbled on the thick pillows that were meant for writhing in creative pleasure, not resisting a personal invasion by a warrior. "Okay, so, Mari, then."

"We've got five minutes for you to tap into your power source and get me cleared up." He tugged her the rest of the way, and she fell into his chest.

She managed to get her hands free to catch herself, but his body was hard and hot beneath her hands. "We already tried. I can't affect you. I'm not that kind of Mystic—"

"I don't care what you think you are, or what you think you're not." He tucked her against him, her body flush against his. "But I know that two of my friends are trapped because I screwed up. Plus, I almost killed you." His grip tightened, and regret flashed in his eyes. "I can't afford to lose it again, and you're my best chance to make it happen. Got it?"

"With sex? I'm not really comfortable—"

"I know you're not." He softened his grip and stroked her hair gently. "But do you want to turn into a deedub?"

"No, of course not—"

"Do you want to eat Maggie?"

She glared at him and thumped him lightly on the chest. "It's not fair to ask me that! You know the answer!"

"I'm just trying to get you to look at your choices and decide which is the better option." Nigel rubbed his hand over her hip, his touch seductive and alluring. He bent his head so his mouth was inches from hers. "Do you want to be able to save yourself against the deedubs? Do you want to own your life again?"

Her breath caught in her chest, and hope flared to life inside her. "Oh, yes." That would be a gift, a true gift. What good would a gold star rating for her store do if the deedubs could destroy the store, and her, whenever they wanted to?

His face softened with understanding. "Then you need to tap into your power source, sweetheart, and I'm going to help you. I need it, you need it, and the people counting on us need it." He moved his hand around to her lower back, his palm searing hot through her shirt. "Do you trust me?"

"Of course." She didn't even hesitate. It didn't matter that he'd snapped. It made no difference how lethal his expression was. This was Nigel. She would always trust him.

He smiled. "Then let me kiss you."

Her heart began to race. "Um—"

"You need to tap into your power source, and that's your sensuality." He thumbed her lower lip. "Let me kiss you," he said again. "I'll keep you safe."

Her blood was rushing so hard she could barely hear herself think. Her hands were trembling, and her belly was dancing with anticipation.

"Nat?"

She nodded once.

Nigel smiled. "That's my girl."

Then he kissed her.

Chapter 12

NATALIE'S ENTIRE SOUL CAME TO LIFE AT THE FIRST touch of Nigel's lips.

With the tension and battle-ready adrenaline racing through him, she would have expected a hard, controlling kiss. A kiss of possession and duty. A kiss of urgent demand.

That, she'd been prepared for. That was what she'd gotten from the Godfather. That was the kind of kiss her body and soul had betrayed her for.

But this... this... this was something she wasn't ready for.

It was a kiss of tempting tenderness. A brush of his lips against the corner of her mouth. Then the other. The loosening of his grip in her hair until it was a soft caress, a coaxing massage.

This was the Nigel she knew. The artist who would sit for hours with his paints and contemplate. A man who had retained his sensitive side despite years of torture. She sighed with delight, and she raised her face to his, accepting and encouraging his kiss.

The kiss was of bright sunlight, of fresh air, of the silken touch of rose petals. It awakened in her a sense of freedom, of lightness, of carefree delight. It was the kind of kiss that a young girl's dreams were made of. The kind that would turn a raggedy washer girl into a princess.

Nigel's arms wrapped around her, burying her in the

protective strength of his embrace. She snuggled against him while he continued to kiss her. She felt delicate and cherished, adored and honored, liberated and elevated. It was a kiss she didn't need to fear. A caress that made her spirit laugh with delight, not stress, under the burden of uncontainable desire.

Nigel's shoulders bunched, his muscles strong and protective, while he continued to kiss her. He caressed her lower back, then ran his hands over her bottom, his touch featherlight, as if he could barely believe she was real.

His lips slid over her throat, and she leaned back, delighting in the surge of relief, of rightness, of peace at the feeling of his warmth surrounding her.

"You taste magical." His whisper was low and guttural, and it tapped into something inside that was more than peace, more than safety... into something more decadent and sensual. A heavier, weightier urgency. A yearning for him to kiss deeper, to touch more assertively. To take ownership of the kiss. Of her. It was aching hunger fueled by erotic desire and irreverent recklessness. She buried her fingers in his hair and pulled him closer.

"Yeah, that's right." He backed her against the wall. The plaster was cold against her back as he deepened his kiss, as it turned to a powerful seduction like the one she'd been expecting.

Excitement roared to life inside her, and she grabbed for his shoulders. She basked in the torn fabric of his shirt. She cherished the ridges in his skin from the scars of battles gone by. He was danger. He was strength. He was unbridled rage. But he was also tender, compelling seduction. And it made her crave more, more, more—

His hand moved between her legs, caressing the seam of her jeans, touching, teasing—

Desire pulsed in response, the sensual power within her she'd tried so hard to destroy after the Godfather. But now, under Nigel's kiss, it was coming alive, fighting back, striving for freedom, thriving with more force than she could contain.

Natalie began tremble, and then she was kissing Nigel back harder, more fiercely, with passion that drove her so relentlessly she didn't want to question it. She didn't want to stop, but she didn't mind. Somehow, in Nigel's arms, she still felt safe enough to allow her passion to roar to life. She wanted it to go on forever. She needed to take it further, further, further, as far as it could go. She yearned for that high, that sense of indomitable power, that soul-deep conviction that nothing could ever bring her down.

"Tell me." Nigel's mouth was by her ear, his hand on his breast, flicking her nipple. "Tell me I don't want to draw." He bit her nipple, and she gasped at the fire that sparked through her. "Tell me I don't need art." His eyes were dark, and the rose on his cheek was pulsing with energy. "Tell me I'm in total control."

And then he kissed her with a fire, a passion, and a desperation that undid her. Passion leapt through her, her belly lurched, and she gasped for air.

"Tell me," he ordered. "Tell me now!"

Natalie closed her eyes, and she concentrated on the seduction of his hands across her hip, of his lips on her throat. On the pulse of desire throbbing deep inside her.

"Come on, baby." Nigel kissed her again, and he slipped his hand down the front of her jeans. He palmed her belly, and then his finger slipped lower, flicked her swollen nub.

She gasped as her whole body shuddered, and she laid her hands on Nigel's face and felt the roughness of his skin. She searched his face, saw the man she knew buried in the depths of his dark eyes. His humanity. His desperation. "You don't need to draw," she whispered. Her voice was hesitant, rough. Tentative.

"Again," he demanded. He caught her hair, heat simmering in his eyes as his other hand moved lower between her legs. He thumbed her with a precision that made her body writhe with pleasure. "Say it like you believe it." He squeezed her breast, his hand was hot, almost burning. Her legs nearly buckled and he had to brace her harder against the wall to keep her from falling. "Make me believe you're a woman with power," he whispered into her mouth between kisses. "Make me tremble on my knees before you. Own me like you own all those other men who come to you for help."

Despite the strong conviction of his voice, she saw the plea in his eyes. The desperation. The fear. Her heart tightened and she held his face again, but this time softly, with tenderness, with passion. "Nigel. You're a powerful warrior. You own the world. You don't need art. You don't need to draw. You're in complete control of yourself, your weapons, and your destiny. *You know it*." She felt the power of her words, of her statement, and it reverberated through her.

Nigel jerked back, releasing her suddenly, and cold air rushed over her.

Wariness flashed over his face. "I felt that."

"Really?" She grinned. "That's great!" Could she really do it? *Had* she done it? Her heart started to race with anticipation. "Do you feel like drawing?"

But Nigel was staring at her as if her head had spun off and she'd sprouted tentacles instead. "You are one powerful woman."

She grinned and sort of felt like doing a little tap dance. "Really?"

"Hell, yeah." Smoke began rising from his palms, and a metal blade flashed threateningly from his fingertips, which made her smile even more. She'd been so powerful that she'd triggered self-defense instincts from a great warrior?

Rock on, baby!

She cheerfully watched as Nigel tossed the knife aside and flexed his empty hand, happy to see he was sane and in control. Yay!

"How can I tell if it worked?" he asked.

"Oh, right. That's true." She supposed it was true that a burst of power didn't necessarily mean her suggestion had been successful. Back to business. Romantic interlude and delightful self-love moment over. But even though they'd been a call to duty, those kisses, his touches... it had been amazing. For a moment, she'd forgotten to fear who she was. She'd been immersed in the present, loving life, and completely free of her baggage. Exactly how she'd wanted to be. That moment had been such a gift!

She wanted to be like that all the time. To always feel like she could sail through life with joy and be able to rise above baggage and worries and fears, and to crush any deedub who tried to upend her life or her business. And that was exactly how Nigel should be feeling if her suggestions had worked. "Do you feel like you own the world?"

He grinned at her. "I always feel like I own the world."

"Oh… I'm a little jealous. I want to own the world too."

His smile widened. "You keep that up and you will. I'll have to chain you down to keep you from making the world do your laundry and kiss your toes on a regular basis."

"Really? Wouldn't that be cool to make the deedubs kiss my toes?" She paused to picture that. "No teeth, though."

Nigel laughed softly, and she laughed with him. They shared a moment of relief and hope between them, and it felt so good. "I guess we won't know for sure, not until there's a time when you would normally need to draw. If you overcome it, then it worked. If you can't—" She sighed, some of her excitement fading at the mere idea that she'd failed. "Then it didn't." She folded her arms, annoyed at how quickly she could retreat into a feeling of powerlessness. "But I did feel something happen, though, so it's at least possible. There was power there, and that was good."

"Yeah, I agree. You made progress. Nice job."

She grinned. "Thanks."

"But I need more than 'maybe the suggestion worked' to ensure we get out of the Den. Your suggestion has to be infallible and unbeatable, even in the face of direct attack."

"Oh. Well." She sighed. "I don't know about that." That seemed to be rather high standards for a woman who hadn't even influenced a human two hours ago.

"Yeah, no way to know until the fire's roaring." He nodded and rubbed the back of her neck in a reassuring gesture. "Which is why you're coming with me. If we have to do it again, we'll do it again, but for now, we've got to go." His phone rang, and he looked down. "Christian's ready." He shut his phone and unlocked the door. "Let's hit the road."

Um… yeah… she wasn't feeling that everything was in order for invading hell. "But what if it didn't work? What if my suggestion doesn't hold? And we, um…"

"Get our asses kicked?"

"Well, yes."

"Better to at least try. Death is always an option." He held the door open for her, and his eyes were grim and ready. "Welcome to my world."

But that wasn't the part of his world she wanted to join! Why couldn't he give her a golden ticket to feeling like *she* owned the world, huh? So much better than being in the part of his life that treaded on the edge of death on a regular basis.

Been there.

Done that.

And quite frankly, she'd vote for not doing it again.

Which, she supposed, meant she had to get it right when influencing Nigel, and let him do his thing successfully.

On the plus side, that might mean more kisses and caresses…

Oh, wait, that was a minus, right?

No, plus.

No…

"You coming?" Nigel was holding the door open, and his eyes were dark and ready for war. "Or are you daydreaming?"

"Both." She ducked under his arm before he could ask her what she'd been daydreaming about. Telling a warrior that she was reliving his kisses was probably not the best thing to do, you know, right before they had to walk into battle.

And she was a battle girl, right? She always knew what to do in the middle of war.

Always.

Ahem.

After leaving Maggie and Ella in charge of the store, Nigel and Natalie were halfway out the front door of Scrumptious on their way to invade the Den when a six-horse chariot coasted to a stop in front of them. The scent of rotten bananas floated through Natalie's nostrils before she even saw the hunchbacked, far-too-successful assassin poke his swarthy and grizzled face out the window.

It was the man who'd murdered more immortal beings that most adults could even fathom existing, let alone actually snuff the life out of.

When Augustus saw her, his face lit up, and he waved at her with enthusiasm more fitting of a five-year-old extrovert than a suicidal loner who had fewer friends than a cannibalistic rattlesnake. "Natalie Fleming! I've come for you!"

Natalie stopped. "You have?" It was *never* a good thing when Augustus came for you. What had she done to bring *him* down on her? Clients paid him unfathomable amounts of money for his murdering talents, and if he was after her, she'd pissed off someone really, really impressive.

"Uh, uh. You don't get to have her." Nigel pulled Natalie behind him in a completely endearing statement of protection and possession that she really wasn't going to argue with.

"You are sadly mistaken, my good man. You cannot keep her from me." The world's most well-decorated assassin climbed out of his hot pink chariot and eased to his feet in front of them.

Well, he landed on his truncated feet. They looked like they'd been cut off in the middle, leaving him with little flesh-colored clubfeet.

Augustus had pissed off a talented black witch a few weeks ago, who'd dumped an impressive leprosy type spell on him that had taken him a while to overcome. It looked like he was finally feeling beautiful enough to go public, a feeling of self-confidence that might be debatable. After all, his skin was still a rather odd shade of green, his nose was reminiscent of deformed mold, and the crust forming where an ear used to be… well… it was just a little disturbing.

But even half-falling apart, as Augustus drew himself into a vertical position, there was power pulsing from him that made Natalie forget about his appearance and remember only the number of bodies he'd left behind.

Nigel let a blade slide out of his palm and gripped it with a silent threat as the crusty old man tipped his fedora and bowed low. "Miss Natalie, I have been dreaming of you for much time. We have a date, remember?"

Nigel growled and pulled her closer. "There will be no date."

"A date?" A vague memory of Augustus inviting her to something drifted into her mind. It had happened while she'd been under the influence of the deedub poison, and her memory of that time of her life was a little fuzzy. Intentionally, she was sure. "Listen, I'm a little busy—"

"Of course we have a date," Augustus said, scratching the crust where his left ear was supposed to be, apparently oblivious to the rising tension emanating from Nigel. "It's time for tea. We discussed this several weeks ago. But I was too busy trying to kill your friend, and you were too busy dying. But we've both moved on, so the time is right!"

Well, on the plus side, he wasn't there to kill her, which was always a bonus. She glanced at Nigel, whose skin was taut. His face was cold and hard, and he looked far more deadly than she'd ever seen. "Um, it's not a good time for tea right now—"

"Nonsense. I am ready, therefore it is a good time." Augustus placed his hat on his nearly bald head and tipped it back. "My therapist says you are the only bright light in my life, and I must tap into that, or I will kill myself. Then the world will be deprived of the most premiere assassin, and I am far too altruistic to let the world suffer like that just because I cannot find joy in my day, in my night, or in my heart." He set his hands on his hips. "It is time for you to become my new therapist, Ms. Fleming. I need your help!" He grabbed for her shoulders, and Nigel stepped between them, his blade at the old man's throat.

"Now is not the time," Nigel said, his voice like barbed steel. "I've got dibs on her time, and I've got an agenda." Nigel's hand tightened on the blade and his skin began to glitter, as if more weapons were beginning to form beneath his skin. Just like before.

Only this time, it was to protect her. Nigel was on

edge because her safety was being threatened. Because another man was trying to stake a claim to her. Hello? How adorable was that? A mightily powerful warrior brought to his knees by danger to her?

It was beautiful. He made *her* feel beautiful—

Then she noticed a sharp metal tip poking out of his shoulder. Um, yeah, that wouldn't be so adorable if he exploded again... Oh, crap! Did that mean he wasn't in control? That her suggestion was a total failure? "Dammit! I'm so sorry, Nigel!"

He didn't look over, concentrating instead on the lethal assassin he was staring down.

She supposed it was possible he was calling them on purpose to be intimidating. But still, unmitigated launching of blades couldn't be good. "Nigel? Calm down." She touched his shoulder and was startled by how cold his skin felt. She could feel the sharp pricks of blades beneath his skin.

Nigel jumped at her touch, and then he grabbed her hand with his free one and clasped her hand tightly. Using her to ground himself? His palm was hot, and there were embers sloughing off it. She sensed his unrest and realized that all that metal wasn't his choice. His fear for her safety (or possessiveness in the face of another man's attention?) was triggering a reaction he couldn't control, just like before.

"Nigel," she said quietly. "I'm okay. It's okay." She moved closer, giving him reassurance through her touch. "I'm not in danger."

Nigel didn't look at her, but he took her hand and pressed it to his chest. "Yes," she whispered, touched by his need for contact with her. "It's me. I'm here."

He took a shuddering breath, and she felt the blades retreat back into his body.

"Don't let go of me," he muttered, as he tightened his grip on the dagger he had at Augustus's throat, which was the only blade he would need.

I will never let go of you.

Augustus turned toward her, appearing to ignore Nigel, but she knew he was intricately aware of every breath Nigel took, just as Nigel was of him.

"My dear," Augustus said conversationally. "I am desperate, and I will scale the highest mountains and cross the widest seas and slay thousands of rabid and wealthy vampires for ten minutes of your time. I *need* to know how you stay so positive! If you do not tell me willingly, I will be compelled to slay your protectors and kidnap you—"

"No!" For God's sake, she had enough on her plate right now without being stalked by a suicidal assassin or worrying about Nigel snapping because of it. "I already told you! I don't know anything. I was insane from the deedub curse, and now that it's over, I'm terrified and miserable and scared and—"

"Oh, no! Warrior-man has stolen your spirit!" Augustus hurled his pink star at Nigel's face. "My beautiful flower will not be severed at the stalk and left to die! I shall protect you!"

"Oh, for hell's sake." Nigel raised his palm, and a dozen blades exploded from his palm and shredded the star into a thousand pieces that sprayed across the cement sidewalk like pulverized dust. "You can't beat me when you're healthy," he said, his voice calm and precise again but loaded with threat. "Why try when you're injured? Be smart, man."

"You bastard!" Augustus plunged his hand into his pocket for another star. "I will preserve my fruitcake's spirit from your beastly influence—"

Nigel swept his boot under the assassin's rickety legs and upended the assassin into his coach. "Enough." He slammed the door shut and clucked to the horses. "Take him home."

The steeds swished their magnificent tails and leapt into the air. The coach lurched off the street, and Augustus rolled against the door, his stumped feet poking out the window. "I will punish you severely," he shouted.

"Let's go." Nigel grabbed Natalie's arm and propelled her down the street. "Interesting choice of admirers."

"He's not an admirer. He just wants to use me." Natalie looked back as Augustus tried unsuccessfully to right himself, apparently hindered by the lack of functioning appendages. How long until he was fully healed? Even Nigel would have trouble with him once his body was rebuilt.

Augustus might be pathetic, overmatched, and weak right now, but the man was legendary. He'd taken down an entire camp of bloodlust vampires hiding out behind a demon-backed cloaking shield, and he done it in less than five minutes without so much as a nick on his skin. He could find anyone, anywhere, break through any safeguard, and kill anyone. No one had escaped or survived him. Ever. And now he was after her.

Granted, as a woman, it had been kind of endearing to have Nigel step up to protect her.

But she kind of thought the trade-off of manly protection wasn't going to be an even swap with being stalked by Augustus.

Because they were going to be a little bit busy, fending off deedubs, tracking down Mari, rescuing warriors, cleansing smut, and, of course, doing round two of "seduce Natalie so she can influence Nigel."

Hmm... One of those just wasn't quite as scary as it should be. One of those was much more tempting than a smart woman would allow it to be.

She'd always prided herself on being smart.

But now, apparently, Nigel was also turning her into a real woman with a sensual, feminine side, and she just wasn't sure what she thought about that.

Chapter 13

"AUGUSTUS WANTS YOU TO SHOW HIM HOW TO EM-brace life and be happy." Nigel's dark tone suggested he wasn't so impressed with that.

"Yes, I know." Neither was she. Because it made her think too much about the person Augustus had met before. She'd been on her way to death, but he was correct that she'd been happy. Irreverent. Not worrying about whatever fate might hand her. It had felt good, but it had led her right to her death, so, she wasn't exactly jonesing to be that out-of-control person again. But at the same time, she couldn't help but remember what a gift it had been to do exactly what she wanted and love every minute of it.

"Augustus thinks I'm someone else." She shivered as she hurried along. "Someone different than I really am."

"Does he?" Nigel stopped in front of an enormous charcoal gray Mercedes sedan and opened the passenger door for her.

It was a luxury vehicle designed for financial gurus wearing three-piece suits, polished black shoes, and monogrammed diamond rings. It was not a car for a blood-drenched warrior. "Shouldn't you have an Escalade? Or a tank?"

Nigel chuckled and guided her into the opulent machine with a hand on her back. "It has the smoothest, quietest ride in existence. Total peace when I'm in it."

"Oh." Well, that made sense. At least relative to the old Nigel, who exuded serenity and peace, even when he was in the middle of battle. It was logical that he'd gravitate toward a car that gave him spiritual harmony, as opposed to a vehicle with a loud engine, jacked up suspension, and too much instability around sharp corners.

And boy, oh boy, was his choice magnificent. The leather was baby-soft-plush as she slid across it, the dove-gray material breathing with life and sensual pleasure. She ran her palm over its lushness, a fabric so rich with texture and depth that she wanted to bury her face against it and breathe it into her soul.

The dashboard was immaculate, a display of high-tech gadgets, gleaming mahogany, and the richest leather. She slipped her shoe off and ran her foot over the wood. It was smooth and cool, not a single ripple, just an endless stream of perfection. No flaw to break up the smoothness. The leather was decadent sensuality, but the wood was cold perfection.

Nigel opened his door and slipped inside, a tattooed warrior in a bloody shirt and torn clothes, behind the wheel of a car that should belong to a bank exec. His woodsy scent filled the car with life, with heat, with the dark smell of man, of warrior, of life, of death. The blood on his clothes, the dirt on his hands, the turbulence of his aura… it upset the tranquility of the car.

There was no more peace in the vehicle. Just two sides opposing each other, each striving to be heard. Violence and harmony.

Nigel shut the door with barely a murmur and the engine whispered to life.

As he pulled out, she could barely sense the car moving, could hardly feel the bumpy roads. It was a car designed for a man who didn't want to experience anything but a life of emotional quietude. It had not been created for a man who thrived on passion.

Not a car for an artist. Not a car for a warrior. Because both lived with passion. It was the wrong car for Nigel. Wasn't it?

Nigel looked over at her as he pulled into traffic. "I was present the day Augustus met you. When he got that in his head about your zest for life."

Natalie tucked her arms against her and leaned her head back against the deliciously tantalizing leather. "It wasn't me. It's not who I am."

"Yes, it was. I was there. It's still a part of you."

She bit her lip and looked out the tinted window at the overpriced storefronts rushing past. She didn't want to be reminded of who she'd been back then. The sex-crazed lunatic willing to trade life for a high. "You don't know me."

"I see souls," he said. "I've seen yours. There's more truth in that than in your words or actions any day."

She turned her head slightly to look at him. "What do you mean?"

He ran his hands over the leather steering wheel, as if he were caressing the splendor. "When I'm sketching, I see my subject's soul. If their spirit is thriving, I see their passion, both the positive and negative. If there's no passion, I see nothing. They're a blank to me. I don't draw people like that." He merged onto the highway and unleashed the ride. "You had passion. You had life."

The wind was silent, the car felt completely still, the

interior more like a luxurious spa than a vehicle speeding down the highway. Her only hint that they were moving was the number on the speedometer. Other than that, the car had stripped them of any sense of movement or energy or life. It was a car without a presence.

"It wasn't my passion." She shifted, suddenly not liking the leather anymore. The car was stifling her. She didn't want to catapult toward her death, but as God was her witness, she didn't want to *feel* dead anymore either. She wanted to feel alive *and* know she wasn't going to die for it. "When I was under the deedub thrall, I was insane—"

"Your spirit was alive." He moved into the passing lane and started zooming past other cars as if they were taking a nap on a hot day, and still, the interior of the car was silent and still. "And you were also tortured by being so vibrant, and for your love of how great it felt to have your spirit zinging with life. You were terrified. Exciting. Yearning. Conflicted." He glanced over at her, his face pensive and thoughtful. The artist creating an image in his mind even as he spoke. He was drawing her in his head, she was sure of it, and the intimacy of that concept made her heart begin to thud.

"You intrigued me," he said.

Well, hmm. She wasn't sure she'd ever intrigued anyone before. That didn't sound bad. And he was exactly correct in his assessment of her. And that was okay with him? He didn't think she was crazy? It wasn't a deterrent? "Why did I intrigue you?"

"Because you were life fighting to get out. But at the same time, you were death, fighting to finish your descent." He grinned and swerved around a car that was impeding his forward progress. "A conundrum that in-trigued me."

"And now?" She hugged her knees to her chest.

"Now you're only death fighting to stay dead. The life, the light, it's fading. It's almost gone."

She stared at him, startled by his words. "No, no, I'm—"

"Feel it, Natalie. Look inside you and feel it."

"I'm alive," she retorted. But as Natalie hugged her-self and looked out her window at the cars whizzing past them, she sensed the truth of his words. She had been hiding. Cringing. Buried in fear of herself and of life, in a desperate attempt to stay alive. Suppressing the sensuality that made her who she was. Yes, sure, she'd been committed to getting that Gold Star Michelin-O Rating, but that desire was undercut by the lockdown of her soul. "The truth is, I've been dying my whole life," she admitted quietly. "Except for those few days when I was under the deedub thrall, which is, ironically, when I was closest to actually dying." And minutes ago, when Nigel was kissing her. She'd come alive then, and it had been beautiful. If only she could be like that all the time—

"That's why your Mystic talents are on the fritz," he said. "You gotta let it go, sweetheart. Tap into that inner vixen. You can do it. Just step up and—"

"I don't want to let go like *that*." Well, she did, but she didn't.

"I can see that." He swerved around three cars and whipped past them in the breakdown lane. His driving was effortless, calm, and utterly precise. He was using his car as a weapon to get them where they needed to go, and his control over it was mesmerizing. The monstrous vehicle responded to his lightest touch; they were a perfect team. Okay, so yeah, she could kind of see the connection now between Nigel and his car.

Maybe the car wasn't quite as innocent as it seemed. Just as the artist wasn't quite as simple as he had seemed.

"You need to get past your need to shut down that fire inside you," Nigel commanded.

She sighed. "I'm beginning to realize that, but it's not that easy." She managed a small laugh. "I have a hefty amount of self-preservation instincts trying to keep that side of me at bay. It's a little challenging to overcome a lifetime of habits of keeping myself calm, cool, and collected."

He cocked an eyebrow at her. "Not that hard."

Her cheeks heated at the way his gaze slid over her mouth, reminding them both of the spark that they'd lit together. "Apparently, it is. Remember, it didn't work?" She sighed and closed her eyes. "I don't know if I can do it, Nigel."

"Natalie." He reached over and lifted her hand. His touch was warm and solid, and she felt a part of her body reach out for his comfort. Her insides released and relaxed. And there was peace. "Look at your hands."

She saw that her fingers were gray now. It was no longer just her cuticles. The skin on her arms looked taut and strained. "It's still coming." She'd lived a lifetime watching her slow march toward death. She'd beaten it, and now it had come again. New format, same fate. She fisted her hand in frustration. "Dammit."

"Hey, you've got me on your team now. It's not the same as it was." He folded his hand around hers and squeezed lightly. "I'm a phenomenal warrior."

"I'd assumed that." He was still holding her hand. On purpose, or by accident? "You all are."

He got a smug look on his face, the kind of arrogant expression worn by a man who knew that he was the best, and he would never be kept from his goals. "But I'm different."

"You're the only artist?" She curled her grayish fingers into ball. Her fist looked so small and delicate next to Nigel's. In good way, like the big, strong man could protect her. But also like, what chance did she have of defeating the monsters coming for her?

"I'm phenomenal because of my rigid mental control and my ability to focus so intently."

"Really?" She thought of his explosion in the back of her store. "You're losing that edge, though, aren't you?"

"My art is my source of control." He stroked his thumb over her hand. "I *have* to get it back." His grip tightened, and his voice became lower. More fierce. More focused. "We need to take Mari, and it's got to be now. If we go into the Den and screw it up, we're never coming out, dead or alive." His jaw was hard, and she thought of the stories her sister had told her about the torture that the men had endured at Angelica's hands.

They'd all been through hell, and Nigel was going back in to save his friends, and he needed *her* to make it okay? Hello, pressure? "Nigel. I'm not sure it's the best idea to count on me—"

"That's it." He swerved across four lanes, skidded up onto the grass on the side of the road, slammed on the brakes so fast the car spun out, whipping in six circles before it skidded to a stop halfway up the embankment. He ripped off his seat belt, grabbed her, and pulled her across the seat. "Natalie. There is no room for can't. I felt the power pouring from you just before you died three weeks ago. I felt it again in your store. You're the most sensual woman I've ever encountered in my life. It burns in you, and you've got to stop castrating yourself. Let it go, dammit."

"That power killed me! It took me over, ruled me, and eviscerated any sense of self-preservation!" She shoved at his unyielding strength. "Do you have any idea what it's like to be running toward your death and to not be able to stop yourself? For God's sake, Nigel, I never want to feel like that again!"

"All you need to do is channel it—"

"Channel it!" She ripped out his grasp. "It was an *orgasm*, Nigel! An orgasm! I was going to die because it felt so damn good to have an orgasm! With a man I didn't know and didn't care about! A man who had killed hundreds of women like me, women who were sucked into his spell! And I didn't care enough to stop myself from doing it." Her stomach churned, and she clutched her arms around her belly. "I was a monster. I couldn't stop. I was so terrified of death, but I got so caught up in the high that I didn't care. If my sister hadn't been there at the end, if she hadn't interfered, I would be *dead*. Dead!"

"Who the hell cares?" Nigel grabbed her again, but his grip was less desperate. More understanding. But still forceful. "The moment you let fear of death control you is the moment you stop living. I can't even *see* anyone who doesn't have passion. Because they're dead, even when they're living."

Tears filled her eyes. "I don't want to die, Nigel. I

don't want to spiral out of control like I did. It wasn't what I wanted, and I did it anyway—"

"Maybe it was what you wanted." He leaned closer, his hands softening on her shoulders. "Maybe your soul wanted to live, and once you got hit with the deedub poison, you lost the ability to destroy your own spirit." He thumbed the back of her neck. "Did it feel good? In that moment? When you let go?"

Natalie sighed. She knew the truth. "Yes, it felt good. So good I was willing to die for it. Like a drug addict—"

"No." He rubbed his palm over the front of her neck. "Like a soul that wanted to live. Your whole life has been an exercise in terror, because you were afraid that if you unleashed your passion, then the deedub poison would take root. Then your soul finally said no, and it wouldn't let you suppress it anymore."

"And it triggered the deedub poison. It killed me."

"You're here now, aren't you? That's not dead, is it?" He put his hand over her heart, and warmth filled her. "We are nothing without passion, Natalie. Whether it's love or sex or art or whatever. The minute we let it all go and follow our souls, that's when life becomes good."

Her heart began to thud. "I don't know how to make it good. I'm afraid to let it go."

"I know." He cupped her chin. "Trust me for a second?"

She shook her head at the sudden sensuality in his gaze. "No more kissing. It didn't work and—"

"If you want to save yourself, and Maggie, and one desperate warrior, you need to trust me for one minute."

Maggie. Dear God, she couldn't become the monster that would steal life from her. She clenched her hands in her lap. She had all this power inside her, and she was crippling herself from accessing it. And because of that, people who needed her help, including herself, were all in danger.

Castrating her own power gave the deedubs the victory, even if they never touched her again.

And she was tired of losing. So, she took a breath, squared her shoulders, and met the gaze of the one man in this world she could possibly trust. "Okay. You have one minute."

"Good." A satisfied expression flashed across his face. "No resistance allowed. Just total capitulation." He brushed his finger over her cheek. "Close your eyes."

Oh, um... that felt a little defenseless. She shook her head. "Nigel—"

"No, babe. No words." Nigel brushed his lips over her jaw. "I'm going to show you how good a kiss can be when you trust it. How good your soul can feel when you let it celebrate being alive. How you can tap into that power and still be entirely the woman you want to be."

"But—"

"I'm not the Godfather," he interrupted. "I'm not going to kill you. I'm going to save that pretty little ass of yours, and a few others along the way." He grinned. "Besides, as good as I am at sex, I've never killed a woman with an orgasm, and I don't think I ever will. So you can trust me."

She couldn't help but laugh at his comment. "That's a good point." She knew the honor by which he lived. He was tortured and desperate, being haunted by his own demons, and he needed her. She could trust him, but more importantly, she needed to trust herself.

And a part of her wanted so desperately to tap into

that side of her that she'd denied. To know she could let down her barriers, allow her spirit to soar, and to know she wouldn't destroy herself in the process.

Maybe Nigel could show her that. Even that chance would be worth another try. She could trust Nigel not to kill her, but it was herself that she needed to trust. Right now, he would keep her safe. This moment, in the car, with no enemies bearing down on them, was her moment. This was her chance to try. "Okay."

He smiled. "Now, close your eyes."

And this time, she did.

A century and a half of seduction training had seemed like pure hell at the time, but as Nigel gazed down into the trusting face of Natalie Fleming, he was damn glad he knew exactly how to woo a woman.

Not that he'd be sending Angelica thank you notes anytime soon, but maybe he would grant her a shorter suffering before she died, when he finally got that chance. Or maybe not.

Nigel traced his index finger along Natalie's jaw. Shit, her skin was soft. Warm. Fragile. Alive. He followed the curve of her neck, along her tendon, and around the front of her throat. He watched her swallow nervously.

That was the cutest damn thing. She was skittish about being kissed?

Protectiveness swelled inside him, and he cupped her throat. No woman he'd ever been with had been nervous. They'd been minions, trained to torture him into giving them what they wanted. Every woman, again and again, had critiqued his approach, punished him for not doing what her specific requirements entailed. There had been no nervousness, no vulnerability, just brutal demand that was so far from sensual it couldn't even qualify as sex.

But now... he bent forward and brushed his lips over Natalie's neck.

Natalie sucked in her breath in a quivering awkwardness. "Nigel—"

"I like hearing you say my name." And he did. She wasn't issuing a command. It wasn't an order. It wasn't a condemnation. It was a request for reassurance. It was a whisper of intimacy. And it brought out a side of him that felt good. Empowering. Worthy.

She made him feel like a man.

He wrapped his hand around the back of her neck and pressed his cheek against hers, so his mouth was by her ear. "I will keep you safe," he whispered. "Forever and always. Do you understand?"

She nodded once, and a feeling of power surged through him. Was this what being a man felt like? Because damn, he felt like he could rule the world.

And he hadn't even kissed her yet.

Slowly, his body twitching in anticipation, he pulled back until his mouth was a whisper from hers. He could feel her breath on his face, taste her nervousness, and feel the tiniest hint of desire pulsing at her. "I want you to release all judgment, all thought," he said, gently massaging her neck. "I want you to simply open yourself to the sensations. To the feel of my mouth on yours."

Her breath quickened, but she didn't pull away.

"Like this." He kissed the left corner of her mouth.

Sweet Jesus, her lips were like angel's breath, like

the softest silk, so delicate, so tender, so female. Her mouth was a woman's mouth, just like he'd dreamed about, just like he'd painted so many times, creating a magical image that he'd never experienced in real life. Until now. Her mouth was a decadence of sensation, of wanting, of shyness…

Desire surged through him, and his body responded with a ferocity that made him feel like a load of his blades had just been unleashed in his pants. *Jesus*. This was what it was supposed to be like?

Mother of God.

He wanted more.

Then he realized she had tensed, and tenderness consumed him. The need to protect. To keep safe. To fend off her fear.

He thumbed her cheek with a softness he'd practiced a thousand times that, for the first time, felt natural. "Feel the tenderness of my lips," he whispered. "Focus only on that. Let yourself bask in the sensation."

Then he kissed the right corner of her mouth. The brief touch was like a moment of utter stillness in his mind, in his soul, a pause in the turmoil constantly racing around inside him. It was pure beauty.

She swallowed again, but her eyes were still closed, and she didn't pull away.

She was trusting him.

Triumph made his muscles bunch, and he lightly spanned her waist with his hands. "Let yourself want to be kissed. It's okay, Natalie. It really is."

Then he kissed her full on her mouth.

Her lips were softer than he could have imagined, like the rose petals on the flowers he painted. Like velvet, only alive with tenderness and vulnerability. He kissed her again, and she tentatively kissed him back with a fragility that made him want to erect a barrier around her and protect her from the world.

He could feel her response to the kiss.

Right now, her body was soft and pliant, her lips were tentative and real. She was kissing him with her soul, with trust, with delicate exploration.

"I'll never let you down," he whispered against her mouth.

She didn't answer, but she laid her hand on his shoulder. Gently. Tentatively.

Desire surged suddenly to life and he gripped her neck a little harder. Deepened the kiss. Explored with his tongue.

She allowed him access, and he framed her face with his hands, striving to be gentle and protective. He concentrated on allowing her the freedom to pull away. He prayed, God did he pray, that she wouldn't, but he knew he had to give her that choice.

She didn't shut him down.

She kissed him back.

A small noise of pleasure emerged from the back of her throat, and her other hand went to his shoulder. Holding tighter now. As if she didn't want to let him go but was afraid to grip too tight.

"Lose yourself in the kiss," he whispered. "I've got you. I won't let you take it too far."

He kissed her again, deeply, and she met him with all he gave her. He felt her body respond, felt the heat burning beneath her skin. And he felt right. It felt good. She was putting herself in his hands, in his kiss, in his protection, trusting him. There was no manipulation by her. No agenda. Just tentative, hopeful trust.

And damn if that wasn't the biggest turn-on he'd ever felt.

He wanted to be the man who she could entrust with her safety. He'd never felt that way. Never really gave a shit about women, because, well, when all they were good for was hellfire and damnation, it didn't create a whole lot of incentive to be nurturing.

And he'd thought that was fine.

But now, feeling that burning need to protect her... He finally understood what it meant to be a man.

"I've got you, babe." He gripped her hair and coaxed her head back so she could see his expression and *feel* the truth of his words. He searched her face, those deep green eyes of hers. "I'm trained in battle. And I grant you my protection. You don't need to protect yourself anymore."

He fought to make her comprehend, needing her to know, needing her to trust him. He didn't know why he needed it, but he did. It felt like his very core was screaming to be given the role of protector.

Her face softened, and a tentative, fragile smile curved her lips.

And that was all the feedback he needed. He tightened his grip on her hair, pulled her against him, and he did what he'd been wanting to do since the first time he'd met her, and she'd made him realize he was damn glad he was a man.

Chapter 14

NIGEL KISSED NATALIE AGAIN, AND THIS TIME, IT wasn't gentle, it wasn't sweet, it wasn't nurturing. It was the kiss of a man who had just learned what it was like to feel like a man, who had the woman who'd validated him in his arms.

He gave of his passion, he took of her vulnerability, he took of her soul and gave his own, he wrapped his being around hers and gave her his protection.

He cupped her breasts, he palmed her hips, and he groaned when she kissed him back. When she moved against him. When she began to stop fighting her own desires and give into his, into hers, into the heat driving them both.

The kiss turned frantic. Carnal. Deep. Hot. Wet. Until there was nothing between them but the need for more, for skin, for intimacy, for passion. He had no idea how much time had passed, or how long he'd kissed her, but he couldn't stop himself, couldn't break away from the connection. He cupped the front of her jeans, thumbed over her sensitive parts. She shuddered, and he caught her in his arms. "I've got you, babe. You can let it go. You're safe with me."

She opened her eyes, her lids heavy with passion and heat. "Nigel," she whispered. "You don't need your art. You're in complete control of your weapons and your mind. You feel powerful. You feel mentally calm. You are focused, and it is easy to be so. You are all you strive to be."

The words plunged into his chest like blades, they hit his brain like hot wind, and they raced through his body like electric shock rippling and rippling and rippling. His muscles went rigid, and for a moment he couldn't move. All he could do was feel her words shooting through him, eviscerating his own thoughts, his own needs, his own identity.

He tried to stop it, he tried to resist the flood, but it was relentless, streaking through him. He saw art in his head, pictures he'd drawn. They were falling off the walls, burning up in white-hot flames. He envisioned the blades in his own body shriveling up. He felt the metal disappearing from his own flesh, felt the coolness of the metal vanish, replaced by burning heat, by fire.

"Stop!" He grabbed her shoulders and shook her. "Make it stop!"

She caught his face and held tight, her expression confident and calm. "Let it in, Nigel. It hurts only because you have resistance. It's what you want. You asked for it. Stop fighting."

But he couldn't. He could feel her words stripping away at his own mind, at his own emotions, trying to inject themselves over his. He didn't want to lose who he was. Didn't want to put himself in someone else's hands. "No!" He shoved her off his lap and stumbled out of the car onto the embankment.

"Nigel!"

He heard her voice, a female voice, and he swore. A blade came out and he spun around. Ready to attack. To protect himself.

She stopped, her palms up in surrender. "Nigel," she said. "It's okay. It's just me. I'm not one of them. You're not in the Den."

The cars were whizzing by on the highway. He heard the hum of the engines. The high-pitched whine of the tires careening past. The click of the gravel flicking up to the undercarriages. Noises of action. Of the real world. Of life outside the Den.

He saw Natalie, then. Really saw her. The brown hair. Those haunted green eyes so wide with worry. Not aggression. Not threat. Not satisfaction. Concern. For him.

"It's okay," she said quietly. "I helped you. I didn't hurt you. I didn't take away your will. It's all okay."

But it wasn't okay. He knew it wasn't. She'd stolen something from him. "No. It's gone—"

"It's just temporary, I promise. You're still you."

It's just temporary. He saw the truth in her expression, heard the honesty of her tone. *It's just temporary.* Like all the other hell he'd been through. Each had been a blip in his lifeline, even the worst moments. It had all passed. Like this would pass… oh, *shit.* This would pass? "You mean, we're going to have to do it again?"

She stared at him for a second, then burst out laughing. Laughing? *Laughing?*

"Oh, Nigel." She walked over to him and set her hands on her shoulders. "You're afraid of me? I'm a nothing."

"Shit, woman." He realized he was on his knees and started laughing too, relief breaking through the tension that had strung them both so tight. "You rocked me back on my ass. You could bring down the world if you wanted to."

Her eyes were still sparkling with laughter. "I have

to admit, seeing a big, mighty warrior like you run away from me like that is really good for my ego."

"Run away? I was practicing my footwork for a scrimmage I'm playing in tomorrow." He caught himself grinning like a school kid in response to her amusement. "You are one gorgeous woman when you're smiling like that, Natalie Fleming."

Her smile widened. "You don't have to compliment me to get a kiss. Just threaten me with deedubs and I'm all yours."

"That's all it takes?" At her amused nod, he snapped his fingers. "I knew Angelica left out some key things in Seduction 101. She said it was all about flowers and poetry. Threat of death was never mentioned."

"Yes, well, if all you know about women is what she taught you, you're in trouble." Natalie was still laughing as she held out her hand. "Need a hand, big guy?"

As if he was going to turn down that offer. She was captivating as hell with that levity in her spirit. He grasped her hand and let her assist him to his feet. But once he was vertical, instead of letting her go, he swept his arm behind her and pulled her up against him. "Woman, if all it takes to get that gorgeous smile on your face is for me to fall on my ass, I would do it every day for the rest of my damn life."

Her eyes danced. "Now that is something I'd like to see. Wouldn't that damage your reputation?"

"Hell, no. My reputation as a badass is completely intact." Then, because he just couldn't help himself, he kissed her again.

Her laughter bubbled up in the kiss, turning it into a playful exploration of fun and levity dancing on top of the desire. He was grinning as he pulled away. "That's the first time laughter has ever been involved in a kiss for me."

She raised her brows. "And how was it?"

He paused, trying to think of the right word. "Exhilarating."

She smiled again, but this time there was more tenderness than mischief. "Sex shouldn't be a torturous experience, Nigel."

"And it shouldn't be scary, Miss Natalie." He brushed the hair back from her face. "Seems like we both could use some new experiences in that category."

She leaned into his touch. "Probably."

He closed his eyes and rested his forehead against hers, surprised by his desire to simply cart her off and do nothing but lose himself in her. No art. No battle. No weapons. Just exploration, laughter, and passion. In a moment like this, he could almost convince himself that he had the ability to get close to her and not put her in danger of him snapping.

Almost, but not quite.

He wasn't the man she deserved to have.

Not yet, anyway. He brushed his lips over her forehead. "Do you think it worked?" he asked quietly. "Your suggestion?"

"I don't know." She laughed softly. "I've never knocked a man over before, so that's got to be something."

"You have the tools, that's for sure." He flexed his hand and called forth a blade, just to make sure he could still do it. A razor-edged dagger slipped free of his hands, and dark embers began sloughing off his palms. Yeah, okay, he still had his blades, so she hadn't taken that away from him. He rubbed his thumb along the edge of the blade, checking the sharpness.

Natalie lifted her head away from his to look at his weapons. "Do they feel any different?"

"No." He tossed the blade aside. "I'll you tell you, though, Angelica and Mari would love to have you working for them."

Natalie cocked her head. "Is that why you freaked? Because you thought I was them?" She wasn't joking anymore. She was actually serious.

"I didn't freak out." Nigel palmed her back to guide her to the car. "I was engaging strategic, evasive moves."

She raised her eyebrows at him as she stepped into the vehicle. "No man has ever reacted like that to me before."

He suddenly wasn't all that happy with the thought of her delving into the souls of other men to try to bone up their sex life. "Had you kissed them first?"

Her eyebrows shot up, and she looked amused again as she slipped into his car. "No, you're the first."

"Well, then, that's probably why." He slammed the door shut. End that conversation now. Yes, granted, he wasn't arrogant enough to think he was going to endanger her by keeping her, but that didn't mean he wanted her to be getting up close and personal with other guys. What if she'd said he wasn't the first? He already knew. The metal was stirring beneath the skin at the mere idea of it.

Yeah, any wonder why he wanted to ship her off to the tropics? It was going to be a severe test of his control to keep her around and not trigger another episode like the Dunkin' Donuts coffee drawing fiasco.

But when he opened his car door, he discovered she wasn't finished. "You know, I think the reason you're different from the other men I've influenced is because you're so tough," Natalie said.

"Well, that's true. I am tough." He started up the car, sort of wishing he was driving some big rig with a really loud engine. The whisper-quiet of his ride didn't quite feel like the message he felt like sending. "Much more manly than any of those other... men." Did he have to call them men? Couldn't he call them spineless wimps not worth noticing?

"I've only influenced Dullets before, and they tend to be men who are weak, and they want to feel like a man. So, when they feel my power, they like it, because it's more than they've ever felt before. But with you..."

Okay, that was a better slant. The other men were weak who couldn't feel like a man on their own. "But I'm not like them."

"No." She tilted her head. "You felt like I was stealing your power."

Shit. She was dead right. He had felt like that. "Wow. Did you see that move?" He gestured randomly at a car that had just whizzed by, trying to distract her with traffic. What? Like he was going to admit that she'd scared the crap out of him? That might even put him lower on the manly scale than the wusses she'd empowered.

"So, that's why you wouldn't let Ella talk to you," she observed. "You're afraid—"

"I'm not afraid," he growled. There were some things a man simply had to defend himself against, and being classified as "afraid" was one of them. "Here's the deal. For the last one hundred and fifty years, the one thing I've been able to claim for my own is my mind. They fucked with my body, they stole my freedom, they manipulated my powers, and still are apparently, but they never got to my mind." He pulled out onto the highway, and then gunned the engine.

He needed to get fast, get out, feel the speed.

"But I did." Her voice was quiet with understanding, with empathy. "I got into your mind."

He rubbed his hand over his whiskers. Yeah, still had them. He was still a man. "You got close." Had she actually gotten there? It felt like she had.

"I felt it. We were connected."

He heard the concern in her voice, yeah, but there was also a hint of awe. Of amazement. She had her feet up on the dash and was hugging her knees, a thoughtful expression on her face. She wasn't one of the women from the Den, and she had no desire or intention to hurt him. The only reason she'd been able to get to him was because he'd empowered her, and he'd made the conscious choice to let her in. It had been a team effort. Yeah, he'd been unprepared for the sensation of her in his head, but it was okay. He was still who he was. And she was still Natalie.

She'd done exactly what he'd asked of her, despite her deep fear of tapping into her sensuality. And what had he done? Panicked instead of taking advantage and encouraging her to raise her weapons to an even higher level. She was his partner, and she'd done something extraordinary that just might save their asses, and it was time for him to act like it. He touched her hand. "What you did back there was good. Really good."

She set her hand over his and smiled at him. "Thanks."

"Just don't do it again."

She laughed then, a sound that was relief and

happiness. "I will direct all my powers of suggestion toward other hapless souls." She grinned. "Seriously, if I could command you, then I could tell a deedub not to attack me. Think of the freedom!"

"You were impressive," he agreed. Enough to defeat Mari? Who the hell knew what it would take to defeat Mari? If she'd become as powerful as Angelica, it would take luck, the alignment of the universe, and some damned good fortune on his part. Translation: killing Mari would be impossible.

But to shut her down enough to rescue Pascal and Blaine, and cut off the delivery of smut into Natalie's soul?

Well, he was sane now. Able to avoid art and still keep his head clear enough for battle. Even if Natalie didn't repeat what she'd just done, it would be enough.

Mari was going down.

Together, they were going to do it.

And when she squeezed his hand, he knew that she was feeling the same optimism.

For the first time in a long time, perhaps ever, they both had a chance to control their own destiny. And damn, it felt good.

━━━⚬━━━

The dream genie was back, and he was rocking this world!

"Charlie? You awake?'

Charles Morgan straightened his new suit jacket and turned toward the door as the knob turned and in strolled the magnificent female that was feeding him powers in ways she couldn't begin to comprehend.

Mari was followed by a young woman pushing a wheeled chair in which was strapped a massive male of the warrior persuasion. The male was alert, and smoke was rising from his skin where the stainless steel chains were locked down on his bare skin.

Not a grimace of pain from the stoic hero.

"Right here, Danielle." Mari gestured her assistant to a stop. "Charlie, this is Pascal. He's the one you're going to practice dream-purging on today."

Danielle set her hands on her hips. "Mari, this isn't right. You have no right to steal dreams from these men." She shot an accusing look at Mari as she grabbed a napkin from Charlie's dinner tray and wedged it under one of the chains to protect Pascal's forearm from the steel. "You said that the torture was over. It was all lies?"

"It's not a lie," Mari protested. "Pascal is here for you. I want you to get his love, Danielle. That's why we're here."

Danielle looked over at Pascal, who was glaring at the women with a combination of quiet stealth and a hint of amusement, as if he knew something the women didn't know. "You want to set me up with Pascal?" Danielle asked. "But he's... I hardly know him."

"You don't think he's sexy?"

The maiden's cheeks turned pink as Pascal cocked an assessing look at her. Yes, yes, the warrior definitely had some sort of plan. "Well, yes, I guess," Danielle stammered. "But that's not how it works. You can't lobotomize him into loving someone—"

"Stop!" Oh, for all that was a waste of good time. People not living in the vortex of his vision were just a drain on his brilliance. Charles had no time for the emotional bickering of those with fragile personal auras. He was a man on a mission, and he needed to hone his skills.

Mari was studying him as if he'd gone insane. "I need to take more smut off you, don't I?"

"Nonsense. I am fit and amazing and fantastic." He flexed his palms. "Just aggravated by non-visionary peons."

Mari touched him with her wand anyway, and his whole body lurched as sunlight, excitement, and freedom surged through him. He did a backflip and landed sprawled on his back on the ground, twitching uncontrollably. "Wow. That's more of a rush than peeing on an electric fence."

She smiled down at him and tucked the baton back under her arm. "I'm just helping you out, big guy."

"I appreciate it!" He bounced to his feet, feeling a thousand years lighter. There was less of the thick, dark hair on his arm, and his fingers were straighter. But most importantly, his soul felt different. Lighter. Like he owned it. "Let's do it, Mari!"

"You got it." Mari strode across the room, fired up the computer, and turned on the PowerPoint. "Okay, Danielle and Pascal. I want you to sit back and watch the show."

Charles reclined his La-Z-Boy, grabbed a beer from his minifridge, helped himself to the bag of chips, and put on his fuzzy slippers. "Yes, yes, let's begin." How delicious did he feel? Hardly any smut holding him back. Life was so grand! He was the man!

Mari set a tray on Pascal's lap and handed one to Danielle. "Hold it in front of you."

"What are we doing?" Danielle asked, standing in front of the warrior, as if she could protect him.

So very cute. And naive, but cute.

"Just watch." The lights went out, and the presentation began. First up," Mari said. "We have an image of a double chocolate fudge brownie with chips. It is warm out of the oven and smells like the decadent warmth of cocoa. It will melt in your mouth—"

The image of a fudge brownie flared in Danielle's mind. It glowed bright and powerful. Pure unfettered longing without any baggage.

Bingo.

Charles tapped it a split second before guilt about the fit of her new jeans dimmed it. A gooey chocolate chip cookie appeared on the tray in front of Danielle.

Shit. A fucking cookie? Where was the brownie?

Danielle jumped back. "Where did that come from?"

"Your mind," Mari said. "Charlie's not very good, but he'll get there. Next."

Charles took another swing of beer and settled more deeply into his chair. "Don't be frustrated," he muttered to himself. "It always takes a little while to warm up." Yeah, sure his pappy had always told him that any halfway decent genie didn't need to warm up and could get it right from the start, but his pappy was a conniving bastard who thrived on squashing his son, so screw that.

The next slide was of a harsh, penetrating sun in a brazen blue sky above a parched desert. The next slide was one of high noon on the Sahara Desert. There were pictures of bones scattered across the sand, and a man reaching out with an empty cup.

Charles could almost feel the sweat dripping off the audience. The desire was being created.

The image of a frosted pitcher of lemonade flashed on the screen.

Mirror images of lemonade flared in the minds of both viewers, raw and desperate longing.

Charles gritted his teeth and tapped both of them.

Beer for the warrior and a pitcher of sangria for Danielle.

"Oh, for God's sake," Mari snapped. "It's not that hard, Chuck! They were both thinking of lemonade!"

"Shut up." Charles chugged the last of the beer. "Stop pressuring me, woman. You have no idea how the complexities of my power work." Shit, shit, shit! How was he going to save the world if he couldn't pull his shit together? "Next!"

The next slide was of a climber on Mt. Everest sitting on an ice floe, with blackened and frostbitten fingers. And then a shot of dumbasses leaping off an iceberg into frozen waters wearing nothing but bathing suits.

He shut out Mari droning on about frigid and cold things, ignored the picture of Russians huddled against the bitter cold. He focused on preparing for the moment. For the slide of the fuzzy, warm, fleece boots.

He hit Danielle's mind at the exact second the image appeared in her head. He threw all his force into it, then slammed her with power so extreme he felt his own head burn.

Danielle screamed and flew back off her chair into the wall behind her.

"Dear God! What did you do to her?" Mari raced across the room and knelt beside the girl. "Danielle? Are you okay?"

Charles didn't even have to look. He felt it. He'd aced it. He just sat back. Ate a chip. And waited.

It took almost two minutes before he heard Mari gasp. "She's wearing the boots!"

He grinned. "And they're her size, too."

"Wow." Mari looked up. "You've never gotten it that right before."

Pascal didn't move, but dark energy was pulsing off him with a force that made Charles just a wee bit happy the man was under lockdown. Charles rubbed his hands together, basking in the sensation of his power pulsing through him. He was back. Better than before. His power was surging, and it was time. "Fantastic. Bring the warrior forward. It's time to work on him."

And it was.

One mind, one soul, one heart... *prepare to be stripped.*

Chapter 15

NIGEL GLIDED THE MERCEDES UP NEXT TO THE PINE trees caressing the entrance to the cave. He was pleased to see Christian was already there waiting for them. He parked the car and turned to Natalie. Her face was tense and her hands were fidgeting restlessly in her lap.

He set his hand over hers and was rewarded with a brief flash of a smile. "Ready, Natalie?"

"I'd rather be making virility balls and polishing the crystal for the inspection." She peered out the window at the black opening of the cave. "You know, cleaning the toilets would probably be preferable as well."

Nigel grinned. "Cleaning toilets? I don't believe you." He squeezed her hand. "Fighting for your freedom and possibly having to seduce a manly warrior is much more fun."

Her cheeks flushed as she looked back at him. "I'm way too tense for seduction."

"I could take care of that in a heartbeat."

Her gaze flicked to his mouth, and suddenly the atmosphere in the car heated up several degrees. His hand tightened around hers and he bent forward and brushed his lips over hers. The spark was instant, and he grinned when she sucked in her breath.

Oh, yes, he could turn her on in a heartbeat.

"Hey!" Christian shouted and began walking toward the car.

"There goes our chance for a make-out session," he said ruefully as he trailed his fingers through her hair.

"Good. I don't like sex."

He laughed then. "Even with me?"

She eyed him, but her eyes were sparkling again. "The correct answer would be yes, I don't even like sex with you."

He grinned. "Too bad you can't say it, can you?"

She signed. "No."

He laughed at her obvious chagrin and kissed her forehead. "It's okay, I like kissing you, too. We'll find a way to hate it, I promise."

She laughed then. "I don't know about that."

"Neither do I, to be honest." Christian was nearing, so Nigel forced himself to focus on the situation they were about to walk into. He'd managed to relax Natalie, and it was time to get into battle mode. He pointed past her at the opening in the hillside. "That's our entrance point into the Den. It's the Cavern of Murderous Poltergeists—"

"Seriously?" She looked over at the cave with a cute grimace. "That seems a little melodramatic—"

"Unfortunately, it's not melodramatic. It's highly accurate." Nigel caught her arm, suddenly feeling apprehensive about taking Natalie into the Den. He already presented enough danger to her safety, and now he was adding more danger to her life? Shit. This wasn't how it was supposed to be. "Listen to me, sweetheart."

She met his gaze, those huge green eyes staring into his with such trust. "Okay."

He rubbed her arm, needing to touch her, to know she was safe. "Stay close so I can keep you safe. Your only job is to be near in case I snap and need to draw, okay? That's it. Leave everything up to me and Christian, so we can protect you. Got it?"

She nodded. "I'm completely okay with leaving hand-to-hand combat up to you."

"Thank you." He grinned, relieved at the honesty in her voice. "We're not going to engage in any extra battles. We're going straight in to find Pascal and Blaine, to cut Mari's ties to you, and then we're out. Got it?"

Her forehead furrowed. "How do you know where they are?"

"We'll find them." Nigel kissed her hand once and then it was time. He shoved the car door open as Christian reached the vehicle. He climbed out of the car. "You good?"

Christian's skin was shiny, as if he were already morphing into metal. He walked up and slammed his fist into Nigel's jaw. "You drew Blaine, you son of a bitch."

Nigel stumbled, caught his balance, and righted himself. But he didn't raise a hand to Christian. "You spoke with Jarvis, I take it. He told you about Blaine and Trinity getting snatched."

"Yeah." Christian's arm flared with metal and he pulled a sword out of his skin. "We can't risk it, brother. I'm taking you out."

"No!" Natalie scrambled out of the car and threw herself in front of Nigel. "Don't—"

"Hey!" Nigel yanked her behind him and pinned her up against the car. "Never, *ever,* put yourself in front of a blade again. Do you understand? That's not acceptable!" His heart was pounding and blades were prickling beneath his skin, on his shoulders and back at the thought of her putting herself in danger. He couldn't believe she'd done that. Hadn't she seen the instability in Christian's eyes? The man wasn't thinking clearly, and he very well might have staked her. Nigel went cold at the thought and his grip tightened on her. "Don't you get it? You need to stay safe. You're important."

Her face softened and she laid her hand on his cheek. "I'm okay, Nigel. I'm not hurt."

She wasn't hurt. He bowed his head and felt the blades recede. "Don't do that again."

She smiled. "I won't—" Her attention went past his shoulder, and she tensed. "Nigel—"

He spun around and blocked Christian's sword as it came down toward his chest. "Christian. You're not going back."

"Damn right." Christian ripped his sword free. "There's no chance—"

"Hey!" Natalie shoved off the car, but she didn't move into the line of battle. *Good girl.* "I worked on Nigel. He doesn't need to draw now. You're safe, Christian. It's over."

Christian didn't even look at her. "Nigel betrayed us." He whipped out his sword, and Nigel pulled one out and met him halfway, playing defense only. The clang of blades was ominous and dangerous, especially given that they were friends.

Nigel swore as Christian lunged again, at the betrayal on his friend's face. "Yeah, I blew it. I know I did. But it won't happen again. I've taken measures, and we're going to get them out." He sandwiched the blade up against Christian's chest. "I'm not the enemy, big guy. You know I'm not!"

"You drew them," Christian growled. "You got them sucked back in—"

"I know! Mother of hell, I know!" Nigel didn't back down. "You don't think Mari did that on purpose? She intentionally used my talents as a trap. She wanted to split us up. Come on, man! I don't know what the hell happened to you in there, but don't let them mess with you. We're on the same team!" He shoved hard and sent Christian flying backwards into a tree.

Christian stared at him in fury, then lunged for Nigel with a killing blow in his eyes.

"You know who I am, brother." Nigel let his own sword drop out of his hand and raised his palms in surrender. Natalie gasped behind him, but he willed her to trust him. She placed her hand on his back, but she didn't interfere or get in the way. "If I was the enemy, I wouldn't trust you, would I?"

Christian's blade plunged toward his heart, and still Nigel didn't move. Natalie's fingers dug into his back, but she didn't interfere. *Come on, Christian. Find your place again, big guy. You can do it.*

The tip of his sword pierced Nigel's chest, then Christian stopped, watching the small drips of blood trickle down Nigel's chest. He frowned at the sword and then at Nigel. He looked confused and shocked.

"You're good," Nigel said quietly. "You're good, big guy."

Christian slowly lowered the sword and Natalie's sigh of relief was so powerful that Nigel felt it in his soul.

"I'm toast," Christian said.

"No." Nigel strode forward and slammed his hand down on his shoulder. "We're out of the Den. We're free. We're in control now. You'll shake the residual aspects of whatever they did to you."

Christian raised his gaze to Nigel. "We're not in control, Nigel. Not any of us. They're still ruling us. For hell's sake, I was ready to kill you." He wiped his forearm over his brow, and it came away streaked with sweat. "That wasn't me."

"I know." Nigel flexed his hands and noticed the grayish tint was spreading over Natalie's skin. The smut was hitting harder. "It ends now for all of us."

Christian looked past him at the opening in the cave. "I'm not going to go in and get taken," he said quietly. "If I get caught, kill me."

"Kill you?" Nigel shook his head. "I won't leave you behind—"

"Not good enough." Christian shoved off him and began to walk back toward the street. He didn't look back. Didn't hesitate. He was leaving.

What in God's name could have happened to Christian to make him walk away from battle? From a chance to rescue his friends? To ask for death instead of torture?

"Give him death," Natalie said, moving up beside him as she tucked her hand around his arm. "Give it to him."

"No chance." Nigel shook his head. "I won't kill him—"

She squeezed his forearm, her touch gentle and reassuring. A moment of beauty and gentleness in the whirling inferno of hell brewing around him. He took her hand and held it tight. "You won't leave him behind, either, but he doesn't believe you. He knows it's possible you won't get out. But he knows you'll be able to kill him, even if you guys get trapped there. Give him that relief. Tell him you'll kill him."

Shit. She was right. Christian honestly didn't trust that Nigel wouldn't leave him behind. Where was the faith? His heart twisted for the damage that had been done to his friend. Somehow, Angelica had stolen his heart. "I will kill you," he said quietly.

Christian didn't say a word. He just swung around and strode straight into the cave. He didn't look back. Didn't wait. Just walked into hell. All it had taken was one word from Nigel, and Christian had trusted it. So, that was something at least. Maybe Christian couldn't trust him to pull him out, but he trusted him to kill him.

That was a good sign.

Nigel pulled out some blades of his own and kissed Natalie lightly. "Let's do it, sweetheart." He didn't miss the look of apprehension as Natalie followed him inside, and he sure as hell didn't miss the first hint of fear he'd ever experienced in his own soul. Not fear of getting caught, like Christian. A fear that he would let everyone down. A fear that he would let Natalie get hurt.

He'd already endangered Pascal and Blaine. He had betrayed his parents before that, when he was a kid. What if he blew it with the rest of them? What if Christian was right that he should be killed before they could take the rest of them down? He looked down at the blades in his hands, searched his mind, and found no answers. He might not need to draw right now, but he was unfocused and tense. If he had drawn, he could have settled his mind and gotten into battle mode. But he hadn't, so he was scattered and on edge.

Now was not the time to be less than his best.

But now was the only chance they had.

———～～～———

It was third time Nigel had been back to the Den since the escape, and the prospect wasn't any rosier this time. Even having Natalie beside him couldn't penetrate the shadows and doom weighing down on them.

Nigel tightened his grip on Natalie's elbow as they strode into the Cavern of Murderous Poltergeists. The sky grew cloudy, and the air became thick and acrid, burning his throat.

Natalie coughed, and Nigel pulled her against him and covered her face in the crook of his elbow. "Breathe through the jacket," he ordered.

She nodded and buried her face against him. She didn't complain, didn't hesitate, didn't pull back. He knew she was scared, but she was stepping up. For herself, for him, for his friends, for Maggie. She might not be a trained warrior, but she was one in her heart. He held her closer and fisted the dagger in his free hand. "We're going to make it," he told her.

"I know." Her voice was shaky, but her words were strong. "I can't miss my appointment with the Michelin-O team. They get cranky when you try to reschedule."

He chuckled at her comment. "Yeah, well, we can't have them getting cranky on us. Guess we better survive, eh?"

"Definitely."

Christian led the way across the graveyard, carefully watching as the smoke drifted and the ghouls began to circle. The spirits were a dark gray and black, and weapons glinted in their hands.

"They've upgraded since we were here last," Nigel commented. "Don't remember them being armed."

"No one's been around to feed them," Christian said. "You know how they liked Angelica's cookies. Mari probably ignores them, so they're going through sugar-detox."

A banshee let out a high-pitched scream, but Nigel didn't even bother to glance that way. He was focusing on the swirl of energies around them. Right now everything was cold and heavy, which meant the dead hadn't started to go corporeal yet, so they couldn't hurt their uninvited guests. Once the temperature of the cavern began to rise, that's when things would get dicey.

A serpent-headed wolf dove at him teeth bared, but he went right through Nigel and crashed through the wall behind him. Natalie yelped and grabbed her chest. "Oh, God. That was weird."

Nigel frowned at her. "You felt that?"

"Yeah. It was like someone knifed me with an icicle." She eyed him, her face suddenly wary. "You didn't feel it pass through us?"

"No." He exchanged looks with Christian. "It was of demon blood."

"Oh." Natalie's face paled and she managed a rueful smile. "A cousin of mine? I should have invited her to dinner."

"Probably good old Aunt Edna." Nigel squeezed her shoulder as they neared the portal where Mari had been standing. Natalie was running of time. He could feel the taint in her energy. *Shit*.

Christian shimmered, and then he went into full chain-link mode. From flesh to chain mail in a heartbeat.

The fact he was suiting up before even setting foot in the Den said exactly how much Christian respected the place they were entering.

Nigel walked up beside Christian, keeping Natalie between them. The portal was pulsing black light. "It's open."

Christian nodded. "The spirits make it hard to keep it closed. I heard Angelica talk about that before. That why she fed them, to keep their loyalty."

Natalie looked up above them at the murderous spirits circling. "They're not guarding it now."

"No." Nigel didn't like that fact. "I don't know what they're waiting for."

"Maybe they think we're sexy and they're hoping for a prom date." Christian pulled a sword out his arm and readied it. "Ready?"

Or maybe Mari had specifically bribed the spirits to allow them entrance into the Den. He saw the grim look on Christian's face and knew his teammate was thinking the same thing. "They're waiting for us," Christian said quietly.

"I know." Of course they would be. Mari had two of their men. It was automatic that those remaining would go in after them.

"You know she's expecting us?" Natalie stopped. "And we're still going in?"

"You bet. She might be ready for us, but we're ready as well." Nigel's palms began to smoke. He tested his mind, felt it was still clear. He was going into battle, and he was focused, with no need to draw, which he usually liked to do before heading into war. Having Natalie beside him was helping, not because of her Mystic power, but because she made him happy. Shit. That sounded weird. Happy wasn't something he'd spent a lot of time thinking about, and he didn't have time to start now. So he nodded at the portal. "We're on."

Christian squared his shoulders, and his skin was shimmering. "Nigel."

"Yeah?"

"Don't forget our deal."

Nigel swore. "Yeah, I'll kill you."

Christian nodded, and then he stepped up—

"No." Nigel moved forward. "I take the first hit."

This was his fault, and Mari clearly knew they'd be coming in. Whatever she had waiting for him, he would be the one to take it.

He readied his blades, made sure Natalie was safely behind him, then strode through the darkness into the hell that was waiting for him.

Inside the entrance to the Den was silence.

Blackness.

Utter stillness.

Nigel waited as he heard Christian and Natalie step through the portal behind him. "Don't move," he whispered. "Something's wrong."

He searched the night, searched the blackness, used every sense he had, but it was as if he'd been stripped of all his senses. As if he'd stepped into a void.

"What is it?" Christian asked.

"I don't know." Nigel called for a blade, and he heated it up, like a blacksmith would do in a forger. The glowing orange tip that he usually used for cauterizing injuries cast an amber light over the interior of the tunnel. And over the body of one of the warriors that Nigel knew all too well from his days in the Den. Max Bruta. Another young one, like Pascal, irreverent and a brutal badass. He'd come the closest to hurting Angelica before she'd cut him down. He was an angry son of a bitch, and that was what had kept him alive.

He was too damn mad to die.

"Max!" Nigel strode across the stainless steel floor and crouched beside the warrior.

Max was splayed on his back, staring blankly at the ceiling. Eyes sunken, face empty, his sword lying across his gut. He didn't even look at Nigel, but Nigel sensed life still present in him.

"Hey, Max." Nigel put his hand on his chest and found that his heart was still beating. Slowly. But... "Son of a bitch. His soul is gone."

Christian hadn't moved from the doorway, his metal skin glistening in the glow of the light from Nigel's weapon. "What do you mean?"

"His soul." Nigel searched the body, but there was nothing there. Just an emptiness. A blank. "It's been stripped. There's nothing left but an empty body."

Natalie was beside Christian, her hand over her chest. "He's a vampire?"

"No. He's just done." Nigel rose to his feet. "Mari killed his spirit and left his body to rot."

Christian swore. "She's stealing our will to live." He ran his hand through his hair, a telling gesture he made only when under extreme stress.

"Looks that way." Nigel exchanged grim looks with Christian. So many times, the only thing that had kept them alive was their will to live, their fight, the soul that beat at them to stay alive. The spirit was the essence of life, something they all had been able to cling to no matter what else she'd done to them.

And now Mari was stealing that? Screw that. It crossed a line that was beyond acceptability, even in war. "We need to get to Pascal and Blaine. Now!" They were going in now. No more were going to die.

He grabbed Natalie's hand and sprinted down the tunnel, Christian on his heels.

The battle had begun.

Chapter 16

PASCAL NARROWED HIS EYES AS SMUTTY HEADED toward him. The dream genie's shiny new loafers were nearly silent on the hardwood floors of the plush suite. Pascal had felt bad for the guy when he'd been Angelica's smut monster and had been condemned to a life of running around as an oversized puppy dog.

But stealing another man's soul?

The way he figured it, that was even worse than kicking another man in the nuts. Smutty had to go down.

"Oh, come on, Pascal." Mari patted his arm, and Pascal let his gaze drift toward his captor. "Have I hurt you yet? Have I tortured you at all?"

He didn't bother to mention the two-inch-deep burns on his arms from the stainless steel chains that were currently locking him down to the steel chair that had brought him from the bowels of the dungeons to Smutty's lab of demented activities.

Much as he'd enjoyed his path toward becoming a manly man in the Den, now that he'd been out, he was proud to admit that he now preferred Francesca's organic pizza and apple beer over being chained down. Go figure.

Mari, apparently, was able to read his mind. "Well, I wouldn't have to chain you if you'd trust me," Mari said defensively, as she knelt in front of him, forcing herself into his line of vision. "Listen to me, Pascal. You've got all this pain and anger inside you, all these thoughts of revenge and punishment. I know it's awful. I don't want you to suffer like that, so I want to help you. You'll never be able to find peace in your heart while all this horrible stuff is running around in there. I'm going to give you peace."

"Actually," he said, "I'm generally a pretty chipper guy. The only time I get cranky is when I'm here. Funny how that works, isn't it?"

"Chipper is completely inadequate." Smutty pulled up a bar stool and perched on the edge of it. "We're talking about total salvation of the soul."

"Sounds too dull for me." Pascal scanned the room, searching for options. He knew he would get one chance to make a break, and he had to make sure he accounted for everything. "My soul likes being a little tarnished, and the girls seem to appreciate it." He saw Danielle stifle a smile, and he winked at her.

The woman might be working for Mari, but she'd slipped him some peace when she'd tried to protect him from the metal chains, and he was down with that.

Mari smiled sadly. "Sweetheart, you say that only because you don't really understand what real peace is. I'll help you. You'll see."

Pascal sighed. The woman was going to be stubborn and shortsighted, wasn't she? Apparently, once again, it was up to him to manifest his own destiny. He ran his fingers over the palms of his hands, and felt the tips of spines poking out from under the skin. *Come on, baby.* Mari had no clue that Nigel had healed Pascal before she'd snatched him. He wasn't back to full potency, but he was pretty damn close. A lot closer than she would be prepared for.

He had one shot.

And he was going to take it.

He wanted to get back to his pizza.

"Oh, come on, Pascal," Mari said. "It's not that bad—"

"It is!" That little chit, Danielle, who he'd never seen before today, shoved her way past the two psychotic beasts and stood in front of him. Blocking his access to the bad guys. "This is wrong. You're worse than Angelica. Stealing their inner souls. It's wrong!"

Well, he had to admit that he found her gumption somewhat endearing. It was clear she absolutely meant what she said. He liked that. And quite frankly, it was damned cute that the little thing was trying to protect him. Hello? Who was the badass warrior in the room? That would be the big guy strapped to the chair.

Despite his appreciation for her willingness to give Mari grief, her audacious little move had the unfortunate side effect of placing her right between him and the bad guys, which meant that she would be caught in the cross fire once he went to work. He got no bad vibe from her, and he wasn't really interested in hurting her. Which meant she had to move that cute little fanny of hers aside. "Get out of my way," he said quietly, the command barely a whisper in the air. "Hide."

Danielle whirled around, a startled look on her face. Her bright blue gaze met his, and he saw the anguish on her face. He knew then that she was as much a victim as he was. She was trapped like the men in this place. Seemed to him that he was going to have to take her with him when he left, didn't it?

Always fair damsels to be rescued. It made a warrior's life such a challenge.

"What did you say?" Mari leaned forward, disrupting the vibe Pascal had going on with Danielle. "I'm just giving you love, for heaven's sake. Doesn't anyone understand how important love is?"

Pascal ignored Mari and kept his gaze fixed on Danielle, willing her to understand.

For a moment, she didn't move, then she raised her brows and took a step to the side. At his nod, she flashed a brief smile and eased behind the huge wooden wardrobe housing Smutty's new designer suits. Trusting him.

Good girl.

"Pascal is too thick-minded to understand the gift we give him," Smutty said. "I will take care of it."

Pascal turned his focus back to Smutty. He'd seen them carry Max down to the tunnel, and there was no way he was going to allow them to do it to him. He liked his own mind just fine.

Smutty pulled the chair up and leaned forward, staring intently into Pascal's eyes.

Pascal met his gaze, unflinchingly, and he allowed himself to feel the threat. His easygoing relaxation rolled away, and a powerful strength began to build inside him. He drew on the fire Nigel had given him. His skin began to prickle everywhere as spines began to form. Lethal, acid-laced spines. He would have preferred something less hostile, like a whiffle ball, but this wasn't the moment to tap into his softer side.

Because, as he'd said, he liked his brain exactly how it was. He bunched his hands and felt the scales beginning to harden.

His fingernails began to extend, digging into his palms. His teeth began to lengthen.

His scalp started to itch as the hair shifted into scales.

Smutty leaned closer, his gaze intent, and then Pascal felt pressure in his head. Tingling in his brain. He knew that the son of a bitch was inside his mind now, attempting to strip away who he was.

Yeah, good luck with that. He was not going down.

"Wait!" Mari shouted. "Pascal's going—"

Pascal unleashed the beast.

The chains exploded as he ripped free of his human form. Smutty leapt back as Pascal erupted to his feet. He whirled around and expelled the spines from his body. They screamed through the air and embedded themselves in the furniture, Mari, Smutty, and the walls. Sparks exploded from the computer, and the television went haywire. Smutty shouted with pain, and the monster inside Pascal came to life. Feeding upon the fear, the pain, the anguish.

Pascal fought to stay in control, to direct the beast, but he felt his mastery slipping as the monster became stronger. The girl. He wanted the girl. Pascal leapt across the room and ripped aside the wardrobe. She was huddled down behind it, and her face was stricken as she saw the beast gazing down at her.

Pascal tensed, expecting the monster to kill her, as it always did. Killing whatever was around. But instead, the beast reached for her, palm up in invitation.

In a crazy move that spoke either of insanity or a suicide mission, Danielle instantly set her hand in his with total trust. And in some bizarre unfolding of events, the beast did not chomp her for dinner, but instead pulled her to her feet—

Something crashed into the back of his head, and

the monster howled with agony as Danielle yelped and shouted his name. Pascal's body went numb and he fell to the ground, writhing in pain. He felt the monster begin to retreat, felt humanity returning. *No!* What was happening? Where was it going? *Come on!*

But his skin reappeared and his vision went back to normal as Mari came to stand over him. His spines were sticking out of her body everywhere, and she wasn't even wincing. She yanked one out and tossed it aside. "I'm so sorry I had to take away your beast, but I can't let you walk away from happiness. Don't you understand? I'm trying to fix what we did to you. Please, stop fighting and understand that it's different now."

Weirdly, it didn't feel real different than the last time he'd been here. He tried to release another barb at her, but he couldn't move his arm. Just agony, raw, sheer agony ripping through him. Jesus. She really had taken away his beast, at least for the moment.

Well, that was different, he'd give her that. But not one of those *good* changes.

Smutty came hurrying up. Spines were poking out of him, but with one shrug, they all spewed out of him and dropped on the floor. "Smut comes in handy. I'm carrying the smut from the spell that created your spines, so it can't hurt me." He squatted next to Pascal. "You are so tormented by frustrated dreams and desires, my boy. Let me take care of that for you."

"No!" Pascal fought, he struggled, he tried desperately to shut his mind to the invasion, but his head began to ache, to tingle, to pulse with pain… And suddenly, he didn't hate Mari anymore.

And then the rest of his soul began to be torn away.

Dammit.

He'd really liked himself.

———∿∿∿———

"Get away from him!" Nigel charged through the door and hurled a red-hot dagger at the man leaning over Pascal.

The man leapt up as the blade plunged into his chest, and he instantly dissolved into a dozen rats. The blade cleaved harmlessly through the pack and thudded in the wall behind him. The rodents sprinted for the door, merged into one big pile and then transformed into a giant troll wearing a "Trolls kick ass" shirt.

"It's Smutty." Nigel had already spent plenty of time fighting the black magic smut monster, and he'd seen it shift forms faster than a teenage girl could change her mind. None of the forms were good news. And none of them were stoppable, at least from what he'd seen.

But anyone could be slowed down.

Nigel peppered Smutty with blades as he sprinted across the room toward Pascal. The kid was comatose on the floor, like Max had been. "Cover me, Christian."

Smutty shimmered and resumed his human form. "Warrior. I can take away your pain. I can take away your discomfort. I can give you peace!"

Well, damn. That was almost worth investigating. But the timing just wasn't quite right. You know, the middle of battle and all that.

Instead, he tossed a handful of blades at Mari, intending to lock her down against the wall. But she held up her hand, and his blades stopped in midair and went careening right back toward him.

He opened his palm to take control back, but they

sailed past him and headed right toward Natalie, who was standing just inside the door.

"Shit!" He screamed silent orders for the blades to divert, but Mari had stripped his bond with his weapons. He couldn't stop them. They weren't his anymore, and they were going to take out Natalie.

Son of a bitch! He charged for Natalie. "Get down!"

She dropped to the floor and he threw himself over her as the blades peppered his back, hammering at him like a machine gun.

The pain struck him with brutal force, and his body shook with the agony of trying to fight it off.

He was vaguely aware of Christian engaging in battle, but he couldn't move quite yet. Couldn't think. It was taking all of his concentration simply to stay conscious. In hopes of at least slowing Mari down, he'd unleashed killing blades, every one of them with enough force to knock out an army of demons, and now they were camped out in his body.

But, better than Natalie's body, so he was counting this one as a victory for the good guys.

"Nigel!" Natalie held his face in her hands, her face stricken with worry. "Are you okay?"

"Yeah, just a scratch." Her hands were warm and soft, a feel of humanity and warmth. He focused all his attention on her touch, tried to hang onto the feeling she gave him while he tried to figure out what Mari had done to him. No one had ever broken his link to his weapons. He felt impotent and weak. Not powerful. Not driven. "Can't—"

Tears filled her eyes. "Come on, Nigel! Don't die on me—"

He snorted. "Die? I'm not going to die—"

"You!" Mari grabbed Natalie and ripped her out from under Nigel.

"Hey! She's mine." Nigel lunged for Natalie as Mari pulled her out of his reach. "No!" He swore at the terrified look on Natalie's face as she fought to hang onto Nigel.

"Welcome to my home, little smut monster." Mari dragged Natalie over toward the door, her iron grip leaving no chance for escape for a woman whose talents lay with chocolate and sex. "Charles," Mari announced. "Here she is. She's the one. We can take more off you much faster with her here."

Dizziness began to take over Nigel's brain, and his mind clouded as the poison from his knives penetrated his defenses. Through his dimming vision, he saw Christian thrown back against the wall by Charles, landing beside Pascal. And then Smutty crouched over Christian, his eyes focused.

Christian shouted and went scaly, lashing out. Being stripped of his mind. "No!" Nigel fought to get free of his own poison, struggled to help his friends. *Come on!*

Natalie shrieked and recoiled against the wall, holding her belly as Mari poured more smut into her. Her skin flashed dark cobalt, and then he smelled sulfur, the sulfur of demons.

Natalie! She was in danger. She was getting hurt. And he couldn't protect her—

Son of a bitch.

His skin began to prickle, and he realized he was going to lose it. And with fear for Natalie's life driving him, he knew it was going to be even worse than in the alley.

They were all going to die, and he was going to be the one to kill them.

Son of a bitch. He knew he shouldn't have kissed her. It had done him in, and now they were all going to pay.

———

Natalie's vision began to blur, and her muscles began to shake. Dark, crimson nails began to extend out of her fingertips, and her skin began to glow like bronze metal. And it hurt. God, it hurt—

Chocolate! I smell chocolate! Like some weak-willed chocoholic, she whirled around, searching for the source of the soul-wrenching aroma. But instead of chocolate, she saw Nigel twisted on the ground. "Nigel!" She started to run for him, and then saw an old chocolate chip cookie abandoned on the floor near him.

Her mouth began to water. Nigel. Chocolate. Nigel. Chocolate. What should she choose? Her heart was screaming Nigel, but she changed tracks and headed toward the dessert, driven by the compulsion inside her. "No!" She grabbed for Nigel as she passed by him, saw his eyes open.

The agony in them was unreal. Not just agony, but brutal, searing fury. Anger. Coldness. Death. The monster that had shown its face at her store was coming to life again, only with far more aggression. He reached for her, his fingers outstretched. "Natalie—"

"I'm here. I'll help—"

Her body convulsed with pain as another onslaught of smut hit her (was that a bad sign that she knew what it felt like to get hit with smut? She was kind of thinking it was). She screamed as it rocked through her, and she was flung backwards. She crashed into the wall and landed beside the cookie.

She stared blankly at it for a second and could practically hear it calling out to her. *Natalie. Natalie. Come eat me. You know you want me.*

No. She wouldn't succumb to the demonic poison racing around inside her. She was not turning into her worst nightmare. She *wasn't*. Chocolate would never trump saving those she cared about. "Nigel," she gasped. "I'm coming."

In an impressive show of willpower, Natalie raced across the floor and kneeled next to Nigel. He opened his eyes as she laid her hands on his cheeks. "Okay, Nigel, let me in."

He grabbed her wrists. "If this doesn't work," he managed, "get away from me. I won't be able to stop myself."

"You would never hurt me." She laid her finger over his mouth, silencing his protests. "Just let me in." He nodded once and closed his eyes, and she felt him try to relax, trusting her. *Please don't let me let him down.* She leaned closer, breathing deeply. He smelled great, like total man and power and control. She tried to recreate the feeling of his kisses, of the way he'd made her feel. "You are in control," she ordered. "You're an effective and smooth warrior—"

Mari grabbed her arm and hauled her back to her feet. "What are you doing? What are you?"

"Nothing!" She tried to twist free, desperate to get back to Nigel. "Let me go—"

"You have the power of suggestion?" Mari's eyes were gleaming with anticipation that didn't comport with an appropriately submissive response to Natalie's suggestion. "You can influence these warriors to respond to anything I want them to do, can't you?"

Uh oh. Natalie recalled all too well Ella's horror at what she'd done to the warriors. She remembered Nigel's revulsion when she'd touched his mind. What greater nightmare than to have that power in the hands of this woman? "No, no, I don't—"

"You lie!" Mari tightened her grip. "You're a Mystic. You're powerful! I need you—"

"I'm not! I can't influence anyone!" She didn't dare look at Nigel to see how he was doing. She didn't want to direct Mari's attention to him.

"You can!" Mari leaned closer and sniffed. "You really stink of smut. How did that happen? It was Gina Ruffalo. How did she dump that on you?"

"It was *Gina*?" Gina had been the altruistic self-sacrificing angel who'd traded bodies with Natalie so she would die instead of Natalie. She'd told Natalie that she wanted to go to the Afterlife to be with her true love. But it had really been to escape an eternity as a smut monster? Um, hello? That definitely went on the list of "things that would have been good to know *before* trading bodies with someone." "Gina was your smut receptacle?"

"Yes. Gina had betrayed Angelica long ago, and she got smutted as punishment." Mari cocked her head. "I'm so sorry that you got loaded with it. I assumed that I was hitting up Gina."

"Well, then, you can stop, right?"

"Well, yes, but it has to go somewhere." Mari glanced over at Charles leaning over Pascal. "I'm all for girl power, so I'm willing to make a deal. If you come work for me, I'll put the smut back on Charlie." She lowered her voice. "Honestly, he's not that easy to control. And I really feel like he brings out the worst in me. You and I could fix things so gently and so easily."

Nigel bellowed, and Natalie whirled around. His skin was gleaming with metal, his body was rigid, the tendons rigid in his neck. He'd broken the hold she'd put on him back at the car, and her second attempt to bring him back hadn't worked. He'd trusted her to keep him sane, and she'd failed him. "Nigel! You are in control—"

"No!" Mari yanked her back as she tried to go to him. "Don't you realize what we could do for all these men? We could teach them about love and bring them peace." She nodded at Nigel. "You could save him from the pain. Open his spirit to love."

Natalie's heart tightened as she saw Nigel writhing on the floor. The anguish in his face. The monster rising within. Could she really save him? Mari was powerful with her magic. She could help Natalie tap into her own magic. Make her powerful enough to save Nigel, to save others, to save herself—

Dear God! What was she thinking? She would be no better than Mari if she went that route. She wouldn't force anything on them. "No!" She pulled free. "I could never work for you."

Disappointment flashed in Mari's face. "I respect your decision, but if that's the case, then I've got to use Smutty, and I need you to carry his smut. I apologize, but I don't have time to track down someone who deserves the smut." Mari picked up a black baton and pointed it at Natalie. "Are you sure you want to turn down my offer?"

Natalie backed up a step. "You could just let the guys go and stop messing with them."

"No, I can't. I have to fix things. Everything is too broken." Mari's voice broke with frustration and guilt, and she pressed a button on her black baton. The end of it flashed with a bright blue light, and more smut flooded Natalie.

"Trust them to fix themselves," Natalie said, gasping for air. "Just stop interfering!" It felt like demons were gripping her lungs and stealing her breath. The smell of chocolate was hammering at her, making it difficult to think.

"They're too damaged," Mari said. "I owe it to them to clear the scars from their soul."

"They're warriors!" Natalie hunched over, hugging her belly against the pain. "They like scars! It gives them something to talk about over dinner!" She saw Smutty sit up and rub his eyes, looking decidedly more cheerful and sprightly than Natalie was feeling.

"Does no one understand my vision? It's about love. Is there any greater good?" Mari twirled her wand like a baton, her face twisted in frustration. "If you won't help, I'm going to have to clear Smutty enough to make him able to function better. I promised everyone love, and love they shall have." She raised the wand again and aimed it at Natalie. "One last try—"

And then, in a display of excellent timing for an act of dubious horror, Nigel erupted.

Chapter 17

NIGEL LEAPT TO HIS FEET, POWER AND EMOTION ROARing through him like he'd never felt before. It was a thousand times worse than the day he'd killed his mother. His mind was a white light of heat, of aggression, as he saw Mari's hand close on Natalie's neck. As he saw that baton coming toward Natalie's heart. "No!"

A roar ripped out of his chest and he flung his arms up toward the ceiling. Drawing in all the energy he could find, letting it fuel the rage within him. Embracing himself in a way he'd fought against for a hundred and fifty years.

"Shit, Nigel! You're going to bring us all down!" Christian raced over to Pascal and threw his chain-linked body over the prostrate warrior.

Power filled Nigel, and a lethal coldness filled him. The coldness of living metal, rushing toward the surface, toward his skin.

He turned toward Natalie, saw her ashen face. "Oh, no," she whispered.

Oh, *yes*.

Mari was staring at him as well, and her face was delighted. "Angelica always said you were far more of a man than you'd ever let yourself be." She raised the baton to Natalie's thigh. "Bring it on, Nigel. Show me what you can be. Let out all your anguish and fury. Face it, release it, and then you will be ready to move on."

Something in his mind, buried in the depths of where his sanity used to be, registered Mari's excitement, realized that he needed to stop, to be strategic, comprehended that he was playing right into her plans. He needed to stop, stop, stop.

Then Mari flung the zapper at Natalie and hit her.

Natalie yelped, her skin began to smoke and then she was down on the ground.

I have to protect her. The blades ripped out of Nigel's skin. They hammered everywhere, ceiling, walls, floors. They thudded into Mari, but she simply stood there and smiled. "I accept the pain, and I deserve it," she said. "But if you kill me," she continued calmly, "Natalie will get all my smut. The demons will come to collect, and she will be taken by them."

"You lie—"

"I do not." Mari began to back toward the door. "Smutty!" she shouted. "Take away his dream of killing me!"

"No chance of that." Nigel allowed the blades to fly. He had to stop Mari. Had to stop her from hurting Natalie and Christian and Pascal—

"If I die, so will Natalie," Mari shouted. "And it will be your fault!"

Her words were like a shock to his system. Shit! Natalie couldn't die! It his job to protect her. He realized his blades were spewing in all directions. Just like when he'd killed his parents. "Natalie," he shouted, falling to his knees as he tried to reel the blades back in. "Get out of here!"

Smutty leapt to his feet. "I take your dreams, warrior!" he shouted.

Nigel's head suddenly felt like it was going to explode. Pure golden light raced through it, and thoughts of Mari swirled around in his head, darting in and out of his conscious and his mind. "Jesus!" He stumbled backwards, clutching his head. "No!" He whirled toward Smutty and directed all his weapons onto him.

"Not me!" Smutty shrieked and dove behind the wardrobe. "I'll steal your aggression, too! Stop, you silly boy!"

Nigel's head billowed with pain and he fell to his knees, holding his head against the invasion in his brain.

Mari crouched beside him. "Come on, Nigel," she begged. "Stop fighting this! I'm trying to help you, and if you just let me, everything will be okay."

"Losing my mind will never be okay," he gritted out. Shit. He was losing it. He couldn't stop the fury, couldn't hold onto his focus. Everything was sliding out of control. "Run, Christian," he gasped. "Get Natalie and run!"

Christian leapt to his feet, his chain-linked body intact despite Nigel's assault. He grabbed Pascal, flung the inert warrior over his shoulder, whipped out his sword, and hurled it at Smutty.

The sword diverted and sank itself into the wall beside him.

Nigel swore. Christian never missed. None of them did. "He's in your head too. Get out!"

"Not without you." Christian called his sword back and raced for Nigel. "Get up, you bastard! We're leaving!"

"Don't let them leave, Charlie," Mari shouted. "Make them want to stay!"

"Jesus." Nigel's head felt like it was going to explode, and he lurched to his feet. "No!"

"Stop!" Natalie suddenly leapt to her feet. Her hair was strung out, her face was ash-gray, and her skin was tight and shiny. Her eyes were black and her teeth were pointed. "Stop hurting them!" And then Natalie flung herself toward Mari, unleashing a scream of anguish that made Nigel's soul crack.

"No!" He intercepted Natalie in midair. "You don't want to be that person. Let me do it." He wrapped Natalie against him, shutting down her struggles. "This isn't you," he shouted at her. "It's the demons! You don't want to be a killer!" He threw a knife at Mari. The blade sank deep into her heart, and she screamed. It was a living blade, and he knew it was growing strong, taking over her body almost instantly.

Mari's face paled, and she grabbed her chest. "Stop, you idiot! You can't kill me!"

But he knew she was wrong. She was dying. He could feel her soul dying. It was over. *It was over. Mother of God, it was over.*

Christian had been sprinting toward the door with Pascal, but he stopped to watch Mari crumbling. "And the wicked witch of the west finally gets hit with her bucket of water. Justice reigns."

Nigel saw relief in his friend's eyes. Hope for a brighter future, or any future at all. For them, and for everyone else still trapped under her reign. "It's over, buddy—"

Natalie screamed suddenly and lurched in Nigel's arms.

"What—" Then the walls came alive. Monsters began to emerge from the plaster, bronze ones with oversized teeth, black, soulless eyes, and more horns that any living creature could possibly put to use.

"Demons!" Christian charged the nearest one, took off its head, and another head sprung up out of the neck, hissing. "Shit!"

One of them leapt off the wall straight at Natalie. Nigel took the beast out with a single swipe. Then more appeared. And more. Dozens. All of them circled Natalie, hanging on the wall like demonic spiders. "What the hell?"

"It's the smut," Mari gasped as she went down on her knees. "If you kill me, the demons come to collect payment, and since Natalie's carrying my smut, they'll take her instead."

Another beast leapt off the wall, teeth bared to reveal a bottomless throat. Screams of dying souls echoed in is belly. "Holy crap! That's not good." Nigel slammed his blade down its throat, and it kept coming—

Christian bisected it, and odious sulfur smoke assaulted Nigel's nose. Burned it like acid. The two halves each sprang into a new demon, and the walls began to shift as more and more appeared. "There's too many," Christian shouted. "We can't stop them all!"

Mari groaned and held her hand to her stomach. "Pull the blade out, warrior. Now. Save me, or Natalie will get taken by them."

A demon sprang from behind and tried to eat Nigel's head. He engaged it, and then another pried Natalie out of his arms. There was a screech of victory, and then it began to drag her across the floor. Natalie fought, but she had no chance against the monsters of hell.

"No!" Nigel raced after her, and then the demons closed ranks, shutting him out. He couldn't see her. Could just hear her screams. He fought, he sliced, he jabbed, and there were more and more... He couldn't get through them!

He spun around and raced over to Mari, threw her down, and slammed his hand over her chest.

"What the hell are you doing?" Christian raced over to him. "Don't save her!"

"Get off!" He backhanded a huge blade at Christian. It caught him in the chest and flung him backwards. Nigel barely registered the fact he'd taken out one of his best friends. All he could feel and think was that Natalie was being taken by demons. He had to save her. At any cost. He threw his healing energy into Mari, found the blade, and ripped it ruthlessly out of her.

She shrieked and gasped, a gaping wound open in her chest. And still more demons came, called by Mari's approaching death. They surrounded Natalie, who was screaming like she was being skinned alive. "Shit!" He tried to focus on healing, couldn't think, couldn't focus, too frazzled.

"Nigel!" Natalie's shriek of horror, her last plea for help.

Nigel saw a pad and pen set carefully on a nearby table, placed there as if it had been waiting for him. He knew it probably had been set there just for him, as part of his trap, but he didn't care. He raced across the room and snatched it up. His fingers flew across the page as he sprinted back to Mari, and the image was complete by the time he crouched beside her. He didn't even know what he'd drawn. Didn't care. But his mind was clear and focused, at least enough to heal, and he flung healing light ruthlessly into Mari's body. The white light glowed, the blood flow slowed, her chest began to knit together. He threw every last bit that he had into him, and then there was a flash of light, and the demons vanished.

"Nigel!" Natalie's upper body was halfway through the wall. Her feet were out of sight, sucked partway into hell. She had dug her claws (claws!) into the floor and there were drag marks across the wood as she'd tried to hold herself. Her eyes had bronze flecks in them. "Help me," she whispered, as if she were too exhausted to fight any longer.

"Nat!" He bolted across the floor. He caught her under the arms and pulled on her... and she continued to disappear further into the wall. "Mother of hell!"

Tears streamed from her eyes. "I can't stop it. I can feel the monsters inside me—"

"No!" Fury raced through him, white-hot rage, and suddenly there was an enormous serrated blade in his hands. The metal was glowing purple. He had no idea what he'd just created, but he knew instinctively what to do with it. He jammed it into the wall that was trying to suck Natalie into the abyss of doom. The wall pulsed and shrieked, and then exploded.

Nigel cradled Natalie as it flung them across the room. He shoved her into the protective shield of his body as they careened into the opposite wall.

They hit hard and crashed to the ground. He had no time to check on Natalie before his head was hammering from a new assault by Smutty. He jerked his gaze up to see Smutty staggering toward him, hands out, invading his mind.

"Enough already!" Nigel grabbed Natalie, flung her under his arm, and attacked. The blades spewed left and right, hitting everywhere, but he could still feel Smutty in his head, trying to take away his fury. "Hell—"

"Get out!" Christian shouted. "We have to get out!" Christian sprinted past him, Pascal over his shoulder. "Go out the hole!"

Nigel tucked Natalie up against him and ran after Christian. He leapt through the cavernous opening he'd created with his sword, and then they were flying through space, through a void, through blackness. To hell? To salvation?

They were about to find out.

———

Natalie heard the demons screaming as Nigel carried her through the opening. She felt them clawing at her arms. Oh… wait… those were Nigel's weapons digging into her as they tried to emerge from his body. He was going mad. He was going over the edge.

"Nigel!" She shouted at him as they fell to whatever hell awaited them. "Stop!"

"No chance of that, sweetheart—" And then the demons came.

Real demons. Just like in her dreams. Claws, snarls, howls of torture and death, bursting out of the darkness. She fought off the claws, hit at her assailants, gagged at the scent of sulfur. She realized they were catapulting down a black chasm, glowing eyes watching them—

Then Nigel went ballistic, attacking, and Christian did the same. Their weapons were moving too fast for her to see, and somehow, miraculously, nothing hit her, nothing gouged her. The creatures stopped going for her, fought for survival against two powerful and enraged warriors. And then there was a wail of capitulation, and the demons were gone. A battle cut short by the guardians protecting her.

Utter silence, and then the rock walls disappeared, and they were free-falling in darkness, in stillness—

"Nat!" Nigel grabbed her and pulled her against him. "Hang on to me," he gasped, his voice harsh and raspy. She threw her arms around him and buried herself against his body. She could feel his chest poking at her as knives fought to free themselves from his body, but he kept them in control, never actually stabbing her (always a good quality in a man).

He buried his face in her hair. "God, I could hold you forever," he whispered. "You're the serenity of my soul."

Warmth filled her and she hugged him tighter, needing his touch as much as he seemed to need hers. The wind whistled past as they fell, but in Nigel's arms, there was peace. She needed his support and his embrace after the hell they'd just been through. She concentrated on the feel of his whiskers against her cheeks, allowing the sensation of his body against hers to ease her tension.

The world disappeared, until all that was left was Nigel, their bodies tangled together as they fell in the blackness. She had no idea where they would land or how much it would hurt, but she didn't really care. With Nigel, she knew that everything would be all right.

"You're smiling," Nigel said. "I can feel your face against mine. Why?"

"I just realized that after a lifetime of being terrified of one bad ending after another, now that I'm in a situation with high potential for serious negative impact, I'm not worried. I'm just happy to be where I am."

He pulled her more tightly against him and brushed his mouth over hers. "That's my girl," he said softly. "A giant first step. Feel good?"

She raised her face to his. "Oh, yes."

He kissed her then, a tender and gentle kiss. A kiss that spoke of their mutual need to replace the experience they'd just had with something that felt good, with something that restored their souls and brought lightness to their spirits.

"Incoming," Christian called out. "Brace yourself."

Nigel broke the kiss and shifted their position in the air so he was below her. "Hang on, sweetheart. This could get rough."

"Okay—" She didn't even have time to brace herself before they crashed to the ground. Nigel absorbed most of the impact and rolled them as they landed, diffusing the impact, but she still felt like she'd just had a load of cement blocks dropped on her chest. "Oh, God."

Nigel grunted and let her go as he rolled away from her. The loss of his body was jarring, and she skidded another few yards before coming to a stop. She lay on her side and tried to catch her breath as she heard Nigel groan. "Nigel? Where are you?" She reached for him but felt only cold steel flooring. It was so dark, she could see nothing but blackness.

"Here," he growled, his voice harsh and throaty, as if he'd been hit with a sudden case of laryngitis.

Natalie raised her head as her eyes began to adjust. They were in a dimly lit tunnel that smelled of death and rot. "Where are we?"

"We're back at the portal," Christian said. "Let's go."

"The portal?" Hallelujah! She was so on board with getting out right now. She stumbled to her feet and saw the decayed body of Max against the wall. That was what she'd been smelling. The abandonment of life. She didn't need Nigel's expertise to tell her that Max's physical being had finally abandoned the effort of clinging to life.

She heard Christian run for the door, but she didn't move. There was only one set of footsteps heading for freedom, which meant Nigel was still down somewhere. "Nigel?" It was too dark to see much, but she could make out a shadowed outline of his body. He was on his hands and knees. She stumbled toward him, her body aching from the crash landing. "Are you okay?"

"No, sweetheart, I'm not." His body shuddered again, and he bowed his head, as if he was willing all his strength into suppressing the weapons. "Get out," he ordered. "Both of you. I'm going to lose it." Metal glinted in his shoulder, then a tiny razor-sharp shard split free and sideswiped her arm.

Natalie winced and grabbed her arm, realizing suddenly that even though he'd seemed crazed back in the Den, he'd actually been managing the blades. But not now. Because she knew he would never hurt her if he could help it.

He drew his head up, his face stricken. "Mother of God," he whispered. "I'm going to kill you." And then another blade went off. And another. They were going in all directions now, and another careened recklessly toward her head. She ducked, and it skimmed past her ear.

Nigel dug his fingers into the steel floor, and the

pads of his hands were sizzling from the burning of the stainless steel that all the warriors were so sensitive to. "Can't fight it off much longer," he muttered. "Get out."

It was like the alley again. All over again. "No!" Natalie raced over to him. "You can control it—"

"I can't!" He grabbed her shoulders and flung her away. "I can't control it without my art—"

She landed on her bottom and slid across the floor before she could stop herself. "Then get your art—"

There was a roar of fury from Christian, and Natalie whirled around in time to see Pascal convulse in Christian's arms. The younger warrior shuddered, began to sparkle, and then he was jerked out of Christian's arms. He flew past them and bolted down the long hallway, out of sight. "Oh, *no*."

Christian roared his protest and started to run after Pascal, and then one of Nigel's blades hit him in the chest. "Shit!" He whipped out his sword as he staggered. "Pull yourself together, man!"

"Can't," Nigel growled. "Get away from me."

"I have to get Pascal—"

Then Natalie heard footsteps pounding down the hallway toward them. Christian went rigid and raised his head. "It's Smutty and Mari." He fisted his sword. "They're going down now—"

"Run," Nigel gasped. "We can't beat them. Not right now." Another blade hit Christian. "Shit!"

Christian turned metal, and the next blade bounced off his skin. He took one last long look down the tunnel that had stolen Pascal, then he turned his back on the missing warrior and faced Nigel and Natalie. "Get behind me, Natalie!" Christian ordered. "Now!"

"No!" She wasn't going to leave Nigel behind to be taken by Mari and Smutty. No way! She grabbed Nigel's arm and began to drag him toward the entrance. "We're not abandoning him—"

"Of course we're not." Christian's metal-encased hands turned to flesh, and then he grabbed Nigel's wrist and hauled him toward the portal. "Go!"

Nigel was writhing on the ground, his eyes were rolled back in his head, and blades were flying everywhere. Natalie grimaced as another knife cut her thigh, and she ducked behind Christian, whose suit of armor seemed to be protecting him.

"Go!" Christian roared as more blades thunked off his skin. "Now! I'll cover you!"

She ran, and she heard Christian break into a sprint behind her. Nigel's body screamed over the stainless floor, his blades tearing along the ground as they burst from his body into the now-rutted floor.

"Stop them, Charlie!" Mari's shout bounced off the walls, and Natalie felt sudden pressure in her head.

She hesitated, suddenly no longer driven by the need to get away. Why was she running? There was no need to leave… Then a knife sliced across her arm. The pain jerked her back to consciousness as Smutty rounded the corner, and she realized he'd tried to steal her dream of escape. *Too late, jerk off!*

"Go!" Christian yelled.

She went. Natalie reached the portal mere yards in front of Christian. The air shimmered thickly around them, and then they were through.

Never had a Cavern of Murderous Poltergeists looked so fantastic! She paused long enough to make sure that Christian still had Nigel, and then they ran. They sprinted past screaming ghouls that now didn't seem quite so scary, after facing down Mari and Smutty.

They burst out into the night, and Nigel was still releasing blades like he wanted to eviscerate the earth. Christian threw him into the trunk of the Mercedes, and Natalie blocked him when he tried to close it. "You can't lock him up like some monster—"

"He is a monster." Christian yanked her back from the car and slammed the trunk shut. Inside was the loud crash of metal hitting the metal, of the car groaning in protest. Christian handed the keys to her. "Meet me at his place. Go!"

Without waiting for a response, Christian sprinted off to a motorcycle. He jammed on the engine and then peeled out. He shouted something at her, and then he was gone.

Natalie raced around to the front of the Mercedes, leapt inside, and gunned the engine. The tires squealed and then the car lurched forward just at Mari and Smutty came racing out of the cave. *So sorry. Gotta run.* The car careened across the gravel shoulder before she caught control.

She slammed the gas pedal down and hurtled through the darkened streets. She just drove. As fast and as far as she could. She didn't know where she was, and it didn't matter. They just had to get away, away, away. But as she looked in her rearview mirror and saw Mari and Smutty watching her, she knew it really didn't matter how far she drove.

Running away wasn't an option. Not for the long term. What were they going to do now?

Chapter 18

MINUTES, HOURS, EONS OF TIME PASSED BEFORE Natalie finally slowed down. She looked over her shoulder, but there was no one following them. Of course no one was following them. There was no car for the bad guys to chase her with.

Natalie unclenched her hands from the steering wheel and flexed them, trying to get the cramps out. They'd made it out alive. They weren't being followed. They were alive for chance number two... and heaven only knew what that was going to be.

It took several more minutes, but she finally found the highway and pulled out on it, heading back toward the city. The car purred effortlessly as she edged up the speedometer, but this time, the ride wasn't smooth and relaxing.

This time, there was the rapid thumping of hundreds of knives peppering the interior of the trunk. How long would Nigel continue the assault? How long until he cut through the metal and started destroying the world? Where could she take him to get help?

Christian said to meet at Nigel's house, but she had no idea where he lived. She'd seen Nigel only at her house that she used to share with her sister, when he'd come by with Jarvis to see Reina, before her sister had moved into Jarvis's place.

So... where was Christian? Nowhere she could find. Not before—

A blade hissed past her shoulder and thudded into the dashboard.

Okay, yeah, so apparently, they were now out of time. She didn't have time to find Christian. It was up to her, which really weren't the odds she was hoping for. She rifled through Nigel's glove box and found a sketchpad and pens. She hated to violate his oath by giving him drawing supplies, but he had to get sane, and quickly. He'd be more upset if he killed everyone… wouldn't he?

She took the next exit off the highway and pulled off onto a side street. Ahead was an empty ball field, a local park that was quiet and apparently shut down for the evening. She yanked the steering wheel to the right, and the car lurched over the curb with a clank that couldn't be good for a luxury vehicle. She careened down a steep embankment, floored it to the outfield, and then slammed on the brakes.

She dove out of the car as a series of metal darts escaped from the trunk. A knife slammed through the headrest right where her head had been. Yes, okay, this was going well.

She grabbed the drawing supplies, dropped to her belly, and inchwormed along the side of the car, trying to stay beneath the range of killer metal. She reached the back door and gripped the trunk. "Okay, Nigel," she shouted. "I'm going to throw you a sketchpad—"

"No!" His roar was deafening even though the metal.

"Yes! Just don't finish the picture!" She pulled the cover off so he could access a blank page, and then froze when she saw the image he'd drawn on the book.

It was of her.

Sitting on the windowsill in her family room, knees

hugged to her chin, staring out the window. She was wearing slippers, sweats, and a tattered pink teddy bear T-shirt. Her face was in shadows, her eyes heavy, and a single tear was on her cheek. She remembered that moment. It had been the first day after she'd nearly died. Her first morning alive without the deedub curse.

She'd been too terrified of who she was to even step outside, so she'd sat there in the window and watched the flowers.

Nigel had sat in that room all day with her. Never speaking. Never intruding. Simply being there, providing reassurance that if the Godfather came back, if all hell broke loose, Nigel would be there to help her manage it.

He'd been drawing all day, but never looking at her.

She hadn't thought he'd drawn her. She hadn't realized. But...

She flipped to the next page.

Another drawing of her. The same pose. The same clothes. The same moment.

But this time he'd drawn her with a smile on her face. A twinkle in her eye. She was laughing, and her arms were outstretched, as if she were reaching for him to give him a hug.

Her heart tightened as she looked into her carefree eyes. It was a face of peace, a face of laughter, a face that had learned not to fear life, or who she was, but to simply love.

He'd drawn her as she wanted to be. Courageous. Happy. Dear God, she never thought she'd see that expression on her face. And there she was. He'd seen it. He'd caught it. He believed in her. She looked beautiful.

Tears filled her eyes. Dammit. Why couldn't she be that woman? Why couldn't she just be happy? Why did she have to live in fear? Maybe Smutty was right. Maybe the answer was to cleanse the hell out of her and let the inner peace rise to the top.

Angry now, angry at herself, angry at Nigel for making her see what she wasn't, she tore the paper off, and then gaped at what he'd drawn on the next page.

She was on a bed. A huge bed with white posts and a white comforter. She was on her side, wearing a sexy black silk nightgown. Simple, edged with lace, with thin straps so decadent and tempting. It was the Natalie of Sex. Natalie of Orgasms. The Natalie who had gotten herself killed.

Her body wrenched, and cold fear coursed through her as she looked at the decadent woman she'd once been, the one who had died for sex. Of course he would see her like that! He'd been there when she'd lost it. When she'd gone over the top toward her death. When she'd been drugged out on the big O...

Then she noticed the bouquet of roses on the table by the bed. Pink roses for love, not red for passion. And then she saw the expression on her face. It was a half smile of peacefulness, of invitation, of softness. There was no desperation in her eyes, and her body was relaxed and at peace, as if she was waiting for romance, for lovemaking, not for random hot sex with an almost stranger.

She gripped the pad, her throat tightening. The picture was beautiful. It was sexy but peaceful. Safe. It was lovemaking, not raw, hard, dangerous sex. It was lovely. It was sensuality in its most beautiful form. Passion that would never hurt, never endanger, never threaten.

Tears filled her eyes, and she pressed the pad to her chest. Nigel really saw her that way? She hadn't thought of lovemaking in such a beautiful way since her awful experience. Nigel's kisses had been beautiful, and they'd created a yearning in her, but never had the vision of the kind of love and passion she craved been so vivid.

Nigel's picture, the way he'd captured the tenderness on her face, the love shining in her eyes... he made her see a future she hadn't taken the time to conceive of. He gave her hope. Was it really possible for her to get there? A man like Nigel, with his art, and his vision, could he take her there? Keep her safe and make her a woman at the same time—

A blade sliced through the sketchpad. She jumped at the intrusion and looked up to see a gaping wound in the trunk of the car. She could hear grunts now, Nigel's courageous battle to defeat the monster within.

She looked down at the sketchpad, at the picture of her being the woman she wanted to be. Seductive, loving, embracing of life. Passion in a world of beauty and commitment of the soul. Nigel had seen her in that way and he'd believed in her enough to bring her along on his foray into the Den. He'd trusted her to keep him safe, to keep the monster at bay, to keep him from betraying his friends. He'd known she had that sensuality inside her, and he'd counted on her being able to access it when it counted.

Her fingers closed over the pen. How could she abandon him? Take a shortcut by forcing him to draw and endanger someone else he cared about? If Nigel saw so much peace and serenity in her, if he perceived her as a sensual being who basked in the glory and wonder of desire and passion, then so could she.

She threw the pen aside, tore the sensual picture out, and tucked it in her back pocket. She would treasure it always, use it as her inspiration for the future she wanted.

Then she turned to face the trunk. She took a breath and set her hands on the handle. She closed her eyes and focused on the image he'd drawn. The pure, beautiful passion of it. She imagined his hands caressing the paper as he'd drawn her body. As he'd created her lace night-gown, the curves of her body, and the beautiful spirit that he saw flowing from her soul.

She envisioned the woman she wanted to be, allowed the sensual part inside her that had been dead for so long to come alive. At the first pulse of desire within her, fear came fast on its heels, dampening the budding passion. Dammit! She wasn't going to be able to reach that place of powerful sensuality by herself. She couldn't break through those barriers on her own. The fear was too deep, and quite frankly, the high pressure situation was just not making her feel sexy.

But men could feel sexy at any time, right? They were like steam pistons. And Nigel could make her feel safe… even while he was unloading knives and daggers into her? Well, only one way to find out.

She'd responded to Nigel before. Why not again? This time she wanted it. She needed it. She needed to be the woman she had never been.

It was time to take control. Or rather, make him take control of her. If he could trust her to bring him back from the edge, then she could trust him not to hurt her.

Another blade cleaved through the trunk and skimmed her side. She grimaced and pressed her hand over her hip. Okay, maybe she did trust him, but clearly, there wasn't time to dally. It was time to bring Nigel out and allow him into her soul, into her heart, and into the very core of who she was. And that was far scarier than any blade could ever be.

But as she gripped the latch on the back of the car, she knew that if there was anyone she would trust with her greatest terror, it was the man who had come to mean so much to her. "Nigel," she called out. "I need you!"

And then she kicked the trunk open and turned herself over to him.

Natalie was shocked when she saw Nigel in the dim light of the trunk. His clothes were shredded, his hair was caked with sweat, and the muscles in his upper body were rigid. His body was covered with cuts from the blades that had torn so ruthlessly from his skin, and he was glittering as more fought to rise to the surface.

His gaze shot to hers. For a split second, his face softened and he reached for her. Then he jerked his hand back and pressed it over his chest, trying to suppress another blade. "Get away from me," he growled.

On one level that didn't seem like a bad idea. Really. But on the other hand, this was Nigel. She'd already made her choice. She was committed, and she wouldn't let him down. "I can help you," she said. "Seduce me and—"

He groaned and his head arched back. "I can't—"

"You can! You've had sex through much worse than this! If you want me to help you, you have to help me." Tears were streaming down her face at the agony he was enduring. She kneeled on the bumper and took his hand, pressing it between her palms. His hand was warm and strong, the same hand that had caressed her so tenderly. "This is your chance to seduce me the way you've always dreamed of—Ow!"

Sudden pain ricocheted through Natalie's belly, and she slipped off the bumper, gripping her stomach. "You know," she gasped, "with Mari's timing, you would think that she didn't want us to get it on or something."

"Nat!" Nigel launched himself out of the trunk. He landed on top of her, but supported himself on his arms so he didn't crush her. "You okay?" Turmoil roiled in his dark eyes. Violence rippled beneath his skin. Nigel wasn't currently the tender artist who had painted her. Right now, he was a lethal monster in a dangerous place. This would not be tender lovemaking. This would be dangerous and possibly deadly.

She shuddered at the thought, and then anger raced through her. Afraid of Nigel? Afraid of lovemaking? More than the demons? Screw that! She focused on his dark eyes, on the soul of the man she knew was fighting to stay in control. "Take me, Nigel."

He tunneled his hand through her hair. "You sure?" He could barely get the words past his gritted teeth, and his body lurched as another blade tried to rip out of his chest and into hers. The skin flexed and pointed, but he didn't let it through.

"I want to die on my own terms this time. Not hiding anymore. I want to fight to live. And I want to fight for you, too." And then, before she could change her mind, freak out, and run away screaming, she pulled him down and kissed him.

His lips were cold and hard, as if they were made of the metal that was spewing from his pores. Then he growled, and he took over the kiss. He buried her in the force of his kiss, as if he were releasing all his darkest emotions into the connection. It wasn't tender, it wasn't lovemaking, it was violence, fury, and danger.

For a split second, she hesitated, not sure of what she'd done, of what she'd unleashed, and then he sank down onto her, crushing her beneath him as he kissed her. His shoulders were broad and rigid beneath her palms, and she felt tiny, safe, protected in the circle of his body… and yet he was kissing her like she was a fierce warrior who could handle anything.

Excitement surged through her. *Yes.* Somewhere deep inside, a fierce, dangerous, powerful being came to life. A woman who didn't fear, who wasn't afraid to tap into her own power. She felt strength rock through her, and the cells in her body began to burn, as if they'd been injected with some sort of energy. Her soul began to hum.

She gripped his shoulders and felt the pricks edging at his skin. "You're in control," she whispered.

But there was no hum of power, and her words were flat. Nigel's kisses were aggressive and desperate. His hands gripped her hips as if to hold her still and fight her down. There was excitement, but not sensuality. Adrenaline, but not tenderness. Her soul was still trapping her emotions too deep. She caught his face and forced him to stop kissing her. "Nigel," she whispered.

His face was contorted with agony and desperation. "What?"

"Seduce me."

"Shit. I can't—"

"The Godfather took from me." She couldn't keep the desperation out of her voice. "He took my body, but I need you to take my soul. It has to be different. I can't—" She couldn't finish, her body starting to shake at the memory of what had happened at the hands (and lips) of the Godfather.

Something flashed in Nigel's eyes, a brief insight as to the humanity that still existed within him. He bowed his head for a split second, and his body lurched as more metal exploded out of his back.

"Oh, God. I'm such a dork." She lifted his face to hers. "I can't believe I'm such a wuss that I'm asking you to seduce me when you're about to snap. Just take me, Nigel. I can get there on my own. I'll figure it out—"

"Hey, Natalie," he interrupted softly, his eyes dark as he searched her face. "The tenderness you want from me is the greatest gift I could give you. You heal me simply by your needs."

She felt her body relax at the husky intimacy of his voice. "Really?"

"Really." He managed a small smile, and then he kissed her. And it wasn't a kiss of carnal need. It was a kiss of gentleness. Of beautiful desire. Of a deep craving. His mouth was soft. A kiss here. A kiss there. His hand lightly tangled in her hair. His hips moving against hers in a seductively tempting rhythm, an invitation, not a command.

And she responded, her body and soul coming to life under Nigel's touch. Of her beautiful, powerful artist. Desire flared through her, and her heart began to race.

Then he pulled back and framed her face. "Sweet love." He brushed her hair off her face. "Feel the strength of my arms holding onto you. It's okay to let yourself go."

Her eyes began to burn at the honesty of his tone. She felt the truth of his words, that he was really going to keep her safe.

"I'm not the Godfather." He kissed her again, a deeper kiss, nudging her lips apart. "I'm Nigel. Always Nigel."

She whispered his name, trembling at the amazing sensation of his tongue brushing over hers. Warm, soft, intimate, an offer, a gift, not a ruthless demand that was forcing a response from her unwilling soul. Instead it was a seduction, an invitation to play. To dance, just a little bit.

His body convulsed against hers, and she gripped his shoulders. "Nigel!"

"I'm fine. Don't worry about me." He cupped her face and kissed her again, his lips so gentle and seductive, with just a hint of the desire driving him. "Kiss me back, sweetheart. Kiss me." His deep voice was so gentle, so tender, and yet so tightly strung with pain, with desire, with heat, all of which he was keeping under ruthless control so as not to scare her. To allow her time to find her footing. He was of such rigid, iron will that he was controlling a monster just to help her feel safe (and of course, to make sure he didn't kill her, which was always a fantastic trait in a man).

Nigel wasn't an artist.

He wasn't a monster.

He was a warrior, a protector, a guardian of all that fell under his protective wingspan, and he was granting that protection to *her*.

And with that realization in her, the wall of iron fear that had been holding her back… it disintegrated.

And suddenly Natalie couldn't get enough. She wanted

him to touch her. She wanted Nigel's hands on her, his mouth on her. She wanted to feel his skin against hers. Her soul began to glow, alight with the passion that had fought for freedom her whole life.

She kissed him with all the passion that she'd been holding back for so long. For in this moment, in his ruthlessly strong arms, in his embrace, pinned beneath his body, it felt safe to let it all go. He wouldn't kill her. She wasn't going to die. Not right now. And embracing her true, passionate self was her fast-track toward *life*.

Nigel apparently sensed her change, because his kiss went from seduction to passion in a split second.

It was exactly what she wanted.

Chapter 19

NIGEL'S KISS DEEPENED, PROBING, THRUSTING, TAKING, and he palmed the sensitive skin on Natalie's belly.

She shuddered when she felt the warmth of his hand splayed across her stomach. Such strength, such desire. It made her feel adored and admired. Wanted for who she was, not simply because she was some oversexed chick in the thrall of deedub passion. *Yes.*

He kept kissing her, kept up the marvelously decadent assault, and then shifted his weight to the side. He slipped his hand between her legs and tugged on the button of her jeans.

She tensed in anticipation as she heard the burl of the zipper being undone. He moved his hand over her belly, then lower. A touch, a brush, lower, and lower.

Her body began to throb, and her soul began to dance. She felt light in her heart, excited, like this was where she was supposed to be, the place she'd been striving to access for so long. The place of oneness with her soul, with her desires, with the passion that was the very essence of who she was.

"You okay?" He whispered the question against her mouth, his forehead against hers, a position so intimate, only between lovers who were emotionally connected.

Her heart opened to him then, to this man who was so dangerous, so tortured, who wanted nothing more than to find peace in his soul and to retreat into a world of art and sensuality. A warrior who was giving it all up to fight for those he loved.

She loved the feel of his whiskers against her cheek, basked in the sensation of his hand gently stroking her lower belly. "Oh, yes," she whispered. "It's perfect."

He kissed her again, hard and deep, and her soul lifted in response. Pressure pounded in her chest, and she knew it was her heart opening for the first time in her life.

"I've been wanting you since I first saw you so insane on that street," he whispered as his hand slipped beneath her underwear and touched her. "You were a contrast of passion and fire and terror." His face softened and he smiled tenderly. "There was such anguish in your face. I wanted to save you. I still do." And then he plunged deep with his fingers, claiming her most intimate parts and making them his.

I wanted to save you. It was like the gift of heaven, the feel of him inside her. His words still echoed in her mind. He'd seen her for who she was, even through the deedub thrall, he'd seen her truth, and he'd been attracted to that? Not to the passionate crazy woman. But to the woman who had walked through life afraid. And yet he'd also seen her passion, and he'd drawn it. "I want to live," she whispered.

"I know you do, sweetheart. I know you do." He pulled back then and pulled his shirt off. "We're both going to. The battle is ours."

His upper body rippled with muscle, and there were scars riddling his body. A red and gold phoenix was emblazoned across his chest, a magnificent drawing of the bird who could rise from the ashes. There were dozens of puckers from the blades that had been tearing out of his body, bright pink scars that were already healing.

Her heart bled for the pain he'd endured, but as he rose to yank off his jeans, she saw his muscles corded and flexed beneath his taut skin, and she felt his power, his strength. His body trembled and he stopped for a second and fisted his hands, willing his blades to stay in control. The tendons on his neck were bulging with the effort. Sweat was dripping down his brow, and agony twisted his face as blades exploded out of his upper body, shooting in all directions.

Natalie flinched and covered her face, but none came near her.

He swore and dropped to his knees, tugged her jeans off her and then lowered himself on her. "Takes a second for them to rebuild," he whispered as he brushed his lips over her neck. "We have a window."

God, the feel of his hot skin against hers was magnificent! With all the weapons expelled from his body, he wasn't prickly anymore, just smooth, hard muscle. It was seductive, amazing, and it felt so right.

Nigel kissed her breasts and then went to work on her body, activating every nerve ending, touching every inch of skin, caressing every curve. Desire swelled through her and she shifted restlessly, unable to focus on anything but the onslaught of sensation. Of his thighs between hers. Of his mouth on her breast. Of his hand gripping her hips, stroking over her skin, over her belly. Of the strength of his body as he loomed over her. Sensation rushed at her from all directions, until she couldn't keep track of where his hands were, what his mouth was kissing, of what part of her skin was touching his.

Her mind was consumed by Nigel, by his touch, by his body, by his kiss, by the connection between them. Desire was pinging in every cell of her body, but it was more than desire. It was need. It was the very depths of her soul wanting it all, tapping into a fire, a power, a truth that had eluded her for a lifetime. And it was there now, in her hands, in her heart, in her soul, beating with life, with love, with power.

And then Nigel was between her thighs. Silky hardness nudged at her body. She needed him inside her. She craved that completion. She was desperate to lose herself in him. To abandon all fear, all resistance, all caution, and to simply ride. To live without fear, even if just for that moment.

He met her gaze, and she saw the question in his eyes. His skin was rippling now, as another round of danger began to form. There were more now, and she saw his anguish. His desperation.

"Yes," she whispered. "*Yes*."

He didn't take his gaze off her face as he raised his hips and positioned himself.

She grabbed his forearms where they were braced on either side of her head, gripping the taut muscles, feeling his raw strength.

"It's me," Nigel said, his deep voice laced with the agony of what he was enduring, raspy from the monster within. "It's *me*." And then he thrust.

She gasped at the invasion, and her whole body shook with the magnificence of the sensation. She was there with him, with every move, with every touch.

Nigel swore. "Jesus, this is unbelievable." And then he pulled out and thrust again. And again.

The sensations were overwhelming, amazing, magnificent waves of such intense pleasure. Passion raged inside her and leapt to the conjunction of their bodies, of their souls. The connection burned between them. She could feel Nigel's pain, his passion, his anguish, and she opened her heart and her soul to him, to herself, to them.

His hips moved more quickly, taking her, and he kept his gaze desperately and tenderly on hers, demanding her attention as her body convulsed. She gasped as a tiny convulsion ripped through her. Oh, dear God. Her first orgasm since—

"Again," Nigel demanded. "Again!"

And another one. Small, but rippling all the way down to her toes. Another one, and she was still alive. She was still sane. "I'm okay," she whispered. "I'm okay." She was trembling now, scared, but excited.

"Let it go," he ordered, gently demanding her capitulation. "Go all the way. *Trust me*." And then he shoved her knees up toward her shoulders and thrust again.

The orgasm plunged through her with a glowing passion that made her body thrum and her soul sing.

Nigel thrust again. "Tell me," he ordered. "Tell me now."

She fought through the cloud of ecstasy, and she focused her energy on the passion pulsing through her, on the unstoppable desires that illuminated her body. Her core rippled with power, and her entire being began to throb. Her soul glowed, and she drove that power into her vocal cords, and then fed it to Nigel. "You don't need to draw," she gasped. The words echoed in the air, pulsing with force and power. She felt them in every cell of her body, in her throat. A high. A rush.

His body shuddered. "More, Natalie, give me more," he urged, driving deep again. An orgasm hit him, and he shouted her name.

An answering orgasm ripped through Natalie. She welcomed it, drank in the rush, the full sensuality of the experience. She took his face in his hands and brought him down to her, riveted by those beautiful brown eyes that carried so much emotion. "Nigel." She stroked her fingers over his cheek. "You do not need art to control your monster. You can restrain every blade at any time. You can be in control simply by deciding that's how you want to be."

"I feel you in my head." His body began to shake, and his face tensed. He began to pull away, and she felt his resistance spring up. "I need to block you—"

"No, you don't." She put her hand on his heart. "Trust me, Nigel, the way I trusted you. You *are* in control. You're at peace and there is no pain in your heart anymore. No anger. There is simply you, in utter control of what you want and who you want to be—"

"Holy crap." He pulled out, lurched off her, and rolled away, cutting her off.

Oh, God. Tears filled her eyes in dismay. She'd failed again.

Nigel couldn't believe it.

He absolutely couldn't believe it.

It was gone. The anger. The fury. The crazed insanity. The metal stabbing him in his own back. Gone!

He ran his hand over his arm and felt smooth skin. No blades poking at him or brewing deep inside his flesh "Hot damn!" He grinned at Natalie, who was propped up on her elbows, looking utterly distraught.

He leapt over to her, grabbed her hands, and tugged her to her feet. "You did it!" He pulled her against him and began to waltz with her across the grass. God, it felt so amazing to hold her.

"Did what?" she sounded confused. Wary.

"Oh, sweet girl." He framed her face and smiled at her. Her green eyes were like emeralds sparkling in the moonlight, and her skin was so soft. More than he'd ever been able to experience before. "Dear God, you're beautiful." He bowed his head and kissed her forehead, closing his eyes as sensations assaulted him from that innocent act. Fire, passion, sensuality, desire, possessiveness. He pulled back, gazing into her upturned face. "You're my angel, my guardian angel, delivered to me to bring my soul back from hell."

A smile of disbelief softened her lovely features as she placed a gentle and tender hand on his forehead. "You're better?"

"You cleared it all away." He raised his arms to the night sky, basking in the sensations delighting his heart. His soul felt unburdened, his body felt light, his mind clear and effortless. "There's nothing but peace in my body."

Natalie frowned. "But you shut me out after we made love."

He swept her up in his arms. "I'm so sorry about that. You know how I am when you get in my head." He kissed her again, marveling at how soft her lips were.

"You threw me for a loop. In my state as an ungrateful and uncouth male, I was unable to express my appreciation at that precise moment." He nuzzled her neck until she laughed. "Forgive me?"

"Never," she teased, her face lightening. "Men who don't appreciate me are forever punished."

"No, not men. Just me. There can never be another man. I couldn't possibly share you."

Her eyebrows shot up. "Really?"

"Absolutely." He placed her gently on her feet, cupped one hand around her lower back, and then took her other. "May I have this dance, my angel?"

"What? Here?"

"Of course here." He tugged lightly, and she smiled as she allowed him to guide her into a waltz. Together, they spun across the grassy infield as he hummed a waltz. "Do you realize what this feels like?" He twirled her and then enfolded her against him again, marveling at the magnificence of two naked bodies pressed together. Natalie's and his. A fit beyond perfection. "My heart is light. There's no dark monster inside me that I'm trying to fight off." He set her hand on his chest. "Do you feel that? It's peace, Natalie; it's utter and complete peace."

Her fingertips curved into his chest, a delightful, sensual move that made his whole body warm. "Really? We did it? The monster is gone? Without art?"

"You did it. I know it worked. I feel completely different than I ever have before. There is simply no violence inside me. Not even a whisper." He hauled her close and kissed her. Her mouth tasted luscious and sweet, pure, unadulterated pleasure. Even the kiss was different now. "There's no darkness. There's no taint.

There's just the purest of beauty. Of sensation. Of life."
He kissed her again, delighting in the sensation of beautiful longing and sensual lust racing through him. No resistance, just the purity of the moment. "It's amazing."
He nuzzled her neck, feeling giddy like a little boy. "I want to dance," he said. "I want to sing." He twirled her away, laughing at her surprised giggle.

"You're crazy," she laughed.

"No, I'm sane, finally, for the first time in my life. There's no inner violence trying to threaten my serenity. It's just me, how I've been trying to be for so long." He threw his arm around Natalie's shoulder and pulled her against him, then pointed to the sky, the endless canvas of perfection that was far more dazzling than it ever had been before. "Do you see the beauty of those twinkling lights? The magnificence of all that endless space? The stars are so bright. The night is so black. Isn't that contrast amazing? It's sheer beauty." He breathed in the crispness of the night air. "I want to paint it."

Natalie tensed. "You do? But that's not good—"

"No, no, my girl." He turned her toward him. "I want to paint the beauty now. It's different."

"What did you paint before?" She frowned, her captivating green eyes so full of question and interest.

He stroked her hair, marveling at how soft it was. He could feel things he'd never been able to sense before. It was incredible. "Before, I painted to try to soothe my soul. I painted out of need." He didn't remember anyone ever being that concerned about what was going on in his mind and his soul, and he wanted to lift her to the heavens and kiss her until angels came down and blessed them both. "I painted anguish. Conflict. Angst."

He brushed his thumb over her cheek, stunned by how soft her skin was. It was as if all his senses had come alive, no longer fettered with all the baggage that had been weighing him down for long. "I had to paint suffering so I could put my negative energy into the painting and take it out of my own soul."

Understanding dawned on her face. "That's why you drew me. Because I was suffering."

"Yes, yes." He pulled her close, breathing in the magnificence of her bare body against his. Sheer pleasure. Unfettered joy. Utter perfection. "But now I can see your beauty, only your beauty." He trailed his fingers through her hair. "I see the golden highlights in your hair. I feel the silkiness of each strand as it slides through my palm."

Her face softened, and she smiled.

"I can taste the delectableness of your mouth." He bent his head and kissed her. *Perfection.* "I could kiss you all day long." He kissed her again, unable to stop himself from partaking in the beauty of that gift. Of the intimacy of the connection, of the poetry of the kiss. He felt like the world was shining brighter than it ever had. There was only peace in his soul. He brought her close. "I want to make love to you again. With just us. No anger. No metal. No desperation. Making love. Nothing but the beauty of our connection."

Her cheeks turned pink in the most deliciously tantalizing expression. "Nigel—"

"Dance with me, my love." The feeling of unfettered freedom was simply too magnificent to deny. He began to cavort across the grass, the blades soft beneath his feet. When had he last cavorted barefoot?

Ever? Most likely not. "No more boots. I love the feeling of the grass."

Natalie was staring at him in confusion. "You seem so different."

"I am, my love." He kissed her again, stroked his hands over the magnificence of her curves. "I have yearned for this kind of peace my whole life." He tasted her collarbone, he suckled her nipple, and his whole body shook with sheer delight at the feeling of her body against his. "I sought this through my art, but it was all about pain, about suffering, about trying to manage the hell." He scooped her up and cradled her against his chest. "Dear God," he whispered. "Your body feels so magnificent against mine. They way your breasts are pressed against my chest, the feel of your hip in my stomach, the curve of your bottom in my hand—" He laid her on the grass and kissed her again. "You are my angel, my light, my delight."

His heart felt like it was exploding from his chest. There was no pain, no torment, just peace, peace, peace. He saw only beauty. He felt only purity. He heard only the most beautiful music.

"Stop." Natalie pushed at his shoulders. "We don't have time for this. Mari is after us, and Christian and—"

Ah… Mari and Christian. Such bad energy from them. He didn't have time for that. This was his moment. "They will wait." And then he summoned all the beauty in his soul and he kissed Natalie, pouring the music, the angels, and the beauty in his kiss into her body.

And it took less than an angel's song for Natalie to melt into his kiss, to grasp his shoulders with the delicate grip of a woman so beautiful that the world would stop for her. She kissed him back, and it was a dance of perfection, of connection, of the ultimate grace.

Just two bodies, two souls, to spirits, losing themselves in the beauty of their physical connection.

Her breast was perfect in his hand, her small noises of exultation were like the sound of an archangel's choir. He kissed her belly, and lower, and it was the most luxurious taste of honey and sweet plum and the purest of sugars, straight from the beauty and flawless perfection of the great earth, as only Mother Nature could provide.

The beautiful orchestra of heaven's bells was playing in his ears as he moved over, as her body parted for him like the great seas tapping into the soul of eternity, and then he slipped inside her, a mating of such rightness, of a thousand years of harmony reaching its peak and coming into flawless alignment.

He moved inside her, smiling at the softness of Natalie's expression, and the utter peace in her face as she tapped into that spiritual bond calling them together. He held up his hand and she entwined her fingers with his, and together they held on as he moved, as she responded. It was a coming together of such perfect unison, of flawless harmony, of the culmination of all the beauty and peace and magic in existence.

And when they orgasmed together, it was the fireworks of heaven igniting the sky above them, it was the chorus of angels glorifying the night, it was the beauty of perfection blanketing them.

Chapter 20

"I UNDERSTAND NOW."

Nigel's softly spoken comment gently nudged Natalie awake. She opened her eyes to find that she was stark naked in a little league field, and she was cold. It was still nighttime, so she couldn't have slept for long. Nigel was sitting beside her, also naked, and he was leaning forward, his arms wrapped loosely around his knees.

He was staring across the lumpy ball field with a look of awe on his face as if he were sitting on a mountain top, gazing down upon a valley vista of untouched, breathtaking magnificence.

She followed his gaze and saw only the chain-link fences separating the neighboring houses from the field. Some scraggly brush. And a slightly crooked and peeling equipment shed next to a Porta-Potty. "What do you understand?"

"I understand Smutty and Mari." Nigel seemed barely aware of her, and she shivered.

When they'd made love the first time, it had been so intense, so amazing, and she'd felt so connected to him. She's felt his pain, and his anguish, and her own, and they'd connected over the burning within both of them.

The second time (she'd made love with him twice!) it had been amazing. Magical. Totally different. A seduction of utter peace. But at the same time, something had been missing. He hadn't been connected to her. He'd been off in some other place in his mind, just like he was now. She realized, with some surprise, that she preferred the former. Passion and connection were better than too much serenity.

Her clothes were strewn over the field as if they'd been ripped off in some lovemaking frenzy of such passion that they hadn't even known what they were doing. Which is what the first time had been. A connection that had overruled her fears and his monster. Her body warmed even at the memory of that intensity.

She crawled over to her bra and pulled it on. Nigel didn't even turn. Didn't even seem to notice that she'd moved away. A warrior who used to be so tuned in that he would have noticed the slightest shift in the wind was now oblivious? A chill rippled down her arms. "Nigel? Are you okay?"

"Smutty and Mari want to remove the pain," he said, not even hearing her question. "And that's when peace comes in. That's when life becomes the magic we have always wanted."

"Smutty wants to castrate everyone's dreams," Natalie corrected. Why was Nigel speaking of Mari and Smutty as if they were logical, sane do-gooders? "And Mari wants to scrape your mind empty until all that's left is a vegetable without enough brain cells to realize that you don't want to fall in love with whoever she wants you to love." God, the very idea made her stomach turn.

She knew what it was like to be stripped of your ability to choose who you slept with. It had been so awful to find herself walking so willingly into the Godfather's arms when her mind and her soul were screaming at her to stop.

"No. That's not what they want." Nigel rested his chin on his knees like a little boy, not a big, tough warrior. "They want peace, and now I understand how their idea will work. It was when you took away my anger that I was finally able to experience beauty and the peace I've been striving for my whole life."

Natalie paused as she reached for her underwear. "I did this to you? Turned you into…" A zombie who actually thought Mari and Smutty were right?

He turned toward her, and his face was utterly serene. Almost without expression. It was as if he was no longer human. Just a shell of a creature with no inner passion. "I've sought peace my whole life. I thought I found it with my art. But this—" He laid his hand over his heart with a gentleness that made chills bump on her arms. "This is different. This is serenity all the way down to my core. There's no monster that I'm trying to quiet. I simply *am* at peace, all the way through to my soul." He smiled, a distant expression. "I am happy."

"Really?" Natalie pulled on her underwear. "Are you sure?" It sounded good, theoretically, but the way Nigel was sitting there, naked, relaxed, and utterly unmindful of anything, it was wrong. Where was his passion? His fire? He was flat.

Then he smiled, and she told herself to dismiss her worries. It was good that he had peace. Now he could focus and do his thing, right? "So, you're ready to take on Mari?"

Nigel returned his gaze to the Shangri-La he was apparently viewing. "Ah, Mari."

"'Ah, Mari?' What does that mean?" She was getting a little concerned over his lack of response to Mari's name. "She's coming after us. Like now." She found her jeans over by third base and pulled them on. She picked up her shirt and Nigel's clothes, and then headed back over to him.

"I see her point." He didn't even notice when she held his clothes out to him. "Perhaps the greatest gift I can give Pascal and Blaine is this peace."

Natalie dumped the clothes at his feet. "It's not right to force it on them. They don't have the choice if you leave them there—" Her stomach rumbled suddenly, and she caught the scent of chocolate. Her head whipped around and she scanned the neighboring houses.

She immediately pinpointed the scent as emanating from the third house on the right. She took a step closer and sniffed again. "It's a person," she said. "A Sweet." Her teeth began to elongate. She took a step. And then another. And ano—

A child's scream pierced the night. She froze. Then she heard another scream, followed by laughter, and then she saw three young girls running through the backyard of the house she'd been headed toward. "Oh, my God. They're children. I was scenting *children*." She stumbled backwards. "Nigel—"

His arms closed around her and he pulled her against his chest. "I've got you, babe." His arms were like steel around her. "We'll take you to see Smutty. He'll clear that—"

"Smutty? Are you insane?" She wrenched out of his grasp and whirled to face him. "I don't want some unseen force directing my actions. I want to control myself. I want to be able to fight, to keep myself safe—"

"I can still fight. But I don't need to." He set his hands on his hips, proudly in the buff like some nature boy. "It's about peace."

Oh, no. What had she done? She ran over to him and grabbed his shoulders. "You're a warrior," she shouted, throwing all of her soul into the words. "You have fire and passion and—"

"Stop!" Nigel grabbed her arms and slammed his hand over her mouth to silence her. "You don't get to take this peace away from me. I won't let you."

She shoved his hand away. "But this is wrong! You won't want to be like this! You're empty and—"

"And I'm safe, dammit!"

"Safe?" She stared at him. "But you're always safe. You're a warrior. You're so tough you can—"

"I mean that I won't hurt others." He touched the bleeding wounds still in her body, the ones she hadn't even noticed. "Like I hurt you."

She looked down at them and saw that the cuts from the blades were already healing. "Why am I healing it this time?"

"The smut's turning you into a demon." He thumbed a wound thoughtfully. "Demons are pretty immortal."

"Oh, God." Her legs started to shake. "I can't handle this."

"You can." Nigel patted her shoulder. "Just chill out and you'll feel good."

"No, I won't! I'm going to start preying upon innocents if I don't stop this! That's not okay, and getting a lobotomy from Smutty isn't going to make it okay! And you're some tree-hugging freak now, and you can't keep me safe. For God's sake, you're actually thinking of handing Christian over to Smutty? What's wrong with you?" Dear God, what had she done to him?

"Hey!" He caught her arm. "I killed my own parents."

She stared at him, trying to grasp the sudden change of topic. "You what?"

His jaw was ticking, the only sign of the old Nigel she once knew. The one driven by passion. "When I was five, Angelica came to steal me away from my family. She had heard about my talents for art, and she thought I would be a good addition to the Den. Be a good example of how a man could tap into his inner artist."

Natalie rubbed her arms against the encroaching deedub numbness and tried to breathe through her mouth so she couldn't smell the chocolate. "Did your parents turn you over to her?" She remembered Reina telling her that Blaine's parents had sold him to Angelica.

"No, they tried to stop her." He sat down on the grass and crossed his legs. His face became distant again, as if he'd shut down the emotion that had just started to come to life. "They were gardeners. Simple people who spent their days with flowers and beauty. They weren't warriors." His body was relaxed, his voice devoid of the emotion that he should have had when talking about his dead parents.

She knelt next to him and touched his face. His skin was cool, lifeless. "Did you love them?" Anything to get him to tap into his passion again.

"Of course." But his voice was flat and he continued with his story, barely even registering her question. "My parents had no chance to stop Angelica." He picked a clover out of the grass by his feet and tickled the leaves over his forearm, smiling faintly at the sensation, like he was some drugged-out man. "My dad pulled me aside and told me to let Angelica take me, and then he would come after me with proper reinforcements and get me out. But that if I fought now, they would all lose."

"Seems logical, I guess." Angelica was tough to beat even by those trained to do so. What chance did ordinary people have against her?

Nigel set the clover on his bent knees and blew softly, so its tiny leaves rippled gently. "He was right, of course. That was our only chance. He was a brilliant man, and I knew he would find a way to get me. He'd never failed at anything in his life."

"But you didn't listen?" Natalie felt a sinking weight in her belly. "You fought?"

"I didn't want to go. I knew I was strong." He picked up a blade of grass and smoothed it across his knee beside the clover. Creating art, all the time. "So I unleashed my blades at Angelica."

Natalie grimaced. "It didn't work?"

He laughed softly. "Hell, no. I was five. She was a highly talented witch. She knocked me on my ass." Nigel's gaze returned to hers, and she could see hints of understanding in his eyes, but still a lack of emotion. It was as if he was talking about a movie he'd seen, not a life he'd lived. "I was terrified and angry as hell that she would take me. I lost it. My knives went everywhere. Living poison. I killed my parents almost instantly. I still remember the way my mom reached out for me before she fell." His voice got quiet. "She didn't blame me. She loved me until the end, and I murdered her."

Natalie's heart ached for his loss, for the anguish that had stalked him his whole life, pain that he now refused to feel. "I'm so sorry."

"My parents deserved better than for their son, who they loved, to turn on them." Nigel stood and turned his back to her. He clasped his hands behind his back and raised his face to the heavens. "I kept my talents under lockdown after that," he said quietly. "I drew until my fingers bled, keeping that anger and self-hate at bay. Using my art as an outlet, I shut down who I was so I could keep those around me safe."

Natalie walked up behind him and slid her arms around his waist. "I understand now." She understood his fear of being who he was. It was the same as her own fear of tapping into her own core. "It sucks to have to suppress who you are. To be afraid of the repercussions if you let your true self out."

He leaned against her, an intimacy that made her yearn for the old Nigel, the one who lived and fought and kissed with his soul. "And then, yesterday, I snapped. Nearly killed you." He turned toward her, his face grim, but still empty. Devoid of anguish and pain, but also of the happiness and joy he'd so recently displayed. The euphoria hadn't been real. He wasn't real now. "So, yeah, I'll take an emotional void over killing the people I care about all day long." He set his hand on her throat, gripping lightly. "And I won't let you take it away from me. Your safety, the safety of my team, it is more important than anything else."

"No, it's not! What's the point without you being a part of it?" She flung her fist against his chest. "I want to make you care! For God's sake, you want to leave Pascal there! That's awful you killed your parents. I get that. I stood around and couldn't save my family when they died. It sucks! I'm all alone, too! But dammit, I'm alive now, and I want the chance to live, to care, to not be afraid—"

"That's what I'm doing," he snapped. "I'm shutting down the crap so I won't endanger everyone."

"No, you're not!" How could she get through to him? He wasn't thinking. His aversion to hurting others was so strong he couldn't even see the value of his passion and his fire anymore. "You wanted to stop drawing so you didn't trap anyone else in the Den. You wanted to find a way to get focused so you could go in there and rescue your friends from the hell that you all suffered in for so long! And now you're flat, emotionless, and you don't care! You aren't even going to go get them back, are you?"

His fingers dug into her throat, a hint of the passion that had once driven him. "I'm going to give Pascal the gift of peace. That's what we all want, right? Everything we do in life, everything we yearn for, it's because we think it will make us happy." He knocked her hands off his shoulders and locked down her wrists. "You want to be free of fear because you think it'll make you happy. Well, I've got news for you, sweetie. Taking away my anger and my monster gave me peace, and it'll give him peace too, and that's what we all want."

"No, Nigel." She ripped her arms free. "Apathy is not the same thing. Taking away free will and passion and desire is a not a gift."

"Yes it is." He lightly thumbed her cheek. "You just don't understand, sweet girl."

"Oh, I understand! You want to hear my story?" She was so frustrated! She could feel darkness coursing through her, the pointiness of her teeth. She was turning into a demon and that was not acceptable! "My dad died when I was little, so I never knew him."

Nigel raised a brow that was far too cavalier. "Did you kill him yourself? Because that's what I did."

"No, I didn't." She shoved at him. "But a deedub attacked me, six of my sisters, and my mom when I was little. Do you know what happens when you get bitten by a deedub?"

"You eventually die."

"But do you know *how?*" She glared at him, angry that he was discounting her story. He wasn't the only one with a haunting past. "At some point, and no one knows when it will happen, the victim starts to get healthier and stronger and happier. They get this feeling of invincibility and pure euphoria for life, and then they go off on this high and push their limits until they get themselves killed. It's like a suicide drug." She hugged herself. "I spent my whole life terrified of every good mood I had, petrified each time I lifted something heavy, got stronger or taller or experienced any of the benefits of actually growing up, afraid that it meant the deedub poison was starting to work on me. Every time I faced a challenge and felt like I could overcome it, I'd do a double take, afraid that it was the first step down that path of suicidal invincibility."

Nigel was watching her now. Listening.

"I spent my whole life terrified of being happy or feeling good. As long as I was scared, miserable, weak, and afraid of life, I knew I was going to live another day."

"That's a crappy way to live," he observed.

"I know it is. I know now." She rubbed her arms, suddenly cold, despite the restlessness rampaging through her. "And then the deedub poison finally hit. I got caught in that thrall. I experienced what it was like to feel wildly carefree and unstoppable, to feel that life is about embracing every minute and not caring about the consequences."

He was watching her closely. "And it felt good?"

"It drove me to my own death." She kicked at a clump of grass. "But yeah, it felt good not to be afraid." She looked at him. "And that's what I want, Nigel. I want to enjoy life, to feel good, to appreciate the fun and the good moods, but I don't know how."

"Easy. Get Smutty to work on you."

"Even if I did want to abandon my brain over to some crazed dream genie, it won't solve my problem." She held out her hands, which were black with smut now. "It's happening again. Just like before. I'm headed down that same path again, toward a future I don't want, to becoming a person I don't want to be and can't stop." Her palms were blackened now, her fingernails growing longer and twisted, a deep demon-colored bronze.

Nigel brushed his finger over her palm, as if inspecting the change.

She looked at Nigel. "For me, there is nothing more terrible, more terrifying than having your free will to act taken away. And that's what Smutty and Mari are doing. They're taking away the free will of your friends. It's not peace. It's awful." She looked at him. "Like when you killed your parents. Your mind and your soul wanted one thing, and you were unable to make it happen." She searched his face. "You're betraying Pascal and Blaine by leaving them there. Your own friends!"

Nigel's eyes flashed with anger. "I am not going to

leave them there," he snapped. "I'm going to get them out. Is that really the kind of man you think I am?"

She blinked. "But I thought that's what you said? That Smutty will give them a gift—"

"He is. I'm going in there, I'm going to have Smutty give them peace, and then I'm taking them out."

"What? No—"

He grabbed her arm. "I owe them my life," he said. "And I'm going to give them the chance to look at a flower and see beauty instead of remembering the acid-laced toothpicks that jammed into their groin if they didn't stop to smell every flower. I'm going to give them the chance to sleep through the night instead of having nightmares about all the surprise, middle-of-the-night hellions that came to visit them." He gripped the back of her neck and his thumb caressed her nape with a tenderness that made her whole body tremble. "And I'm going to give to them the gift of being able to kiss a woman and feel the sheer poetic beauty of a female, instead of cringing at the pain and torture they know is coming." He kissed her once, and again, with such sensual beauty she almost started to cry.

How could this tortured warrior be capable of such beauty? How could this kind of passion have survived this hell? Because this was the real Nigel, not some creation of her Mystic powers. She'd taken away the anger, and this is what had remained. Would it really be that easy for the others? Take away the pain and then they could be happy? Was that all it took? Really? God, was Mari right?

But as Nigel began to kiss her again, so sweetly and so intently, as if he had all the time in the world, and no bad guys were closing in on them and the people they cared about, she realized that he wasn't actually his true self. Nigel was a man who loved with passion, as evidenced from his reaction to his parents and his need to protect his friends. By taking away his pain, she had also taken away his connection to those he loved, she'd taken away his desire to protect, to bond, and to connect. She'd taken away his fire, his understanding and appreciation of what it meant to be alive.

And she had her answer as to whether Mari was right. The answer was no. Which meant Nigel was wrong too. But how was she going to fix this?

Chapter 21

AH, YES. THIS IS WHAT HE'D BEEN LIVING FOR.

Nigel kissed Natalie again, basking in the feel of her lips. In the softness of her body. His mind was finally at peace, allowing him to absorb the beauty around him, allowing him to experience the full sensations of—

Natalie suddenly grimaced and pressed her hand to her stomach. "We really should have taken Mari's smut rod when we left."

"I'm so sorry, babe." Nigel gently caught her arm. He grasped that she was in pain, but he couldn't really register it. It felt like he was watching a movie in the distance. He was supposed to do something, wasn't he? Be upset? But he wasn't sure why. "We'll give Mari a call, and she'll clear up all the negative energy inside you."

"What?" Natalie smacked him lightly on the side of the head. "Are you insane? Get yourself together, Nigel! This is not the time for serenity—Ahh!" Bronze tendrils of smoke began to drift up from her head.

Uncertainty rippled through Nigel. This was a problem. He could see that it was. Something he should be concerned about, but he couldn't quite find his way to that place. It was like he was trapped in a gelatinous fog of tranquility.

"You bastard!" Christian shouted the warning a split second before he slammed his blade into the back of Nigel's head.

Nigel shoved Natalie behind him and whirled to face Christian. His teammate's face was pale, paler than a living creature's should be. His clothes were faded, and he looked almost like a specter. A ghostly image. "Holy crap. What happened to you?"

"This!" Christian held up his hand, and Nigel saw it was gone. Christian the Handless.

Nigel felt his fingers tingle, readying themselves for blades. "Where is it?"

"Where is it?" Christian whipped his sword out and had it at Nigel's chin. "You fucking drew me, you bastard. I'm getting sucked back in."

Nigel swore. "No, I didn't. I swear I didn't—"

"What did you draw in the Den when you were trying to heal Mari?"

"I didn't—" Nigel stopped, suddenly remembering he had drawn something. He tried to visualize the image in his head, but he couldn't place it. He shook his head. "I don't know." He'd been such a wreck then. He patted Christian's shoulder reassuringly. "But I'm good now. Natalie cleared me—"

Christian slammed his boot into Nigel's chest and knocked him down. He lodged the tip of his sword in Nigel's throat. Pressing.

Nigel didn't arm himself. His buddy was ticked, and engaging would just escalate the situation. It was time for de-escalation. Peace to everyone. "It's all going to be fine, Christian. There's nothing to worry about—"

"I can hear her voice." Christian pressed harder on Nigel's throat. "I can hear Smutty's. I can feel the wind that's too warm for out here." He looked around, a frantic, desperate glance that made something cold take root deep inside Nigel. "She's taking me." He jerked in pain suddenly and looked down at his left hand. "Shit!" Christian's left arm dissolved from sight.

"Huh." Faint alarm pulsed through his serenity. Something was wrong. Peace was an illusion? His mind was shouting at him to be on the alert, to take action, but his body was consumed by a great lethargy, an inability to generate any action or urgency. Nigel rose to his feet just as a white light began to glow over the pitcher's mound. In the middle of the globe, Mari appeared. "Check that out."

"Mother of hell," Christian whispered. He raised his sword and charged the mound.

"No!" Nigel tackled him and brought him down. "Don't attack her. It's going to be all right." Yes, yes, it was. Mari was here to give Christian peace. "Trust me, it'll be worth it. You'll feel so good after she gets done with you." But something tugged at his mind, a nudge that all was not well. That all was not right. But he couldn't wrap his mind around it.

"I'm not going back!" Christian began to be dragged across the ground toward the mound. His face was stricken and sweat was beading down his cheek. "I can't stop it." He jammed his sword into the earth, a pickax against the demons of hell. Not really going to be effective.

"Listen to me," Nigel said. "It sucks to be emotionally tortured. Let her heal your soul, and then I'll come in and get you. I swear it."

"You swore you'd kill me before you'd let me be taken." His sword was ripping a chasm in the field as he was dragged slowly toward Mari. "Kill me."

Nigel didn't like the look of terror, of hell, of pain

on Christian's face. "It's not worth it to die, trust me. Aren't you tired of suffering? Let her clear you—"

"No, mother fucker! I won't let her touch my mind. Not again!"

Nigel hesitated. Something felt wrong. Yes, Mari taking Christian was good because peace was the greatest gift he could give his friend, but deep in his mind, something was resisting, something wanted to fight.

Christian was suddenly jerked away from him, tumbling across the infield toward the glowing human bubble. He let out a bellow of fury.

Nigel watched him go. "Christian! I swear I'll come get you. Let yourself go. It's worth it—"

Christian looked over his shoulder, saw Mari getting closer. Inches away now, he flipped his sword around so the tip was pointing at his own chest.

"Oh, *hell*." Nigel broke into a sprint. "Don't—"

Christian plunged his own blade right into his own heart.

Mari screamed, Christian's head fell back, his sword dropped to the earth, and then he was swept into the bubble.

"No!" Nigel lunged for his friend, his fingers brushed over the toe of his boot, and then he was gone.

Nigel somersaulted over the mound and landed on his feet. He whirled around and raced back to where the portal had been, but the air was still. It was gone. "Son of a bitch."

He grabbed Christian's sword off the dirt and ran his hand over the blade. The blood was thick and purple, and he felt its contamination immediately. It had been a killing blow. Christian was immortal, but even he wouldn't survive it. He'd be dead within the hour, and his last moments of life were going to be at the hands of Mari. "Son of a bitch."

He sank to his knees in stunned shock, staring at the blade. Christian had chosen death over being taken. Nigel bowed his head. Why hadn't he seen that coming? Why hadn't he understood Christian's desperation?

He gripped the sword in disbelief. He'd let Christian be taken? He threw back his head and roared with fury, with all the anger that he'd been deprived of three minutes ago. What had he done? What price had he paid for peace? Everything Nigel had wanted his whole life, and he'd gotten it, and it had led to the death of his closest friend? What the hell was he doing? Anger that would unleash killing blades into those he loved? Or peace that would render him incapable of saving his own friend? What was right? *What was the goddamn answer?*

"Nigel!" Natalie's faint scream penetrated his subconscious, and he sensed the desperation in her voice. He couldn't *feel* it in his empty-as-shit soul, but instinct made him look up. Natalie wasn't near him, where he'd last left her.

"Nigel!" Her voice sounded distant now, desperate, fading, but he couldn't tell where it was coming from. Which was weird, because he always knew every threat, every move, and could sense anything.

Nigel stood up and turned, scanning the field. More and more quickly. A sense of urgency was beginning to build in his mind, even though his body was still relaxed, unable to respond to the threat.

And then he saw her. She was being dragged toward a chariot with six white horses by a man who was too hunchbacked to ignore. Augustus. The assassin had her.

How had Nigel missed out on that happening? How had he not sensed it? He hadn't simply lost his anger, he'd lost everything that made him who he was.

"Hang on!" Nigel grabbed Christian's sword and sprinted toward the chariot. "Natalie—"

Augustus threw her into the chariot with ease. His body had grown back, and he looked almost whole. "It is my turn to have her," he shouted at Nigel. "You can come pick her up at her store in two hours." And then he hurled a three-pointed pink triangle at Nigel.

"I need her now!" Nigel blocked the triangle with Christian's sword, but his movement was awkward and sluggish. The assault weapon dodged the sword easily and plunged itself into Nigel's chest.

The pain was impressive.

The fact that every muscle in his body froze up as he was flung backwards onto his ass? Not good.

His feeling of uselessness as he watched the chariot and Natalie zoom over the very spot where Christian had just disappeared? Complete and total hell.

He'd fucked up.

Big-time.

Christian dead. Natalie abducted. Pascal gone. Blaine gone. It was all because of his obsession with peace. His inability to control himself like the man he was supposed to be, which had prompted him to ask for outside aid. Screw that. He was taking his old self back, and it had to be fast, before it was too late to stop the slide. There was only one woman who could fix it. *Natalie*.

Slowly, willing strength into his body, he reached up and tried to dislodge the triangle from his chest. But he had as much control over his body as someone who'd been on a six-day bender. Something in the weapon had petrified his muscles, and he had a bad feeling that it was going to last for the full two hours that Augustus had claimed. He couldn't afford two hours. By then Christian would be dead, and Natalie would be a deedub. Two hours would be too late.

Which meant he had to find a way to get this shit out of his system, and fast, or everything was going down.

Natalie had never really considered herself a tea and crumpets kind of girl.

Being chained up to one of her own brass stools, while a crusty old assassin, who smelled of rotten bananas and too many dead bodies, served her tea and virility balls in her own store, was not going to change her mind.

Augustus crossed his legs and picked up a plate of balls. "Would you like some?"

The chocolate scent hit hard, and Natalie's stomach cramped. "Please take that away from me." Even as she said it, her arms twitched and strained against the chains. They weren't metal but were some kind of pink, glowing gelatinous substance that felt cold and clammy against her skin. They stretched with her movements but never gave her room to navigate. They were tight, alive, and keeping her bound.

Where was Nigel? What had happened to him? He'd turned away for a split second when Christian had arrived, and Augustus had grabbed her.

She couldn't afford to be here. She needed to fix him after she'd pretty much destroyed him. She needed to bring him back to his deadly, out-of-control state of mania to stop Mari. To stop the smut. To help him rescue his friends. Dammit! With every minute, she was catapulting toward hell, and God only knew what had happened to Nigel. For all she knew, he could have joined a meditation choir by now and was on his way to some retreat in Vermont! *Nigel!* She screamed his name in her mind. But of course, there was no answer. Funny, that.

"Nonsense, my dear. Chocolate cures all." Augustus took a bite, and then frowned when one of his teeth came out lodged in the ball. "Look at that, will you? I'm still not healed." He sighed and set the plate of goodies down. "Listen, my dear, we really need to talk." He looked around and lowered his voice. "I'm really worried that I'm going to kill myself."

Sharp pain hit her in the belly, and Natalie winced. How much more smut could she take and stay sane? Remain herself? "Listen, get yourself bitten by a deedub. Then you'll be on a high."

"No, no." Augustus leaned forward. "You had a passion in you that day that transcended any kind of poison. It was you, not the deedub effect." He touched her knee. "What were you thinking about? How do you keep your faith?"

"It's my faith in Nigel that keeps me sane." Her head was starting to throb, but she knew she was speaking the truth. She wasn't as terrified and weak as she'd felt before, and the difference was Nigel. He believed in her, he'd showed her she could make love without becoming insane, and he'd showed her that she had strength. She smiled, realizing that somewhere along the line she'd started to feel better. Yeah, the deedub future was a drag, but other than that... she was different.

"Nigel?" Augustus snorted. "He's an artist, not an inspiration."

"He's the one who grounds me. Let's go ask him." The scent of rich, decadent chocolate assaulted her nose and her head whipped around as Ella and Maggie came rushing in from the back of the store. Oh, man, she did *not* need a chocolate distraction right now.

"Natalie!" Ella looked horrified. "What's going on?"

But all Natalie could concentrate on was Maggie. She could sense the dark amber of her blood rushing beneath the surface of her skin, carrying that magical, powerful chocolate to every part of her body. Her skin looked succulent and rich, drenched with temptation.

"Oh, no." Maggie stopped. "Something's wrong with Natalie."

"No, no, nothing's wrong." Natalie heard the denial of her voice, and she cringed. "No, run," she whispered. "Go…"

But her words were too quiet.

No one heard.

"Go away," Augustus said. "We're having girl time."

Ella was circling, moving closer, a wary look on her face. Ella might be a boring old hedonism professor, but she'd known instantly that something was wrong. Either she had a history of bad news situations, or the hot pink chains had clued her in. Either way, her response had been to step into the fire instead of backing away. A true friend. "Looks like fun girl time," she said gently. "I'm a girl. Can I join?"

Augustus frowned. "Only if you have suggestions on how to find joy in life."

"Oh, that's easy." Ella got nearer, and Natalie saw

she was eying the chains. "Find your passion in life and follow that."

"But I'm doing that," Augustus said. "And I hate it."

The scent of chocolate grew stronger. More tempting. She slowly raised her head and watched Maggie. The girl was standing beside the counter, gripping the edge of it, as if she felt a threat coming on. *Run, Maggie, run.*

But the words were silent in Natalie's head, and she couldn't make them come out. Natalie realized she was licking her lips. Oh, come on! Seriously! This was just pathetic! She was stronger than this! She did *not* have to become a deedub!

"Then you need to find a new career," Ella was saying to Augustus. "It's possible you feel bad about killing everyone and inflicting pain, and it's time you found a career that makes a positive difference in the world to make up for all the damage you already caused."

Natalie realized Ella was behind her now. Fiddling with the chains. Loosening them. Yes, yes. God, yes. They had to get out. She had to get to Mari and stop this demonic onslaught.

While she waited for Ella to work her talents, Natalie closed her eyes and thought of Nigel's kisses, of his body against hers, of how it had felt when he'd made love to her. Of the way he'd unleashed that passion the first time, so desperate for her. She allowed that excitement to pulse through her. She tapped into the power she knew was deep in her soul (if she could castrate Nigel's spirit, she was pretty certain she had at least a modicum of power).

"Yes," Ella said under her breath encouragingly.

"Tap into your power, Nat. Access your inner sensuality and influence yourself."

Oh... good idea! Influence herself to not want to have Maggie for dessert? That was brilliant! "I'm on it." She thought back to that moment of lovemaking with Nigel. Smelled the freshly cut grass. Felt the dust from the in-field on her fingers. Heard the rumble of Nigel's voice as he spoke to her. As he shared his need. As he shared his passion. She recalled the feel of his skin against hers, the intimacy of his hands on her hips.

"Oh, my." Augustus sounded throaty and gruff. "Natalie is quite flushed. Is that from me?"

Natalie scrunched her eyes shut and concentrated on Nigel's face. On the flower on his cheekbone. On the way his eyes carried so much emotion and power. She felt her lower body began to thrum, felt desire pulse through her.

"Do it now," Ella whispered. "You're tapped in."

"You are in complete control, Natalie," Natalie said aloud, focusing all her energy into herself. "You are not tempted by Maggie. Your mind is your own, and your body will do exactly as your mind and your soul desire. You are a powerful, courageous creator." Her body hummed with the power of her words, and she gasped as shocks and fire ripped through her, and her body convulsed from the force of her emotion.

Ella caught her as she fell off the chair. "You're okay. I've got you." She helped Natalie to the floor, and Natalie rolled onto her side, hugging herself as the tremors ripped through her.

Wow. She understood now why Nigel had been so startled. "That was weird."

"It was awesome!" Ella squatted next to Natalie and grinned. "All I've got to say is wow, girl. You knocked yourself out with your own words. Impressive." She winked. "I knew you had it in you."

She grinned back. "You were awfully insistent about it, if I remember. A bit bossy, actually."

Ella winked. "No one ever accused me of being too genteel with my opinions."

"You smell like sex." Augustus dropped to his knees in front of her, his eyes wide. "I've never felt that kind of sensuality in my life. It's not raw, empty sex, like I've been leading. It was passion. Sensuality. Desire." He leaned closer. "No wonder you are so alive, with that passion coursing through your body. That's it! That's what I've been missing. Passion!" He reached for her—

"No, thanks!" Natalie quickly squirmed out of his reach. See? Look at her? All worked up and *not* tempted to jump into any man's lap, except Nigel's! Not crazy sex woman! Go her! She moved to the right and froze when she realized Maggie was right next to her.

Maggie was peering at her with great concern. "How are you doing?"

"Um…" Oh, wow. The scent of chocolate was nearly asphyxiating, it was so powerful. Natalie tensed, her heart racing. "I don't think—"

"You're not bronze anymore." Ella slapped Natalie on the shoulder with delight. "You did it! You released the deedub from yourself."

"Really?" Her skin had returned to its gray smutty color that was so much more comforting than the bronze demon tint. A quick teeth check revealed that there were no more pointy fangs. Smutted? Yup. Demonic? Not today, baby! Carefully, she took a deep breath through her nose. The chocolate smelled delicious, but Maggie no longer looked like dessert. "I did it." She grinned at Ella. "I really did it."

She had just won the battle. Maggie was safe. Everything was going to be just fine.

Chapter 22

THERE HAD BEEN TIMES THAT MARI HAD SEEN Angelica cry while standing over the dying bodies of her warriors, but Mari had never really believed it. How could a woman who inflicted so much pain on others have feeling in her heart?

But as Mari sat on the edge of Christian's bed and felt his life force seep away, she finally understood what her mentor had endured, watching the deaths of the very men she wanted so desperately to protect and nurture. How had this happened? She had tried so hard to help. To protect and not hurt. And yet somehow, everything had spiraled out of control.

Mari took Christian's hand and held it to her heart. "I'm so sorry," she whispered. Her body felt numb, her chest painful and heavy as she stroked his hair.

Pascal groaned and twisted in his bed, and Mari looked over at him. He hadn't woken up from Charlie's manipulations to his mind, and she had no way of knowing if it had worked, or what kind of brain function Pascal had retained, but she had a bad feeling. His energy aura had been mottled and weak, not at all like his usual one.

The door opened, and in walked Danielle carrying a smoothie. She paused when she saw Mari, then her jaw tightened and she averted her gaze as she strode across the room. She sat down on the far side of Pascal's bed and settled herself against the headboard. She pulled him onto her lap and gently nudged the straw between his lips. "Come on, Pascal. You don't want Mari to win, do you? If you live, you can defeat her."

Mari stiffened. "I'm not the enemy—"

"You are." Danielle's voice was nonjudgmental but very matter-of-fact. "You're perpetuating the same hell that Angelica had going on, and you're hurting the warriors. And us."

"That's not true!" Mari felt like smacking the wall in frustration. "Angelica didn't want us to love, but I believe in love and I'm trying to bring it to all of you."

"Whatever." Danielle began to stroke Pascal's hair, and Mari saw his throat move as he tried to swallow.

Hope filled her, and Mari raced over to the bed. "You got him to drink!"

Danielle held up her hand to block Mari. "Get back. You'll screw him up."

Mari saw Pascal's throat had stopped moving, and he'd fallen back onto the bed. She'd become the kiss of death toward all these men she wanted to help? How could that have happened? Mari sank back on Christian's bed, watching as Danielle lifted Pascal back onto her lap and began to talk to him again. Mari stroked his hair, like a lover would do in the most intimate of moments.

Mari remembered sitting by Christian's side so many times as he'd fought death, and she'd felt so helpless. She'd wanted desperately to offer him comfort like Danielle was giving Pascal, but she hadn't dared go against Angelica's orders.

No kindness to the men.

No love for the men.

No softness for the men.

Mari had blindly followed the rules, and then when her heart had found Christian, she'd fought those rules. When she'd finally found the nerve to reach out to him, the magic between them had been magnificent... until Angelica had found out and convinced Mari that betraying Christian and his friends would be the greatest act of love she could perform.

How wrong she'd been.

Christian had been all that she could have hoped for. He'd been on his way to break out of the Den, and then he'd come back for her. He'd rescued her from Angelica at risk to himself. He'd played the role of the knight in shining armor, and then she'd betrayed him.

And now, he'd killed himself to keep from coming back to her. First, she'd ripped out his heart, and then she'd been responsible for the obliteration of his life.

No! She wasn't giving up! "Danielle. Give me the smoothie."

"What?" Danielle cradled it protectively. "Get your own drink."

Mari held out her hand and crooked her finger. The smoothie flew out of Danielle's grasp and careened across the room and smacked into Mari's hands.

"Hey!"

Mari ignored Danielle's outburst and turned to Christian. After a moment of hesitation, she snuggled herself up against his headboard and pulled his head onto her lap, just like Danielle had done. Just like she'd always dreamed of doing when he'd been suffering. As the weight of his head settled on her thighs, she knew this was who she wanted to be. A woman who nurtured and loved. Who didn't torture or abuse.

"Christian," she said gently. "I swear I'll never hurt you again. I just need you to eat." She touched the straw to his lips. "Give yourself another chance. I know you can heal this. Nigel will draw himself soon, and he'll be in here, and then he'll heal you. It's not over. You deserve love, and I have that for you—"

Christian gagged and his body convulsed. His skin flashed once, and then his flesh morphed into steel. The metal burned her side, and she wrenched herself out from under him, stumbling away as her skin turned purple and began to seep with toxins from his scales. "Dammit!"

A small smile was playing at Danielle's lips. "He poisoned you on purpose?" Danielle was still stroking Pascal's hair. He hadn't moved away from her touch. Hadn't gone into his scaly assault mode to fend her off. He was allowing her to comfort him. To heal him. To bring him back.

Christian's skin returned to a flesh state, ashen and gaunt. The wound on his belly was a deep purple and black. Mari bit her lip. Never had she felt so helpless. "What do I do? I'm trying to make it right."

"He's a warrior. They never forget." Danielle laid her palm on Pascal's forehead. "Turn him free, and then let him kill you. That's what he needs to do to heal."

Mari set the smoothie down beside Christian, in case he changed his mind. "Ha, ha."

"I wasn't joking." Danielle snuggled closer to Pascal. "If you truly love Christian, let him kill you. He won't be whole until he releases the hate and betrayal he is carrying."

"There are ways to release it without killing me." If Christian wouldn't save himself, she would do it for him, just like she'd originally planned. "Charlie can fix him."

"No!" Danielle stood up. "Don't you dare subject Christian to that incompetent loser. Look what he did to Max. And Pascal."

Mari bit her lip. "I know, but he was still heavily smutted. If I clear him completely, then—"

"He's incompetent and insane—"

"He's my only chance." Mari leaned down and kissed Christian's forehead. "I know you want to die," she said quietly, "but I won't let you kill yourself because of me." She squeezed his hand, and then jerked back as he turned to metal again.

"Smutty will have to lobotomize him to rid Christian of that hate," Danielle said. "He won't let it go that easily."

"It's worth the chance to give Christian life. If I can free him of the hatred, then he'll want to live again." No more men would die because of her. *No more.* It ended now. Mari grabbed her baton from beside Christian's bed. "Stay alive," she ordered him. "I'm going to go clear all the smut from Charlie and give him full power. Then you'll have the gift of happiness that you deserve."

"No!" Danielle tried to block her path. "Charles wants to strip all of us of all our dreams, not just the warriors! The minute you give him that power, he'll come after us all—"

"I won't let Christian die." Mari stepped out in the hall, gripping the baton in her hand. "I can control Charlie."

Danielle ran after her and caught her arm. "He's a

dream genie, Mari. No one can control them. You can't give him full power. You can't!"

Mari tugged her arm free. "I'm doing it for you, too."

Danielle made a noise of despair. "I don't want it. I don't want a man to love me because you stripped his mind of everything else. That's not love—"

"It's the purest form of love, because it allows the soul to be heard." She nodded at Christian. "He has the most beautiful soul, and I'm giving it back to him."

Christian groaned. His skin flickered and little sparks started shooting off him. "Oh, no." She had minutes left to save him.

"Don't—"

Mari shoved Danielle aside and raced for the tower room, toward Smutty, baton in hand.

Natalie felt strong. Powerful. A woman in control. It felt brilliant. She'd talked herself out of a future she didn't want and suppressed her deedub infatuation with Maggie. Nigel had helped her finally overcome her phobia of letting go. Ironically, it was the act of giving up restraint that had given her the most security over her life she'd ever had.

"You're amazing." Augustus leaned forward, trying to shove his face way too close to her girly parts.

She cheerfully smacked him in the head, feeling so empowered and strong that she wasn't even afraid of the world's most deadly assassin anymore. "Back off, old man."

His pupils were dark, expanding over nearly his entire cornea. "You are so sensual. I've never thought of sex as anything but a slap and tickle. But that..." He put his hand over his belly. "That hit me right here. I've never felt so alive."

Yeah, okay, so he was still creepy. "Well, there's your answer then. That's how I stay happy. I tap into my inner sensuality. Now call off the chains. I have things to take care of."

Augustus eased back onto his heels, staring into the distance with a vacant expression too reminiscent of Nigel's recent one. "I've been missing passion in my life. Who knew?"

Ella touched Natalie's shoulder. "Are you sure you're okay?" Her brow was wrinkled with concern. "I mean, your aura feels good, but those inclinations could still be beneath the surface—"

"Yes, I'm great." Natalie tugged at the chains. "I need to find Nigel. He needs my help." She kicked Augustus, who was still staring off into space, rubbing his chin contemplating his discovery that he'd been having too much superficial sex. "Let me go!"

He glanced vaguely at her. "Oh, yes, yes, fine." He waved his hand and the chains dissolved.

Natalie tumbled forward into Maggie's lap as the chains suddenly released her. "My power of suggestion works on Magicks now," she told the younger woman. "When a deedub comes, I can handle him. Do you understand? We're safe now—" Sudden pain hit her in the gut, like a knife to her belly. She gasped and went down to her knees, clutching her stomach. More smut? Come on! Couldn't she get a break for one minute?

Ella and Maggie grabbed her, and Augustus stepped over her, strolling toward the door while scribbling notes on a pad. "What's wrong?" Ella asked.

But Natalie couldn't answer. The pain was too extreme. It was attacking every cell in her body. She felt like millions of needles were stabbing her soul, and an acid-laced sword was carving out her belly. Her hands clenched, her feet cramped, and her head began to pound.

"Natalie!" Ella grabbed her shoulders, and she pulled Natalie close. "You are stronger than this. Talk it down."

But she started to tremble, and the odor of sulfur burned her nose. *Demon sulfur.* She pushed Maggie. "Get away," she gasped. "Run!"

Maggie's eyes widened, and she stumbled to her feet. "Oh, no." She bolted for the front door.

Natalie's body went rigid, her throat felt like it had closed up, and then fire spewed through her veins, burning her from the inside. *Nigel!* She screamed his name in her head. *Nigel! Help me!*

"Get control," Ella yelled at her. "You can do it."

And suddenly the pain was gone, replaced only with a feeling of utmost power. She stared at Ella with a sinking feeling. Ella's face fell. "It's too late?"

"It's too late," she whispered as she inhaled the most delicious scent of chocolate. "I need Maggie." She pushed Ella away and leapt to her feet in time to see Maggie race past the front window. As her soul recoiled in horror, even as the memories of her own sister's victimized bodies flashed in her mind, Natalie turned and sprinted toward the window.

She lowered her shoulder and shoved through the glass. The glass splintered everywhere with the delicious sound of breaking crystal. She leapt through the opening and tackled Maggie. They skidded across the pavement, and the asphalt scraped Natalie's skin.

But she didn't care. All she could think about was the amazing scent of chocolate, of how delicious Maggie would taste.

They crashed to a stop against the front tire of Natalie's Hummer. Natalie pinned Maggie to the cement and grinned down at her. "Hello, my Sweet."

"Please, don't," Maggie gasped. "Please, you know you don't want to."

"I—" Maggie's terrified expression broke through the thrall holding Natalie so tightly. She pulled back, horrified. She couldn't do to this girl what had been done to her. She couldn't be that monster. She couldn't—

"Welcome to the family, my dear."

She looked up and saw the deedub that had killed her entire family sitting on the bumper of her car. Fear ricocheted down her spine and at the same time, a pulse of recognition. Of admiration. "Oh... this can't be a good thing."

He was wearing a tuxedo with a red rose boutonniere, and a black and silver evening gown was draped over his arm. A pair of diamond-studded pumps were sitting on the hood next to him.

"Tell him to leave," Maggie gasped. "You can do it."

"Right." Natalie tried to summon her power, but the deedub interrupted before she could focus.

"Welcome, my dear," her deedub said with a cheerful smile. "You know, it's really not good PR for Sweets to start thinking they can escape a deedub bite, you know? My rep was a little sketchy there for a bit, but now that you're coming over, I'm a hero." He grinned, a thin, evil smile. "You're the first conversion in over a thousand years, and I did it." He held up a ring that had a blood red diamond on it and flashed a fanged smile at her. "My name's Ricky Freese, and thanks to you, I'm inner circle now. It's going to be some kind of party tonight."

"Party?" she echoed, her mind still trying to focus. What was wrong with her? Why couldn't she summon up the energy to shut him out? And why did she have an urge to leap up, run over to him, and hug him like he was her long lost best friend?

He held up the dress. "This is for you. For your inauguration ball. We don't get new deedubs very often, so we always celebrate." He grinned. "I'm your date."

A deedub ball? Would Satan be the emcee? Would there be cauldrons of boiling acid positioned strategically around the corners for bad little girls and boys? "I can't." She tried to let go of Maggie, but she couldn't peel her fingers out of the girl's shoulders. Her teeth began to elongate—

"Natalie!" Maggie shouted, jerking Natalie out of her stupor.

"I won't do this." She ripped herself off Maggie and slammed her foot into Ricky's crotch. "Run, Maggie!" Natalie whirled around and sprinted down the street. Away from Ricky. Away from Maggie. Away from herself. *Run. Run. Run. Run*—

The deedub appeared in front of Natalie and slammed his hands into her chest. She careened backwards and landed on her butt. Thick, noxious smoke swirled around him. "Sorry, sweetheart, but I'm not losing again. You're coming with me." He had Maggie under his arm, her struggles useless against his strength.

Natalie lurched to her feet. "Let her go!" She threw everything she had into those words, but they were empty, meaningless, powerless. Oh… no. Was her power linked only to Nigel and how he made her feel? Was he the only one who could summon her true self?

He shoved Maggie at her. "Smell her!" he commanded.

"No, no, no." She stumbled backward, away from her desire to do exactly what he wanted. She could almost taste the chocolate. Almost feel the rush. And the horror. She felt like throwing up. "No—"

He grabbed Natalie by the hair and shoved her face into Maggie's neck. "Breathe! Now!"

She struggled against his strength. She wasn't going to fail again. Wasn't going to succumb. Wasn't going to be the woman she didn't want to be—

And then she caught a whiff. A delicious amazing tease of the most decadently delicious scent she'd ever inhaled in her life. Longing pulsed through her, a sense of absolute rightness. This is what she needed to do. Who she was meant to be.

"Yes, yes." Ricky's hand softened on her hair, and he stroked it. "Bite her. Bite her now. Become one of us."

She opened her eyes and saw Maggie's terrified face. Something lurched inside her, something screamed at her to stop, to listen to who she was… and then it died.

It simply died.

And all that was left was the demon.

Chapter 23

NIGEL SPRINTED AROUND THE CORNER AND SAW Natalie at the far end of the block, locked down by a kid in a tux, with Maggie shouting furiously in the boy's arms. "Shit!" Fangs had elongated past Natalie's beautiful lips. Her delicate, flawless skin was bronzed sandpaper, her silken hair like copper wire. He could smell the chocolate from here and knew she was about to cross the line from which she could never go back. "Natalie!"

She looked up, and her face crumpled at the sight of him. "Nigel!" Her voice was desperate, and she reached out to him with one hand, reaching for him. Begging for his help.

"I'm here!" He ran harder, and his palms burned as he called forth his blades. He would not fail her, too. *He would not fail.*

"Bite her!" The deedub grabbed her hair and shoved her face down into Maggie's neck.

"Don't touch her!" Nigel whipped his hand back to throw the blades... but nothing was there. What the hell? He looked down at his hand and saw no metal. Just charred palms. His body went cold, ice cold. *He'd lost his blades.* Peace had stolen from him the very essence of who he was? Not good!

Maggie screamed as Natalie bared her teeth over the girl's throat. "Stop!" He sprinted toward them, but he knew he wouldn't get there in time. "Natalie," he shouted. "You can defeat this!"

And it was like some hellacious vision, watching Natalie's face twist in horror as she descended toward Maggie. He saw the look of triumph on the deedub's face, and Nigel couldn't do anything. Couldn't get there. Had no weapons. *Mother of hell.*

He launched himself into the air, still yards away, bellowing.

Natalie looked up at him, met his gaze, horror reverberating in her eyes, and then sank her teeth into Maggie's neck.

———※———

Natalie gasped as Nigel tackled her, pulling her away from Maggie and the deedub. They skidded across the pavement, and he protected her in the shield of his body.

The deedub let out a triumphant roar and held his arms up toward the sky. "And she belongs to us!"

"No, I don't." Natalie twisted in Nigel's arms as he shoved her back, away from Maggie. The Sweet was unconscious on the asphalt, two tooth marks in her neck. Infected. By Natalie. "Oh, my God."

Ricky thrust the dress at her. "Come, come, my dear. It's time for the party."

"Get away from me!" She'd become her worst nightmare. The very thing that had destroyed her whole family. "Maggie? Are you okay?" She started to crawl toward the girl, caught a whiff of chocolate, and her fangs elongated still further. Oh, come on! "Um, Nigel?"

"I've got you." He pulled her back just as the deedub turned toward Maggie and sniffed.

"Well, well, lots left to eat," Ricky said. "Can't give up a chance for a Sweet." He started toward Maggie.

"No!" Natalie commanded. "You will leave her here!"

He snorted, her orders useless against him. "No chance—"

"I disagree." Nigel set Natalie aside, then grabbed the deedub and threw him against Natalie's car. "You don't get to have the girls. They're mine." Nigel's voice wasn't as dark and deadly as it used to be. It was almost conversational, but his eyes were tormented. As if the warrior in him was fighting to get free, but it was trapped by the spell she'd put on him. Which, apparently, was exactly what was going on.

"Don't take away my rewards," Ricky snapped. He wrenched himself out of Nigel's grasp, ripped a parking meter out of the street, then upended it into Nigel's head. Nigel went flying and landed in a pile near a trash can.

"Nigel!" Natalie dropped beside him as he hit the dirt, his head bleeding from a crevice in his skull. This was her fault. The normal Nigel would never have been vulnerable to a second-rate assailant like Ricky. But she'd stolen everything that made Nigel who he was.

"I'm fine. Just need a second." He struggled to his sitting position as the deedub threw Maggie over his shoulder.

"Get yourself cleaned up, Natalie," Ricky said. "Just a note regarding proper deedub etiquette: It's not polite to sic your pathetic boyfriend on your dates."

"No! Stop!" She tried to grab him, and he backhanded her back to the pavement.

"Be nice. I'm taking the girl. Others would love a bite of this succulence. You can have the leftovers when you get there. I'll be back in twenty minutes to get you." His upper lip curled. "Be dressed and ready, my pretty."

"Don't take her!" Natalie stumbled to her feet. "Don't—"

Nigel yanked her back and forced her to face him. "Undo it, Natalie! Take the peace off me! Now!"

She fought to get free. "I can't—"

"You can. In order to stop him, you need to free me." He held her arms so tightly she knew he was leaving marks. "Tap into it, Natalie. I know you can. Bring it on. I can stop him."

She started to look over her shoulder at the deedub to see if he'd left yet, but Nigel turned her back toward him, his touch gentle on her chin. "No, sweetheart." His voice was eerily calm, not him, but it was still soothing to her. "It's only about me right now." He set his hand on her heart. "Feel my presence and my comfort. I can keep you safe when you tap into your sensuality. Trust me. Just trust me."

She saw the fierceness buried deep in his soul, the warrior who had once been free to take on the world. She felt his determination to shed this artificial peace consuming him. She felt his soul reach for hers, and suddenly a deep warmth was surrounding her, penetrating the coldness of her body. She gripped his hands and opened herself to his strength. "Your blades are violent and dangerous," she said. The words were tingling, heavy. Not powerful, but at least they were alive. "You are the man you were before I interfered."

Nigel's shoulders shuddered, and his body rippled with strength. "More." He cupped her face and pressed his forehead to hers, his lips to hers, the ultimate in intimacy. "I feel your spirit wrapped around mine," he whispered. "Let me have your whole soul. Open your soul to me, Natalie."

Power swelled in her chest like a hurricane, and she felt her walls tumble down. "Your blades are deadly, and you live and fight with passion, with anger, with every fiber of your soul," she said. "You're a warrior!"

He flew backwards, his hands ripping out of hers as he was slammed into a fire hydrant. His face contorted with fury, with fierceness, with the eyes of the warrior. He was back!

Relief cascaded through her, and she felt like cheering. Who knew she'd be so happy to see the monster again?

Nigel blew her a kiss as he leapt to his feet. "You don't get to take the girl," he called to Ricky. Dozens of blades flashed in his palms, and he hurled them at the deedub.

Ricky yelped and staggered backward as the blades hit him. "Too late, you dumb bastard. All the women are mine!" Then he disappeared into a thick wall of purple smoke with Maggie.

"Too late? We're too late?" Natalie was too stunned to move, riveted to the pavement in shock at the disappearance of Maggie and Ricky. "I bit her." Her soul was black, black, black. She'd fallen into the trap, and this time, it wasn't herself she'd killed. It was someone else.

And Maggie was only the first. What about those little girls she'd seen running in the field? They were Sweets. Those girls could be next!

She pictured the young Sweets, and suddenly her revulsion was replaced with thoughtfulness. Then anticipation roiled through her, and she rose to her feet. She knew where to find them. She would just go and—

Oh, no. What was she doing? "Nigel," she gasped. "I think I need help."

But when she looked over at him, he was hunched over, hands on his knees, taking deep breaths. "The blades are trying to take over again." He bunched his fists, and his body vibrated with the effort of containing them. "We went too far."

Natalie's stomach cramped, and she thought of those girls again. Took a step toward her car. She could drive there. Be there in ten. "Nigel. I'm going to go kill those girls."

He looked up, and his face was stricken. "Don't tell me that. Pisses me off that I didn't protect you. Need to pull my shit together. Can't think of a plan when I'm losing my mind over worry for you." He gave her a grim smile. "You distract me, my love, which is lovely, but it's really not helping right now."

My love? She really wished she had time to delve more deeply into that comment. But she was at the car now and about to head off onto a deadly field trip. "Don't suppress your weapons. Unleash them. Take me out." Tears filled her eyes at her request. But what else was there? She would not hurt anyone else. She wouldn't. "Hit me with them. Make it end."

"No!" He grabbed her and pinned her against the car, but there was a thoughtfulness to his expression, as if an idea was ruminating in his mind. "Don't even say that. We're going to save you, and I'm going to get Christian—" A blade exploded out of his shoulder and impaled itself in her car door. "*Shit.* You have a really nice car. Sorry."

"I'm not really worried about the car, but thanks." Natalie began to struggle against his grip, the compulsion to go after those little girls taking over her determination to be a responsible citizen and let the little darlings continue wreaking havoc all over the neighborhood. "Nigel! Stop me. Kill me. I won't be this monster."

"You're not a monster."

"I am!" Tears were streaming down her face now, and she didn't care. "Don't you get it?" She held up her hand, saw the bronze highlights to her skin. "I'm a demon," she whispered. "If Maggie comes back, if I save her, I'll just bite her again. Or those girls—" Dark, lethal need began to grow inside her, and she felt power surging through her. "Nigel? Something's happening to me."

"I can feel it. Demon strength." He met her gaze. "You'll be stronger than I am in a minute. More desperate, too."

She closed her eyes and leaned her head back against the car. "End it now, then."

"Fuck, no. It's never over."

"Really?" She opened her eyes and stared into his tortured face. "Can you stop me? If I took away your fury, could you still stop me from killing those girls?"

Nigel shook his head. "No. It wiped me out when you stripped me before. I had nothing. I need to get control on my own."

"With art?"

"It's my way."

"But you'll draw someone else—"

"I know—" He grinned suddenly. "That's it!" He grabbed her face and kissed her. "That's what we'll do!"

She had no clue what he was talking about, but she was so happy to see his excitement. Her warrior was back in the game, and she was totally okay if he accidentally hit her with a blade or two because he was a little too deadly for his own good. "What is?"

"Do you have a pen and paper in your car?"

"I don't know. Why?"

"I'm going to draw us. I'm going to turn us in." He gritted his teeth against another wave. "It's the only way to get access to Mari fast enough. She needs to take the smut off you, and I'm going to get my boys."

Oh, man. Because that last trip into the Den had gone so well. "But then we'll be there on her terms. She'll destroy our minds and—"

"Not this time." He grinned. "I'm done castrating my own powers. I'm taking control, and I'm doing it now. You just told me to embrace my weapons and use them, and I realized you're right. I'm not going to try to suppress them anymore. I'm going to use them the way they're meant to be used. A brilliant idea, Nat." He kissed her hard once, his eyes dancing with anticipation. "You in?"

She thought of Maggie. Her sisters. Pascal. Her only chance to save Maggie was to become sane again.

They would succeed. Because there was no other acceptable result. Yes, she wasn't having success at calling up her power unless Nigel was seducing her, but she knew it was there. She could do it. She *would* do it when it mattered. "Yes, I'm in."

"Good." He stepped back and released her. "Get the pen. We're shutting you down."

"Great—" *Shutting her down?* As in, taking her away

from her deedub destiny? Protest boiled inside her, a demon that was not so happy about that proposal. "Uh, oh—" Fire ripped through her body, an explosion of pure demonic expulsion. It threw Nigel onto his back as only demon fire could do. Flames encased him, burning him alive as he fought against them, fighting to break free while they buried him in their tainted fury. "Nigel!"

"It's okay, sweetheart," he yelled. "I know it's not personal. Give me a sec and I'll be fine."

"See? I told you to kill me!" She tried to go to him, to help him, but instead, she turned toward the car that would take her to those girls.

"Never. A man likes a woman who's a challenge." He rolled over, and the flash of metal became visible behind the flames. "Trying to murder me doesn't change the beauty of your soul, sweetheart. You're still what I would choose to draw if I could have only one subject for the rest of my life."

Okay, was that the sweetest thing ever? "You kind of make me melt, Nigel." She reached for the door handle to her car, unable to stop herself from leaving him to become toasted marshmallow. Did demons have no sense of romance whatsoever? Choosing chocolate over romantic words and heart-melting declarations?

"Kind of made you melt?" The flames grew higher and louder, and she could barely see him behind the wall of demon light. "Clearly, I need to work on my tactics."

"No." She pulled the door open and slid into the seat. "You're perfect exactly as you are." And as her hands folded over the steering wheel, the protests in her soul faded, replaced by a growing glee. She was having twins for dinner! "Good-bye, Nigel."

"I'm coming after you," he yelled.

"I hope to God you do." Then she slammed the door shut, cutting herself off from the only man she'd ever let into her soul. She revved the engine, shifted into drive, and pulled out before the towering wall of flames destroying the man she loved had even begun to reach full strength.

The squeal of the tires as she peeled out almost drowned out her soul's wail of anguish.

Almost.

But as long as she could hear herself over the din of demon, she knew she still had a chance.

Nigel had partaken in demon fire celebrations, he'd been burned at the stake, and he'd even been hit with Blaine's flames, but that didn't compare to being upended by a Mystic-demon inferno. His eyes felt like they were burning to a crisp, his skin was shriveling, and his balls were on fire, and not in the good way.

Natalie could inflict severe pain with her words alone.

But combine that with fire, aggression, and some bronze demon?

She could be Angelica's latest torture goddess.

And if he didn't get his ass out of there, she might end up being just that.

Except, of course, for the fact that he was done letting down the people he cared about.

Nigel fought his way out of the flames, then fell to his knees just outside to regroup. His eyes were burning, and his lungs were aching. Blades were exploding out of his body like he'd become a popcorn fest, and his hands were smoking. Yeah, hellish and crappy to become a one-man-murdering-machine, but at the same time, it felt brilliant to have his weapons back at his disposal. Thanks to the demon fire, his vision was blurred, but he knew instantly that Natalie's car was gone.

No problem. He was on it. *Hang on, Natalie. I'm on my way.*

He vaulted to his feet. His vision was blurred from the demon fire, but he knew exactly where Natalie's store was. Instincts were back, baby! He raced into Natalie's store and immediately sensed a female presence right away. "Ella?"

"Nigel?" She was sitting on the floor by the door, holding her head as if she'd taken a hit during the battle when Natalie had gone over the line.

"Stay down. I'm dangerous." The sound of blades careening into the walls was like the rat-a-tat of machine guns. "I need paper. Where is it?"

Ella was already crawling behind the counter. "Back room. At the desk."

Nigel sprinted back there, his head so crazed he could barely think. His vision and other senses were distorted from the demon fire, and he crashed into the wall instead of turning. "Shit!" He felt his way to the door and tried to find the papers. Fumbled along the countertops. Found boxes. More boxes.

"No, not there!" Ella ran up beside him. She shoved a pencil into his hand. "Here—" She gasped suddenly, and he knew he'd hit her.

"Dammit! Why'd you come in here?"

"Because I could help. I owe you. I owe all of you." She gasped, holding her side. "Forgive me, Nigel. Forgive me for all I've done."

Nigel shoved her under the desk, trying to get her out of range. His vision was already returning. Self-healing at its finest. "When I come back, I'm going to heal you. Don't you dare die, do you hear me?"

"I'll be fine. It just nicked me." She huddled back against the wall as he stood up. "Paper's in the printer to the right."

"Got it." He began to draw. Not fast. Precise. With utter care. Because this time, he was going in on his terms, and he was going to get it exactly, exactly right.

Natalie had never been to that field before last night. She had no clue where it was or the right roads to take to get there. But she didn't need to know. Her sniffer took her right to where she wanted to be.

She drove onto the yard of a three-story, multifamily red house, her Hummer careening over a flower bed in a nauseating display of reckless power. She had a vague thought that she was disgustingly similar to the last time she'd snapped, believing she was above the laws of life and society.

The thought made her smile. Because this is the moment that felt good. When she felt above all the crap.

She stepped out of the car and slammed the door. Breathed in the flowers. The freshly cut grass. And chocolate. Living, breathing chocolate.

She noticed that her side was still bleeding from Nigel's knife, the poison turning her skin green as it tried to combat the demon immortality. Hah. It couldn't stop her. Excitement rippled through her, and she strode powerfully up the walk. She owned this house, she owned this street, she owned her life. No fear. No submission. No victim.

Just power.

Glee.

Delight in who she was.

She reached the door and decided it would be a fun bit of irony to ring the doorbell. Like she was some guest for tea. She tapped her finger to the bell and delighted in the cheerful chimes.

"Just a moment," a woman called out.

"No problem," she replied gaily.

Now that she was here, and that she was following her soul, she was at peace. Basking in the enjoyment of the process. Savoring the anticipation. She felt lovely. Just like before.

Yes, yes, yes, she was now a murderer and would have many bodies to her credit, but there was no judgment in her mind. Simply acceptance, just like she'd accepted herself before as a sex-crazed orgasm junkie.

And it felt good to accept herself. To allow herself to simply feel the joy of being alive, of loving herself no matter who she was. Of not being afraid of her true self.

The door opened, and Natalie found herself staring down at two curly-haired little cherubs. Twins. She breathed deeply and delighted in the scent of chocolate.

"Mommy will be right down," one of them said. "She's brushing her teeth."

Natalie smiled. "That's okay. How about if I wait inside?" She imbued her voice with her power, and the two girl's smiles became wooden, no longer their own.

"Yes, okay." They stepped back and gestured to the

front hall. "Mommy tells us not to let strangers in, but you seem okay."

For a split second, she hesitated. Grabbed the door frame. Tried to turn away. Heard a voice screaming in her head not to do it. And then it was gone, and she stepped across the threshold.

Chapter 24

NIGEL'S PEN WAS GOING FASTER NOW AS HE SKETCHED every little detail. His own face, his weapons. He drew himself as a warrior hopped up on adrenaline, with a clarity of mind that would make him unstoppable. It was how he needed to be when he got sucked back into that hell.

Another tremor wracked his body, and he gripped the pen as he tried to fight it off, tried to hold back the blades, the rage in his mind. He fought for focus and saw that he'd drawn the wrong boots. He hadn't drawn the boots he liked to wear for battle.

He had to go in right. Had to go into the Den with everything in order. His fingers clenched the pen and it snapped under his strength. He yanked open a drawer, then another. "I need a pen."

"Here." Ella reached up and opened the middle drawer. Her hand was ashen and pale, and it was shaking.

"Woman, don't you dare die, or I will not be happy with you." He found another pencil and began reworking the boots. He finished them off, and swore, realizing that he'd almost finished off the drawing of himself. *Not yet.*

He broke off from his own image and began to sketch Natalie on the same paper, tucking her right up against him. He didn't know if it would work. If it would pull her in if Mari wasn't looking for her.

No. He would make it work.

He sketched Natalie's hand grabbing onto his shirt. Her legs around his waist. Redrew his arms around her. One anchored on the back of her neck. His other clamped around her hips. His leg over hers. His body against hers. So tight. So close. One body. One soul. He brought the connection to life. He opened his mind to the connection that he'd felt when she'd reached into him and plucked his hell right out of his body.

He drew her hair drifting down over his face. He could feel the silkiness of it against his skin as he drew it waving gently in a soft wind. He could feel the heat from her thighs where she was wrapped around him. He knew the curve of her hip beneath his hand. He could smell the scent of her body, redrew his own nose while he breathed the scent of honeysuckle and cocoa, the scent that was beneath the smell of sulfur. He knew her real scent. He knew the real her.

Her hands were tangled in his hair. He closed his eyes, reliving the sensation of her gentle touch on his head, her tentative exploration, that moment when her grip had tightened, when she'd no longer been afraid. When they'd been connected. On fire. Aware of nothing but each other.

He erased his shirt, drew his bare torso against hers. Had to feel skin to skin. Bound them so tightly in the drawing that it would impossible to pull him into the Den without bringing Natalie with him. He had to make them one unit, one soul, one being, so that Natalie would come with him.

He could feel her breasts against his chest, could feel his erection pressing into the seam of her jeans.

No, not jeans. Needed more contact. Couldn't make her naked. Didn't know where they'd land. He drew a skirt, a long, loose flowing skirt. Hitched it up around her hips with one of his hands hidden beneath it. He didn't draw it, but he knew where his hand was, felt the warmth of her body. The connection in the most intimate way.

No, no, not enough. Mari was too smart.

He tossed the sheet, grabbed a new one. His mind was clearer now. The act of drawing already soothed him, helping him focus. He knew what he wanted. How he needed to format it. This time, he drew a different position. Natalie on his lap, skirt shrouding them, but he drew their connection in their faces, in the passion in their eyes, in the way they held each other. Anyone looking at it would know that beneath that skirt was the most intimate passion and connection. They were one, in their souls, in their bodies, in their spirits.

He felt his own body harden, felt the desire pulsing though him, his need for connection with Natalie, the intimate weaving of two souls that happened whenever they were together, whenever they made love. He poured those emotions into the drawing. One of his hands was anchored around her waist, holding her tight, ready to toss her to the side, behind him where he could protect her. His other hand was fully armed, poison blades sliding out of his fingertips. Ready to show up fighting.

He drew his eyes again, shrouded in passion, but with fierce determination, clarity of mind. He drew Natalie's skin vibrant and flush with humanity. He drew her teeth perfectly white and flat. He drew her eyes alive and passionate, filled with courage and power.

He drew them both the way they wanted to be, except the final line on both their jaws. He'd planned the drawing so one line would complete both images at the same moment. And it would take them to the Den, or else everyone who mattered to them would die.

He swept his pen through the line and completed the picture.

———*m*———

Natalie shut the front door of the Sweet's home and leaned against it. Her heart was pounding, her head was starting to ache. She had to stop. Had to run. Had to find Nigel. *Nigel.* Tears burned as she thought of Nigel dying, destroyed, all because of her. Her spirit screamed at her to go back and help him, but her body wouldn't turn away from the temptation before her, like she was some pathetic chocolate addict in need of one more fix.

Oh, wait. She was.

One of the girls flipped her ponytail out of her face, and the decadent scent of chocolate drifted toward Natalie. Cravings rippled through her body, and she knew she was gone.

Her mind screaming in protest, Natalie levered herself off the door and took a step toward them.

The blue-eyed girls went still, their eyes widening, sensing danger.

The air became heavy.

The room descended into silence.

No one moved.

No, I am not this person.

Then, in rude and utter disregard of her deepest desires, Natalie promptly launched herself at the cherubs, fangs bared and all. Her claws reached for the cupcake twins, and—

No! This was unacceptable! She would not do this! *She would not.* And then, for the first time in her life, she took control, and she stopped fighting Nigel's poison and allowed it to rush through her. *Yeah, baby, bring me down.*

Debilitating, numbing, paralyzing pain was instantaneous, and she crashed to the hardwood floor inches from her prey. Fantastic! For the first time in her life, she was no longer afraid of dying. Dying was the ultimate statement of her own power that even a deedub couldn't decide who she was going to be.

Death was hers, and so was victory.

But she really, really wished there could have been another way—

Her hand vanished. Natalie gaped as her entire arm disappeared, and then her other hand. Her legs. Was she dying? Getting sucked over to the deedub party? Or had Nigel done it? Had he managed to draw them? *Please let this be Nigel!*

Granted, being fêted at a ball was every girl's dream, but in this particular case... not so much.

Then raging heat rocketed through her body. Especially between her thighs.

Now, what was a girl to make of *that*?

———

Nigel had never been one for extensive fantasizing about interesting and unusual places and ways to make love, because getting personal with women hadn't generally led to the most positive results for him.

But when he felt the heat of Natalie's body crackling on his lap and he had confirmation that she was on her way, he couldn't quite manage to contain the rush of sheer, raw anticipation. Intimacy with Natalie, on the other hand, was so worth fantasizing about. *I'm waiting for you, sweetheart.*

His arms were already around her when Natalie appeared, exactly as he'd drawn her. He was deep inside her, her hot warmth was wrapped around him, and her body pressed against his. Connected so intimately that not even Mari had been able to pry them apart. *Success.* But as hell was his witness, those seconds that had passed after he'd been taken and before Natalie had arrived had nearly scared him shitless. For a moment, he thought he'd blown it.

But he hadn't. His woman was right here in his arms, on his lap, holding onto him as if the world would stop turning if she let go. As it should be.

Natalie's eyes were slitted with passion, just as he'd drawn, and she was wearing the same white peasant skirt he'd sketched. It was draped over his lap, concealing the intimacy below. Her head was tipped back, leaning up for his kiss.

"Welcome to hell, my dear." He kissed her.

Natalie tensed in his arms, and she pulled back in startled surprise. "Nigel?"

He nodded. "You got it, babe."

She touched his face, as if she couldn't believe he hadn't melted into a pile of rubble. "You're okay?"

"Oh, yeah." Understatement. His weapons were quiet but humming with energy. His mind was focused and clear. He was in the exact state he'd draw in his art. Hell, yeah. He was the *man.*

Natalie flung her arms around him and hugged him. She said nothing, but the strength of her hold on him made him want to cart her off and spend the rest of his life thanking her for making him feel that important. She just held him so tight, as if afraid she'd lose him again, and buried her face in his neck.

"Hey, sweetheart, it's okay." He moved her hair to the side and lightly rubbed the nape of her neck. "I'm here. You're here. We're okay."

"I know." She sighed and snuggled into him. "I've just had a tough day and it's really good to be with you."

Nigel laughed softly and pulled back, gently lifting her face out of his neck. Her green eyes were shimmering, her skin was tinged with bronze, and he was absolutely certain he had never seen anything as beautiful in his entire life.

She smiled. "When you look at me like that, I feel like an angel."

"You are. My angel." He traced his finger lightly over her jaw and kissed her. Slowly. Taking the time to savor every moment of connection between them. They had so little time before the battles would begin, but this moment, this precious, beautiful moment, was a gift he would always cherish.

He kissed down her jaw, and Natalie turned her head to give him access. "Where are we?" she asked.

"In a jail cell in the Den." Nigel tunneled his fingers in her silken hair as Natalie tensed.

"We are?" She pulled back. "We can't sit here like this—"

He grabbed her hips, moving her back onto him, closing his eyes at the amazing sensation of sinking deep inside her. "No one realizes we're here," he said. "I'll know if someone's coming."

"But—"

"I'll keep watch. We'll have plenty of warning." He smiled into her worried face and rubbed his thumb over the silken softness of her cheek. "I need to kiss you," he said. "I need you in my soul."

Her expression softened. "I need you too."

"Simpatico, as always." He kissed her again, slowly, needing her touch. They were in a prison cell, alone with magically enhanced stainless steel bars. Mari had been anticipating his arrival, that was clear.

The witch had spliced allergic reactions to stainless steel into all her warriors, and being surrounded by so much was already weakening Nigel. Having Natalie on his lap eased him. Grounded him. Gave him a sense of balance. "Kiss me, sweetheart."

She looked around again, and he knew she wouldn't be able to relax. Then she smiled at him, and he saw trust shining in her eyes, trust that made warmth soar through him. "I could never disappoint my warrior." Then she buried her hands in his hair and kissed him.

Yes. The kiss quickly turned into more than a gentle moment. The adrenaline firing both of them roared to life, and they channeled it into each other. Together, they connected, their souls reaching for each other as their bodies began to move in rhythm, drawing strength from the passion rising between them.

He held her hips and moved her, shifting inside her. He thrust deeply, and she grabbed onto him. No words needed, none spoken. The connection was exactly as he'd drawn it, and he felt it all the way to his soul. This warmth growing and expanding until he felt like his spirit was going to burst.

He didn't hold back, and neither did Natalie, and the release was almost instant, simultaneous, and with a blinding force that nearly knocked him off his feet.

Natalie hung onto him, her body trembling as the final shocks hit her.

He held her tightly, not wanting to let go. She was holding just as tightly, her body trembling against his. "I want to stay here like this forever," she whispered. Her green eyes were luminescent, her face radiating with a beauty that awed him. It was her spirit that he was seeing, freed from the constraints she'd had it under for so long.

"I do, too." He kissed her forehead. "Promise me something?"

She nodded. "What is it?"

"Promise me that when this is over, you'll give me a chance."

She frowned. "A chance to do what?"

"To make love to you and not have to leave."

She blinked, and she looked confused, and adorably hopeful. "What do you mean?"

"This is it," he whispered, stroking her hair. Her silken, soft hair that he could touch for hours and still not get enough of.

She wrapped her arms around his neck, her demonized bronze glowing. "This is what?" she asked.

"This is the peace I've been searching for my whole life." This moment. With her. This was the elusive answer he'd been chasing for a hundred and fifty years. He smiled down into her flushed face. "I—"

Then Christian bellowed.

⁓

Christian's shout still reverberating in the air, Natalie jumped off Nigel, clothes were replaced at an impressive rate, and then he raced to the entrance of the cell. He grabbed the steel bars, then jerked his hand off them, but not before his palms had burst into flames and blistered.

"We're going to have to work on your hypersensitivity to steel," Natalie said as she hurried over. "You're so lucky you have a woman who can talk that kind of thing out of you." She clasped the metal rods. She could feel the hum of energy racing through her, and she recognized the answering energy in the bars. "I'm carrying the smut from that spell. Can I do something with that?"

"Sweetie, you're carrying the smut from almost all the spells in this place, I'd guess." Nigel blew on his hand as he assessed their options. "It'll get you a free pass to the Christmas party, but I'm not sure how we can work that in our favor. Stand back." He pulled her out of the way, then a long, dangerous looking blade slid out of his fingertips. It was the size of a pirate sword, long and thick, with a blade that was red hot.

He gripped it tightly, and then raked it across the bars. The bars glowed orange and then his blade turned black as if it were poisoned. He dropped it with a clang on the floor. "The blight travels up the blade. I can't let it touch me."

Christian shouted again, pain evident in his voice.

Moving fast now, his mind apparently clear and strategic, Nigel flicked his hand and another blade came out, also glowing. He held it out to her. "Take it. I'll guide it, but you've got to catch the contamination before it hits me."

The thought flashed through Natalie's mind that grabbing onto a burning blade might not be the best plan for a mortal girl, but hey, what's a near-death evasion without a little risk? Fried hands just didn't really scare her anymore. "You got it."

He grinned and kissed her nose. "You are so cute when you're gathering your courage. I think I want to make love to you."

She smiled back, her cheeks heating up. "Of course you do. Why wouldn't you? There's something incredibly sexy about a murderous demon with black cuticles."

"Sweetheart, sexy is an understatement." He slapped the handle in her hand. "You rock my world."

Her smile got bigger. "You're trying to sweet-talk me so I do something really crazy for you, aren't you?" The sword began to burn her skin, and then her hand turned to bronze and cooled. "Hey, did you see that? It's handy to be a demon."

"Don't get used to it. Your time as a demon is limited." He set his hand over hers, engulfing it in the grasp, and he guided the blade across the bars with a quick slice. "And I'm not trying to sweet-talk you. It's just that recent events have conspired to give me some perspective on life. And you."

She glanced at him. "What does that mean?" It almost sounded like... well... that he was getting a little mushy on her. Her heart began to pulse, like little angels had started to dance in it. Did she want him to get mushy? After the Godfather, she had thought her answer would have been no for the rest of her life. But she realized it wasn't true anymore. She did want Nigel to be mushy with her. "Nigel—"

Black crud crept down the blade, and she paused to watch the taint racing toward her hand. She grimaced as it banged into her palm with an audible thud, but then it stopped. It didn't continue through her hand onto Nigel's. "Hot damn," he said. "It worked."

He swiped the blade across the bars a second time. Then again, and again, he carved up the bars, rotating her hand so quickly she could barely track its movement. But in less than a minute, dozens of glowing red bars were strewn across the floor, permanently dislodged from their restraints. Yay! They were free already! Warriors with clear heads were such a boon to have around when locked down in the Den of Really Nasty Things.

Nigel's blade was mottled with taint, but his hand was clean. "Drop it. We're done with it."

She released and it clattered to the ground with a thud. Nigel nodded, then grabbed her hand. "Let's go find my boys."

"And Mari."

Their hands joined, they leapt over the carnage, just as another scream echoed through the hallways. It seemed to be coming from a hallway on the right, but Nigel paused. He cocked his head. Listening. His eyes were clear and focused, and his skin was devoid of wayward weapons trying to poke through. He was in utter control. A warrior in his element. Without even drawing.

Impressive.

"This way." He turned to the left, the opposite direction of the screams.

Natalie hesitated. "But isn't it coming from the other direction?"

He cocked a jaunty brow in her direction. "Who's the one who's been trapped here for a hundred and fifty years? Who knows her tricks?"

She looked back down the hallway. It sounded like Christian was just around the corner. Then she looked back at Nigel and saw the man she would trust with her life. "Let's go."

"That's my girl."

His girl? What did that mean?

But it wasn't like there was time for a subtle inquiry to pry info out of him. Nigel took off down the hall, never losing his grip on her hand. Together they ran toward a hell they couldn't predict, an ending that would most likely destroy them all.

But as Natalie ran with him, her mind was calmer than it had ever been in her life, devoid of all the noise that made it impossible to appreciate the moment. She didn't feel afraid. She didn't feel alone. With Nigel, she knew she could take on anything.

It was time for her to step up and face her life, and this time, she believed they could do it.

And if they failed? She was no longer afraid of dying. Did that make her a warrior? After a lifetime of living in fear, had she finally become the woman she wanted to be?

She suspected she was going to find out soon enough.

Chapter 25

THREE MINUTES INTO THE DREAM GENIE'S INVASION of Christian's mind, Mari couldn't take Christian's suffering anymore, no matter how much it might help him. "Stop!"

But Charles kept his hands in the air over Christian's head. "I'm not hurting him." The genie's cheeks were flushed and his eyes were excited. "He just has so much hate and baggage inside him, and he doesn't want to let it go. So many dreams of inflicting massive amounts of damage to you and this place."

Mari was cradling Christian's head between her palms. She was wearing nylon gloves to protect her from his metal skin, and he'd gone alloy several minutes ago. The nylon was starting to smoke, and it was burning her hands. "It's not right. If he's fighting it this much, then I think we should respect his wishes."

"No!" Smutty smacked Mari in the shoulder. "That's the whole point! To get rid of his wants so he can have peace." He gestured at Christian, who was silent now, his body trembling. "Is that living? Is it?"

"God, no, but we're causing him more pain." She felt like she was going to throw up. "I can't do this anymore. It's been too much." She stumbled to her feet and pushed the genie back. "It's over, Charles. I can't do this anymore." Where had she gone wrong? This wasn't how it was supposed to turn out. It had all made so much sense when she'd first read Smutty's file and found out he was a dream genie. No more abuse. No more torture. Just love and peace for everyone who had been tormented for so long. "No more suffering. It ends now."

"Suffering is subjective." Smutty eyed her thoughtfully. "Which is worse? Physical or emotional ordeals? The crushing of a hand, or your soul?"

"I'm tired of it all!" She threw up her hands in frustration. "No one should suffer! Just let it go, for God's sake —"

He grabbed her hand and thrust power into it. She yelped and tried to jerk away, but he kept pressing mercilessly. "Do you want me to do this for an hour, or torture Christian for an hour?"

"This, this. Don't hurt Christian anymore." But holy cow, it hurt. An hour? Really?

He released her hand with a look of triumph. "When I hurt Christian, it hurts your soul. You'd rather take physical discomfort than torment in your soul." He leaned forward. "It's the same with Christian. We're only causing physical pain right now, but we're taking the pain off his soul. Isn't that what trumps?"

Smutty was right. When she'd fallen in love with Christian, Mari had still been able to administer the experiments on him that caused him physical pain, because they both knew that kind of pain didn't really matter. He'd still loved her and she'd loved him, even amidst the torture. But his emotional grief when she'd betrayed him? That was what had done her in. And him.

Smutty nodded. "It hurts because he's resisting, but I'm giving him peace in his heart." He leaned forward. "He'll be able to love again. Isn't that what you want?"

Mari's head snapped up at his words. "You don't believe in love."

"No, I don't." Smutty nodded at the baton in the corner. "But you gave me back my own soul, and for that, you get a break. If you want love, I'll let you go for it. Can't promise it, because you're not clear enough in your desires, but I'll do what I can to help."

Mari caught her breath. "Really?"

"Swear." He leaned forward. "But as soon as I'm finished with Christian, I'm walking out of here, and I'm following my own dream and creating a utopia for all. Got it?"

She nodded. She would be happy to let him go. Christian was her last project, and then it was over.

"Very well." He turned toward Christian and settled beside him. "Let it begin."

Mari sat beside him and took Christian's hand in hers. "Will he still recognize me when you're through with him?"

"Depends on if there are any positive feelings about you in there. I'm stripping every bitter, vengeful, and torturous dream he has." Smutty raised his brow. "How confident are you that there's love somewhere in this big guy? Because if there's only this bad shit, there's not going to be a damn thing left inside him when I get done."

Mari bit her lip. "He loved me once."

"You sure? Or were you simply his salvation from a hell that was destroying him and everyone he cares about?"

She raised her brows at him, and he shrugged. "I had a couple affairs when I was the smut beast. Women mistook my desperation for love. It happens." He cocked his head. "How sure are you? You willing to risk his soul? If there's no love in there, then there's going to be nothing left when I'm through."

"And if there is love?"

He shrugged. "He'll be like your favorite lap dog."

Mari hesitated. What was she doing? She—

Christian shuddered, and his self-inflicted wound in his belly sparked. It was septic now, bleeding out what looked like thumbtacks. He was dying. He would be dead in minutes, unless she gave him a reason to live. "Better to give him a chance," she said quietly. "I owe him that much."

Smutty raised his brows. "And you won't try to stop me? You'll let me do what I need to do? Take it as far as I need to?"

"Yes." She took Christian's hand and snuggled close. "Christian, this is for you. Please let him help you."

But Christian's skin turned to metal, as it always did when she touched him. Trying to poison her. Not that it mattered. She would do what was right. "Do it, Charlie."

Smutty grinned and rubbed his hands together. "And let the genius begin." He set his hands on Christian's head, and this time, the screaming started for real.

Whatever Smutty was doing, it was the real deal.

Christian would not be the same when he was done.

"Come on, Christian," Mari whispered. "Tap into your love. It's the only way to live."

But when the screams kept coming, she had a bad feeling that she'd made a horrible, horrible mistake. And it was too late.

—∿—

Nigel rounded the corner just as Christian's screams reached a crescendo that would invoke the master of death himself. Nigel whipped out a dagger and flung it straight into Smutty's head. It thudded into his skull, wedging itself hilt-deep.

Amen, brother. You be going down.

The genie roared with fury and leapt up. He pulled the blade out of his head and hurled it right back at Nigel with impressive aim.

"Well, that's interesting." Nigel ducked, yanking Natalie with him. "He's faster than I thought he'd be."

"Didn't that go in his skull?"

"Yep. Dream genies are apparently plucky little fellows."

Mari leapt to her feet. "Don't kill him, Nigel. He's halfway through. If he stops now, Christian will never recover—"

"I don't believe you." Nigel hurled a set of barbed wires at Mari. They wrapped around her and flung her back against the wall, the barbs anchoring deep and trapping her. Well, damn. He'd never made those suckers before. Barbed wires, eh? He supposed it made sense. Metal weapons were metal weapons, right? Stood to reason that he would be imbued with a limitless and impressive ability to manipulate it in countless unpredictable ways, especially now that his head was clear.

Mari closed her eyes and started whispering. Another spell? Now *that* he didn't like.

"Ow!" Natalie lunged forward, her hands on her belly. "More smut. Have I mentioned how tired I am of this?"

"Stop!" Nigel raced over to Mari and slammed his hand down over her mouth. "No more spells." But her lips were still moving, racing, and he heard the distant

howl of creatures coming to life. The wolverines. Damn.
He hated the wolverines. Granted they were cute little
things, but their personalities needed a bit of work.

Christian groaned again as Smutty continued to lobotomize him. Behind Smutty, against the wall, were
Pascal and Blaine. Pascal was unconscious, and Blaine
was encased in a stainless steel iron lung. Smoke was
pouring out of it, as Blaine was apparently trying to burn
his way out of it, but there was no way. The stainless
steel alone would kill him.

Natalie was down on the ground behind him, gripping her belly. "Hang in there," he commanded. "Don't
let it take you. I'll be right there."

"Trying," she managed. "But hurry up, for God's
sake." Black smoke was rising from her skin, and the
ends of her hair were starting to burn.

Christian screamed again and Nigel threw a dozen
blades at Smutty. *Take that, you scum!* The blades thudded rapidly into Smutty's body, but the son of a bitch
dislodged them all into a pile on the ground. Damn.

But then the insolent pug looked intently at Nigel,
and Nigel felt him digging in his mind. Audacious
little bastard!

"Shit." The tendrils were digging in, searching for
his dreams. *Christian. Blaine. Pascal. Natalie.* The
names tumbled through his mind, and he knew Smutty
had found his dreams of keeping them safe, of rescuing
them. "You don't take my family."

The click of dog toenails grew closer.

Nigel whirled around and faced Mari. "Call them
off!" He wedged a blade under her chin.

She shook her head. "If you kill me, your girl gets

taken by demons, remember? Do you really want that? For heaven's sake, Nigel! This is all for your own good! Let me help you!"

"You're insane, woman." And yes, he remembered what would happen to Natalie if he killed Mari, what other option was there? Natalie would die—*Natalie*. Natalie was the option. Natalie was their key.

Amidst Christian's screams, Blaine's howls, and the sound of wolverines closing in, Nigel raced across the room and gathered his woman into his arms. "Natalie, sweetheart. I need you to focus."

Her body was trembling, her eyes pitch-black, bottomless depths. "Nigel—"

"Listen to me! You have to talk Mari into taking her smut back. You have to do it."

"I'm not feeling sexy right now—"

"Fuck that!" He grabbed her tighter. "You don't get your power from me! It's in you. It's that same passion that comes to life when you're under the deedub thrall. You've got it. Feel the love. Do it for fun, dammit. Feel good, love yourself, and let it fly!"

She convulsed in his arms. "I'm way too screwed up. I can't focus on anything but chocolate. On those girls. On Maggie. Thinking about how good she tasted, and how I want more—"

"A perfect dream!" Smutty suddenly leapt to his feet. "I can't believe it!" He raced over to Natalie and kissed her forehead. "Bless you, my girl! You restore my faith! I was beginning to think that no being in existence had the ability for a perfect dream I could grant!" He bowed deeply and gestured with a grand flourish. "And here she is, my queen."

There was a flash, and then Maggie was in Natalie's arms. Because they didn't need another challenge.

———— ⁓ ————

Natalie nearly screamed with frustration and dismay when she found Maggie in her arms. The girl's neck was a ragged mess, her clothes were covered in blood, and the girl was ashen. She smelled like chocolate, like chocolate, like chocolate—

Maggie's eyes opened, and she met Natalie's gaze. For a moment, Maggie didn't react, and then the most lovely smile dawned on her dazed face. "You came and got me. You saved me, just like I knew you would."

That trust, that pure, unadulterated trust made something twist in Natalie's belly. It struck past the darkness, past the demon, to a place so deep inside her. She wanted to be that woman. She wanted to be that hero. She didn't want to be the crazy, destructive one. She wanted to be the woman that made everything right. "Oh, Maggie—"

"Natalie." Nigel gripped Natalie's shoulders. "Look at me."

She did and found herself staring into the most intense face she'd ever seen. He flinched each time Christian screamed, he had a knife ready and angled toward the door, but his attention was solely on her. "Maggie's—" He stopped and pressed his hand to his head.

"Nigel?" She gripped his arm. "What's wrong?"

"Nothing." He shook his head as if to clear it. "Maggie's presence doesn't change anything. You can do this. And—" He stopped again, as if he'd forgotten what he was going to say.

"And what?"

"Sex." He muttered the word. "You don't need me, or sex."

"What's wrong?" Her heart started to race. "Nigel, talk to me. What's wrong with you?"

"Smutty's working me over." He scooped up Maggie and set her gently aside. The girl's eyes were mercifully closed again, sliding off into unconsciousness.

Natalie saw that Smutty was staring at Nigel, and his lips were moving. "Put up your shields. Don't let him steal your mind."

"Dream genies are a little tough to block." Nigel winced, and his pupils began to dilate. "We need to shut both Mari and Smutty down. Do you understand?"

"Yes, yes, how? Tell me what to do."

"I'm going to engage Smutty." He paused to throw two dozen glowing blades into Smutty's face. The dream genie snorted with disgust and started spitting them out. Nigel took a breath. "He's distracted for a second. We have a window. Listen, I'm taking my weapons to the highest level. The shit I was throwing at you earlier."

She sucked in her breath. "On purpose? But you can't control them." Smutty was plucking the barbs out of his face way too fast. He'd be back onto Nigel in a heartbeat.

Nigel shot her a disgruntled look. "Hey, babe. Support would be nice."

"I'm sorry. Right, you can do it." But of course he couldn't. Those poison blades were like her deedub curse. He would take out everyone in the room. He was just like her. Unable to control the lethal beast inside.

"Hey! Don't give me that look." He gripped her arms and gave her a determined look of unflappable self-confidence. "I'm done fearing my dark side, and I'm going to make it work for me. I used my art to control it, and it's working." He grinned. "I'm going to let it all go, and it's all going to go just fine." He tapped her forehead. "And you're going to do it too. You have to work Mari over until she takes the smut off you. I distract Smutty. Two-pronged attack. It has to happen, and it has to happen now."

Well, that was great that he believed in her, and she wanted to jump and help take down the bad guys, but there was a fundamental flaw with that plan. "Even if I could call up my powers at will, it's nearly impossible to influence someone who doesn't want it. It has to be a cooperative event—"

Nigel yanked her close and kissed her. Hard. With fierce passion. Then he thrust her toward Mari, turned toward Smutty, and held his hands up to the sky. "Bring it on," he shouted.

And then the blades began to fly.

Natalie stared in awe as the implements erupted from Nigel's body. They were glowing red, they were twisting and turning, living entities seeking life to exterminate. She could practically see their teeth, she could almost feel their black hearts, could sense the darkness of their intention and their energy.

She ducked as one flew toward her, but it diverted at the last second, careened over Mari's head and slammed into Smutty. Natalie covered her head as more blades swirled around like a swarm of furious wasps, but then she realized that none of them were coming near her. No matter what direction they came out of Nigel's body, they were all spinning around and hammering Smutty.

He was controlling them.

Somehow, someway, Nigel had figured out how to harness them. Sudden hope swelled inside her, and power rolled through her. If Nigel could do it, so could she. *I can do it!*

The dream genie leapt to his feet and started ripping them out, but the blades were coming faster than he could manage. Faster and faster. Nigel was winning the battle and—

A two-toned pink wolverine with nine-inch claws, matching teeth, and a fuchsia hair bow launched itself through the doorway and landed on Nigel's back. "Nigel!"

"I'm okay, sweetie!" He waved cheerfully as another beast and another hammered him to the ground. "This part is fun. You just go do your thing." Nigel's knives went right through them, harmlessly, as if they had been bred to withstand his attack, which they probably had. Smutty leapt to his feet and flung his hand toward Nigel.

Nigel staggered, and his hand went to his head as Smutty attacked his mind again.

Okay, enough observation. It was time for her to step up. She fisted her hands and turned toward Mari. "Call them off! Shut down the magic!"

Mari didn't even look at her, and Natalie heard the scrabble of more feet. Pain clubbed Natalie's belly, and she stumbled, gripping her stomach. Her hand was curving into a claw. A real claw, with black scales and tainted nails.

Okay, fine, if Nigel was going to tap into his inner beast, then so was she.

She faced Mari, steeled herself, and then dropped her resistance to the monster within. Claws burst out of her fingers, scales ripped down her back, and her nostrils grew larger than any woman should ever have to be burdened with. The energy felt deliciously powerful, and she recognized it, not as a monster, but as that same feeling of unstoppable delight that she'd experienced as Orgasm Queen and as a deedub. And for the first time, she saw it through a nonjudgmental mind, and she saw that the power within her wasn't the poison, it wasn't the curse, it wasn't the monster.

The power within was her own energy. It was her Mystic power. It had manifested in a negative way because she'd locked it down so fiercely. But now, as she tapped into it and allowed it to be what it really wanted to be, it was different. It was *hers*. It was working for her, not against her. She breathed deeply, let the lure of chocolate race through her, let her fangs elongate, and she let out a loud hiss that, well, was just fun.

Mari finally looked at her, and she grinned. "Hello, my new smut dump. Don't you know you can't hurt me? It's a natural safeguard—"

"Mari!" Natalie's voice thundered out over the room, and the walls shook with the force of her voice. Holy crapoly! That rocked. This was what she was meant to be. She strode across the room and parked her face right in Mari's personal space. "You will call off the wolverines right now."

Mari's gaze swiveled to her, and her face was wary. "What are you doing?"

Shit. It wasn't working. Natalie could feel the power in her voice, but Mari didn't want to be influenced. Oh, yeah? *Nice try, Mari*. She grabbed Mari's face, and she summoned all of her own willpower and thrust it into her words. "You will call off the wolverines."

But more came in the door, and another off-load of smut crashed through Natalie. Argh! It wasn't working. They were losing. There had to be something else she could do! Something she was missing. But what was it?

Chapter 26

YEAH, SO NIGEL'S DECISION WAS FINAL.

He was never getting a pet. Finding joy in four-legged creatures had simply been ruined for him.

Teeth scoured his back, and he grimaced as another creature leapt onto his shoulders. His head felt like an anvil had been smacked into his head. Yeah, sure, this used to be fun, but now that he'd realized what it was like to find peace with Natalie, this kind of thing had kind of lost its appeal.

He'd moved on. Good to know. Who says men can't evolve?

Time to ditch these puppies, and now. Nigel threw another set of barbs at Smutty. The dream genie staggered under the attack, and the pressure on Nigel's mind eased slightly. He had room to think. "Nat? How's it going over there?"

"Having a little trouble, actually," she called back.

Not the words he wanted to hear from his woman right now. Nigel flung a furry rodent off him long enough to turn to Natalie.

She was hanging onto Mari, and he could see her whispering to the other woman, but it was clear from the look on Mari's face that it wasn't working. His heart softened as he watched how hard Natalie was trying. His woman had courage, she was a warrior, and she was accepting nothing less than victory. *That's my girl.*

His sweetie's hair was on fire, her skin was smoking, and scales were beginning to form on her arms. Two horns were beginning to peek through her hair. His darling was turning into a hellion. How much time did she even have left of sanity? He remembered all too well what Smutty had been like when he'd been fully smutted. That simply couldn't be allowed to happen.

Another wolverine tackled, and Nigel went down under the impact. He rolled to the side, throwing it off him as he unleashed more living deaths into his assailants. They hit with unerring precision, hammering the monsters on all sides. Energy and power were rushing through him, and he knew that he was in total control of his weapons. He could take down Smutty, he could defeat the weasels, he was so close. He just needed a tiny window.

Then there was a bellow and he jerked his gaze to see a huge clawed foot appear in the door, then a two-toned purple snout with teeth the size of Mount Everest.

Holy crap.

The wolverines attacking him were *babies?* And mama was pissed. His head started to throb again, and he saw Smutty back on his feet. "Son of a bitch." This circus had to be cut short, and now. Mari was so powerful that Natalie needed extra juice. Chocolate or sex?

He was engaged at the moment so... Nigel spun around and saw Maggie hiding under a bed in the corner. "Maggie!" Ducking another furry assault, he sprinted across the room. He scooped the girl up, cradled her against his chest, and shoved his way through the carnage. He could feel his adrenaline fading. Smutty was stealing his power, his desire to fight and defend. He was stealing his aggression.

The metal that had been racing around in his soul began to cool, and he swore as the blades stopped flying. The wolverines intercepted him, took him down. He tucked Maggie into the shield of his body, and he heard Natalie shouting at Mari, fighting desperately to make her listen. It was all going to shit.

He needed to draw. He needed that sense of peace. He needed to clear all the crap out of him right now—

Then a wolverine jumped onto Natalie. "Get off her!" He felt his entire soul scream with terror for her, for the woman he loved. *For the woman he loved.*

The emotion swelled inside him, exploding like sunshine and fire and passion. It pierced Smutty's iron grip on his mind, it filled him with power. It was what he'd always drawn, that passion, that fire, that crazy, convoluted empowering emotion that had come alive on his page so many times. It wasn't anger anymore. No violence. No fury. It was love.

And this time, he didn't need to draw to access it. He *owned* it. It was in his soul. *Love.* He channeled it into his body, his passion flared brightly, and the blades came alive again. He threw every weapon he had into the monster trying to kill his woman, and the wolverine exploded. Natalie leapt to her feet, and her skin was pure bronze, horns ten inches long, and her face was contorted like only a demon's could be.

Now that was a woman with power. Was she a goddess or what?

He kept up his assault on the clawed furballs and Smutty, but still they came as he shoved his way through the crowd to his woman. He dumped Maggie into her arms. "Use your chocolate power to make it happen! Now!"

Natalie looked at him with horror, and he suddenly realized he could have made a huge, huge mistake.

Ah, screw that. There was no time for mistakes.

He was right.

—∿∿—

When it came to battle, Natalie trusted Nigel. She really did. But somehow, it seemed that delivering her Achilles heel into her arms in the middle of a particularly high stress moment wasn't the absolute best choice that could have been made. "Nigel—"

He took her face in his hands, and she felt his warmth and support flowing into her. Going past the darkness that was pulsing with her, easing her pain. "I love you, babe."

Her heart went still. "What?"

"Natalie, your power comes from your soul. From your passion. From your heart. From your love." A wolverine started gnawing on his ankle, and he ignored it. "It's not your sexuality. It's your love, your love of life, of victory, of yourself. Stop fearing who you are, stop fearing your passion, ride it, embrace it, and live it." And then he kissed her, the most tender, loving kiss she'd ever experienced, which was just insane given the deadly chaos going on around them.

And that's what made it so special.

Because it was pure beauty in the midst of hell. It was proof that even in the middle of all sorts of dark and negative energy, she could still find purity and peace simply by opening herself to it.

Nigel pulled back and smiled. "I believe in you, sweetheart. Tap into that zest for life, that passion that has driven you over the edge, and let it flow."

A wolverine landed on his back and bit his neck. "Nigel!"

"It's about love." He put her hand on his heart, seemingly oblivious to the wolverines bearing down on him, to Smutty giving him the evil eye, to the blades flying out of his back in a valiant and somewhat successful attempt to slow down the oncoming assault. "Feel the magic of the love within you, within us, and of the pure zest for life that is so powerful. Feel the ride."

His words were the poetry that had been in his art, the peace that had once been in his drawings. The juxtaposition of fire, passion, danger, along with peace and love. He had become his art. He had found his own place in the balance of everything. And it wasn't coming from his drawing. It was coming from within.

Her heart filled, and she smiled, suddenly, finally understanding the beauty of the power within her. "I love you, too."

"That's my girl." He kissed her. "Love yourself too—" The mama wolverine swooped down, clamped her jaws around his waist, and ripped him out of Natalie's grasp.

Nigel blew her a kiss. "Enjoy the ride, my love. That's what it's all about." Then he twisted around and began to fight for his life.

And she could fight, too. Still feeling Nigel's warmth wrapped around her, Natalie picked up Maggie and pressed her face into the girl's neck as the wolverine flung Nigel against the wall. He landed beside Smutty, and the dream genie leapt on top of him, and Nigel gave her a cheerful thumbs up before he disappeared beneath the onslaught.

He loves me. Natalie opened her heart to that emotion, and she felt her walls fall. Power rushed through her, courage and strength. She smiled at the sweet young girl, the one she wanted to save, and she released the fear of hurting her. And with that, the need to kill her also left.

Maggie's eyes widened. "You're okay?"

"More than okay." For the first time in her life, Natalie wasn't holding herself back from who she was. Instead, she was tapping into it, and embracing who she was, and loving it. "Maggie, you need to make Mari smell chocolate."

Maggie's face paled. "Won't you kill me?"

She grinned at the love warming her spirit. "Actually, I'm fine. Do it. Now."

"Okay." Trusting her with her life, Maggie touched Mari's face, and then the most delicious scent of chocolate filled the air. Mari took a deep breath and then shuddered.

Chocolate contamination complete. Natalie looked at Mari with love, instead of fear, instead of desperation. This time, when she spoke, the power rolled off her tongue like a thunderstorm. "Mari, look at me."

The witch's head swung toward her. It was working!

Maggie put her other hand on the witch's face, and more chocolate filled the air. So delicious and so decadent, it was so thick the air was almost brown as it dissolved Mari's resistance and empowered Natalie.

"You will call off the wolverines," Natalie said quietly. "You will make them disappear right now."

Mari gaped at her. "No, I—" And then her attention went to the wolverines, and she whispered something, and then the furry beasts vanished.

Nigel leapt to his feet, surprisingly unbloodied given his activities of the last few minutes.

Oh, God. He was okay. Relief cascaded through Natalie, and she felt her knees grow weak. Then he pressed his hand to his head, and she realized he was still fighting off Smutty. "Nigel—"

Nigel blew her a kiss. "I'm fine, my love. Now take care of yourself." He turned toward Smutty and began to hammer at him with his weapons. "You will not take away my mind," he shouted.

"And the smut." Natalie's heart began to race as she turned toward Mari, desperate to get to Nigel. "And you will take the smut off me. Now! All of it!"

Mari stared at her, and suddenly the room began to shift. Natalie's body began to tremble, and then a hot burst of sunshine blasted the room, knocking her down.

For a moment, an eternity, the light was so bright Natalie couldn't see, and she felt as if her eyelids were being scorched. But at the same time, the heat felt marvelous, as if it were healing the deepest recesses of her soul.

The light finally faded, and she opened her eyes. She was on the ground beside Maggie.

"Hey, hey, I've got you." Nigel was beside her, holding onto her. He was covered in blood, his skin was shredded, and he was missing several chunks of flesh that were already healing. But he looked happy, and so proud. He grinned. "You are one tricky girl."

"I am?" Tricky was good, right? "What happened?"

Maggie leaned over her and applauded. "You did it! You shut her down and took the smut off."

"I did?" Hot damn. She would be so impressed with herself if that was true.

"Yeah, babe." Nigel held up her hand and kissed her palm. "Look at your skin, sweetheart."

Natalie looked down at her hand encased in his and saw healthy, human flesh. No bronze metal, no claws, just herself. Disbelief, glee, and delight sprung up inside her, and she sat up. "Oh, my God. I did it!"

"You did it." Nigel hugged her, and Maggie tackled her, and Natalie laughed gloriously. Nigel and Maggie, the two people who had been such a threat to her when she'd met them. The sexual side of Nigel, the chocolate side of Maggie, and yet they had both turned out to be her greatest strength.

She stroked Nigel's face, her fingers running over his prickly whiskers. "Thank you for showing me how to not be afraid."

He kissed the tips of her fingers. "Sweetheart, you're the one who taught me not to resist myself. You showed me the peace I've been searching for." He touched her cheek. "You are my angel, Natalie Fleming."

Natalie felt her heart begin to swell with love, and she didn't hide from it. Instead, she allowed the fullness of the emotion to fill her, and it felt wonderful. "I love you."

"Well, I'll just go check on the others." Maggie cleared her throat and hurried across the room.

Natalie suddenly remembered where they were. "No, watch out for Smutty—" Then she stopped in surprise. Across the room, sitting down and looking very confused, was a large, black shaggy dog. "Smutty?"

"When Mari took the smut off you, some of it went back to him." Nigel grinned. "Now he's back where he belongs. Insane and in dog form, where he can't take over the world. We'll have to lock him up before he goes back into murderous serial killer mode, though. The dog form won't hang around for long."

"What about Mari?" Natalie saw Nigel's chains were empty. Mari was no longer trapped. "Where'd she go? Did she get some of her smut back?"

"I'm not sure—" Then Nigel grinned and nodded behind her. "Check it out."

Natalie followed his gaze and saw a giant black lizard slithering across the floor toward the door. "That's Mari?"

"Think so. Everyone gets smutted differently." Nigel pulled her into his arms and kissed her. "Looks like Mari went reptile when some of the smut bounced back to her. I think it's a nice look for her."

"She's getting away—"

"We'll get her. But right now—"

"Christian's still alive," Maggie called out. "But barely."

Nigel stood up and pulled Natalie to her feet. "I need to go heal them, darling."

"Can you? It is too late?" She pushed past him to go to the men, but he caught her arm.

"There's so much energy pulsing through me right now, I could heal the world. But I need to focus, and for that, I need a moment with my woman." Nigel took her face in his hands and searched her face. "I just want you to know, my dear, that words spoken in the midst of stressful situations don't always reflect true emotions."

She jerked her gaze at him. "You mean you don't love me?"

He grinned. "Oh, no, sweetheart, just the opposite. I just wanted you to know that I really did mean it." He cupped her face. "The first time I saw you, I thought you were beautiful. I was entranced by the contrast in your eyes, by the fire and zest for life, combined with the angst and turmoil." He thumbed her cheeks. "I was always interested in drawing conflicted faces, in drawing others in pain."

She felt her heart warm as the artist began to reemerge from the warrior shell. She loved this side of him. "Because you were conflict. An artist and a monster?"

"Exactly. But now the beast is simply an extension of who I am, and it's good. Everything is in alignment. Once I accepted all levels of myself, the conflict ended." He kissed her softly. "And I look into your eyes and I see a woman with courage, and strength, with incredible power, with a heart that is so strong and so loving that it transcends it all."

She could feel the fullness of his love, and it felt so wonderful. "You made me come alive. You took away my fear."

"Team effort." He kissed her palm. "Natalie, I don't need to draw, but I want to. I want to draw you, because I want to capture your beauty on the page. May I draw you? After I heal everyone?"

She smiled. "All day long." She leaned forward and lowered her voice. "And I will even pose naked for you."

A lascivious grin curved his wicked mouth. "A woman who is not afraid of her own sexuality. I love it."

She grinned, feeling so delightfully powerful. "Never, ever again."

"My kind of woman." And then he kissed her, and it was perfect.

Chapter 27

"It's beautiful, isn't it?" Natalie sighed as she placed the diamond-crusted Gold Star on the center of her counter.

"It is." Ella grinned. "You and Maggie blew that inspector away with your desserts." She winked. "I still love the thank-you note from his wife the next day. It was so cute how she said it was the most romantic evening of her life, wasn't it?"

Natalie chuckled softly as she thought of the whispered plea that the inspector had offered while she'd been showing him the newly fixed freezer. "He was a good man."

"A man who will now be loyal to you forever." Ella laughed softly. "You did good, girl."

"I did, didn't I?" Natalie smiled as she looked around her. She, the girls, and Nigel had worked like fiends for two days getting the place in shape for her inspection, and she and Nigel had easily kept at bay the assorted deedubs who had tried to stop by for a snack. The store was beautiful, the displays nearly overflowing with new and delicious treats, and the air was positively crackling with the power flowing from her.

Her dream, her beautiful dream, had come true in every way. Her store, her friends, and—

"So, how about these double Dutch chocolate raspberry torts?" Maggie held a tray of still warm delicacies as she walked into the front section of Scrumptious. She was grinning with delight, and her cheeks were flushed with glee. "I think you'll find they're quite fantastic."

Natalie smiled at the girl. "Your talent is amazing, Maggie."

"It's getting better and better." Maggie set the tray down. "It's amazing how creativity can expand when I'm not afraid of getting eaten—"

Natalie's deedub walked in the front door of the store, a cocky grin on his face. "Well, hello, Sweets. I was in the neighborhood and I thought I'd pop in for a snack—"

"Down on all fours!" Natalie ordered. "Bark like a dog!"

The shocked murderer's face registered surprise, and then he dropped to his knees and began yapping like a poodle.

Maggie's grin grew wider. "I love that he can't keep himself away from here, and he keeps coming back for more."

Ella chuckled. "He is a great source of amusement." She beamed at the other women. "That's what life is about. Making yourself happy. You girls are great examples for my dissertation." They'd finally finished the interview, and Ella had been thrilled at how her dissertation was turning out. A few more days, and she'd be turning it in. Fingers crossed by everyone!

"I have to admit, it feels brilliant to be happy instead of afraid of who I am." Natalie grabbed a stick of chocolate off the counter and walked to the front door. "Fetch this, crazy boy." She waited until a taxicab was speeding down the street, then she tossed the chocolate into its path.

The deedub cavorted out the door on all fours, tongue hanging out to the side, and promptly got himself squashed by the cab. He disappeared in a cloud of purple smoke that dissipated almost immediately into the afternoon air. Natalie grinned. "It's sort of fun that he's immortal, I must admit. How many times have we killed him so far this week?"

"Seventeen," Ella said. "Gets more delightful each time."

The front door opened, and Nigel strode inside. "Good afternoon, my lovelies."

Excitement and awareness pulsed over Natalie as she watched his broad shoulders fill the doorway. He nodded at the others, then walked directly across the room, gathered Natalie in his arms, and kissed her.

His body was lean and hard, his skin hot and magnificently strong, and it was marvelous to be buried in his arms. The kiss was decadent and sweet, and hot, and—

"Did you find Mari?" Maggie asked.

Nigel broke the kiss, tucking Natalie under his arm as he smiled affectionately at the young woman. "I have to admit that it's damn fun going after her when she's too lizarded up to cast any spells."

Natalie smiled at Maggie's nervous face. "Don't worry, Maggie. As soon as we find her, we'll switch your soul in her body, and hers into yours. The deedub poison stays with the body, so you'll leave your curse behind, and Mari will get it. As soon as we find her, we'll have my sister switch your souls and you'll be free."

"Giving Mari the smut in her new body, right?" Maggie asked. "I don't want to be a lizard."

"Absolutely. She'll be a lizard with a deedub curse,

and you'll be free." Nigel grinned. "Let her wiggle her way out of that one."

The door flew open, and in walked Blaine and Pascal. Blaine looked the same as ever, a towering warrior with a raw intensity. She'd never actually seen Pascal upright before, because he'd been on the verge of death ever since he'd been rescued. His white-blond hair was short and askew, and he was grinning. "She's a slippery little thing," he said. "I think she's finally in the form she is supposed to be in."

"You found her?" Nigel asked.

"Found her in the rubble after we destroyed the Den. Seems like she had nowhere else to go."

"So, where is she?"

Pascal nodded. "Christian's got her. He's on his way."

Maggie clapped her hands. "Really?"

Natalie put her arm around Maggie's shoulder. "It'll be only a few minutes, and then you'll be free." Yay! Everything was working out perfectly—

And then Christian walked in. Natalie was shocked by how gaunt he was. His body was nothing but muscle and skin, his face was sunken, and his body was tense. He was carrying a metal carrying case, and in it was a black, slithering lizard that was hissing with displeasure. His face was rigid, and he looked so tense he was about to snap. He held up the cage, and his grip was white knuckled. "She's in here—"

He stopped mid-sentence, and his face went white as he stared across the room.

Everyone turned to see what he was staring at, and Natalie saw Ella had gone equally pale. Her hand was over her heart, and she looked stricken as she stared at Christian.

"Christian," Nigel said slowly. "This is Ella—"

"I have to go." Ella grabbed her computer and backpack, then turned and sprinted out the back door. She knocked over three boxes on her way, and there was a loud clatter as she crashed into something in the back room.

"Ella!" Natalie started to run after her. "Wait—

Christian caught Natalie's arm and forced her to stop. "She's your friend?"

"Yes, she's—"

Christian released Natalie's arm as if she'd shocked him. He dropped the cage, and it landed with a clatter on the marble floor. He looked at Nigel. "Take care of Mari."

Nigel nodded. "Of course, but don't you want to do it—"

Christian turned and walked out.

"Christian!" Blaine strode after him. "What's going on?"

"Back off." Christian held up his hand and a steam of molten metal shot out and slammed Blaine in the chest before he strode out the door. He leapt into the Blaine's Escalade and then peeled out.

"Dude," Pascal said. "He's got some serious PTSD going on. You should have heard him howling last night during his sleep. For him to not want to deal the final blow to Mari? He's got issues, man."

Blaine and Nigel looked at each other. "Ideas?" Blaine asked.

But Natalie wasn't surprised when Nigel shook his head. It had been a team effort by all the warriors and a nearly debilitating healing effort by Nigel to pull Christian back from death. Christian had fought hard to die, and even though his body was living, he'd succeeded with his soul.

"I'm really worried about him," she said.

Nigel took her hand and squeezed it. "So am I." Then he pulled her into his arms, and she felt the safety of his embrace and knew that even though she was worried about Christian and Ella, she no longer had to fear herself, because Nigel had taught her not to fear herself. The artist, the conflicted, tortured artist, had taught her about inner peace, about embracing the excitement of life.

And he'd done it by giving her the greatest gift of all: love.

From *Kiss at Your Own Risk*

WHEN THE BLACK SKULL AND CROSSBONES CARVED into Alexander Blaine Underhill III's left pec began to smoke, he knew tonight wasn't the night he was going to get his newest cross-stitching tapestry finished. His escape from the Den of Womanly Pursuits, the hellhole he'd been imprisoned in by a black witch for the last hundred and fifty years, was about to get complicated. "Look pretty, boys, we're going to be entertaining."

"Shaved two days ago. Good enough?" Nigel Aquarian was sprinting beside Blaine, his shitkickers thudding on the stainless steel floor of the Hall of Embroidery. He was wearing only dark leather pants and a pale pink rose tattooed on his left cheek. His palms had turned to blackened charcoal, and burning embers were sloughing off onto the floor. "Forgot the cologne, though. Never remember to smell nice after I party with starving piranhas." He held up the pinkie finger he'd had time to grow back only halfway. "I hate fish."

Blaine leapt over a breeding pit for vipers that was blocking his path. "Spiders are worse."

Nigel grimaced. "Bet the witch is good with spiders."

Blaine refused to revisit that particular hell in his mind. "Toughened me up. It was fun."

Nigel shot him a knowing look. "Yeah, I bet it was."

One hundred and fifty years at the nonexistent mercy of Death's grandma, Angelica, had given new meaning to the definition of hell. The black witch was diabolical in her quest to become the most powerful practitioner in history, and she wasn't exactly the nurturing type when it came to her experiments. Ruthless evil bitch from hell was probably a better way to describe her. But after a century of planning their escape, it was finally *hasta la vista* time for Blaine and his boys.

Blaine flipped a grin at one of the security cameras he'd disabled only moments before. "Hope you miss us." He was so jonesing for a little *mano a mano* to make her pay for all she'd done, but his brain was the one thing she hadn't managed to mess with, so he was hitting the road instead of gunning for a battle he couldn't win. Embarrassing as hell that one grandma could kick the shit out of four badass warriors. Not going to be posting that on his online dating profile when he got out.

Green and pink disco lights began to flash, and the screams of men being tortured filled the air.

"The fire alarm? Come on, guys. Can't you two keep the smoke in your pants for five minutes?" Jarvis Swain sprinted up beside them. A checkered headband was keeping his light brown hair off his face, and he was streaked with sweat and blood from the spar he'd been winning when Blaine had pulled the trigger on the escape. For Jarvis, a practice session ended only when his opponent was on the bleeding edge of death. He was clenching his samurai sword in his fist.

"Nice pants." Nigel nodded at the yellow tulip cross-stitched on the hip of Jarvis's badass martial arts outfit. He raised an eyebrow at Blaine. "Is that your delicate touch, Trio?" His question smacked with friendly insult.

Blaine ignored Nigel's sarcastic reference to his pedigree. Far as he was concerned, everyone he was related to could go to hell. Hoped they already had, in fact.

He looked over his shoulder to check on the progress of the most important member of their team, Christian Slayer, but the Hall of Embroidery was empty. "Where's lover boy?"

"He detoured for his girlfriend when we passed through Flower Appreciation." Jarvis hurled his sword at a small black box tacked onto the seventeen-foot high ceiling. "He caught her scent, said she was nearby, and took off to get her." The blade hit cleanly, sparks exploded, and the alarm went silent.

Without breaking stride, Blaine leapt up and grabbed the sword. "We're in the middle of a daring escape from our own personal torture chamber, and he's taking time to get a girl?"

"That's what he claimed," Nigel said. "He can't lie worth shit, so I tend to believe him."

They continued to haul ass toward the door at the end of the hallway. Freedom was less than fifty yards away. "Well, damn." Blaine hurled the sword blade-first at Jarvis's heart. "That's really sweet of him."

Jarvis snatched the sword out of the air easily, his hand unerringly finding the handle. "You think?"

"Sure. It's not every man who will strand his team in a war zone so he can go rescue a girl." Still running hard, Blaine pulled out a pair of small blue balls from a sack strapped to his hip. "Of course, I'm going to have to kick the hell out of him for doing it, and there's no way he's going on future missions with us, but I admire that kind of choice."

The three men he'd handpicked to escape with were the only residents of the Den of Womanly Pursuits he'd trust with his life. He didn't take loyalty lightly, and neither did his team. Yeah, Christian's detour showed that honor could be a liability, but Blaine was down with that kind of cost. Anyone who refused to leave someone behind had his vote, no matter what the repercussions were.

He heard the muted pitter-patter of little feet skittering around the corner behind them, and he swung around to face their pursuers, spinning the blue balls in his hand. Instinctively, one hand went to the long tube he'd strapped to his hip. Just checking to make sure the one cross-stitching project he was taking with him was still secure.

It was.

"Personally, I think he's lost his sense of perspective." Nigel planted himself at Blaine's right shoulder and extended the burning embers of his hands toward their oncoming pursuer. "Getting laid has completely compromised his ability to think clearly. I'm thinking celibacy is the way to go. You boys in?"

Blaine snorted. "Sex can be good for the brain. Depends on the situation." Blaine's blue balls caught fire, and he swiveled them in his palm. He wanted to toss those suckers at the bastards on their tail, but he'd blow Christian to hell if he were in the middle of the pack. Where was the slacker?

"How would you know whether a man's brain gets fried when he gets laid?" Jarvis asked. "When was the last time you got some, Trio?"

"A real man doesn't discuss his conquests." Blaine caught the faint scent of kibble and he stiffened, hoping he was wrong about what was after them. Yeah, a good battle was fantastic for achieving inner peace, but some things really were the stuff of nightmares.

Jarvis barked with laughter. "A real man keeps a journal and reads it to his sex-deprived buddies. Last action we got was the stick figures Nigel painted on the bathroom wall with toothpaste."

They'd all agreed long ago that the forced intimacy with Angelica didn't count as sex. Some things had to stay sacred.

Nigel shot Jarvis an annoyed look. "Don't knock my artistic talents. You're just jealous because you can't knit your way out of a weekend of torture with the witch."

"I choose to suck at knitting. Being subjected to another of her experiments makes me tougher." Jarvis began to whip his sword over his head in a circle. The air crackled with the energy he was generating. "You're the pansy, choosing to make beautiful pictures so she's happy with you and lets you skip out on the torture."

"I like to paint." Nigel's unapologetic tone was a truth that Blaine knew they all felt. Anything they could do to get through another hour, another day, under the blonde despot's reign was a victory. Nigel was lucky she'd chosen painting for him, because the lightweight actually dug it.

Counted cross-stitch hadn't exactly been a mental haven for Blaine.

His team was comprised of the only four men left from the batch of thirty boys kidnapped and brought to her realm that night a hundred and fifty years ago. Most had died. A few had been rescued. Jarvis and Nigel had hoped to be saved for a while, but Blaine had never bothered.

Even as a four-year-old, he'd known no one would come for him. He'd heard his own parents make the deal with the sorceress. Still remembered sitting there at the top of the stairs, clutching the wolf he'd just finished carving for his mom's birthday. The clunk of the animal hitting the wood floor, the snap of its leg breaking off, as he'd sat there in stunned silence, listening to his own mother hand his soul over to the devil.

He'd been no match for Angelica when she'd come to get him, and the thick scar down the length of his forearm was proof. He rubbed his hand over the mark, the last injury he'd gotten before he became her plaything and developed the ability to heal from anything.

That scar was his reminder never to trust a soul with anything that mattered to him. The day she'd dropped him on his ass in that cellar was the day he'd decided to save himself. There were times when his thirst for freedom had been the only thing keeping him going. Lying there, his life bleeding out, the witch standing over him... his refusal to die a prisoner had often been the only thing strong enough to pull him back from the edge of death.

His resilience had made him one of Angelica's favorite playthings.

And now he got to win. Rock on.

"I hate knitting. My hands are too damn big for all those little knit/purl things." Jarvis flexed his fingers as he moved beside Blaine. Shoulder to shoulder to shoulder, in strict formation. The witch tried to emasculate them with womanly pursuits so she could control them, but she'd also wanted her warriors to be tough as hell. She had no idea how far they'd taken it.

Today was her lucky day. She was about to find out.

"Knitting is about finesse, not the size of your hands." Thick black smoke flowed out of Nigel's palms. "It seems to me that you have a mental block about it."

"Nigel does have a point, Jarvis." Blaine focused his energy into his chest. The skull and crossbones mark burst into flames, and he opened himself to the pain. *Bring it on.* "I've seen you do some good detail work with the knitting needles when you're in the zone." The flames licking at his chest were orange. Not hot enough. He thought of the last time he'd been alone with Angelica, and what she'd done to him. Fury rose hard, and the flame turned blue-white. Now that's what he was talking about.

Then their assailant arrived. The first of the schnoodles rounded the corner, teeth bared, ears pinned. Blaine tensed as it erupted into frantic yapping. *Dammit.* He'd wanted to be wrong.

It could have been the demons.

It could have been the pit vipers.

But no. She'd sent the schnoodles.

Their odds of making it to freedom had just gone to hell.

From *Touch If You Dare*

SOMETIMES RESCUING A BUNCH OF ALMOST-DEAD warriors from black magicked pit vipers was just the kind of thing a man needed to help him forget the fact that he could not, for the life of him, figure out how to knit.

Jarvis Swain, the Guardian of Hate, ducked as the bright red snake launched itself at his throat, sprouting wings as it hit the air. He whipped his sword up just in time to de-fang it before it clamped its gums onto his jugular. "Since when do these suckers fly?"

He ripped the scaly mutant off him and tossed it out the door of the Hotel of Love and Healing, the pit of doom and despair where injured warriors were taken to recover or die after Angelica, Death's psychotic grandma, had tortured them until they were on the bleeding edge of death.

After a hundred and fifty years of incarceration, Jarvis and three others had escaped from Angelica's Den of Womanly Pursuits two weeks ago. They'd kicked Angelica's crazy-bat-shit-ass, saved a girl, and made a deal with Angelica's heir, Mari Hansen, to free the rest of warriors.

Two weeks post-escape, and Mari was stonewalling (so much for thinking Angelica's dethronement would make Mari become sane and reasonable) and the remaining warriors hadn't been released. Jarvis and his team of fugitives had decided to start plucking out the good guys one by one. First stop was the Hotel of Love and Healing. Any poor bastards still in there needed help—and in a big way.

Jarvis and his teammate Nigel Aquarian were rocking the sick bay rescue while their cronies, Blaine Underhill and Christian Slayer, played decoy with Mari and her assistants (no need to deal with a bunch of overly talented, lethally brainwashed, estrogen vessels of hate, if it could be avoided).

"These vipers aren't pure snake." Nigel flexed his hands, and two dozen three-inch knives exploded from his fingertips, careening across the cavernous room. Twenty-two vipes dropped to the cement floor, graphite blades winking in the centers of their murderous little foreheads.

Nigel might be an artist, but the man also had the aim of a Roman god. "Angelica cross-bred the snakes with ladybugs a few weeks before we bailed." Nigel's hands were charcoal black now, and ash was sloughing off his palms. "Bastard went right for my left nipple. Still healing from it."

"Angelica's a she-bitch-from-hell, but I gotta tip my hat to her vision. I always felt ladybugs had more potential than anyone gives them credit for." Jarvis thwacked another swarm of incoming vipers as he took inventory of the Hotel. Only six beds were still occupied, and every occupant was slow dancing so intimately with death that not one had even cracked an eyelid at their entrance. How many nights had he spent here, flipping off Death?

He swore as he remembered Death sitting on his headboard, waiting for him to finally give up. Those deadly shadows looming over his bed, daring him to accept the peace and relief they offered. Reminding him that if he decided to revive this time, he'd be back in the Hotel again, dying again, fighting for his last breath, *again*, in another week. A day. An hour. A never-ending cycle of torture, torment, and hell.

Jarvis saw the cleave marks in the first bed's posts, ones he'd left his last time here, when the pain had been so intense he'd left raw strips in the wood, clawed by his own fingernails. His grip tightened on his sword, and a bead of sweat broke out on his brow. "Coming home can be a bitch," he said quietly.

Nigel inclined his head in silent acknowledgment. "What do you say we retrieve these poor bastards and get the fuck out?"

Get the fuck out. Jarvis glanced toward the door. Yeah, still unlocked. They weren't trapped this time. They were in control now. They could leave whenever they wanted. He forced his grip to loosen and shook out his arm. "Let's torch the place on the way out."

Anything to wipe the nightmares from his soul. Nigel had his art. Blaine had his cross-stitching and his woman. Everyone on his team had something to cleanse the boils from their souls. But not Jarvis. The hell he carried inside him wasn't about to be placated by a session with a pair of lavender knitting needles and turquoise angora. He had no artistic reprieve, and he'd never be soothed by the tender touch of another human being, let alone a woman.

He could imagine it, though. He'd bet his ass it would feel like a fucking angel to have a female touch him the way he'd seen Trinity touch Blaine.

But peace was not for him.

He'd have to settle for torching everything that had ripped the marrow from his bones over the last one hundred and fifty years, in hopes that turning his aggression outward would keep the monster within from ripping him to shreds.

"Yeah, let's blow this place to hell," Nigel agreed. "Eliminate all evidence that it ever existed."

"Sounds good to me—" Jarvis swore as a reptile shot out from behind a pile of chains and went for his crotch. "These snakes must be female." He whacked it aside with his sword. "No male would fang a man's balls with a neurotoxin. Necrosis of the testicles is just not done between guys."

Nigel thudded him on the shoulder. "I'd protect your boys with my life."

They'd all done exactly that a thousand times already. It was why they were all still alive. And intact. "Back at you, my man."

"As always." Nigel took out another trio going for his own manly bits. "Plentiful little suckers, aren't they?"

"Breeding like rabbits. They have no idea what's coming now that we can fight back." Jarvis began to whip his sword over his head in a dizzyingly fast circle, channeling the dark energy of the room into his weapon. Adrenaline rushed through him at the realization that this really was different than it had been for the last two centuries.

He wasn't hog-tied and strung up by his balls, forced to take whatever hit came at him. He was in control now, and he was going to embrace every damn minute of it. He drew even more dark energy into the blade, turning himself from an ordinary combatant to one more lethal than any human being could comprehend. Stacking his sword with extra hate was kind of like the difference between sticking a match into a pile of newspapers or a stack of dynamite. Explosives were always an excellent choice when the lives of defenseless victims were at stake.

His blade began to glow with that heinous purplish mutant color. He smiled.

He casually nicked the wing of an incoming bug. It immediately exploded with enough force to take out ten more of its buddies and a chain-link chandelier. "Now that's what I'm talking about—" Then he caught sight of the poor sod in the nearest bed and noticed a shock of white blond hair on the filthy pillowcase. Mother of hell. It was one of his favorite newbies. "Pascal," he barked. "Get up. It's time to bail."

The kid didn't move, but a scaly beast dive-bombed the youth, fanged teeth going right for the pretty boy's charming dimples. "Hey!" Jarvis lashed out with his sword and bisected a snake a split second before its teeth sank into Pascal's face. "This kind of shit doesn't happen anymore," he snapped as he scooped the rookie up and threw him over his shoulder.

"I'll take him out," he shouted at Nigel. Granted, the kid was a disrespectful pain in the ass with more guts than strategy, but the kid's appreciation for life had helped keep Jarvis sane for the last fifty years. He sure as hell wasn't going to leave him behind to get turned into dinner for Angelica's pets. "You deal with cleanup."

"You got it." Nigel's palms began to smoke, and then dozens of micro-sharp knives exploded from his palms. They shot across the room, hitting his prey with unerring precision. "This kind of action is good for my muse."

Jarvis paused as Nigel engaged the enemy in a full-scale assault. His skin itched with the need to unleash some of the hate festering inside him. "Next time, I get ass-kicking duty."

Nigel grinned. "Stop whining, and go rescue the kid. You know you love the hero role. It's your shtick."

"Shut up." Yeah, he'd taken the hit when Angelica had intended to kidnap his brother a hundred and fifty years ago, but that was his job. Protect his brother. It wasn't about the glory. Assigning him a hero complex was insulting as hell, and they all knew it. One of these days, he was going to behead the next one who said it.

Pascal's muscles began to twitch. Incoming torture-induced seizure? Jarvis lightly squeezed Pascal's shoulder, trying to give him comfort. "Easy, kid. We're almost out." Jarvis turned toward the exit just as the door flew open.

He whipped his sword into position, ready for murderous breasts and hostile mascara wands—

A cosmetic dentist's wet dream glided into the Hotel instead, and Jarvis relaxed at the sight of another male. As with all soulless bloodsuckers, the vampire was too thin to be taken seriously as a badass, and giving him a spray tan would be an act of mercy.

What was a vamp doing inside the Den? The undead were too emotionally fragile to make good subjects for Angelica's studies. They were going to be destroyed if they stayed. "Get out," Jarvis warned, striding toward them, ready to shove them to safety if they didn't respond. No more suffering. No more. No more. *No more.* "This is not the place for men. These women aren't the ones you want to be using to satisfy the bloodlust thing."

The vampire held up a melodramatic hand with long, well-manicured fingernails and a way-too-stereotypical large black ring with a family crest of some sort on it. "I'm here for you, warrior."

"My soul's already got a lien on it." Pascal twitched again and let out a low moan of distress. Urgency tightened Jarvis's muscles, and he gripped the kid more securely. Pascal needed freedom, and he needed it now. "Call me on my cell next week. Kinda busy right now."

Twelve more tuxedo-wearing vampires appeared behind the first one. A baker's dozen of the undead. Arms were folded, shoulders were back, and chins were raised loftily in that "I am so much better than you" disdainful look they must practice diligently as soon as they were converted.

Jarvis raised his sword and let it burn with his poison. "Get out of my way." He kept his voice low. A promise of no mercy—

The lead vampire's eyes flashed red, and his fangs elongated. "My Lord, you are not going anywhere." Behind him, his cronies went caveman: fangs as long as tusks, skin like stale marshmallows, eyes going cherry-bomb. Battle stance for hemoglobin junkies.

Under normal circumstances, thirteen parasites with big canines and bad fashion sense were no match for two magically enhanced ex-torture victims with serious attitude problems. Odds were with the good guys. But throw in a nearly dead kid fading fast on Jarvis's shoulder and his buddy occupied with a bunch of rabid pit vipers?

Well, shit.

Acknowledgments

Thank you to Deb Werksman, whose insightful suggestions and great vision helped make this book the best it could be. Your unflagging and enthusiastic support is a gift. Thanks also to Deidre Knight for everything. Special thanks to Susie Benton and Danielle Jackson for their tireless and magical efforts behind the scenes. This book would never make it to the shelves without the tireless and wonderful efforts of all the people at Sourcebooks, including Cat Clyne and Liz Kelsh and so many others. And, as always, my deepest love and appreciation to my family for being my hugest fans, most ardent followers, and my core of strength and love.

About the Author

Nationally best-selling author, Golden Heart® award winner, and four-time RITA® Award nominee Stephanie Rowe is the author of more than twenty books. A former attorney, she resides in New England.